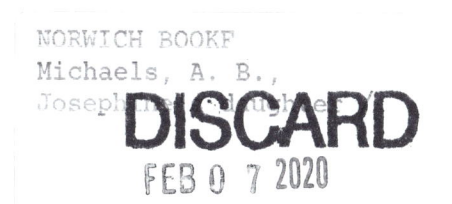

# JOSEPHINE'S DAUGHTER

THE GOLDEN CITY BOOK FIVE

AB MICHAELS

*JOSEPHINE'S DAUGHTER*
The Golden City - *Book Five*

Copyright © 2019 by A.B. Michaels

All rights reserved.

ISBN: 978-0-9975201-2-5

No part of this publication may be reproduced, distributed, or transmitted in any form or by any means, including photocopying, recording, or other electronic or mechanical methods, without the prior written permission of the publisher, except in the case of brief quotations embodied in critical reviews and certain other noncommercial uses permitted by copyright law.

For permission requests, please write to:

> Red Trumpet Press
> P. O. Box 171162 , Boise, ID 83716

Cover design by Tara Mayberry

www.TeaberryCreative.com

## ALSO BY AB MICHAELS

"**The Golden City**" historical series:

*The Art of Love*

*The Depth of Beauty*

*The Promise*

*The Price of Compassion*

"**Sinner's Grove Suspense**" contemporary series:

*Sinner's Grove*

*The Lair*

*The Jade Hunters*

*To my mother*

# HISTORICAL NOTE

The Gilded Age in American history saw a sea change in science, industry and culture, making it particularly challenging for women navigating these new waters. Below is a partial list of sources used in providing background for *Josephine's Daughter:*

### History of Medicine and Healing
Lyons, Albert S. M.D. and R. Joseph Petrucelli II, M.D. *Medicine: An Illustrated History.* New York: Harry N. Abrams, Inc., 1978.

Lutz, Tom. *American Nervousness 1903: An Anecdotal History.* Ithaca: Cornell University Press, 1991.

Magner, Lois N. *A History of Medicine.* New York: Marcel Dekker, Inc. 1992.

Porter, Roy, ed. *Medicine: A History of Healing.* East Sussex: The Ivy Press, 1997.

Rothrock, Jane C. *Alexander's Care of the Patient in Surgery, Twelfth Edition.* St. Louis: Mosby Press, 2003.

Toledo-Pereyra, Luis H. *A History of American Medicine form the Colonial Period to the Early Twentieth Century.* Lewiston: The Edwin Mellen Press, 2006.

Zimmerman, Ken Jr. *William Muldoon: The Solid Man Conquers Wrestling and Physical Culture.* St. Louis: Ken Zimmerman Jr. Enterprises, 2014.

Gottlieb, William, ed. *The Visual Encyclopedia of Natural Healing.* Emmaus, PA: Rodale Press, 1991.

Morgan, Barbara J. et al, ed. *Foods that Harm Foods that Heal.* Pleasantville, NY: The Reader's Digest Association, Inc., 1997.

**San Francisco, 1906 Earthquake and Aftermath**

Asbury, Herbert. *The Barbary Coast.* New York: Thunder's Mouth Press, 1933.

Fradkin, Philip L. *The Great Earthquake and Firestorms of 1906.* Berkeley: University of California Press, 2005.

Kurzman, Dan. *Disaster! The Great San Francisco Earthquake and Fire of 1906.* New York: Perennial Publishers, 2001.

Richards, Rand. *Historic San Francisco: A Concise History and Guide.* San Francisco: Heritage House Publishers, 2007.

Winchester, Simon. *A Crack in the Edge of the World: America and the Great California Earthquake of 1906.* New York: Harper Collins Publishers, 2005.

**Chinese Immigrants, Chinatown and Plague**

Chase, Marilyn. *The Barbary Plague: The Black Death*

*in Victorian San Francisco*. New York: Random House Publishers, 2003.

Yong, Chen. *Chinese San Francisco 1850-1943: A Trans-Pacific Community.* Stanford: Stanford University Press, 2000.

*Those whom we love, we can hate.*

Henry David Thoreau

# CHAPTER ONE

### Katherine

### *San Francisco*
### *1893*

The coastal oak, ancient by any standards, stood on the edge of the Firestone estate with branches so thick and heavy that several dipped against the ground before rising again. That made it perfect for a toddler named Kit to climb upon its gnarled limbs and call it her very own "nanny bone" tree. Over the years, she had defended her citadel from both her older and her younger brother with shrieks and tears and flailing arms, so that by the time she turned thirteen, everyone in the Firestone clan indulgently acknowledged whose tree it was.

On this particular September afternoon, during one of the Firestones' many garden parties, Kit and two younger friends, Cecily and Bea, had climbed to the upper branches to perch among the leaves. Kit rucked her blue velvet smock between her knees and leaned back against the trunk with a sigh. "It is my favorite hiding place in all the world," she said. "I've tested it many times. No one can see us."

She was right. Twenty minutes later the three girls saw a man and a woman strolling across the lawn toward the tree. It was obvious they assumed they were alone.

"What's my papa doing with your mama?" Bea whispered to Cecily.

With a finger to her lips, Kit quickly shushed her cohorts. Who knew what secrets they might learn?

"I think she knows," Hazel Anders said to the man, her voice filled with worry. She was a hummingbird, small and fluttery. Anxiety, everyone knew, was her constant companion.

Kit glanced at Cecily and reiterated her silent warning.

"How could she? There's no resemblance." Clarence Marshall, big, blond, and florid-looking, responded with his customary confidence.

"The hair," Mrs. Anders said.

"Nonsense," he replied. "Who would know? Frank barely has any."

"A feeling, then. I sense it every time she and I are together. A certain disdain … bordering on dislike. Covered with a veneer of civility."

"You are imagining things, my dear. But so what if she does? She is nothing to us."

"She has the power to destroy us. One word and —"

"And why would she? She has everything she could possibly want. She's on top of the world. In fact, I should thank her. If she hadn't insisted we move here, you and I would never have—"

"Please stop. I wish it had never happened. I wish we had never met."

As Mrs. Anders began to sniffle, Mr. Marshall took her spindly hand in his large paw. "Don't say that, Hazel. You don't mean it. Somebody had to help you. I'm just glad it was me and that I was able to." He tipped her chin so that she looked up at him.

Kit looked at Bea, whose eyes were wide as saucers. Bea said nothing, however. None of the girls did, no doubt understanding they had heard too much already.

Mrs. Anders looked tearfully up at Mr. Marshall. "No, I don't mean it. I am grateful, really. But … it's just so difficult."

He patted her hand. "I know. We just have to be strong, that's all. Come, we'd better get back. I imagine their game will be ending soon." As they walked back toward the mansion, he added in a light-hearted tone, "Thank God you never liked Russian whist."

By tacit agreement, the three girls waited until the couple had crested the hill before breaking their silence. Ten-year-old Bea, the youngest, spoke first. "Why was my daddy talking about your daddy's hair?" she asked Cecily, giggling. "Or what little there is of it."

Cecily didn't answer, but her face spoke volumes. She was an only child, and twelve, and more than capable of putting one and one together to make two.

"I'm sure Cecily has no idea," Kit said. "But I expect

you'll get a whipping if you tell your papa what you heard him say. Or your mama, too."

"My papa doesn't whip me," Bea said.

"There's always a first time."

Kit began to climb down the tree. Somehow it no longer seemed quite the sanctuary it had been.

Kit and Cecily never talked about what they'd heard that day. Although Kit imagined her friend was ashamed, it couldn't hold a candle to what Kit felt. She knew without a doubt that the woman Mrs. Anders spoke so fearfully of was Kit's own mother, Josephine.

Who else was on top of the world? The Firestone name meant everything in San Francisco society.

Who else passed judgment on everybody and everything from behind a veil of sweetness? Kit experienced that every day of her life.

And who else had convinced Bea's mother and father to move to the Golden City so many years ago? If she'd heard the story once, she'd heard it a thousand times.

Kit's mother had the power to destroy whomever she chose. What Kit overheard only reaffirmed what she already suspected: that her mother was a controlling, spiteful, and dangerous woman.

But does a thirteen-year-old ever know quite as much as she thinks she does, especially when it comes to her mother?

# CHAPTER TWO

*Mr. and Mrs. Edward Firestone*
*request the pleasure of your company*
*at a dinner honoring their daughter,*
*Katherine Madeline Mariah Firestone,*
*on the occasion of her eighteenth birthday*
*at their Pacific Heights home*
*on Sunday, July thirty-first*
*at seven o'clock in the evening*

*Please RSVP by messenger*

Katherine Madeline Mariah Firestone was drunk. Pleasantly so. She'd been sipping purloined whiskey from her father's liquor cabinet on and off for the past three hours, determined to see what all the fuss was about. While she could do without the sourness of the spirit, the way it made her feel more than made up for the abysmal taste. Gone were the nerves that came from knowing this latest party in the string of her parents' never-ending social gatherings was focused on *her*. Kit was turning eighteen, which in her world signified her availability on San Francisco society's unspoken marriage mart.

Not that this came as any surprise. Kit was indisputably beautiful and intelligent, not to mention wealthy by virtue of her inevitable dowry and a trust left to her by her paternal grandmother. She'd known what it meant to be a Firestone by the time she was ten and had long ago pushed aside any discomfort in that knowledge. Hers was a life of extravagant wardrobe changes and catered tea parties, of finishing schools, cotillions, and debutante balls. Her social network resembled a solar system, with friends and acquaintances defined by their proximity to the Firestone family sun.

Above all, Kit's was a life pre-ordained. Like her best friends, she was expected to uphold the dignity of her family name by marrying well and maintaining the status quo. If she chafed a bit under the strictures necessary to her station in life, so be it. But she had to admit, alcohol had the potential to make it all so much ... easier.

She took another sip and watched from the upper library window as a line of carriages dropped off guests for the event. A young man caught her eye. He stood out from the others, not for any physical distinction —he was no taller than she and had forgettable light-brown hair—but for the almost arrogant way he comported himself, boldly greeting those in the line snaking up the steps to their home. She'd seen him before, she realized, at the opening of the new Ferry Building at the city's wharf not two weeks before. It had been a crush, but she'd noticed him, his upright carriage and his inherent sense of self-worth. At one point their eyes had met and held; after far too many moments, *she* had been the one to turn away first, breathless at the contact without knowing why. And here he was, attending her very own birthday party. How had he known? Who had invited him? She was both annoyed and impressed.

*He remembers me*, Kit thought as the young man sidled up to her in the receiving line. He took her hand and stared with a bemused smile as if they had a history together, as if he shared a secret with her and no one else. A wave of dizziness swept over her and she wondered if he or the alcohol were to blame. She glanced at her father standing beside her.

"Kit, I'd like you to meet Mr. Easton Challis," Edward Firestone said. "He's from Chicago and has joined Crocker National as an assistant vice president. Easton, my daughter Katherine."

Mr. Challis executed a proper bow while only briefly taking his eyes off her.

Kit stared back. "I'm very glad you could join us this evening, Mr. Challis. Thank you for coming to help me celebrate my birthday."

He continued to talk with his eyes, his hand slightly

squeezing hers. "Call me Easton, please ... and I assure you, the pleasure is all mine."

"I doubt that, young man," Kit's mother said, standing next to her husband. "An eligible bachelor like yourself is bound to turn at least a few heads this evening. I'm sure several young women are fanning themselves as we speak." Josephine Firestone was her usual effervescent self. At a scant five feet one, she made up for her petite stature with an outsized personality that melded audacity and charm, although Kit felt the charm element was overrated.

"Don't embarrass Easton, darling," Edward Firestone said. "He won't want to come back and visit us."

Mr. Challis's eyes hadn't wavered, but he produced a slow smile. "Impossible," he murmured before turning again to her father. "Thank you again for the invitation, sir. It's most certainly a joyous occasion."

After a final slight press of the hand, Mr. Challis— Easton—moved on, leaving Kit's gaze to linger on his retreating figure long enough for her mother to comment.

"Plenty of time for that, my dear," Josephine said lightly. "Let's see to your other guests, all right?"

A round of cocktails, appetizers, and a five-course, sit-down dinner later, Kit was beginning to feel the effects of her earlier indulgence. She'd been surrounded by her acolytes all evening, giving her no chance to strike up a more casual conversation with Easton. He seemed unperturbed, however. She watched discreetly as he worked the room; he was a natural, understanding that a Firestone social event was ideal for forging relationships, both professional and personal, that could and most likely would benefit both parties in a myriad of ways.

Kit just wanted to lie down.

"That Easton Challis. Oh my." Kit's friend Ellen pretended to fan herself. They were seated at vanities brought in to one of the mansion's upper parlors which was serving as the ladies' retiring room.

Kit remembered her mother's remark about young women fanning themselves over him and set her jaw. Were Kit's friends that transparent? "I hadn't noticed."

"Really? He seems to be all the talk. Cecily knows him already. He works at her father's bank."

Gazing into the mirror, Kit checked her near-perfect coiffure and pulled out the small pot of rouge she'd stashed in the top drawer. She applied a small amount to her cheeks, then took a dab and daintily touched her lips, knowing her father would frown on too much "artifice." "Yes, I heard," she said with just the right touch of ennui. "He seems nice enough."

Ellen was distracted by the lace on her bodice. It wasn't lying flat. "Well, you must be the only one unimpressed." She pinched the lace in an attempt to bend it back. "The rest of us are drooling. Don't you fancy him just a little?"

Kit cocked her head in thought. Did she? He was

certainly a step beyond the usual boys in her circle, most of whom wouldn't have had the courage to boldly stare at her, much less hold on to her hand. "There is something about him, I suppose. He seems ... intense." Even that admission brought her thoughts back to her mother, along with renewed irritation. A persistent throbbing in her temples joined her lethargy. How much longer would she have to hold court? She gave her golden hair one last pat before standing and smoothing down her skirts. "It doesn't matter what I think, though, does it? I doubt any of us will run into him much. I mean, he doesn't exactly travel in our circles, does he?"

"I suppose not," Ellen said, still fiddling.

Without saying a word, Kit pulled a small pin from inside the vanity drawer, brushed Ellen's hands away, and deftly repaired her friend's wayward lace.

Ellen smiled her thanks. "Why didn't I think of that?"

"Because you're not me," Kit said.

"We must keep an eye on her."

Josephine Firestone had a tendency to speak the last of her thoughts aloud, a habit her husband of more than twenty years was used to. As they lay in bed after the party, he didn't look up from the financial report he was scanning.

"Who and why, my love?"

Josephine continued to twist her long, still-blond hair into its nightly braid. "Kit, of course. Did you see the way she looked at that Easton Challis fellow? She was practically salivating. I don't know why you invited him."

Edward's composure didn't waiver. "As a favor to Frank, my dear. If it makes you feel any better, I think he's determined his new protégé is a suitable match for his daughter."

Josephine snorted. "Not if Kit decides she wants him. There's no comparison between the two."

"Spoken like a true mama bear. But if you want to keep her from the arms of Mr. Challis, by all means warn her off him. You know how compliant and eager our daughter is, to always do your bidding." Edward tempered his sarcasm with a grin.

Her hand slowing, Josephine frowned. "I suppose you're right. But I can't help but worry. She is so very beautiful."

Edward put away his report and leaned over. "Shall I tell you why? No, better yet, let me show you how much I appreciate from whence it came."

With that he slipped his hand underneath the covers, causing Josephine to smile. Within a few minutes, all thoughts of their strong-willed daughter were subsumed by the familiar and delicious ritual of marital love.

Sometime later Josephine awoke, warmly cocooned by her sleeping husband, his hand curled tenderly around her breast. Despite her physical comfort, her concern about her daughter had returned. She knew first-hand that beauty was not always an asset.

# CHAPTER THREE

## Josephine

### *1863*

The last words the dashing Colonel Alfred Drummond said to his nine-year-old daughter Josephine were, "Be good, my darling poppet, and take care of your beautiful mama while I'm gone."

And then he *was* gone, off to fight the Confederacy at Gettysburg, which seemed clear across the world, even though it was really only a few days' hard ride from their home in Philadelphia.

He came home ten days later, laid out in a pine box, one of the more than three thousand Union soldiers to die on a blood-soaked southern Pennsylvania field under a hot July sun.

"You are lucky to have him back, ma'am," the officer who delivered the body told Josephine's mother. "We had to bury most of the men right on the spot."

That didn't mollify Marrielle Drummond. She collapsed upon hearing the news, and shortly thereafter, Josephine's Uncle Whitford carried her mother into the bedroom she had shared with Josephine's father, which became her new refuge. Marrielle shed so many tears that Josephine feared her mother's eyes would dry up and pop out of their sockets. Whenever Josephine's own tears threatened, she held her breath to keep them at bay.

But oh, the loss. Josephine felt it straight through to her bones. One day she had led the life of a princess, the apple of her papa's eye; now she had only a ghost of a mother, worse than not having one at all.

For the next several years, she endured what she called "The Darkness." Dark because the drapes in their Delancy Place townhome were almost always pulled shut. Dark because her mother insisted on wearing mourning clothes, even though she rarely went outside. And dark because of the visits her Uncle Whitford paid to beautiful, helpless Marrielle several times a week.

At one point, Josephine gathered the courage to confront her mother about her uncle's intrusive behavior. "He is so much older than Papa. Why does he need to be here so often?"

"He is my rock," Marrielle responded tearfully. "I know nothing about financial matters; what would I do without him?" And later: "We find comfort in each other; we both miss your father so very much."

The visits became more frequent and lasted much longer than Josephine thought necessary. Sometimes, her portly uncle with his mutton-chop whiskers and thinning hair would be the last person she'd see before heading to her room in the evening, and the first one she'd see in the morning, even before Cook arrived to start breakfast. She wondered what her Auntie Pauline thought about his visits. She was a large, round, middle-aged lady who seemed to eat a lot; in the years following her brother-in-law's death she grew even larger, until one day her heart gave out, which left Uncle Whitford with no excuse not to come to Delancy Place and stay.

After that, Marrielle never spoke to Josephine again about the "unconventional" relationship she maintained with her brother-in-law. The servants kept mum about it as well. Only once did Josephine watch from the doorway as her mother talked to Sally, the upstairs maid, from her bed.

"I know what everyone thinks. He is not my darling Alfred, but I-I need him. Do you think me wicked?" she'd posed in a small, little-girl voice.

"No, ma'am," the maid replied, busily plumping her mistress's pillows. "You're copin' the best you can."

Josephine's mother had squeezed the servant's hand and taken a sip of the strange-smelling tisane that Sally always brewed for her.

*Sally needs her job*, Josephine thought with disgust. *What else could she say?*

It came as no surprise to anyone that precisely one year to the day after Auntie Pauline passed away, Uncle Whitford married Josephine's mother in a small, private ceremony. He was fifty-six and she was thirty-one. At last he had the legal right to share her bed.

They did not waste time. Seven months later, Marrielle bore Uncle Whitford a son, and Little Carlton became the center of the new Drummond household, complete with wet nurse and nanny. At fourteen, Josephine's estrangement from her mother was virtually complete.

"The Darkness" was truly an apt description of her life during that time. Thankfully, something—or rather someone—made it all bearable.

## CHAPTER FOUR

Josephine's saving grace came in the form of a girl who had moved into the opulent townhouse next door. If Dinah Clementine Bettancourt were eight inches shorter and twenty-five pounds lighter, she could have been Josephine's twin. They possessed the same thick blond hair, the same fair skin (although Dinah had more freckles), and similar blue eyes (although Josephine's were of a darker hue). It was not uncommon for strangers to remark that they looked like sisters, always assuming that Dinah was the older of the two, despite her being a year younger. Neither girl cared a fig what other people thought; having been the only children in their families when they'd met, they were just happy to have found each other.

Each had started out with her own governess, but a year after his brother death, Uncle Whitford had agreed to share the salary of the Bettancourts' Miss Fishback so that she could teach both girls at once. It thus became routine for Josephine to spend her mornings in the back parlor of the Bettancourt mansion, learning her sums, a smattering of geography, and a bit of French, before sharing a light luncheon and indulging in playtime afterward. It was there that Josephine learned the fine art of dressing well.

Dinah's father—hefty and imbued with bonhomie—was a well-to-do textile merchant. He often brought home samples of exotic silks, satins, and velvet, which the girls delighted in wearing, using pins and ribbons to create dramatic costumes. Their favorite scenarios usually involved royalty of the Egyptian or Chinese variety; Josephine always played the queen.

"I am older, after all," she'd say, and even though such a rationale made minimal sense, Dinah (by nature a follower) always acquiesced and took the lesser role of "princess."

Dinah's mother, Leora, found the girls' playacting absolutely charming—whenever she was around to see it. She was vivacious and plump, a gadabout determined to reach the upper levels of Philadelphia society despite the fact that her money came from trade and not three generations' worth of privilege. Once every few weeks, she'd ask Josephine how "poor, dear Marrielle" was faring, followed by such inquiries as, "Do you think your mama would like to join one of my social groups, darling? Truly, being a Drummond, she could have her pick." Mrs. Bettancourt ticked off the list using her well-manicured and lightly polished fingers. "We play whist on Tuesdays, volunteer at the Orphan's Home on Thursdays, discuss the latest scientific literature every other Friday, to name a few."

And Josephine always replied, "Um, thank you, Mrs. Bettancourt. I'll be sure to ask her and let you know." They both knew what the answer would be, but Dinah's mother must have felt it polite to keep asking and Josephine knew it would be rude to tell her to stop.

When Josephine and Dinah grew too old to play dress up, they developed a zeal for their own wardrobes, spending hours poring over the latest fashion plates, which were also brought home by Mr. Bettancourt. Soon it became a matter of life or death to wear the latest frocks available for young misses, or to engage in the most *au courant* activities, such as cooking or archery lessons. Josephine especially loved the cooking, although she knew at her station in life she would always *have* a cook instead of be one. Mimicking the older generation, the teenagers looked for any excuse to socialize, gathering at house or garden parties to play card games or charades.

Unfortunately, keeping up with the newest trends required money. Josephine learned to treat her Uncle Whitford as she would her late father. Her uncle was a controlling man by nature and it was him and not her mother whose permission she needed in order to go anywhere or do anything, much less make a purchase. She quickly ascertained that her best approach was to couch her requests—whether for a picnic in the park or a new cotillion dress—in terms of how it would reflect on the Drummond name, something her uncle was quite concerned with, no doubt because he had soiled it by marrying his brother's widow. It also helped to suggest how her request would give her uncle more time alone with Marrielle and their little bundle of joy.

But the fashion gods were fickle. Josephine lamented her lack of stature and bosom, while Dinah bemoaned the fact that her outline was too "curvy." Finding satisfactory solutions to such dilemmas was becoming vitally important because of one critical factor.

Young men were starting to notice them.

## CHAPTER FIVE

### Katherine

*1898*

Despite the assumption that their worlds would rarely intersect, Kit ran into Easton Challis with surprising frequency over the next several weeks.

Kit and her mother happened to be patrons of Alice Brown Chittenden and Easton attended a reception they put on at the Mark Hopkins Art Institute for her latest work, a painting called "Roses." Easton demonstrated a surprisingly adroit grasp of the artist's style and abilities, standing close to Kit as he noted certain of Miss Chittenden's brush strokes, comparing her work to others of a similar vein.

A week later Kit saw Easton again, albeit briefly, at a charity ball sponsored by Cecily Anders's parents. That appearance was understandable, since Cecily's father, Franklin, was a partner at the bank where Easton worked. What wasn't so clear was the twinge of envy she felt watching Easton stand next to Cecily and her parents in the receiving line. He looked for all the world like Cecily's consort, an impression strengthened by the sheer delight on Mrs. Anders's normally pallid face.

And one afternoon at Fior d'Italia in North Beach, between the antipasti and the *risotto alla milanese*, Easton approached Kit and her mother, doffing his hat and bowing slightly.

"Oh, how delightful to see you again, Eastie," Josephine said. Kit's mother often addressed people, be they child or head of state, by their nickname, making one up if they didn't already have one.

"The pleasure rests with me, Mrs. Firestone." He smiled at her before turning his gaze to Kit.

"Well, it's kismet," Josephine said. "You must come to our home for dinner. Shall we say tomorrow night at seven?"

The man looked like he'd won the Kentucky Derby, and Kit felt duty bound to clarify the situation. "You'll be one of a select few. Mother's only hosting around twenty or so this time."

If Easton was deflated by Kit's comment, he didn't show it. "I'd be honored," he said. He gave another bow, his eyes once again lingering on Kit's just a moment too long.

"What an engaging young man," Josephine said after he left. She didn't seem to notice the undue attention he was paying to Kit, or perhaps she did and wanted to encourage it. Kit couldn't tell what her mother was thinking, nor was she sure how *she* felt about it. Intrigued, maybe. Curious. A bit titillated, if the truth be known. Perhaps she should test her wiles on someone like him, someone a cut above her usual jejune crowd.

She got more than she bargained for.

Easton Challis held his own and then some at the Firestone soiree. Chatting amiably with the likes of Rudolph Spreckels, the president of First National Bank, and esteemed architect Bernard Cahill, Easton cited statistics on the rise in Market Street retail business thanks to the new transportation hub at the Embarcadero. He praised Mayor Phelan's latest bond issue ("A modern sewer system is critical as we enter the twentieth century") and shared condolences with the group over the passing of ex-mayor Adolf Sutro. He was equally informed about America's recent victory against Spain in Cuba, sharing his enthusiastic belief that "if anyone's going to colonize this hemisphere, it ought to be the United States, not Europe."

Kit found herself enthralled by Easton's intellect. How had he learned so much about the city after such a short period of time? And how did he know just what to say to everyone he spoke to, as if he had been their friend for years? He was sophisticated without being stuffy and he was sure of his place, even in the high reaches of society. His self-confidence excited her, and the looks he gave her said she fascinated him as well. The knowledge left her shaken, unsure of herself, as if she had once again drunk too much and was on the brink of losing control. She was in uncharted territory, certain of only one thing: she wanted to explore it further.

After dinner, when Edward suggested the men repair to a smoking room for cigars and port and the wives join Josephine in another parlor for coffee, Easton asked if Kit might be willing to show him the gardens surrounding her family home. He made the request in the presence of all the ladies, and when Kit assented, he asked if any of the other females would like to join the tour.

"Oh, I'm quite sure you'd love that, wouldn't you?" Josephine leavened her drollery with a smile and shooed them away.

They had no sooner left the house and entered the inky night when Easton took Kit firmly by the arm and pressed her against the side of a tree. "I have been waiting all my life to do this," he said, and kissed her forcefully, his tongue entering her mouth unbidden. It was not the peck or slobber of an untested boy; it was a claiming, the kind of mark a man places on a woman he wants.

Stunned by his aggression, Kit paused long enough for Easton to take even more liberties. He deepened the kiss while his hands began to roam her body, fondling her through her gown. She felt shame at what she was allowing him to do. At the same time, her body began to hum—with something a hundred times more potent than what she had experienced using her own hands, in the privacy of her room. It was ... it was ... too much.

"W-wait," she said, pushing him away. "Stop. Please."

Easton, breathing heavily, immediately stepped back. He appeared as shocked as she felt by what had just occurred. "I don't know what to say," he began. "I shouldn't have taken advantage of you. It's just that you ... well, you are beyond beautiful." He caught her eyes, his expression rueful, his half-smile self-deprecating. How could she take him to task for something she had also enjoyed?

"I think we should return to the house," she said a bit shakily, reaching up to smooth her hair.

"No. Please. Let's walk some more. I promise not be so boorish as to attack you again ... truly."

Seeing sincerity in his demeanor, Kit agreed, and they continued down the garden path. She reached for safe topics, asking about Easton's background. He told her he was an only child and had graduated from Princeton with an eye toward business. He had worked for smaller banks back east before coming out to the boomtown of San Francisco. He wanted to stay out west and establish roots. And yes, he was looking for someone with whom to share his life.

"You really are incredibly beautiful, you know." Stopping, he tipped her chin to meet his gaze. "Do you not think so?"

Kit decided for once not to be flippant. "Yes, I've been told that I'm attractive. But there's so much more than that to consider, don't you think?"

"Oh, yes. Of course. Certainly." He counted off on his fingers as they walked. "There's ... there's intelligence, and, kindness, and, oh, a whole host of things that are more important."

Inwardly Kit smiled. She and her older brother Will had talked on several occasions about the fundamental differences between men and women. A recent Cornell graduate, Will already had a vast amount of experience with the opposite sex. "You women want so much," he'd complained to her during his school vacation the previous Christmas. He'd just broken it off with someone and was not feeling charitable. "You all want brains, strength, a sense of humor. And don't forget money, or, oh my God, *sensitivity*." He'd paused to drive his point home. "But you know what we men want? One word: beauty. We want women so beautiful that other men crave them. It's as simple as that."

Kit had recovered enough from the shock of Easton's kiss to realize she'd liked it. Very much. And if her brother was right, she certainly seemed to fit Easton's requirement for beauty. She glanced coyly at him. "But it certainly helps to be attracted to one's ... mate. Mutually, that is." That elicited a chuckle from Easton. "Yes, it certainly does help." He casually took her arm while they continued their stroll.

That night, in her bed, Kit relived the sensations she'd experienced at Easton's touch. She was attracted to him mentally and she desired him physically. He could be the one, she thought. *He could be the one*.

---

Weeks went by—weeks in which Easton contrived to be in Kit's company as much as possible, preferably sans adults. Lunch at a romantic hideaway downtown;

a stroll in a lesser-known park; a Sunday picnic in a private glade. And on those occasions when they found themselves alone, he wasted no time in leading Kit further into the "pleasures of the flesh," as some of the clandestine novels she'd read had put it. She felt much like the frog introduced to a cold pot of water before the heat is turned up ever so slowly; it feels so good that one doesn't even recognize when matters have gone too far.

Kit told herself that she was still in charge, that the man she was falling in love with—what a heady sensation!—was worth the slightly soiled feeling that passed through her whenever she made up another story to misdirect her family and her friends.

"Let's keep us to ourselves for as long as we can," Easton had said. "I can't bear the thought of sharing you, which is what will happen once we announce that we are a couple."

"But we are a couple, aren't we?" she'd asked.

"Of course, darling," he replied, and sealed his declaration with another improper show of affection.

The passion she felt for Easton grew deeper as she got to know him better.

"I envy you, you know," he told her one warm Friday afternoon as he rowed out toward the center of Stow Lake. He had asked for the afternoon off, he said, because he knew his weekend was filled with other obligations and he couldn't bear not seeing her. Now, floating along with few others on the water, his strokes were languid, as if he didn't care whether they made progress or not.

Kit trailed her hand in the water. "Envy me? Why?"

"Oh, it's not what you think, you having money and all. It's your family. I wish I had what you have — a father and mother who love you, two brothers ready to protect you. I have ... no one."

He had taken a serious turn; perhaps now he was ready to open up about himself. "What do you mean by 'no one'? she asked. "You're not an orphan, are you?"

"I may as well be." He put the oars down and let them drift. "My father is a bastard who beat my mother, and he walloped me when I tried to protect her. I had three broken bones before I turned sixteen, before I got away."

"That's horrendous! What happened to your mother—did she escape him like you did?"

He shook his head. "Alas, no. She died of tuberculosis and afterward, my father drank himself into oblivion. He loved her in his own sick way, but I couldn't take his anger anymore and left. Fortunately, my uncle took me in so I was able to salvage something of my life. But seeing how much your family loves you is something I want for myself." He leaned forward. "I want us to be together, Kit, in every way possible."

She could tell by the way Easton looked at her that he was ready and willing to take their lovemaking to the ultimate level. But was she? She longed to give him the security of a committed, loving relationship—one that he hadn't experienced growing up. But part of her felt the need for a declaration of some sort, an affirmation in front of others that she and Easton were pledging themselves to each other. Her parents already suspected she held a *tendre* for him, but her discretion had kept the extent of their relationship under wraps. Easton wanted to wait until he could offer her more ("It's a bit intimidating to ask a Firestone for his daughter's hand in marriage," he'd told her. "I want to be able to hold my head up high.").

But another, more rebellious, more scandalous part of her longed to know what it was like to join their bodies as one, regardless of what the world had to say about it. Still, she was a planner, even of her own impetuousness. She knew about her woman's cycle, that it wasn't always trustworthy, and she was smart enough not to leave the most important details of such a bold, consequential act to someone else.

She sought Will's advice, knowing that while she couldn't be altogether truthful about her motives, he could still give her perspective on a situation he was no doubt familiar with.

She found him one evening in his suite, standing in front of his Jacobean mahogany wardrobe, perusing an array of trousers, shirts, and jackets. A portable wardrobe stood nearby, ready to receive any transferred garments he deemed worthy. Now back from college for good, he'd displayed a Midas touch and had already tripled his trust fund, earning enough to purchase his own estate on nearby Russian Hill.

"I really think it's time I ordered some new suits," he said, scratching his chin. "This is all so—"

"Collegiate?" Kit joined him, her head tipped in consideration of his wardrobe. Known even then for her fashion sense, she heartily agreed. "I'll help you pick out fabric if you like."

Will took off his spectacles and cleaned them with the tail of his shirt. Like his sister he was tall, slender, and light-haired, with engaging features but myopic eyes. "You pick, I pay. Sounds reasonable."

She thought to ease into her topic. "So, when do you move in?"

"The end of the month."

"I imagine it will be a godsend to entertain the ladies away from Mater and Pater's prying eyes."

He grinned at her as he pulled out a brown tweed vest. "You could say that."

"That one's a keeper," she said absently as she began to analyze his clothing in greater detail. She kept her eyes fixed on the rack, studiously flipping through the garments to hide her nerves. "I was wondering ... when you ... when you make love to a woman, how do you keep her from having a baby?"

That brought out a frown. "What? Why on earth do you have to know that?"

Kit shrugged, trying to look as nonchalant as she dared. "It just seems to me that in all these years of not exactly being a monk, you must have a system in place to keep such, well, inconvenient little details at bay. My girlfriends and I are simply curious, that's all, and they asked me to get your opinion on the matter."

"It wasn't Beatrice Marshall, was it? She seems to be a bit too inquisitive for one so young."

"No, no. Not her. Not anyone in particular, really. Just, well, all of us. You can't expect us to enter the real world ignorant of all that vital information, can you?"

"I suppose not, but heavens, Kit, that's not something you should be worried about right now."

"Oh, I'm not really, but I did say I'd ferret out whatever insights I could. So, how *do* you keep the babies at bay?"

Her brother hesitated, clearly uncomfortable about sharing this aspect of his social life. "Well, if you must know, I invested in a little company run by Joseph Schmid out of New York. He produces rubbers by the thousands. Prophylactics. Pretty profitable business. You do know what a rubber is, don't you?"

Kit had heard of them but shook her head. Rather than describe them, Will casually reached into the top drawer of his nightstand and tossed one of several packets over to Kit. The pack showed a drawing of a pharaoh, presumably Ramses (since that was the name of the condom), lording it over a young blond woman with large breasts barely covered by her sheer harem outfit.

"You roll one of those over ... you know ... and that keeps your essence from comingling with hers, as it were."

Kit gazed at the illustration; it was somewhat salacious. "Why do they call it Ramses?"

He chuckled. "If you ask me, it's a bit of misplaced branding. Ramses was rumored to have fathered a hundred and sixty children."

Kit shared the laugh with her brother and quickly changed the topic, pointing out the various items of clothing that passed muster in her opinion, and those he should most definitely give away. She asked him about his new house: if he was going to renovate it and could she help him pick out furnishings? "Next to clothing and food, you know that's my favorite thing," she said, and continued in that vein until they were called to dinner. Preceding him out the door, Kit congratulated herself on the sleight of hand that had enabled her to slip the mighty Ramses into her pocket without Will's notice. *I doubt he has any idea how many he has; one less won't matter at all.*

---

Ramses made his debut a few weeks later, at another soiree hosted by Kit's parents. There were thirty in attendance this time, a gathering of local pols, mid-level railroad executives, financiers (including Easton and his boss), and various high-level industry types. Aside from Kit and her mother, there were no other women to help keep the posturing and chest-beating under control. Soon after a rather heavy dinner of grilled venison steaks, potatoes au gratin, and chocolate cake, Josephine took her leave and suggested that Kit do the same. Kit was chatting with Easton and two other up-and-coming bankers at the time.

"Yes, well, I have some reading I'd like to catch up on in the upstairs library," she announced to her admiring trio. "Have any of you read the work of Charlotte Perkins?" At the shaking of three male heads, she added with a smile, "I thought not. Try not to miss me too much, gentlemen." She left the room with a swish of her skirts, hoping she'd conveyed the right flirty impertinence while giving proper instruction to Easton.

It took longer than she expected, and she nodded off to Perkins's treatise on the economic inequality of women as she lay on the settee. Eventually there was a slight knock on the door and Easton entered. He walked swiftly to Kit, bent down on his knee, and whispered, "Finally. I thought I'd never be able to break away. I am dying to be alone with you." He pulled her head to his and kissed her almost violently before starting to caress her.

After coming up for air, Kit whispered, "What is happening downstairs?"

Easton busied himself with unbuttoning the top of her modest gown. "They are all in their cups, discussing the latest events and determining that only they have the answers to the world's problems. Typical."

Kit laughed softly, her heart already beginning to beat more heavily. He had trained her to respond to his touch, and she was a willing pupil. In fact, tonight she had decided to bestow upon him what many would say was her most important treasure.

And so she led him to the guest room at the end of the hall on the third floor—a space rarely used except for large weekend parties. Containing just a simple bed and nightstand, it was a small, plain room that overlooked the side of the mansion, a location where no one ever lingered long enough to see a light on or to hear voices from above.

But there was to be no light other than a sliver of moon showing through the curtains. The furtiveness of being with Easton alone in the near dark excited Kit; she had never done anything so bold and so brazen before. Yet a voice inside whispered, *is it him or the idea of him that intrigues you?* The story of his wretched background had tugged at her. She could not imagine growing up without love. He didn't deserve such a childhood, and how noble of him to rise above it! Her heart continued its timpani as she closed the door and quietly locked it. When she turned back, Easton was standing in front of her, his face cast in a somewhat ominous shadow.

"Does this mean what I think it means?" His hopeful tone gave chase to her anxiety. He sounded like a poor little boy about to taste his very first lollipop. She was happy to give it to him.

She smiled, stepping closer and putting her arms around him. This man, whom she was certainly in love with, wanted her as much as she wanted him. "I think it does," she whispered.

"Darling," he murmured before taking the lead in their dance, kissing her deeply and beginning to fondle her.

It didn't take long before Kit had been relieved of every piece of her clothing. They were lying on the bed now, and Easton, still clothed in shirt and drawers, had begun to take his underwear off in preparation for intercourse.

Kit didn't quite know what was expected of her, but a part of her sensed it was time to ask the awkward but necessary question, "Do you have anything to use for protection?"

Easton immediately stopped and sat back on his haunches. She couldn't quite tell, but in the chiaroscuro of the room he looked almost peevish.

"Why, no. I never use ... I mean, I hadn't thought. I hadn't dreamed ..."

Kit reached up to caress his arm. "It's all right. I brought something." She reached over to the book she'd brought with her and set on the nightstand. Inside of it she'd hidden the Ramses pack, which she'd thought was a fitting tribute to the forward-thinking Perkins. Kit tore the pack open and handed the condom to Easton. "Here, put it on," she said.

He held the object in his fingers as if it might bite. "I'm not sure—"

She sat up. "Are you telling me you don't know how to use it?"

"No, no," he said, shaking his head. "I understand the concept." He fumbled a bit before putting the condom on his erection and then turned his focus back on her. "Finally, I'm going to make a woman out of you. I can't wait." He pressed her against the bed and insinuated himself between her legs, saying nothing more as he resumed touching her feverishly.

A barrage of thoughts and emotions careened through Kit's mind. Easton's words didn't sound right. Wasn't she already a woman? Or maybe it was his tone. He sounded desperate, as if *he* was on the verge of discovering something, not them discovering each other. He felt the same passion and oneness that she did, didn't he? Didn't he want what was best for both of them?

She began to shiver, from the cold of the room, yes, but also from anxiety. This didn't feel the way she thought it would. "Easton?" she whispered, hoping his soothing voice would allay her fears.

"Not now, love. I'm just revving up."

The wrongness of it continued to mount in her brain, and all the while she was thinking such things, wondering why she wasn't transported and why he seemed so methodical, he was busy claiming her and it hurt and she thought, *Is this what it's all about?* And as he continued pressing into her, she realized *he* was being transported—but into a world that only he cared about, a world in which his gratification came before hers or anyone else's.

It was over fairly quickly. Breathing heavily, Easton pressed a kiss to her forehead and said, "You were wonderful. It's much better the second time, especially without the rubber. You'll see."

And she thought, *No, I won't. Not with you.* Because something told her it was not supposed to be like that. And the feeling that she had just made a monumental mistake stole over her.

**CHAPTER SIX**

After another perfunctory kiss and a promise to contact her "in the next day or two," Easton got dressed and stealthily made his way back down to the party. Kit put herself to rights and disposed of poor Ramses, who at least had performed *his* role well. Then she returned to her room, grateful for the darkness, feeling ashamed and fighting the urge to cry, knowing deep down that she had no one but herself to blame. In a fanciful bout of self-pity, she envisioned herself the new Eve, eating from the tree of sexual knowledge despite society's admonition not to, and wreaking all manner of havoc as a result. What if someone found out about their tryst? Worse than that, what if her family found out? She began to panic at the thought before reminding herself that Easton did love her, after all. He had said they were a couple, hadn't he? But the idea that they would continue on together, rendering something acceptable out of something unseemly, did nothing to quell her fears. In fact, it sent her further into the abyss. Because a realization came to her with such blinding clarity that she couldn't turn away: *You don't love Easton Challis after all.*

Her new question became: How would Easton react if she rejected him? Would he be angry? Make a scene? Beg her to take him back or threaten to expose her if she didn't? Her imagination ran wild, tempered only by the cold understanding that in the society they both inhabited, he, as a newcomer, surely had more to lose than she. Kit spent the next few days planning how to let him down in the most discreet, face-saving manner possible.

Her plans were a waste of time.

A week went by with no word from the now-elusive Mr. Challis. Easton did not appear at any of the social events Kit forced herself to attend. He did not call, or send flowers, or deliver a letter by messenger. Indeed, she would have thought he'd fallen off the face of the planet, if not for what she learned from her friend Ellen at a long-planned lunch at Fisherman's Wharf.

It was late September and The Golden City was experiencing an Indian summer. Feeling extremely uncomfortable with Easton's lack of contact but determined not to make the next move, Kit was grateful for the diversion. She'd always adored the sights and sounds of the harbor: the Italian fishermen haggling with the Chinese fishmongers, the smell of chocolate from the nearby factory.

"Have you heard the latest?" Ellen asked over *cioppino* at Castello's. "About Cecily, I mean."

Kit shook her head, chagrined to admit she hadn't. She, Cecily, and Ellen had been nearly inseparable growing up, but lately each of them had gone their separate ways. It was part of becoming adults, she supposed. She hadn't seen Cecily since that fundraiser and made a mental note to arrange a luncheon with her.

"The word is, she's secretly engaged! They're going to announce it this weekend at the Cliff House and the wedding's going to be sooner, rather than later, if you know what I mean." In case Kit *didn't* know, Ellen raised her eyebrows higher than a circus clown's.

"Oh really?" To her knowledge Cecily hadn't been seeing anyone special. "Who'd she snag?"

"That dashing fellow, remember? Easton Challis, the one who works for her father?" Ellen heaved a sigh. "I knew he'd get snatched up right away. All the good ones do."

Kit stared at Ellen, too shocked to respond. Easton Challis? *Her* Easton Challis? What?

She must have blurted the last word out loud, because Ellen grinned and pointed her spoon at Kit. "See, I knew you found him attractive. You didn't fool me with that 'I hadn't noticed' routine, not one bit."

Ellen focused on removing the meat from one of the mussels in her stew; otherwise she might have detected something far more serious in Kit's expression. Fighting to remain calm, Kit pretended to look for something in her reticule. "No, I ... I'm just surprised, that's all. He hasn't been in town that long."

"Long enough, I guess. Remember how chummy

they seemed at that fundraiser a few months ago? Apparently, he's been courting her on the side since way before then. I hear she's a couple months along, so they needed to have the wedding chop-chop."

The fragrant fish stew Kit had already consumed threatened to disgorge itself. He had been seeing Cecily the whole time he'd been courting Kit. Even before that, it sounded like. But why? Cecily was a charming, petite redhead, almost doll-like, very pretty in her own right. She was the opposite of Kit, who was sometimes jokingly compared to an Amazon. Why had he pursued Kit at all?

Ellen's next comment offered a possible explanation.

"Daddy says he's heard rumblings that Easton isn't all he purports to be. Warned me off 'grifters and gold diggers,' as he calls them. But I can't believe Cecily would fall for someone like that. She's far too sensible, don't you think?"

"Of course." Kit forestalled further mental humiliation by suggesting they stop by Ghirardelli's for a piece of chocolate. She'd lost her appetite, but anything was better than continuing down this painful and dangerous road.

"Oh, yes! We can watch them coming off the line. I hear their rejects are every bit as delicious as the others. What's your favorite?"

Kit knew she could always count on Ellen to do the right thing—which was to flit on to something else.

The anger and embarrassment Kit felt at Easton's betrayal didn't dissipate as quickly as she'd hoped. Instead it hardened into a crust of indignation mixed with quiet fury. With her parents' understanding (they thought she'd simply been interested in a fickle man), she pled a headache on the date of the engagement party. She did attend the wedding that soon followed but arrived just before the ceremony and sat in the back, apart from her family. Cecily wore an empire-waist gown, no doubt to hide her increasing figure, and she seemed somewhat subdued. It was apparent that despite her "catch," these were not the ideal circumstances under which to tie the knot.

For his part, Easton played the role of serious, committed groom to perfection. He spoke his vows loudly and without hesitation; he kissed his bride decorously; and he wrapped his arm around her thickening middle as they descended the steps of Holy Cross Church.

*That might have been me*, Kit thought as she stood among the crush of well-wishers flinging rice while Easton helped Cecily into the carriage outside the church. *Am I happy or sad that it isn't?* She looked unflinchingly into her heart and was relieved to find she was not only happy, but ecstatic that her relationship with Easton hadn't progressed to such an irreversible point. If she felt animosity toward Cecily, it was only a trace; after all, her friend had captured Easton's interest first.

And yet the "stupidity" with Easton continued to prey upon her. It flared, filling her with shame, whenever the "Cecily Challis affair" came up in conversation. It seemed her friends and acquaintances couldn't get enough of the whirlwind courtship that had led to the first wedding among their circle.

The latest news was dissected during an afternoon tea hosted by Bitsy McFadden a month after the nuptials. Bitsy announced to the group that Cecily and Easton had returned from their Italian honeymoon and were settling into a substantial home on Russian Hill, a wedding gift from her parents, to await the "blessed event."

"Honestly, I would have thought it'd be you," Bitsy said to Kit as she filled each young lady's glass with her custom version of Pisco Punch.

Kit was taken aback. Did Bitsy know something? No, that was impossible. But still ... "Why would you say that?"

"You're the pick of the litter, that's all." Bitsy looked surprised by the frowns of the other women at the table. "What? Can't we be honest, at least amongst ourselves? It's obvious Kit has the best looks and the most money of all of us. She's the jewel in our collective crown, wouldn't you say?"

Before Kit could deride Bitsy's remarks, Bea Marshall stepped in. She was a lesser light in their crowd, often invited just to round out the number of guests. "Well, it's obvious that Easton preferred Cecily." She held up her wine glass. "So, let's drink a toast to us also-rans. Even we have a shot at happiness."

Kit didn't know how to respond, so she simply

smiled, clinked her glass, and said "here, here" with the rest of them.

Bitsy's backhanded compliment stayed with Kit long after that luncheon. She'd known for a long time that she was a "catch," but the fact that she'd sunk so deep into Easton's clutches made her think seriously about her judgment. He had seemed so sincere, and yet it had been a sham. How would she know if the next man she fancied was any better? Her self-confidence began to slide, and she shored it up by pretending nothing was amiss. Not having anyone to talk to about it made it even worse. Like a caterpillar, she began to weave an emotional cocoon around her heart.

## CHAPTER SEVEN

Time heals all wounds, doesn't it? As Cecily's due date approached in the spring of 1899, Kit felt she was finally coming to terms with the horrendous mistake she'd made several months before. Easton had made his choice, and good riddance to him. She rarely saw him at social events, and when she did, he was on his own. The official word was that Cecily was having a difficult confinement and insisted her husband get out and about even though he much preferred being by her side. So it came as a shock when Easton made an attempt to see Kit alone at a large fundraiser for the Presbyterian Mission House. She was on her way back from the powder room next to the Grand Hotel's ballroom when he stepped into her path.

"I must see you," he said in a desperate tone of voice. "When can I see you?"

Kit would have laughed if she hadn't been so mortified. She glanced around to see if anyone had noticed them. "You must be joking."

He made a move toward her, but stopped, as if even he realized the chance he was taking. "I have never been more serious. Just tell me when and where."

She looked at him with the disdain born of generations of privilege. "I can't tell you where, but I can tell you when," she said. "That would be when hell freezes over." She'd never used that expression before. She liked it. "Now if you'll excuse me."

"I want to tell Cecily about us," he blurted out. "I have to. I'm going to."

Kit turned back to him, the rage she had never fully vented threatening to explode into the world's most ill-advised tirade. She paused to rein it back in. "There is no 'us,'" she said slowly. "And if you dare spread such a vicious lie, my father will see to it that you never work in San Francisco again. Doubt me at your peril." She proceeded to walk carefully away, taking pains to hide the tremors that had overtaken her body.

Days later, she was still rattled by the encounter. She knew Easton had no proof that they'd been intimate, but still, he could make an ugly insinuation that would be difficult to defend against. She wished there was some way to excise him from their social circle altogether, but she had no leverage over him.

That changed the evening Ellen's parents came by for cocktails before traveling to a dinner party with Kit's parents.

Kit remembered the doubts Mr. Hart had expressed about Easton Challis and she was determined to ferret out what those doubts were. Well accustomed to participating in her parents' social gatherings, she joined her father and Mr. Hart who were talking business while Josephine and Mrs. Hart gushed over the *tapenade noir* that Josephine had insisted Chef Bertrand embellish with figs.

"I understand Mr. Challis is rising quite rapidly over at Crocker National, Mr. Hart. As a board member, have you been happy with his performance?"

Mr. Hart took a long pull from his whiskey. "He's adequate. I'll give him that. Talks a good game. Now that he's Frank Anders's son-in-law, I guess that'll have to be enough. Still, there's something about him."

Kit smoothed her skirts, trying not to seem *too* interested. "I've heard rumors that, well, he's not quite what he seems. Do you get that impression, sir?"

Ellen's father responded readily to the *on dit* he himself had put out through his daughter. "Yes, that's it —he's not what he seems."

Edward Firestone joined the conversation. "In what way, Larry?"

Crossing one leg over the other, Mr. Hart seemed happy to share what he knew. "I met with the fellow back when he first joined the bank. A 'get to know you' kind of a thing. Challis said he went to Princeton, class of '95, so I asked him what he thought of Penn and Yale moving in on the Tigers, and who he thought had the better case to make for '94. Simple, right? Well, he didn't know what I was talking about."

"No," Edward said. "He must have."

"No, sir. I'm telling you he didn't have a clue. I had

to prompt him before he got the gist of it and chimed in."

"Well, I'm afraid I don't have a clue, either," Kit said. "What do Yale and Penn have to do with Princeton?

"Five years ago, all three teams were named national football champions," her father explained. "That's not a satisfying resolution to a season in anyone's estimation."

"Especially if you'd gone to one of those schools," Mr. Hart added. "Either that young man kept his nose hidden in the books, or—"

"Or he didn't really go there." Kit's mind was already beginning to churn with possibilities.

"Now I didn't say that, but that's what I was thinking. Still, I trust Frank to know what he's doing. He let his daughter marry the man, after all." He said nothing more and took another long sip of his drink.

None of them spoke. They didn't need to. Each of them knew that given Cecily's condition, it was the only thing her father could have done.

Kit had gotten what she came for. "I'm sure you're right, Mr. Hart," she said graciously. "Now I'm afraid I must rescue your wife from my mother's incessant praise of our chef."

---

As usual, Kit made a plan. She didn't care that she might be gaining information through shady means, nor did she think of who might be harmed by that information. She simply set about getting the goods on the man who had betrayed her, and who threatened to betray her still.

As it happened, it was shockingly easy to uncover the truth about Easton Challis. Kit put in a telephone call to Princeton's alumni department, asking for the correct spelling of Easton's name. She was informed that no such student had graduated from the university.

Next, she contacted the two regional banks that Mr. Hart said Easton had listed on his resume. Yes, their representatives said, Mr. Challis had worked at each branch briefly, but as a clerk, not a banker. From one of *those* sources she was able to track down his family address in Chicago. She could not locate a telephone number, so she hired a local private investigator, who went to the home and reported back. The Firestone name, as usual, made her task simple.

"I wish all my cases were this easy, ma'am. I went to the address you gave me and found a Mr. Vern Challis, who lives there with his wife, Maizie. Quite the gabbers. They've been married thirty-five years. He used to work on the docks but has a busted leg that never healed right. They told me about their big shot son who lives someplace out West and asked me to give him a message if I happened to find him. They want him to come on home because they haven't seen him in seven years. They seemed like nice folks."

Kit thanked the investigator and promptly sent him his fee. She wrote up all she'd learned and put it in the drawer of her writing desk, ready to be used whenever and however she wished. Her options were many: she could explain what she'd learned to Mr. Hart and her father, who would likely turn around and fire Easton, regardless of the fact that his father-in-law ran the bank. Word would get around that Easton was a fraud, and his reputation, in San Francisco at least, would be ruined forever. The downside to that plan was that she'd hurt Cecily in the process.

Or she could let Cecily know, so that her friend had a complete picture of who she'd married and could deal with him accordingly. If Kit were in Cecily's shoes, wouldn't she want to know such things?

Finally, she could keep Easton in check by letting him know privately that she had evidence proving his deception. "How's your dear departed mother?" she would say. "Maizie, isn't it? I hear she's come back from the dead and would like you to come home for a visit." That would certainly get the message across.

As time wore on, however, Kit realized that the person most impacted by the envelope in her desk was *her*. It was the first thing she thought about in the morning, and the last thing she thought about at night. *This is crazy*, she thought. *I'm still being affected by a man I despise.*

Kit's brother Will had moved into his new home before the holidays and was just now beginning a few renovations. He'd invited Kit over to see how she could help and she took the opportunity to ask him—indirectly, of course— about what she should do.

They'd been going over paint samples and fabric swatches in the front parlor. It had taken some time to persuade Will that his home might be more inviting if his color scheme consisted of something more than shades of black and brown. While taking a break with coffee and refreshments provided by Will's majordomo, Kit asked, "If you knew something bad about someone, something that could be construed by many as illegal, would you alert all interested parties about it?"

"I dunno," Will said. He sipped his brew and paused before elaborating. "I suppose I would have to know more about what's going on. Do I know the person? Do I like them? Is there a justifiable reason for whatever it is that's under wraps? Things like that aren't always so cut and dried." He reached for a slice of apple and a piece of cheddar cheese to go with it. "So, anything you want to share with your big brother? I can keep a secret, you know."

"Sure, like the time you told Mother I was the one who filched the tarts the morning of that picnic when I was twelve. She didn't trust me in the kitchen for months afterward, and therefore I don't trust *you* as far as I can throw you."

Reaching over the table, Will gently squeezed her forearm. "You seem pretty strong to me."

She appreciated his concern but couldn't bring herself to confess. "No, there's nothing to tell. I was just curious."

Will gazed at her for a moment; she could tell he didn't believe her. "Just remember I'm here," he said.

His words brought a lump to her throat that stayed with her for the rest of the day.

## CHAPTER EIGHT

In late April, Cecily Anders Challis gave birth to a baby girl named Henrietta Joy, but there was little fanfare in the society pages as word was passed around during various highbrow events that neither child nor mother were doing well. Kit was overcome with heart-pressing guilt for wishing her friend ill, even indirectly. It drove her to do the unthinkable: she sent Cecily a letter asking, no, practically *begging* to visit her.

Within a week Cecily responded: yes, she would love to see Kit, in fact she missed her childhood friend and had longed to see her for some time. It was important for them to "discuss matters." Could Kit come on the following Thursday afternoon?

*He told her* Kit thought. *I could kill him*. On the heels of that anger came both embarrassment and dread. Having asked to visit Cecily, she couldn't very well beg off now. But the idea of having her friend chastise her for trying to "steal" her lover turned her stomach.

Somehow, she would have to make Cecily understand that, had Kit known, she would never have gotten close to the man.

Furthermore (and this would be even more difficult to say), given what she'd uncovered about Easton Challis, he was the very last man on earth she would ever want. Should she share what she'd learned? The path forward was steeped in shadow. Still, she had to walk it.

The following Thursday afternoon she knocked on the door of Cecily's new home and was surprised when a nurse wearing gloves answered.

"Mrs. Challis has been looking forward to your visit," the nurse said softly. "I hope you can cheer her up; she's not been in the best of spirits."

Kit followed the young woman through the front of the house, which still had trunks lying about and stacks of pictures waiting to be hung. It was obvious that Easton and Cecily had had little time, or perhaps inclination, to feather their nest. They continued up to the second floor. The nurse led Kit to a room at the end of the hall, then closed the door quietly on her way out.

Cecily lay propped up in a four-poster bed, looking much too small to be a mother; she looked like a child herself. She beckoned Kit to come closer, but when Kit approached her to share a hug, she put up her hand.

"No, please. It's not good for you to touch me," she said. "I ... I am a mess."

Kit said nothing, because Cecily did look terrible. Her once lustrous red hair looked lank, and her skin was pale save for a series of blisters on her face and hands. Most of all, she looked worn out, as if she had been battling pain for quite a while. Kit's heart broke a little. No matter the circumstances, this was not the way a new mother should look or feel.

"What is wrong, Cecily? You look ... You look ..."

Rather than answer, Cecily pointed to the cradle located in a little alcove near the bed. "That's little Henny," she said. Kit walked over to see Cecily's newborn, who was sleeping fitfully. The tiny tyke looked odd. She had what appeared to be large lumps on her forehead, and she displayed a rash similar to Cecily's. And her nose ... her nose was flat in the middle, as if it had been crushed. Had she been struck? No, there was no other sign of trauma—no bruising or cuts. Kit reached out to the baby, but Cecily hissed, "Please don't touch her!"

Mother and child were obviously suffering from the same malady, but she knew Cecily wouldn't have invited her over if it were truly contagious. She turned back to her friend. "Please help me to understand," she said. "It looks like you've caught something."

At that moment Cecily began to cry, the tears solemnly rolling down her cheeks as if they'd been waiting patiently for their turn. Kit once again made to comfort her, but Cecily groaned. "No!"

"What is it, then? You are scaring me. Tell me, please!"

Cecily wiped her eyes with the sleeve of her bed jacket. "It is the wages of sin," she whispered.

Kit frowned. "What? What are you talking about?"

"I'm talking about the price I've paid"—her voice

broke—"and little Henny's paid for lying with Easton before I should have. He was so insistent, you see, and I was so in love with him. He told me we would always be together and so I ... I let him do what he wanted, and he didn't do anything to protect me. He —we— didn't think he needed to."

Kit's encounter with Easton filled her mind. Their tryst would have been identical to his and Cecily's except for Kit's insistence that he use the prophylactic. She remembered he wasn't happy about it. Such a small act. Such a gargantuan difference. She couldn't believe what she was hearing. "You're saying he ... he has—"

"The pox," Cecily whispered again, as if society might not hear if she spoke low enough. "The French pox. He passed it on to me, and I-I passed it on to our little girl." Tearing up again, she looked over at the cradle and then back at Kit. "I didn't mean to. I didn't know. God help me, I didn't know!"

The magnitude of Cecily's nightmare settled over Kit like a pall, bringing with it a thick, dark layer of sorrow. She almost buckled under the weight of it. Because the French pox was no ordinary illness. It was syphilis, for which she'd never heard of a cure.

"My dear friend," she said, wanting more than anything to reach out and touch Cecily to let her know she was not alone. She didn't notice when Cecily's eyes moved to capture those of someone who had just entered the room.

"I see you've discovered our dirty little secret," Easton said.

Kit turned around, ready to excoriate him for the

evil he'd wrought, but the expression on his face arrested her. Although he was attempting to school his features, he looked like a man in the throes of the worst agony possible. After an almost defiant glance in Kit's direction, he walked up to Cecily and kissed her on the forehead, oblivious to her mottled face.

"How are you today, my dear?" he asked as he took her hand.

She offered him a half-smile. "How do I look?"

He didn't answer but gazed at their child in the cradle. "And Henny?"

Cecily merely shook her head. She looked into her husband's face with a forlorn expression. "I had to tell Kit. We cannot keep it secret forever. If you love her and she loves you, then it's something she needs to know."

"But I don't love him, Cecily." Kit looked pointedly at Easton, the temperature of her words dropping sharply. "I never did."

The love Cecily still had for this good-for-nothing shone through her pallid face as she said, with no undercurrent of malice whatsoever, "Please don't say that, Kit. He loves you so, and if I am no longer here ..."

Kit couldn't stand it any longer. She jumped up, furious. "Don't you say anything of the kind. You are sick, yes, but there must be something we can do about it. There must be." She turned angrily to Easton. "What do you know about this ... this 'pox.' Why aren't you sick? What did you do to get rid of it?"

Easton ran his hands through his lank hair. For once his suit looked less than perfect. It was slightly wrinkled with a small stain near the right breast pocket where a handkerchief should have been. "I didn't do anything. I didn't know I had it, all right? By the time I figured it out, it was too late ... too late for Cecily, at least."

"What are you talking about?"

"Look, this happened nearly two years ago, back in Illinois. I came down with what I thought was the flu. I had a little rash, sure, but I thought it was hives. It lasted a couple of weeks, so I went to the doctor and told him my symptoms. He gave me the usual 'drink plenty of fluids, get plenty of rest' song and dance. I did what he told me to do and eventually it went away. *It went away*. I had no idea I was carrying this ... this monster inside me. I swear to you."

Kit stared at him. Was he telling the truth? Did it matter? By the looks of things, Cecily believed him, and at this point, anything that made her feel better, even a lie, was worth it.

But why on God's earth had Easton told Cecily about his pursuit of Kit? That alone was enough to consign him to hell. She turned back to her friend. "Cecily, I am sorry if it pains you, but you must understand that I hold no *tendre* for Easton. He made the right choice in picking someone who loves him as much as you obviously do. So the only thing to consider at this point is how to get you and little Henny well. And once you are well, I am sure that Easton will realize what a treasure he has in you." She stared at the man she'd once been stupid enough to desire. "Isn't that right, Easton?"

He could do little but nod.

"All right, then," Kit said, smoothing down her skirts. "First, who knows about this?"

"Only the nurse," Easton said. "I am paying her handsomely for her discretion. We have told Cecily's parents that she and the baby are in a weakened state and can't be around others for fear of picking up germs. I honestly don't know what else to do, other than have her ride it out as I did."

Kit entered her "take charge" mode. "The first order of business is to find out what our options are. I can do that without betraying your confidence, and that's what I shall do." She turned to Cecily and touched her arm, ignoring her friend's flinch. "I will do whatever I can to help you and Henny," she said. "You can count on that. I will get back to you, but in the meantime, you stay strong, for yourself and for your little girl, all right?"

Cecily smiled and nodded, the tears beginning to fall again.

"I'll walk you down," Easton said. He opened the door and beckoned the nurse inside. When they reached the foyer, he reached out and took Kit's arm. "Why are you doing this?" he asked.

She stepped back from him and let loose. "I know all about you, Easton. I know you didn't go to Princeton and I know your mother still lives. I know you were never a banker before you moved to San Francisco, and I know you're a two-faced liar who will stop at nothing to achieve your dubious ends. You should also know I seriously considered exposing you for what you are." She pointed upstairs. "But for some unknown reason, my friend loves you, and my God, even forgives you for the evil you've perpetrated on her and your child. Right now she thinks it's God's retribution for her dalliance, but you and I know the only person to blame in all of this is *you*. Cecily doesn't deserve any of this, so If I can at least help her get her health back, then I'm going to do it.

"But let's be clear: I am not doing it for you." Kit turned to leave but remembered one more thing. "Telling Cecily about your feelings for me, and making it sound as if I felt the same way was despicable. *Despicable*. So, you'd better make your peace with your wife in that regard, or so help me, I *will* expose your perfidy to all who'll listen. Do you understand me?"

Once again, Easton had no alternative but to nod. "I ... I just want you to know I'm sorry. So very sorry," he said.

"Tell that to Cecily," Kit retorted, "and keep telling her until she believes it."

Still humming with emotion but already making plans, Kit left the Challis household to its misery.

---

Dr. Roland Gage fixed a patriarchal stare on Kit. "You shouldn't be asking me such questions, much less hearing the answers, young lady."

Kit had made an appointment with the Firestone family physician under the pretense of having a "strange complaint." When she arrived at the oak-paneled office adjoining his home, she'd waved off a physical exam and gotten straight to the point, telling him she was inquiring on behalf of a "shy friend." She had even worn her reading spectacles in an attempt to look more studious. Perched upright in her chair, she was poised to take notes in a journal like an intrepid reporter, albeit one with something far more serious in mind than writing a news article.

"For goodness sake, Dr. Gage, a little information about such matters never corrupted anyone; it's probably saved more lives than not."

Sitting behind his rather imposing desk, he leaned forward, peering at her over his pince nez. He had kindly eyes but was obviously taken aback by her curiosity. "And you're being absolutely honest that this pertains to no one in your family?"

*Absolute* was such an extreme term, but ...

"Absolutely."

After a moment, Dr. Gage bent to Kit's will. "Well then, I can tell you it's a nasty business, a nasty business, indeed." He relaxed in his chair, assuming his normally professorial tone. "There are four phases, the first two of which can include painful symptoms and, in some cases, visible manifestations."

"Where are these 'manifestations'?" she asked.

The doctor coughed lightly. "Shortly after contact with an infected person is made, there may be signs in the ... in the nether region, where the act has occurred."

"You mean the penis or the vagina?"

That elicited an outright wince. "Or the mouth," he muttered.

Kim frowned. Oh dear. "And would it be possible to not know it's there?"

"I suppose so, depending on the location, or one's familiarity with their physical self. In any event, it can last several weeks before disappearing. By that time the infection has entered the bloodstream and spread to other parts of the body."

"Then what happens?"

"The disease enters phase two. A rash may occur, or other skin lesions. The patient may feel sick—"

"Like having influenza?" That's what Easton had described.

Dr. Gage nodded. "Precisely. Not everyone reacts the same way. Some experience treatable symptoms, and for some patients, it's not even that virulent. Once it's over with, they don't feel a thing. Some may not even know they've been infected."

"So, it eventually goes away?"

"That is where it becomes quite ... murky. In its third, or latent phase, the disease lies dormant, and can remain so for years and years. There might be flare-ups, there might not. But even though the patient experiences no symptoms, the disease may still be doing internal damage."

"And what about spreading it to others?"

"Unfortunately, the disease remains contagious for a year or more after it enters the latent phase, so that a person might spread it without being aware that they are doing so."

Kit inhaled. Despite the protection, could she have contracted it? Her mind told her no; she knew her body well and she hadn't had any sores or lesions or symptoms of any kind in the nearly eight months since her tryst. Still, the notion sent shivers through her. "I'm almost afraid to ask, but you mentioned it has four phases."

"That's right. Eventually syphilis can rear its ugly head for one, final phase. And that last phase is the most horrific one of all. The germs destroy the entire body from the inside out. Blindness, paralysis, even insanity can result. This isn't for delicate ears, but you wanted to know the truth of it."

Kit put both her notebook and her spectacles away. Only one statement from the doctor had given her any hope whatsoever. "You mentioned 'treatable' symptoms. What treatments would those be?"

Dr. Gage heaved a sigh. "I'm afraid I've not kept up with the latest therapies. I normally refer such cases."

"Those 'cases' are human beings, Dr. Gage. So, who do you refer them to?" She gazed at the man without wavering. Finally, he relented and opened the top drawer of his desk, pulling out a small card.

"You might find better answers with Dr. Landon," he said, handing the card to Kit.

It read:

### A.M. Landon, M.D.
### Obstetrics and Diseases of Intimacy
### Discretion Guaranteed

Putting the card in her reticule, Kit rose and smoothed her skirts. Dr. Gage rose as well, giving her a final stern look. "I am taking you at your word that this does not concern you or your family."

"You would be wise to do so," she said, and took her leave.

---

The initials "A.M." stood for "Alice Margaret," as Kit found out after heading directly over to the specialist's office from her meeting with Dr. Gage. The doctor practiced out of her home in Presidio Heights; fortunately, she had room in her schedule to see Kit right away.

Kit entered a rather large office that must have been a parlor at some point. Two comfortable chairs were placed near the fireplace, and at one end of the room, a long table held a microscope, stacks of medical journals, and several notebooks.

The physician appeared to be a decade younger than Kit's mother and was quite attractive—or would be, Kit surmised, if she wore her hair in something other than a severe bun and dressed in less melancholic clothing. The woman did wear a wedding ring, which at least dispelled the stereotype of the career-driven spinster. Dr. Landon noticed Kit's perusal, glanced at her own drab clothing, and smiled. "I wish being taken seriously did not entail dressing the part of an undertaker. In my specialty I would much prefer signaling hope than despair."

"Is there hope in your line of work, ma'am?"

"There is always hope," she said. "Tell me how I can help you."

Buoyed by that introduction, Kit launched into a more detailed recounting of Cecily and Easton's story, including the sad case of little Henny. The doctor's slight frown at hearing the condition of the baby erased Kit's momentary optimism, but she forged ahead. She'd come for knowledge and facts were sorely needed.

Kit addressed the contagion issue first. "My friend seems to think I could catch her disease by simply touching her. Should I be worried?"

"I wouldn't think so," the doctor assured her. "Syphilis is typically transmitted through sexual relations, or congenitally, that is, passed along from mother to child, as in your friend's case. You mentioned the child's rhinitis—her runny nose. That discharge *is* highly contagious, so you would want to stay away from that."

Kit had to know, so she ventured to ask, "If ... if you had relations with someone who carried the disease, but you used a ... a prophylactic ... would that be enough to ... to—"

"To keep from getting it? In most, but not all cases, yes. Especially if the carrier were asymptomatic."

"In the latent stage, you mean?"

Dr. Landon focused on Kit, apparently surprised at how much she already understood. "Yes, that's right."

"And if the person who was on the ... the receiving end, showed no symptoms, even months afterward—"

"Then yes, I would venture to say they were very lucky indeed."

Kit expelled a long breath and when she looked up, Dr. Landon was gazing at her with a sympathetic smile. Kit smiled right back, a perfect understanding passing between them.

But fate had not smiled on Cecily, and Kit had to find a way to help her friend. "I understand there are treatments one can undertake to get rid of the disease. Can you tell me—"

Dr. Landon shook her head. "No. There is no cure, Miss Firestone. In some cases we can treat the symptoms, but once the disease reaches the latent stage, there is nothing much more we can do except wait. And the wait can take years."

Kit scoffed. "And then you die a horrible death, is that it?"

"Not necessarily. A good percentage of syphilis carriers never see a resurgence of the disease. It lies dormant for the rest of their lives. They can have normal sexual relations, even have children, and not pass it on. One never knows."

"And that's the problem, isn't it?" Kit's voice rose with her anger. "You spend the rest of your life wondering if or when it's going to come back and destroy you."

Dr. Landon's countenance hardened. Kit could tell she was deeply troubled by the limitations of her profession. "You have hit upon our dilemma with regard to this disease. One of its most frustrating aspects, aside from the final phase itself, is its unpredictability. It toys with us who revere science but wreaks havoc on those who must live under the specter of its recurrence." She gestured to the scientific material stacked on the table. "Researchers are getting close to identifying the bacteria responsible, however. Once that happens, we'll be able to determine who has the illness much earlier, and perhaps find an antidote to combat it. Until then ..." The woman shrugged.

Kit sat for a moment, shifting through options, realizing they were much more limited than she'd hoped. "There must be something we can do."

"As I mentioned, depending on your friend's current condition, we can perhaps treat some of her outward symptoms, although the treatment is unpleasant at best and debilitating at worst. Your friend should be made completely aware of her options before we proceed."

It wasn't much, but it was something. "Then by all means, let's begin the process," Kit said. "When can you start?"

**CHAPTER NINE**

Assuring Cecily that her illness would remain confidential, Kit arranged for Dr. Landon to see her friend the next day. Easton was not present. According to Cecily, he was spending more of his non-working hours at the downtown Olympic Club, where Cecily's father had gotten him a membership.

"He says he needs to keep up his physical strength in order to take better care of us," she said. "But I think he simply doesn't want to be here." She smiled without mirth. "I can't say that I blame him."

*Well, I certainly can*, Kit thought. She kept her condemnation of Easton to herself, however; Cecily had enough to deal with.

Dr. Landon examined both Cecily and Henny, taking care to use precautions around the agitated infant. When she finished, she explained, honestly but kindly, what lay in store for both of them.

"I am already seeing signs of cloudy corneas in your

daughter," the physician said. "That is an early indicator for blindness, I'm afraid. In addition, she is experiencing severe joint swelling and bone discomfort. Is she very fussy?"

Cecily nodded, her tears ever-present. "I don't know what to do for her. She doesn't eat much and I pray for her to fall asleep. Even that is fitful, but at least I don't have to hear her tortured little cries."

"I will give you some laudanum drops to put in her bottle, and—"

Kit was appalled. "Won't that turn her into an addict?"

Cecily looked at Kit in disbelief. "Do you honestly think that matters at this point?" She turned back to the doctor. "I would be ever so grateful for whatever you can do to ease my little girl's suffering."

As for Cecily, the options weren't so clear.

"I can put you on a calomel regimen," Dr. Landon said. "That will help with your external rash and lesions, and possibly some of the aching you've been experiencing."

"By all means, do it, Cecily," Kit said.

The doctor held up her hand. "Before you make any decisions, please understand something. Calomel is another name for 'mercurous chloride,' which is basically mercury mixed with other agents. It is a metal, and while it can degrade the bacteria at work in your body, it has harsh side effects."

Cecily struggled to sit up in her bed, pain evident on her wan face. Kit moved to fix her pillow and Cecily smiled her thanks.

"How can it be worse than this?" Kit asked.

"Oh, it can be." Dr. Landon's tone was ominous. She outlined the possible dangers and ended with a less than sanguine appraisal. "It's a Hobson's choice, really. There is no telling when the current phase of your illness will run its course. You already know what that entails. The calomel therapy will help to clear up your outward symptoms but may do even more harm internally." The physician began to put away the instruments she'd used for her examination. "There is no easy answer."

"But there is only one choice," Cecily said. "I cannot hide from society indefinitely with the obvious sign of my wickedness all over my face and body. I must do what I can to get rid of it."

Dr. Landon gazed at Cecily with discreet pity. "And your daughter?" she asked.

Cecily looked over at little Henny, who had relapsed into her fitful slumber. "Whatever can be done to ease her pain—that's all that matters."

---

During the next several weeks, Kit dedicated herself entirely to the resurrection of her friend's health. She went to the Challis residence each afternoon, staying for several hours to give the nurse, whose name was Ellie James, a much-needed break. From Ellie (with whom she'd become friends) she learned how to give injections of the calomel, how to apply dressings to Cecily's sores, how to clear little Henny's nasal passages, and how to change the baby's diapers while wearing gloves to avoid infection.

Although Cecily was able to get to and from the commode, she had very little energy and spent most of the day reclining. Knowing that her most important job was to keep her friend's spirits up, Kit worked hard to keep a smile on her face, reading aloud at Cecily's bedside and regaling her with the latest news and gossip within their social sphere. Time and again she reassured her friend that no one suspected anything other than a severe case of post-partum vapors. "It's all the rage, didn't you know? Women of our class are known to be high-strung; we're prone to bouts of what they call 'neurasthenia'; it's the sign of a progressive society."

If Cecily saw through Kit's façade of joviality, she didn't mention it. Aside from concern that her predicament remain under wraps, she worried primarily about her daughter, who was not responding well to palliative treatment. Little Henny remained listless; her only sign of activity seemed to be that of experiencing pain. The rash on her face, in her mouth, and around her genitals persisted, as did her nasal secretions.

One afternoon, Cecily asked Kit to conduct a small experiment with the infant. She pointed to a locket attached to a silver chain lying on her bedside table. "Do me a favor, would you?" she asked. "Swing the locket gently in front of Henny and tell me how she reacts."

Kit followed her direction and although the baby's

eyes were opened, they did not track the swinging object. One could only conclude that Henny saw nothing, although Kit thought desperately for another explanation. "Well, she ... she seems sleepy," she offered.

"Her eyes—they're open, are they not?" Cecily's voice inferred she knew the answer.

"Yes."

"Then she is blind." There was a curious objectivity to her statement, as if Cecily had accepted the reality of the situation at last.

During this period, Easton Challis spent less and less time at home. He was never there when Kit was, and according to Cecily, he came in late every night, slept in another room, and was gone early in the morning, often neglecting to even speak to her. The nights when he failed to come home at all were growing in number. It was a testament to Cecily's horrific condition that she no longer seemed to care what her husband did. In fact, she seemed almost relieved by his absence. "It's one less thing to worry about," she said.

Kit, on the other hand, began to rage inside. How *dare* Easton abandon poor Cecily after inflicting this nightmare upon her! Kit had never before felt such vitriol for another human being. The feeling was powerful, invasive, like a cancer spreading throughout her body. She was in awe of it—until she realized that her explosive hatred of Easton was her way of venting an even more egregious vexation ... with herself.

Ever since Kit could remember, she had commanded her corner of the world. But her time with

Cecily had taught her the painful lesson that sometimes, putting one's entire heart and soul into the achievement of a goal simply was *not enough*. Despite her daily visits, despite her care and encouragement and even prayers (which Kit considered a last-ditch effort), despite everything, the syphilis would not bend to Kit's will. It would not quickly disappear or cease its malevolent attacks on Cecily's body. Instead, the bacteria magnanimously made room for the assault of the calomel. Perhaps, Kit thought in a cynical moment, the disease relished a challenge like she did.

The two poisons vied for the honor of causing the most destruction. Cecily developed ulcers in her mouth; her teeth grew loose and two of them fell out. The pain in her arms and legs grew worse; even a gentle touch could cause her to wince in agony. Kit seethed with uselessness.

Two months into the treatment, after a particularly bad afternoon, Cecily politely asked Kit to go home. "I really hate to have you sit here, day after day, watching me in my misery." She took Kit's hand, willing now to partake in that much contact. "You can't do anything for me and I would like to sleep."

"Go ahead and sleep," Kit said. "Ellie won't be back from her break for another hour or two; I can wait until then."

"No," Cecily said firmly, in a tone Kit hadn't heard in quite some time. "I really feel the need for some solitude."

Trying not to feel hurt by her friend's dismissal, Kit

reluctantly agreed. "Well, only because Ellie is due back soon."

She felt uncomfortable leaving Cecily alone, but reasoned it might do her friend good to simply be with her daughter for a change. "It's only for a little while," she reassured herself as she quietly left the house.

Unfortunately, a little while was long enough.

---

It was one of the rare evenings in which the Firestones dined *en famille*. Will happened to be over, no doubt relieved he wasn't part of an extensive guest list. Over a *boeuf bourguignon*, their mother took the opportunity to grill Kit about her current "obsession" with Cecily Challis.

"The poor girl simply had a troubling pregnancy," Josephine said. "I can tell you, the act of giving birth is no bed of roses, but it doesn't warrant taking to one's bed for months on end."

"You know nothing about it, Mother," Kit said, taking a sip of wine.

"I don't know about giving birth? I beg to differ, darling. In fact, I remember bringing you into the world with startling clarity."

Kit heard the faint ringing of the telephone in the front of the house. She hoped it was Ellen; she'd even settle for Bitsy or Bea—anyone who could spare her an evening of birthing stories and probing questions about Cecily. She noticed the look exchanged by Will and their father. This kind of talk wasn't their cup of tea, either. "Can we just change the subject?" she asked. "How about—"

"Excuse me. Miss Firestone? You have a telephone call." The family's butler stood at attention.

"Who is it, Geoffrey?" Josephine seemed to think the call was for her.

"A Miss Ellie James, ma'am."

Her heart in her throat, Kit stood up abruptly, her dinner fork hitting the china with a jarring sound.

"Ellie James? Never heard of her," Josephine commented. "A new friend, dear?"

"Yes, she is." Kit smoothed her skirts to calm herself. "If you'll excuse me."

Three minutes after taking the call, she hung up in shock, not knowing if she could hold back the sob fighting its way out. Taking in great gulps of air, Kit hurried back into the dining room. "I must go to Cecily," she announced in a barely controlled voice. "She needs me."

Will rose from the table. "I'm headed that way. I'll drive you."

"This is quite unusual," Josephine remarked. "Is it quite necessary that you—"

"I think it's necessary, darling," Kit's father said, his eyes on his daughter's face. He reached for his wife's hand. "She's a good friend."

Kit sent her father a grateful glance before grabbing her coat and reticule and following her brother out the door. She had barely closed the passenger door of his Winton before the moan she'd been holding back escaped.

"What's happened? Is it Cecily?" Will glanced at Kit with alarm as he drove down the winding driveway of the estate.

Kit shook her head. "No. It's ... it's her baby. Little Henny. She ... she stopped breathing. She's dead."

# CHAPTER TEN

## Josephine

*Do not panic.* In an uncharacteristic move, Josephine drew the curtains closed in the family carriage as her coachman drove home from Dr. Gage's office. Her concern was not for herself. She'd been experiencing some headaches and their family physician had assured her that nothing was amiss. He offered her some powder containing a newly discovered ingredient called "acetylsalicylic acid," but she declined. "I'm certainly not going to ingest anything whose name I cannot even pronounce."

As an alternative, he'd sent her home with a prescription for warm baths and a tincture of feverfew. Since she'd used those remedies for years, it had hardly been worth the visit, except for the information he had shared with her "in confidence" before she left. The suspicion that he might share Josephine's own confidences with others was overshadowed by what he'd told her about her very own daughter. Katherine might, he'd said, be suffering from some sort of unmentionable disease.

For the hundredth time, Josephine revisited her current approach to parenting Kit. It seemed a common enough refrain: most mothers of both daughters and sons swore how much easier the latter were to raise than the former. With the proper combination of severity and cajolery, Josephine could usually bend her sons to her will. Not so with Katherine. Her beautiful girl was stubborn and independent and most likely to say "south" if Josephine even obliquely hinted at "north." Kit maintained enough of a rapport about frivolous things, like parties and fashion, but held important matters close to her breast. Josephine knew she'd been hurt by Easton Challis's defection, for instance, but would she confide in her mother about it? Never.

And now this. Could her darling child really be dealing with a disease even the doctor couldn't talk about?

*Do not panic. At least not now.*

That evening, Josephine and Edward were hosting a small gathering of the city's elite to discuss fundraising for the local teachers' college on Powell Street, which was barely paid for by the state. The legislature had voted to appropriate only a pittance of the money needed to ensure the school's success. As a result, Frederick Burk, the school's president, was lobbying some of the Golden City's wealthiest men in order to make up the shortfall.

Despite her belief in the cause ("How can students

learn anything if their teachers are ill-equipped?"), Josephine found it nearly impossible to concentrate. She therefore headed to one of her favorite retreats—the Firestone mansion's vast kitchen. She had always loved food and the fine preparation of it. As a girl she'd taken culinary classes; as a doyenne of San Francisco society, she put that knowledge to good work. Decision-makers needed to be well fed, after all.

She found her resident chef, Bertrand Laurent, preparing the evening menu of *filet de boeuf en croute* along with *poire belle hélène* for dessert. She immediately took up a wooden pin and prepared to roll out the dough for the pastry that would cover the beef. She had acted as Bertrand's sous-chef on many occasions; it was their secret, shared only with family and the rest of their loyal staff.

"You are worried about something, madame. Is it one of your children?"

Josephine stopped short. "Why do you say that?"

He pointed to the pastry dough sitting on the marble work surface. "You are much less assertive with the rolling pin than usual. I know there are situations that energize you—politicians *désagréables*, perhaps, or a béchamel sauce that is *trop sale*. But your children. They cause you *beaucoup d'anxiété, n'est-ce pas?* Which one gives you *préoccupation* this evening?"

Josephine heaved a small sigh. It was difficult to be anything but honest with Bertrand. "It's Kit. I think she may be keeping something from me, about an illness, and I dare not ask her directly about it or my source will be exposed."

"Is it so important that you must know this matter that she is keeping from you?"

Josephine looked up at her colleague with tears in her eyes. "Of the greatest importance," she said.

Bertrand nodded, taking the pin from her and quickly rolling the dough into three rectangles. He had already seared three sirloin roasts and now placed them onto the pastry sheets before topping them with *foie gras* and a brandied mushroom paste.

"Oh, let me do it," Josephine said, finding comfort in her bossiness and beginning to wrap the roast with the dough.

Taking no offense, Bertrand stepped over to the large iron stove where he stirred the contents of a double boiler. "Then you must keep the lines of communication open, both directly and indirectly. Much like the *chocolat* I have been melting for the *sauce poire*. You need *tous les deux flamme et vapeur*—both flame and steam—in order to achieve the perfect consistency. Was your source certain of his or her knowledge?"

"No, but they gave her a referral to someone else. A doctor who ... who specializes in such things."

"Alors, that is your next move then, *n'est-ce pas*? To meet this doctor and see what else you might discover? It is another layer that you must peel back."

Bertrand saw the world through a chef's eyes, but Josephine understood him perfectly. She bestowed one of her radiant smiles upon him.

"You're right, of course. I shall make an appointment to see him first thing tomorrow." Feeling better with a plan in place, she swept a bit of the mushroom paste onto her finger and tasted it. "Perfection. You are a true genius . . . in many ways."

Bertrand answered with his own Gallic shrug. "I live to serve, madame."

---

The doctor to whom Katherine had been referred turned out to be a woman, which pleased Josephine mightily. Dr. Alice Landon had offered to see Josephine just before lunch the following day and now the two women were seated in the doctor's office. The physician was being quite stubborn, however, and none of Josephine's usual charms were working.

"Dr. Landon, I am not asking you to betray a confidence," she said, an edge to her voice. "I do not care about names. I have been told that my daughter may be suffering from a ... a malady, and I only want to know if that is true so that I may help her."

The doctor looked at Josephine intently before speaking, as if she were deciding upon her worthiness. "Why don't you ask her yourself, ma'am?"

Josephine snorted. "Doctor, you seem too young to have a daughter even approaching the age of ten, but I can assure you that since even before that age, my Katherine has let it be known that she does not want me interfering in her life. She is intelligent and willful, and I am just worried that"—her voice cracked—"that she needs help and is too stubborn to ask for it."

Dr. Landon paused, then pointed to a framed photo

hanging on the wall behind her desk. In it a young girl, about eight, and an even younger boy stood looking solemnly into the camera. "Yes, I have a daughter," she said. "Mrs. Firestone, I am not at liberty to discuss my patients with others, but you will be happy to know this, at least: your daughter Katherine is not a patient of mine. She came to see me on behalf of a friend. Without going into details, I would just like to say you can be very proud of her selfless behavior in this regard. She is the kind of friend we should all be so lucky to have."

Josephine didn't bother to check the tears of relief that began to fall. Dr. Landon said nothing, but handed her a handkerchief, which Josephine took gratefully. "I don't suppose you'd be willing ..."

Dr. Landon gave Josephine a half-smile and shook her head slightly. "You said you didn't want names, which is good, because I would not give them to you. I think this might be one of those cases where you accept that as a parent, there are some areas of life in which your child does not want you to trespass. This is one of them. Surely you had one or two of those episodes with your own parents."

Josephine dabbed her eyes and smiled. "You might say that," she said.

## CHAPTER ELEVEN

*1870*

Boathouse Row was the place to see and be seen for Philadelphia's young elite. It was located on the east bank of the Schuylkill River, along a stretch the Fairmont Dam had tamed into a smooth waterway, perfect for ice skating in winter and rowing in summer. The placid water bred mosquitos, which over time drove out the riverside estate owners who sold their properties, leaving plenty of space for a city park and select sporting societies like the Schuylkill Navy and the Bachelors Barge Club. By the time Josephine and Dinah were old enough to enter that social scene, nearly a dozen such clubs had their own boathouses, playing host to club and school teams who competed against one another in seasonal regattas. Muscular young men, filled with bravado and an overactive sense of their own self-worth, vied for the attention of young ladies from the city's exclusive preparatory and finishing schools who came to watch them perform. All season long, intriguing stories emanated from Boathouse Row; unfortunately, not all of them had happy endings.

Josephine and Dinah were thick as thieves into high school, although they had outgrown their governess and now attended different educational institutions. Being Catholic, Dinah boarded at Mount Saint Joseph Academy, located on the northwest side of the city on Wissahickon Creek. Josephine, still living at home, attended the new, non-denominational Agnes Irwin School. When Dinah came home on the weekends, the girls spent much of their free time together, although the difference in their appearance was beginning to cause a strain.

Because of her petite frame, Josephine continued to be described with phrases like "a perfect little doll." Dinah, on the other hand, was hailed as a "Queen Boudicca" after the iconic Celtic warrior.

"I look like a giant monster next to you," Dinah complained one afternoon as they stood in front of her bedroom cheval mirror dressed only in their chemises and knickers.

"And everybody thinks I'm still a child," Josephine retorted, turning to the side to bemoan her almost non-existent bust line. "At least you are treated like an adult."

Strolling along Boathouse Row started out as one of the girls' favorite outings, but early in the summer before Josephine's senior year, a boorish young rower from one of the posh prep schools saw them walking along the path (both, as it happened, wearing pale-blue dresses) and bellowed, in front of his friends, "Ho, there! Are you two twins? You'd be perfect for Barnum's freak show!"

Dinah, her eyes widening in shock, said nothing, but Josephine couldn't help herself. She gestured at the young man and loudly offered, "Oh, I'd *heard* they'd lowered their admission standards for Friends Select, but I didn't know they'd sunk *that* low."

The young man's dressing-down, sealed by the good-natured ribbing of his cohorts, did little to mitigate the girls' embarrassment. From that point on, Dinah and Josephine made a point to minimize their joint appearances at the river. They would travel to Boathouse Row together out of concern for safety and societal decorum, but once there, they'd part almost immediately and gravitate to their own spheres of influence.

It was easy enough to do. In some ways, Dinah was ahead of Josephine in the courting game. During one sleepover she confessed that she had already caught the eye of a fellow parishioner at Old St. Joseph's Church, an affable young man with bright red hair by the name of Clarence Marshall. At twenty-two, Clarence was six years older and already a college graduate, which to Dinah seemed far too old. "And he's somewhat fat," she confided with a giggle. "He looks too much like Papa."

Clarence, apparently, was willing to wait in the wings. He had worked his charm with Dinah's father to the extent that Mr. Bettancourt offered the young man a job in his textile brokerage. It involved sales and

Clarence was good at it. Mr. Bettancourt was pleased, and often included Clarence in family events.

Clarence came from nothing, which ruled him out as far as the social-climbing Mrs. Bettancourt was concerned. But Dinah's aloofness had a still deeper origin: her heart belonged to someone else.

"Roddy Merchant?!" Josephine was appalled when Dinah finally divulged the name of the man she loved. "Dinah, he's got a ... a reputation." That was putting it mildly. Roddy was a golden boy with wavy, jet-black hair whom just about every debutante on Philadelphia's Main Line wanted to snare. Rampant rumors claimed that the young man was both charming and arrogant ... and that he always got what he wanted. Currently he was escorting a lovely deb by the name of Elspeth Harrington.

Dinah would have none of Josephine's naysaying. "I'll have you know he has paid quite a bit of attention to me," she said with a trace of haughtiness. "What makes you think he couldn't love me back?"

Sensing she was about to walk into quicksand, Josephine proceeded carefully. "Well ... for one thing, he is heading off to Penn in the fall. That makes him two years older than you. And ... and he is not a Catholic."

Dinah scoffed, displaying every one of her naive, not-quite-seventeen years. "Oh, for heaven's sake, that is of no importance whatsoever."

Josephine started to argue but thought better of it. Who was she to judge, anyway? She was outgoing and had gotten to know several of the rowing teams, but the only swain she'd attracted was Bertie Norwich, a large but mild-mannered high school junior whose attraction to Josephine centered on one aspect only: her size.

"You would be a perfect coxswain," Bertie explained to her one morning as she watched his Bachelor Club Mariners crew prepare for a practice run. "You're small but you've got a loud voice, and you're certainly not afraid to boss people around."

"You are a muddle head," Josephine countered with a smile. "In case you hadn't noticed, they don't allow females on crew."

"Not yet, but they might ... someday. How about you come out with us and give it a whirl? You've watched us enough times; you know what to do. Gene's out with the flu and we need someone to steer the boat."

"You need someone who's not going to sink you," Josephine shot back. But as she gazed at the eight young rowers on Bertie's team, a notion grabbed hold of her and wouldn't let go. *Why not? Why not try something that nobody else is doing?* Before she could talk herself out of it, she turned to the rest of the crew. "What do you think? Shall we try it?"

With the exception of two grousing stick-in-the-muds, the Mariners assented, and Josephine climbed into the stern to face them. Eight strapping young men stared back at her, waiting for her command. She trembled with the thrill of it. "Set the boat," she called. "And keep keel!"

That was the first of many practice sessions in which Josephine, weighing in at one hundred and five pounds, got to tell eight muscular young men (any one of whom could have easily thrown her overboard) precisely what to do and how to do it. Gene, the regular coxswain, wasn't happy about being usurped. He complained loudly that using her in his place made everybody think he was a pansy—a misconception he already battled because of his own small stature. He made it through the July Fourth regatta (the Mariners came in third in their division), but his recurring bouts of bronchial illness prompted his parents to take him out west for several weeks to dry out and strengthen his lungs, so his grumblings fell on deaf ears.

"Think of it this way," Josephine said the day he announced his departure. "I try my best to call in your style, and when you come back, you'll *have* to take over because they won't let me compete."

Gene couldn't argue with that.

The rest of the teams on Boathouse Row merely chuckled; word spread that the Mariners were "henpecked" on the water. Opposing teams would call out "Cluck cluck cluck!" to get under the skin of Bertie and the rest of the crew. They thought it was great fun.

That attitude lasted until the Mariners began to win their practice sprints.

Toward the end of July, Josephine (whose crew mates now called her "Jo") realized with a touch of melancholy that her rowing days were coming to an end. Once more she'd be standing on the shore, cheering the Mariners on, only now she'd be second-guessing every move the "legitimate" coxswain made.

The afternoon before Gene was set to return, she was just settling in for a final row when she saw Dinah standing on the shore watching her. Dinah was dressed in a pretty, lemon-yellow dress with a matching bonnet. She held a white lace parasol and looked like a paragon of young womanhood—the highest ideal Philadelphia's high society could lay claim to.

A cold feeling swept through Josephine that had nothing to do with the slight wind that had kicked up over the water. She looked down at the plain brown dress she habitually wore on the shell. They were still close friends, but Dinah looked so distant, as if she lived in another time and place. Jo didn't know if it was an omen or just part of her sadness at leaving the team she had come to know and care about so much. But it just didn't feel right.

"I don't want to leave her," she said abruptly.

Bertie looked over at Dinah, who had begun walking up the steps from the boathouse. Three young men, including Roddy Merchant, were paying her court. "She'll be fine," he said. "There's safety in numbers."

He was wrong on that account. So very wrong.

It was dusk when Josephine and the crew returned to the dock. They had made several runs, Jo coxing the shell and its occupants along a straight and rapid course.

They would have returned earlier but as they were heading back after their last run, they'd been challenged to an impromptu sprint by the Poseidons from Havenhurst Academy.

The Mariners won by half a boat length and Josephine shouted louder than anyone when they crossed the line. Oh, she was going to miss it!

As their shell glided up to the dock, she could see Dinah standing rigidly in just about the same place she'd been spotted before the practice session. She still had her parasol, but she was not wearing her bonnet. By her friend's posture, Josephine could tell that something was off-kilter. Perhaps she'd had some disturbing news about her family, or, God forbid, Josephine's. The coldness she had felt earlier in the day returned.

"Dinah!" she called but got no response. Dinah merely stood there, as if frozen.

Josephine hopped off the boat, heedless of Bertie's calls for her to wait. Dismissing him with a backward wave of her hand, she held her dampened skirts as she climbed the grassy incline leading up from the shore. Her breath hitched as much from concern as exertion. As she approached she could see that Dinah was slightly disheveled, her hair askew and her yellow dress muddied in places it wouldn't have been had she remained upright. Had she fallen? "What is wrong?"

Josephine demanded. Again, Dinah remained mute, only her large brown eyes signaling her distress.

Jo set her jaw, took Dinah's hand and led her away from the boathouse. Bertie ran up to them.

"What's wrong with Dinah?" he asked. "She looks funny."

"Can you call us a cab? Dinah ... doesn't feel well. I've got to get her home."

Instead of going to the Bettancourts', however, they rode the carriage back to Josephine's house. She knew her mother and step-father were out on a rare social visit (part of her uncle's attempt to rehabilitate his reputation), so they'd have the privacy to get Dinah in some sort of condition to face her parents. Once they arrived they headed directly upstairs to Josephine's room.

Sally was dusting the upper parlor. "May I help you, miss?" she asked.

"I think Dinah's been very upset in some way," Josephine hedged. "Would you happen to have something she could take to, well, relax her?" They had grown close over the years and Jo knew Sally's special talents.

Sally gave Josephine a knowing look. "I think I can brew up something for her. A special tea, perhaps?"

"You are first-rate," Josephine said. "Thank you."

Josephine led Dinah to her bed and sat her down. "Now tell me what happened," she insisted.

Dinah had been shivering ever since they'd entered the hansom cab. "I ... I need to lie down. I f-feel tired."

Yet she remained upright, shaking, tears now beginning to flow.

"Oh, my dear friend," Jo said. "Let me help you." She stood Dinah up again and began to untangle the muddied white sash around the taller girl's waist. Eventually she was able to peel Dinah's dress off, leaving her friend in her petticoat and chemise, the latter of which was unbuttoned halfway down the front.

But it was the girl's drawers that told the tale. They were soiled, with spots of what looked like mud, grass, and blood. Jo pulled out one of her own sleeveless summer nightgowns and had Dinah change. She then took her friend's hand ever so gently. Her voice a whisper, she repeated, "Tell me what happened."

"He ... he said he loved me. He liked to touch me and I let him. Just a little. A few times before. Just a little. But this time ... this time he wanted me to prove my love for him. He said, 'Give me everything.'" Dinah stared at Josephine, her eyes bleak. "I said I didn't know what he meant, so he said 'I'll show you' and he took me behind the boathouse with his friends, and ... and started to ... and I said no, but he didn't listen, and I tried to leave but they wouldn't let me. And his friends, they just watched." She frowned, confused, as if she couldn't understand how such behavior could occur. "They just watched."

There was a soft knock on the door. Sally carried in a tray which held two teapots, two cups, and a plate of biscuits. "The green pot is yours," she said to Josephine. "Have the miss drink from the red one."

"Thank you, Sally. Could you wait outside for a moment?"

"Yes, miss."

Josephine got Dinah to drink some of the maid's special tea, then directed her to crawl under the covers. Dinah obeyed like a rag doll, immediately curling into a fetal position and closing her eyes.

"Sleep for a bit, dearest. I'll have a message sent to your parents that we are having a sleepover here." She doubted Dinah even heard her.

Jo took the offending undergarments, slipped out of the room, and quietly shut the door. Sally waited in the hall, running a finger idly along the trim that separated the wainscoting from the papered upper wall. "Is the miss all right?" she asked.

In response, Josephine pointed to the evidence on the soiled drawers. "She did not ask for this. It is unforgivable."

Sally nodded, taking the clothing from her. "It is more common than you think. My two sisters ..."

Jo could feel the blood pounding in her temples; she wanted to throw something against the wall. She glared at her maid. "That is no justification. What can be done about it?"

Sally sent her a look that some might have interpreted as pity. "If I knew that, miss, I'd make a lot of ladies in my line of work very happy. Truth is, there's nothing can be done about it. It's the way of things."

"We will see about that," Josephine muttered.

"Yes, miss." Sally's reply was perfunctory, but before

heading back downstairs, she hesitated. "Miss Drummond?"

"Yes?"

"God forbid, but sometimes there are ... consequences ... to such things. You let me know if anything happens; maybe I can help."

Josephine squeezed Sally's hand gently. "With any luck, that won't be necessary. But thank you."

---

Unfortunately, luck was nowhere to be found. A month went by and Josephine watched, incensed, as Dinah began to exhibit the signs of a most unwanted pregnancy. Her breasts grew larger, straining against her modest shirtwaists, so that even in the dog days of summer she was obliged to wear shawls to cover them up. She began to feel queasy in the mornings, but with Jo's help was able to keep her condition a secret from her parents.

For obvious reasons Dinah had no desire to return to Boathouse Row, but Josephine insisted they keep up appearances, for a while at least, to ensure there was no untoward gossip. Despite the occasional remark about their odd pairing, Jo made sure her friend was never left alone. Fortunately (if one can find anything fortuitous about such circumstances) Roddy Merchant and his minions had seen fit not to bandy about his conquest. In fact, it appeared they'd forgotten about Dinah Bettancourt and Josephine Drummond altogether.

But Josephine hadn't forgotten about them. Not in the slightest. A firm believer in the adage that revenge is a dish best served cold, she began to research ways in which Dinah's attacker could be punished to maximum effect. In the meantime, she had to call upon Sally's herbal "remedies" one more time.

## CHAPTER TWELVE

Sally's two older sisters were members of Philadelphia's demimonde and each had needed to rid themselves of offspring more than once. Personally, Sally saw nothing morally wrong in proactively aborting a child. "Nobody likes a fat mistress," she said to Josephine one afternoon as she measured out herbs from bottles she kept in her room. "'Specially if the father has already left you for someone else. And besides, it's one less mouth to feed."

Josephine was curious. "Why did you not ... follow the same path? You are a pretty woman, and, well ..."

"You think so, do you?" Sally grinned. "Well, it so happens I'd rather be between a woman's legs than have a man between mine, if you get my meaning."

Feeling a blush steal along her neck, Jo could only nod. She had heard of women engaging in Sapphic passion but had never actually met someone who practiced it. Sally misinterpreted her silence as fear.

"Don't you worry none, miss. I can tell you have an eye for the lads, and there's nothing wrong with that."

"No, I wasn't worried. I just ... well, I think it'd be a lonely life, is all. Having to hide who you truly are must take its toll."

Sally looked at her with what Jo took to be a newfound respect. "It can be a trial," she admitted. Then she smiled. "But when you find the one who speaks to you, whoever he or she happens to be, it can be magical."

"You sound as if you have experienced that magic."

Sally winked. "I never kiss and tell, miss."

The two lapsed into a discussion of the ingredients Dinah would be ingesting. Sally had prepared several packets of tea containing blue cohosh and nettle. "You must make sure your friend drinks several cups of this a day," she instructed. "It is not always effective, but it will greatly increase her chances of a natural miscarriage." She also handed Josephine a small bottle with a dropper. "This is squawmint oil, which you might know as pennyroyal. Put a few drops in each cup, but not too many, because it can cause all sorts of problems, such as overbleeding and the like. After several days, your friend will likely begin to feel the need to rid her body of the baby—"

Josephine swallowed hard. "Is it really a baby?" She didn't know if she would be able to deal with such a thing.

Sally shrugged. "Some would call it that; some would call it a problem to be gotten rid of. I guess it's up to you."

At this point in her pregnancy, Dinah was a bundle of emotions, barely level-headed enough to do what Josephine told her to do. The plan, fortunately, was simple: Dinah would drink the tea three times a day until her body began to repel the contents of its womb. Sally had explained it would be like a terrible case of stomach flu, but they mustn't have a doctor examine her or the jig would be up. Josephine would volunteer to nurse her friend back to health and thus be able to help if something went wrong.

"What am I going to do if this doesn't work?" Dinah asked tearfully the first day. She'd made sure to pick a week during which her parents were excessively preoccupied with social engagements.

Jo was carefully putting drops of pennyroyal oil into the cup. Was two enough? Would three be too many? Sally hadn't given her an exact number, and Jo didn't want to put in any more than necessary. "You must remain positive," she cautioned, handing Dinah the doctored tea. "It *will* work."

Dinah drank the potion for several days as instructed, and her body did begin to relieve itself of much of its contents. Nausea took away her appetite, and when she was forced to eat, it caused terrible bouts of flux. As planned, she pled a mild case of the flu and took to her room, refusing all company except Josephine's. Clarence Marshall came to call several times but was turned away.

"He's obviously smitten with you," Josephine teased after yet again passing on Dinah's regrets to the young man.

"I'm sure he would sing a different tune if he knew the truth," Dinah said bitterly. "Oh!" she moaned and ran to the bathroom for the third time that afternoon.

After five days, it became apparent the girl's unlucky streak was holding. Despite severe cramps, the abortifacients were simply not working. There was very little spotting and nothing emerged that resembled the remnants of a pregnancy.

Dinah sank into despair. "I am still carrying this thing!" she cried. "I can feel it. God is mad at me for even thinking of killing one of His creatures. What am I going to do?"

"You are going to stay calm," Josephine admonished. "We will fix this." Inside, however, she was anything but confident. Time was not on their side.

Back at her own house, Josephine sought out Sally for guidance. The maid was in the midst of washing linens in the scullery, her strong arms rhythmically scrubbing a cotton towel against the washboard.

"Those herbs are tried and true, especially the pennyroyal. But sometimes the babe just digs in," she said. "The miss got a raw deal, is all." She dipped the towel in the rinsing tub and began to feed it through the wringer attached to the side. Jo watched the rollers squeeze the water out of the fabric as Sally turned the crank.

*The pennyroyal.* Maybe Jo hadn't put enough drops in. She'd been worried about too much bleeding, but maybe she'd let Dinah down by being too careful. Was it all her fault? She felt a pressure, as if she too were being squeezed. "There must be *something*," she implored. "Some alternative we can consider."

The maid straightened up, rubbing the small of her back. She had a determined look about her. "There are those who can go in and take a babe from the womb, but there's none I can recommend. I've seen a few horror stories and heard of a lot more. Something goes wrong, it could mess her insides up pretty bad. She might not ever conceive again, or worse, she could bleed out. So, no, I wouldn't go down that road."

"I can't believe that's all there is," Jo said.

Sally put the clean towel in the basket ready for hanging and started to wash the next one. "Well, how about putting the squeeze on the man who done her wrong? A marriage license can fix a lot of mistakes."

Jo shook her head. "Out of the question, I'm afraid." Roddy Merchant would laugh at the idea of marrying Dinah; he would simply deny everything and paint her as a whore. Besides, Jo had other plans for Roddy. No, there had to be ...

Wait. Maybe marriage *wasn't* out of the question. Josephine abruptly hugged Sally, catching her off guard. "You've given me an idea," she said. "Thank you."

Now all she had to do was sell the idea to Dinah.

---

"I'm sorry. You want me to do what?" Clarence Marshall, the vest of his brown suit stretching tightly across his expansive middle, stood in the Drummond's informal parlor, invited there by Josephine and, he must have assumed, Dinah. However, only Jo sat across from him on the settee.

"Marry Dinah," she reiterated. "You love her, don't you?"

"Well, I ..."

"Of course you do. And she holds affection for you as well. You could have a short engagement, and—"

Clarence frowned. He was not as gullible as she had hoped. "What is this all about, Miss Drummond? Why the change of heart, and why is Dinah not here to tell me of it herself?"

Josephine plucked at the invisible lint on her skirt. It seemed a fair degree of truthfulness was necessary. She looked up at the young man. "Dinah finds herself in a ... a situation, and to avoid ruin, her only recourse is to marry. You wish to marry her. You have made that clear for several months now. Well, you now have the opportunity to make your dream come true."

The man stared at her for a moment as her meaning became clear to him. "She's with child," he stated in a cold voice. "Whose is it?"

More lint plucking. "I am not at liberty to say at the moment. Suffice to say she is not responsible for what happened, and the perpetrator cannot be counted on to do the right thing. You, however, can step in, and —"

Clarence shook his head, his face red. "Oh, no. If Mr. Bettancourt thought I'd lain with his precious daughter before marriage, he'd kick me out the door faster than parishioners leaving mass. I'm not willing to take that chance for something I didn't do."

Josephine had considered as much. Clarence wasn't

a selfless individual (Who was?), and she couldn't blame him for that. There was no telling how angry Dinah's father might become, even if Clarence appeared to be taking responsibility. The second option would have to do. "I see your point. Alternatively, you could present yourself as a knight in shining armor, offering to save Dinah and her family from social ruin despite the fact that the child isn't yours. Would you be willing to do that, at least?"

Clarence paced the room, obviously weighing his options. Jo could imagine him tallying up the accounting sheets. Marrying into the Bettancourt fortune had always been his goal. Finally, he stopped in front of her. "That is indeed a possibility."

---

The marriage of seventeen-year-old Dinah Clementine Bettancourt and Clarence Henry Marshall took place three weeks later in the parlor of the Bettancourt home. Dinah's father, after being made to see less red and more reason by his wife and daughter, stood grim-faced while Dinah tied herself permanently to a young man she had only months before rejected as being too fat.

Clarence, for his part, played the role of savior well: not too self-congratulating, but letting it slip, now and again, that he was aware of his newfound power. The couple had moved into Dinah's bedroom and now the young man who had wanted so badly to be included was indeed an indelible part of the Bettancourt family.

Dinah reported, thankfully, that Clarence was a decent husband to her in the bedroom. He was insistent that she cater to him but was not cruel by any means. "I think we will rub along fine together," she said bravely. "And we will have a child to care for, which will no doubt give us much joy."

They say that bad luck comes in parcels of three, and Dinah's final portion came three weeks after her wedding, when her body finally decided to rid itself of the baby she carried. She took to her bedroom for three days while her womb shed its lining and the life it had been nurturing. When it was over, the signs that she was pregnant no longer needed to be hidden, because they no longer existed. In turn, the societal tongues ceased to wag about her hasty wedding. As soon as she could, Josephine went over to offer her dear friend support.

"I would have been a good mother," Dinah said through her sniffles as she clutched Jo's hand.

"And no doubt you *will* be one in good time," Jo assured her. "Only then, the baby's father will know it's his child, and that will be a good thing, won't it?"

The light in Dinah's eyes sputtered like a dying candle. It told of romantic dreams cut short, of a union that was no longer needed but could not be broken. It told of innocence irrevocably lost.

Later that night Josephine lay awake thinking about Dinah's fate and the role she had played in it. Guilt gnawed at her, a persistent whisper that she should have done more. She assured herself that if given enough time, Clarence might very well have won Dinah's heart all on his own.

She considered the plight of the women she knew. Some, like her mother, were willing to pay almost any price to avoid responsibility and have a man take control. Others, like Sally's sisters, wanted to believe they were in charge of their lives, but still relied on men to take care of them, even if only for a little while. And women like Dinah? They had it worse than anyone, because they never even got to make a choice. It was so unfair!

Anger bubbled up and out of Josephine, causing her jaw to clench and her heart to pound. *I will never, ever, let that happen to me*, she vowed. *No matter what.*

During Dinah's ordeal, Jo had taken it a day at a time, concentrating on what she could do to help her friend. But now ... now she turned her thoughts to revenge, plain and simple. It was not very Christian-like to think such ruinous thoughts, but in a strange way she felt like Dinah's champion, a warrior who would fight where her friend could not.

But how? Bertie, she remembered, had seen Dinah on the shore and said not to worry, because there was "safety in numbers." He'd been wrong in Dinah's case, but maybe Jo could apply the principle in another way, using it to confront Dinah's attackers. What did every man who took advantage of a woman fear more than anything? Exposure. The censure of society. Jo's stepfather was trying to repair his reputation as a man who took shameful advantage of his brother's distraught widow. The girls of the demimonde were dropped by their "protectors" when evidence of their infidelity began to show in their mistresses' growing bellies. What did someone like Roddy Merchant fear? Losing his status, that's what. A status that had gotten him admitted to the University of Pennsylvania, one of the most prestigious schools around.

But if people knew what he did to innocent young girls like Dinah, they might not be so quick to accept him in high society. The problem was how to expose him with credible accusations and ensure he felt the sting.

One voice wouldn't be enough. But several? That's where the "safety in numbers" came in. Josephine smiled in the darkness as an idea fell into place.

It was past midnight and her mother and Uncle Whitford (she could not bear to call him her stepfather), had retired hours before. Because her uncle always insisted her mother sleep in his bed and not her own, Josephine was able to slip into her mother's dressing room, which was accessed from the hallway, with impunity. There she "borrowed" the article of clothing she knew her mother wouldn't miss (having so many of them already) and which would illustrate her plan to perfection. Tomorrow she would explain to Sally precisely what she had in mind. Reprobates like Roddy Merchants weren't going to stand a chance.

## CHAPTER THIRTEEN

Much to Josephine's delight, Sally highly approved of her scheme. The maid spread the word through her sisters that several women of the demimonde were needed to "make a statement" about their work conditions and could do so dramatically yet anonymously. On a Saturday morning in early October, Sally took time off to bring thirteen of them to West Park, on the opposite side of the Shuylkill River from Boathouse Row. No doubt some of them were there because of political leanings, but it hadn't hurt that their efforts would earn them two new dresses. Josephine hoped they wouldn't be too disappointed to learn that one of those dresses would be black.

The women came in all shapes and sizes. A number of them—Sally's sisters Beth and Amy, for example—were quite lovely. Others had plain faces but curvaceous figures. And there were some to whom God had given very little in terms of physical allure. Yet all were members of the same profession. If Josephine could convince them of her plan, all would have another, more powerful affiliation, one that could strike fear in the hearts of any men who had done them wrong.

Josephine had placed blankets upon the ground where the women now sat, and she stood before them, looking so small that one of the women rudely called out, "How old are you?" to which Josephine responded in her most bellicose coxswain's voice, "Old enough!" She gazed at the women until she had their attention. Then she began.

"Some men do terrible things to women and get away with it because their rank in society is more exalted than ours. A dear friend of mine was assaulted by one of them, and afterward he ignored her. She became pregnant and when she couldn't lose the child by natural means, she was forced to marry another man, a man she didn't love, in order to avoid scandal."

"At least she had that option," one woman argued. "Some of us don't have no choice."

Josephine nodded. "You're right. But that doesn't excuse what the scoundrel did. I want him to pay a price, and you ladies can help make sure he pays it."

An older woman, who looked to be in her thirties, chimed in. "What's the man's name? We'll send one of our boys after him. One session in a dark alley and he won't be goin' after young girls for a while."

The rest of the group tittered. Josephine smiled, but held up her hand for quiet. "His name is Roderick Merchant, and I want him to suffer much more than a simple beating. I want his life to change on account of this."

Sally's sister Beth spoke up. "Merchant, you say? I guess the fruit don't fall too far from the tree." She looked around at her cohorts for confirmation. "Amos Merchant's on our 'look out' list. He likes it rough, and he's a slapper. Maybe this young man you're talking about is his son."

The wheels were already turning in Josephine's brain. "A list, you say? This gets better and better." She stepped to a nearby table and donned the black bonnet and veil she'd purloined from her mother. Then she added a black cape and turned back to her audience. "I hereby invite you all to join an exclusive new club I call 'The Black Veil Society.' United, as members, you will have more power than you ever dreamed possible."

Josephine outlined her plan. "There are three ways that society learns of wrongdoing: through the church, through the newspapers, and through word of mouth. The Black Veil Society will employ all three methods to call out misbehavior—or at least they'll threaten to, in order to see change happen."

"How do you see this coming about?" Sally asked. "I doubt those in power will pay any attention whatsoever to women like us."

"Look at the situation from their point of view. Imagine you are in a position of power, and several ladies insist on presenting their grievances to you. They are veiled, so you don't know if one of them might be your wife, or your sister ... or your mistress. Their demand is reasonable. It's not to have all unfaithful men exposed"—Jo waited for the muttering to stop— "because they aren't in business to shut down their very occupation. No, women in your profession simply want the rogue bulls culled from the herd. If such sensible demands are met, the society's activity stops there; if not, there are reporters who might be interested in which of the city's power brokers frequent its, shall we say, *alternative* forms of recreation. If not reporters, then perhaps church leaders, who you know are always looking to call out sinners, no matter how high and mighty they are. And finally, if not the most visible in the public eye, there are wives and other family members who could be alerted. It's one thing to look the other way when your husband wanders, but to have everyone know about it? That could lead to some very ugly domestic squabbles."

The group chuckled over that scenario, but one woman wasn't so sanguine. "Squealing on our johns could get us in trouble or lose us business. I mean, ain't that blackmail?"

"Remember," Josephine said, "you are anonymous. No one knows you instigated anything; you can deny you had anything to do with it and there's no one to prove otherwise. The point is not to *have* to share any of the information—only to use it as leverage to keep the bad apples from spoiling the crop. No money exchanges hands, and therefore no law is broken. But the behavior stops, otherwise the truth is revealed and there is hell to pay."

One practical young lady raised her hand and

Josephine gestured for her to speak. "So, you said we get two dresses out of this?" she asked.

"Yes. One of them must be black, but the other can be what you want it to be, within reason. I have been saving my allowance, but I only have so much to spend on this endeavor."

"Well, sign me up," the girl said.

Others concurred, until Sally spoke once again. "Who's going to lead this delegation?"

"I hope you will all use the power of the black veil sparingly, because that is where its power lies. It's very difficult to ferret out an organization that does not meet regularly and does not telegraph its actions. And the society will be taken much more seriously if it is not threatening to expose wrongdoers every other day. Since you run no risk of exposure, Sally, I nominate you to be the coordinator of the group." Josephine paused, took a breath. "But in this, our first campaign, I will take the lead ... and I will do it without a veil."

---

The inaugural campaign of the Black Veil Society was launched several weeks later, on the Monday before Thanksgiving. Josephine had insisted it happen after November fifteenth, which was her eighteenth birthday. She told her newfound compatriots that their work was a special gift to herself.

At the University of Pennsylvania, the site of the first confrontation, the fall semester was well underway. Since the target of the campaign was a Penn student (Roddy had enrolled in September), one Black Veil member had cheekily come up with the name "Operation Sheepskin."

Josephine now stood in the large, oak-paneled office of Professor Charles Janeway Stille, the university's current provost. Distinguished by his egret-white hair and matching mustache, the learned historian was not unknown to her. In fact, she'd been granted an appointment with him based on a family connection. Her father, Alfred Drummond, had commanded Charles Stille's nephew, whom the childless provost had considered a son. The nephew had also been a casualty at Gettysburg, and Josephine took shameless advantage of that shared grief.

The professor took both of Josephine's small hands in his. She had worn boots with the tallest heels she could find, and with her high bonnet featuring a plethora of feathers and ribbons, she almost matched his modest height.

"How are you, my sweet girl? And how is your dear mother? I remember how distraught she was back in sixty-three; weren't we all during that time. I heard she remarried."

Josephine made sure her eyes did not leave his. "Yes. She looked to my uncle for comfort and I now have a little brother."

Dr. Stille had the grace to look sheepish. "Yes, well, you're looking fit and pretty. What can I do for you, my dear?"

*This is it.* Josephine willed herself into a taller, more confident version of herself, and began. "I appreciate your seeing me this morning, Professor, because I have news of the utmost importance to share with you. I have some ladies waiting outside whose story may have a direct impact on this university, as you will quickly see."

Without waiting for his permission, she opened the door and beckoned her ladies in. As they entered Dr. Stille's office, a dozen strong, all wearing black from head to toe, with their faces hidden, she could tell by the shocked expression on the professor's face that they were having the intended effect. Josephine shivered, as if a group of specters had entered the room.

"My land, what is the meaning of this?"

The ladies said nothing; Josephine was their mouthpiece. "You have before you, sir, the members of an elite organization with which I have recently become acquainted. They are here to petition you and asked me to speak on their behalf because of my concern for you, a close family friend."

"Why bring you into it? Can't they speak for themselves?" There was a tinge of alarm in his voice. *Good*.

"They cannot, sir. Or rather, they will not. The group, which calls itself the Black Veil Society, consists of anonymous individuals by design. They could be your sister, your wife ... a serving maid ... or your paramour. They come from all walks of life, and all stations, yet they are uniformly adamant about their purpose."

"Now, see here," he sputtered.

Josephine ignored him and pushed on. "They share one thing in common: they are privy to information about members of society who have perpetrated cruel acts upon women, but who have heretofore not been held accountable. In fact, they have a list. A watch list. And they are here today to see that justice is served upon a person on that list."

Josephine fought back a smile. The provost had retreated back behind his desk. Did he think they were going to bite him?

He nervously smoothed the handles of his long mustache. "Justice, you say? Then isn't this something for the law to handle?"

Spontaneously, the group began to hum in a low monotone. Charles Stille looked petrified and the eerie effect had even Josephine swallowing her unease. Hell hath no fury like a group of women mad as an angry bee hive. She lifted her hand slightly to signal *enough*.

"This is something the law chooses to ignore, and therefore these women have seen fit to use what power they have to handle what the authorities will not." Josephine took a paper from her reticule. It was an official-looking document with the serious heading "A Black Veil Society Proclamation." She scanned the page and looked up. "There is a lot of introductory material here, so I will get right to the point: 'Insofar as Mr. Roderick Allen Merchant, currently a first-year student at the University of Pennsylvania, has forced himself upon a young woman, who shall remain nameless, the society asks that he be expelled from the university and never be allowed to return.'"

"That is preposterous," Professor Stille huffed.

"With no proof, with no witnesses, your ... your ladies here haven't a leg to stand on."

Josephine heaved an eloquent sigh. "Dear professor. You know as well as I that in these types of cases there is never any proof and never any witnesses—except for those who will side with the assaulter. In this case, that consists of two malicious young men who are not being singled out only because they do not attend this institution and did not participate in the assault. They merely watched, sir, and did nothing. *Nothing*. The excuse, as you are all too aware, is always that it was 'consensual.' There is no weight given to the female's version of events. Thus we have only the reality of the situation—of both the crime itself and the consequences of not avenging it." Quietly she began to lay out the many ways in which Roddy Merchant and his equally degenerate father would be exposed to society's censure and ridicule, not to mention the "guilt by association" that would be laid at the feet of the university should the word get out. "It is all explained here." She handed him the letter.

"Why, that is blackmail, plain and simple," he charged.

"No, that is justice—the justice that comes from stating the facts for all to see. The only reason I am here is because of the respect The Black Veil Society feels for you and your institution. You should consider yourself lucky."

"Hardly," he countered, glancing at the stygian group. "Why, I could walk over to those women right now and merely expose them by insisting that they remove their veils."

"I wouldn't advise that, Professor. It's my understanding that one or more of the members always carry concealed pistols, and if they felt they were being physically attacked, then it stands to reason they would defend themselves."

Josephine could almost read the professor's mind: *How do I get myself out of this?*

He attempted to deflect. "I am powerless in this regard, you know. My purview extends only to the faculty; I am not responsible for the actions of a few wayward students."

"I know that. Which is why I must add another name for consideration. Do you remember the list I spoke of? This name is also on that list." She passed a small piece of paper to the provost, whose eyes grew wide as he read it. The man named was a member of Penn's Board of Trustees.

"You may wish to deny it, sir, but the truth is, The Black Veil Society 'has the goods,' to borrow a phrase from law enforcement. They also have the means to air this dirty laundry for all to see. They are merely asking for the expulsion of one particular student. That is all. If that can be done expeditiously and privately, then that will be the last you'll hear of these ladies ... unless of course, other transgressions occur. I would ask that you take what you have learned today to the Board. Tell them everything, and I am sure you will all see the wisdom in doing as the society asks to make it all go away."

Charles Stille's anger was intense but controlled. Josephine could tell by the way he regulated his breathing, the way he focused on his desk as he sorted through his papers and his options. She could tell even before he spoke that he had come to the conclusion that his hands were tied.

"And you say this would be the end of it? You would not further pursue the university or"—he held up the slip of paper she'd given him—"others associated with it?"

Josephine felt the giddiness of victory begin to bubble within her. She forced her countenance to remain calm. "Well, yes, although if I were anyone on such a list, I think I would reexamine my future actions. The Black Veil Society has informants everywhere, I've been told. They are watching." She turned to the still-mute purveyors of doom. "Ladies? I think your work is finished here."

The society members filed out, leaving behind a trace of sinister energy, as if a seance had occurred and the spirits had not been happy ones.

Josephine was the last to leave, but the professor stayed her with a touch on her arm. "Josephine," he said.

"Yes?"

"How on earth did you get involved with these ... these freaks?"

"Me, sir? Why, I heard their plight and felt compelled, as a representative of today's ideal womanhood, to do what I could so that others will not fall prey to such cowardly, evil acts. I would think you, as an honorable member of society, would want the same."

The provost stared at her for several seconds and then muttered, "You are not what you appear to be."

Josephine froze. Had she given something away? "What do you mean?"

"I mean you are no longer a sweet little girl."

He did not mean it as a compliment, but Josephine decided to take it as such for her own gratification if no one else's. She smiled at him. "I will expect you to send word within the next ten days that you have taken the appropriate action. You know what will transpire if the Board doesn't act." She held out her hand. "It was nice to see you again, Professor. My best to your wife."

Josephine walked regally out of the provost's office. Per agreement, the girls had rapidly dispersed, filing into a series of hansom cabs in which they changed clothing before heading back into their own worlds. Waiting for her own carriage, Jo felt her eyes prick with tears as her body released the tension she'd been feeling all morning. Elation surged through her, and she laughed out loud. It was similar to what she'd felt as a coxswain, only better, because one didn't have to yell to be understood.

Feeling powerful was heady. To get someone to change his behavior because of the facts you put before him was a type of ambrosia. Was it blackmail if the facts were on your side and you were only seeking justice? Perhaps it was.

It still felt marvelous.

Now, all she had to do was wait to see if their work had paid off. Ten days felt like an eternity.

---

For the past nine years, Josephine had lived as an afterthought in her own home. Anger toward her mother had dissipated long ago; now she understood that Marrielle's method of survival was just one of many her mother could have chosen. Jo had learned quickly that if she went about her business, brought no shame to the Drummond name, and acted the part of an obedient stepdaughter, she was free to do just about anything she wanted. At the age of sixteen she'd been given a modest allowance, drawn from the inheritance she would one day receive in full, so even asking Uncle Whitford for pocket change had ceased to be a problem.

At first such freedom felt liberating; she pitied her friends whose parents seemed to hover about, always imposing strictures and dispensing advice where none had been solicited. Over time, though, the bleak reality set in: Josephine was never censured because she was never being watched, and she was never being watched because she existed apart from the "real" Drummond family, which consisted of Marrielle, Whitford and little Carlton, who was every bit as adorable as Josephine had ever been.

All of which meant that she was caught off guard when her parents summoned her, the Sunday after Thanksgiving, to meet with them in the formal parlor.

Marrielle sat on the settee, dressed in a flowing mauve gown suitable only for family appearances. She was increasing again, her breasts and belly large, her face slightly puffy, her movements languid. Pregnancy had replaced mourning as the excuse for her torpidity. She was still beautiful, however, and she reminded Josephine of a queen bee delighted to be encased in and protected by her hive.

Uncle Whitford, slightly grayer, slightly thicker, stood at the fireplace, possibly hoping it would make him appear more patriarchal. He gestured for Josephine to sit in the upholstered chair he had placed as if it were a witness stand. "Your mother and I have heard some disturbing news about you," he began.

She stopped breathing. Surely this had nothing to do with Operation Sheepskin? But she hadn't heard anything yet, and ... she glanced at her mother, who was looking down at her hands. "Mama?"

Marrielle paused before looking up. When she finally made eye contact, her expression was resigned. She shrugged slightly. "It's true. There have been rumors."

Josephine straightened her spine. "Rumors about what?"

"About your involvement with some sort of mysterious cult," Whitford answered sharply. "A witches' coven or some such."

Relief filtered through her; the professor had kept his accusations vague for a reason. She feigned disbelief. "I haven't the faintest idea what you're talking about. Who is spreading such outrageous stories about me?"

"They aren't stories," her uncle said. "They are ... concerns. And Charles Stille, whom I met at the Philadelphia Club the other night, felt it his duty to relay them."

"And where did such 'concerns' on his part come from?"

"He didn't say. Only that he had heard rumblings that you are caught up in some sort of secret society."

Josephine debated how much outrage she should exhibit; she even considered crying, but felt that would be a bit over the top. Instead she opted for a moderate amount of indignation. "Well, you may rest assured that whatever he heard is totally false. I belong to no witches' coven or voodoo cult, or any other such nonsense. Neither he, nor you, should lend credence to such idiocy. Haven't I been a trustworthy daughter?"

Marrielle sighed and looked at her husband. "I told you there was nothing to worry about, Whitford," she said in her practiced little girl voice. "Josephine has always been a good child."

Whitford paused, seemingly at a loss for how to proceed. He recovered quickly, however, and cleared his throat. "Be that as it may, we feel it is past time to have a discussion with you about your future."

This turn of events gave Josephine pause. When had either of them ever indicated they cared one way or another what she did with her life? "My future?"

"Yes," he continued. You are in your final year at

Agnes Irwin, and we feel it's time for you to start planning ahead."

Josephine frowned. "Well, I have been thinking," she said.

"Oh, have you set your cap set for someone, then?" Josephine's mother looked more animated than she had in years.

"What do you mean?"

Her uncle tapped his fingers impatiently on the mantel. "She means, have you decided which young scion you'd like to marry?"

*Marry?* What on earth? "Um, no, that is, I've decided to—"

"Let us take the lead?" Marrielle said. "That is wise on your part. Whitford should be able to arrange—"

"Wait, wait *wait*," Josephine said. "We are talking at cross purposes. I have no intention of marrying, at least not anytime soon."

"But, my dear, what else are you going to do?" Marrielle looked genuinely perplexed.

Josephine had been waiting for the right moment to share her news, and it appeared that now was that time. "I'm going to go to college," she announced.

She wished she could have captured the expression on their faces. It would be a perfect illustration of the term "befuddlement."

"I don't understand," her uncle said. "You are not going to college. Women don't go to college."

"Oh, but they are starting to. I've been accepted to Cornell University – they just began admitting women. I'll be starting next fall."

Marrielle looked as though her daughter had just announced she was flying to the moon. It was difficult for Josephine to keep the exasperation out of her voice. "It's in upstate New York, Mother. They've just started admitting women to the program."

It was obvious Whitford Drummond was unused to women telling him what they were going to do. Neither of his wives had ever had the temerity to do such a thing. Josephine could tell the notion infuriated him. His voice was tight. "You did not ask our permission."

"I didn't need to," she said. "It was my decision to make."

"Oh was it, now? And how to you propose to pay for such an endeavor that you did not *even once* seek our guidance on?"

There are advantages to no longer feeling the hurt of a failed relationship. Years ago Josephine might have longed for a sign of caring from her mother or stepfather, even if it was couched in anger, as it was now. But too much time had passed. She smiled up at her uncle. "I shall pay for it with my inheritance, which became legally mine twelve days ago."

She had him dead to rights and he knew it. Her real father, no doubt realizing he might perish and that Marrielle wouldn't necessarily know how to handle such matters, had set aside a legacy for his beloved "poppet" to use when she turned eighteen. Months earlier, her family's attorney had contacted her privately to explain the bequest. She was elated and had held the knowledge close to her heart, sending a prayer of thanks to her dear papa every day since then.

Marrielle still seemed unable to grasp the situation. "Do you mean to say you aren't getting married?"

Josephine shook her head, but before she could speak, her stepfather broke in. He spoke to his wife, although his eyes bore into Josephine's, communicating so much more than his words.

"Your daughter has decided to forge her own path," he said. "She will be leaving the family next year for New York. Who knows when we may see her again."

A family, even if you are an extraneous part of it, is still a family, and it hurts to lose it. That night, as Josephine turned her uncle's words over in her mind, she faced their true meaning. As long as she didn't disgrace the family—by joining a witches' coven, for example—he would never throw her bodily out; that stain on the Drummond name would eclipse even the one he'd imposed by his illicit relationship with her mother. But she knew, as sure as she knew her mother would have another child, that she was no longer welcome.

Realizing that took away any satisfaction she might have had by announcing her acceptance at a prestigious, albeit new, university.

Instead, she felt as if there had been another death in the family—her own.

## CHAPTER FOURTEEN

### Katherine

*1899*

The death of Henrietta Joy Challis cast a pall over the highest levels of San Francisco society. A tragedy like that was simply not supposed to happen, especially to such a lovely young couple with everything in the world going for them.

So went the muted conversations at every cocktail reception, gallery opening, and charity banquet. "An unfortunate turn of events, really, but they'll bounce back" seemed to be the standard refrain. "Plenty of time for more children down the road."

Kit had arrived at the Challis home that night to find Cecily inconsolable, Easton stoic, and Ellie beside herself with guilt.

"I don't know what happened," the nurse said. "I came home to find Mrs. Challis sleeping peacefully for a change, and I didn't hear little Henny either, so I didn't disturb them. I was in the other room when I heard Mrs. Challis calling out to me to come quickly, that there was something wrong with Henny." Ellie wrung her hands, clearly distraught. "There was something wrong, all right. The baby was lying on her stomach with the blanket bunched up around her mouth. She was blue, the poor little thing. She wasn't breathing." At that point she began to cry. "I should have checked on her as soon as I got home," she lamented. "I should have ... done something. I just didn't know."

Kit hugged the woman. "It's not your fault, Ellie. If anybody's to blame, it's me. I shouldn't have left early."

Ellie wiped her eyes and looked at Kit. "Why did you?"

"Cecily ... Cecily asked me to. She was quite firm about it."

In the brief silence that followed, an idea skirted through Kit's brain, and she looked directly at Ellie as if to confirm it. The woman's quizzical expression matched her own, but neither dared to speak.

Easton approached them, breaking the tension. "I suppose we should call the authorities." He sounded weary.

"I'll call Dr. Landon," Kit said.

The speculation amongst society as to what had caused the infant's death remained just that. After examining the baby, Dr. Landon determined that Henny most likely suffered crib death by asphyxiation, exacerbated by her underdeveloped lungs. This explanation seemed plausible given the stories of how poorly the child had fared from birth. Still, questions remained. Months later at a fundraiser, Kit would overhear a hushed conversation in which one matron commented to another, "It wouldn't be the first tot to be accidentally smothered."

But first there was a funeral and a burial to get through. Easton barely lifted a finger throughout the ordeal, leaving the details to Cecily, who in turn relied heavily on Kit.

Thankfully, Cecily did attend the memorial service at Holy Cross. Veiled and covered in black from head to toe, she stood next to her husband, who continued to say and do nothing other than to accept condolences for such a tragic loss. Kit's current moniker for Easton was "The Vile One."

There was but one positive outcome during that harrowing episode: Cecily started to recover. A few weeks after the funeral, the blisters on her face and arms began to dry up. Her face appeared less sallow, and her hair more lustrous. Encouraged by her progress, Dr. Landon weaned her off the calomel, and the effects of that wretched treatment began to subside as well. In time, much of Cecily's strength returned and she no longer felt the need for a full-time nurse.

"Are you sure?" Kit asked her friend. "Perhaps Ellie could stay on as your assistant. You know, in case you have a relapse."

Cecily shook her head. "She's been a godsend, but we really can't afford her any longer. It's time I stood on my own."

Reluctantly Kit agreed, and on Ellie's last day, she took the young nurse out to lunch at the City of Paris department store. The elegant tea room on the seventh floor afforded a panoramic view of the city skyline, but the restaurant's interior was impressive as well. Handsome, impeccably dressed young waiters stood by, ready to meet the diners' needs—diners who tended to be female, well-to-do, and ready to part with their money for the latest fashions and accessories.

"You didn't have to do this," Ellie said, "but seeing as how I've always wanted to eat here, I won't say no."

Kit grinned at her before perusing the menu. "You're doing me a favor. It's no fun eating alone."

The two women enjoyed chicken divan and small glasses of crisp chardonnay as they talked about Cecily, her husband, and the couple's travails. At one point, Ellie leaned in and said in a voice barely above a whisper, "If you ask me, that insufferable husband ought to be drawn and quartered for what he did to her. I think we ought to call a meeting of the Black Veil Society."

Intrigued, Kit lowered her voice as well. "Black Veil Society? Who are they?"

Ellie sat back again and sighed. "To tell the truth, I'm not sure they ever really existed, but the story is that many years ago, a group of tainted ladies banded together and threatened to expose powerful clients—at least the mean, dangerous ones—if they didn't change their ways. The members would all dress in black and wear veils to hide their identities. Then they'd show up as a group to some high-ranking official's workplace to state their demands. They say wealthy society women often participated out of solidarity with their cause, and once or twice even a man dressed up as a woman to support them!"

"That is amazing," Kit said. "Were they successful?"

"I don't know," Ellie said with a shrug. "There was a newspaper article written about it with loads of speculation at some point, yet nobody ever claimed responsibility for the society, or wrote anything official. But I'd like to think that at least a couple of villains the likes of Easton Challis got their comeuppance from those gutsy women. Maybe we ought to start a society of our own."

Kit smiled at her jest and the two went on to talk about many topics ... except the one they *should* have talked about. The question of Henny's death hung like a shroud over them, but neither Kit nor Ellie dared to broach the topic. What purpose would it serve? There was no proof that Cecily had done anything, and even if there were, would either of them speak against her?

Over the course of the lunch, Kit discovered that she and Ellie had much in common, despite their disparate stations in life. It struck Kit that she'd made her very first friend—at least first *real* friend—who hadn't grown up in the rarefied atmosphere surrounding the Firestones.

The end of the meal came too soon for both of them. Reluctantly, they said their goodbyes, promised to stay in touch, and gave each other a genuine hug. As she watched Ellie head down the street, Kit found herself grinning. For the first time in a very long while, she felt something other than sadness, and paused to let it soak in.

Although the air was brisk, the afternoon sky was clear for a change, the sun having burned off the city's habitual fog. Kit decided to walk down Stockton to Geary in order to hail a carriage that would take her back to Pacific Heights. Rarely did she walk for any length of time in the downtown area without some type of chaperone, be it a family member or friend. Like making a new type of acquaintance, being on her own gave her a rush.

She passed the infamous passageway off Union Square known as Morton Street and hesitated. Should she explore it, just a little? Ladies of the night plied their wares there; there were stories that they actually danced naked in the windows of the so-called "cribs" lining the narrow street.

*Why not?* she thought. This was a day for firsts. Straightening her shoulders, she proceeded down the alley, which was too restricted for carriages or the occasional automobile. Better to seem purposeful, she reasoned, then almost giggled. What could her purpose possibly be in walking down such a street?

If Kit thought she could get lost in the crowd, she was mistaken. The mid-afternoon foot traffic was light, and she stood out amongst the few pedestrians because of her fashionable attire and elegant demeanor. It took her a moment to realize why. Most of Morton Street's "customers" were probably still at work. The few rough-looking men she encountered gave her odd stares as she passed.

The small houses on either side of the alleyway were ramshackle at best. Most had oversized windows facing the street; through several of them, young women could be seen indulging in salacious activities designed to catch the eyes of those looking in. One sat on a stool with her skirt hiked up. She was examining her black lace stocking, exposing her leg and thigh to public view. In another, a woman wearing an extremely low-cut dress was slowly brushing her long black hair. A third twirled lazily around a pole set in the middle of the room. She wore knickers and a nearly sheer camisole, one strap of which had fallen down. Her breasts were large and pressed heavily against the thin material. As Kit walked by, the lascivious woman caught her eye and winked, tilting her head in invitation. Kit abruptly looked away, sensing a blush crawl up her neck. She was rarely caught in embarrassing situations, so the novelty of it left her distinctly irritated. Did the woman actually think she was interested in ... in going inside? The nerve of her!

Clutching her reticule more tightly than necessary, she continued on, stopping only when she encountered a crudely lettered sandwich board propped up outside another house of ill repute. The board seemed to be advertising the wares inside, much like the specials of a sidewalk cafe:

**Mexican: 25 cents**
**Negro/Chinese/Japanese: 50 cents**
**French: 75 cents**
**American: One dollar**

### *Red-haired (especially if Jewish): Negotiable*

Kit swallowed heavily. These weren't types of food for sale. They were women. Flesh and blood. Maybe somebody's sister, certainly someone's daughter. They didn't have a choice to be "in love" the way Kit thought she'd been, or even *like* the men they lay with; they had to expose themselves to whoever had the money to pay them.

In that moment Kit felt both pity and anger surge through her. She wanted to avenge these women, wanted to wave a magic wand and have them suddenly tell the men who wanted to use their bodies to go to the devil. "The store is closed!" they'd say. "Go someplace else to slake your lust—preferably home to your wives!"

She came to Grant Avenue, relieved to be off Morton Street. Turning south toward Geary, she saw a man walking toward her with his arm around a woman.

It was Easton Challis.

The woman who hung on to Easton was definitely not from Kit's social circle, nor Easton's. She looked older, mid-thirties, perhaps, and her face was heavily made up, as if she thought she could fool others into thinking she hadn't said goodbye to her twenties. The deep blue gown she wore left little to the imagination; it was more suitable to an assignation than an afternoon stroll. She seemed ... she seemed loose, in her attire and in her manner, and Kit sensed the woman was part and parcel of Morton Street; they were headed that way, at least. But what was Easton doing with her?

It struck her then: *He is who those women on Morton Street are waiting for.* In fact, to those women, Easton would probably be considered quite the catch.

Kit couldn't help it; she let her inner demon out. "Mr. Challis," she called when Easton passed by, pretending not to notice her. "How is your dear *wife* faring these days?" She pointedly looked at the woman, who continued to cling to Easton's arm. The woman's only response to Kit's broadside was a smirk. Apparently, marriage to someone else was not a deterrent.

"Ah ... Miss Firestone," Easton said, trying to salvage the propriety of the situation. "I'd like you to meet my ... client, Mrs. Fitz. We are discussing a loan for her company. Mrs. Fitz, Miss Katherine Firestone."

Mrs. Fitz's eyebrows shot up. She must have recognized the name. She inclined her head slightly. "Charmed to make your acquaintance." Of course she was.

Kit had to know. "And what line of work are you in, Mrs. Fitz, that you require a business loan?"

The woman sent her a slow, seductive smile. "Why the business of pleasure, Miss Firestone. An international marketplace of pleasure."

Another first. Kit had just met a bonafide madam. By her answer, the woman thought she was being both clever and cryptic. She was neither. Kit nodded as if putting two and two together. "Ah, you must run the smorgasbord I just passed on Morton Street. Tell me, why do red-haired Jewesses rate higher than Mexican *señoritas?* They're all built pretty much the same, aren't they?"

The woman's disingenuous smile faded, replaced by a scowl. She looked up at Easton as if to say, *You aren't going to let her talk to me like that, are you?*

For his part, Easton looked both angry and chagrined. He obviously wanted to send Kit to the devil, but he couldn't. The devil, already part of her, was off his leash.

"Oh, and another thing," Kit said. "How do you deal with customers like Mr. Challis here, who come to your establishment diseased? Don't you worry about the health of your, shall we say, "merchandise"? Because that's what they are to you and your customers, aren't they? I mean, what happens if word gets out that your girls are infected?"

Kit would have loved to record the panoply of expressions that crossed Mrs. Fitz's comically rouged face, from complacent condescension all the way through disbelief, disgruntlement, and finally dawning horror. It was bad enough for Kit to disparage the woman's occupation, but to imply her very business might be in jeopardy was obviously too much for the woman's sensibilities.

The woman grit her teeth. "What on earth are you talking about?"

Kit's disgust poured out of her as she pointed at Easton. "Why don't you ask him?" she said. "Or better yet, his *wife,* who just lost a baby because of his unclean habits."

Mrs. Fitz turned to Easton. "Is this true?" Her voice had tightened considerably.

"I ... wouldn't say so," he managed.

Now it was Kit's turn to be surprised. "What do you mean, you wouldn't say so? You know damn well what you did."

Easton straightened his shoulders, not quite ready to concede the point. "Do I?" he asked. "Not that it's any of your business, but I'm not entirely sure you have the facts correct in this case, and I would advise you to cease speaking out of turn."

Not have the facts correct? The only alternative was that Cecily had contracted the disease herself before she'd met Easton. That was the very definition of absurdity, and an insult to Cecily in the bargain.

Incredulous, Kit must have stared at Easton a bit too long because he took the opportunity to extricate himself and Mrs. Fitz from the encounter.

"Good day to you, Miss Firestone." He looked her in the eye as if to drive home his warning. "I truly hope you aren't sharing such fanciful notions with others. It would be quite libelous if you did ... and other facts would have to come to light." With that, he firmly took Mrs. Fitz by the arm and guided her away, once again toward Morton Street.

It took several deep breaths for Kit to get her equilibrium back. Not only was Easton denying that he'd done anything wrong, but if challenged, he'd threatened to expose their brief affair. Surely, he wouldn't do such a thing. Yet he'd shared all but the gritty details with Cecily; Kit shouldn't assume he was bluffing.

It was comforting to know he had no proof; it would be her word against his. Still, even to have it bandied about that they *might* have had a tryst was sickening in the extreme. The idea filled her with shame and remorse. If this is what came from having feelings for another person and acting on them, it was simply not worth it.

Heedless of the greater traffic that characterized Geary Street, Kit barely noticed when an automobile nearly sideswiped her, its driver laying a heavy hand on his vehicle's obnoxious horn. Half a block later, a fellow pedestrian pulled her gently back from one of the street cars rumbling by. "Watch the rails, ma'am," he said, doffing his hat before hurrying across the road.

She didn't even pause to call out thanks; instead, she hailed a carriage and returned home, filled once again with the sadness she'd escaped for a few hours that afternoon.

As the days wore on, Kit's imagination went off *its* rails. She envisioned Easton Challis singlehandedly infecting every prostitute in the city and thus spreading the disease to thousands of men who then took the French pox home to their wives, who unknowingly passed it on to their children. Dr Landon had said that nearly half of such babies died in the womb. But imagine if even half of them developed the wretched symptoms and physical abnormalities that poor little Henny had. What then?

She had to stop him. But how? The only way to ensure that women knew the truth about him was to announce his secret to society. The word would get around—it was much faster than the city's newspapers—and he would be exposed for the beast he truly was. She wondered briefly about the society Ellie had mentioned; if only some mechanism like that existed to subject Easton to public scorn.

But what about Cecily? After all she'd been through, what would his disgrace do to her? And would Kit herself be strong enough to withstand the censure, even the hint of censure, that his side of the story would encourage?

It took Kit several sleepless nights to come up with the answer, at least to the latter question. Yes, it was worth some embarrassment to see that Easton was brought to task.

And Cecily? She decided it was only fair to alert her friend as to what she intended to do. Hopefully she would understand that the alternative was so much worse.

The following day she penned a letter to be delivered to Easton at the bank. It read:

*Dear Easton,*

*You cannot continue to harm your wife and others in this manner. You must own up to who you are and what you've done. Perhaps you can get help. If not, then at least your honor will be restored and you can begin to live a life of truth and integrity (for a change).*

*I will be talking to Cecily about how to proceed in this matter. I'm sorry it has to be this way, but too many lives are at stake.*

*Sincerely,*

### *Katherine Firestone*

She would wait before delivering the missive until she could be sure her decision was sound. The delay proved fortuitous.

---

A week later, Kit called on her friend to explain what she intended to do. Cecily greeted her warmly, exuding an aura, not precisely of happiness, but of the calm that comes with the acceptance of a profoundly painful situation, such as death. Kit dreaded breeching that sanguinity but saw no alternative.

Cecily, however, spoke first. "I'm glad you came. I wanted to let you know that Easton is no longer living here."

Kit's jaw might as well have dropped onto the floor. "What do you mean?"

Cecily glanced down at her hands, which rested quietly in her lap. Her nails no longer looked chewed; a crescent of white showed on each tip. "I mean, he's left me. And the city as well. Apparently for parts unknown. He left a note at work saying that he had 'family business' to attend to and wouldn't be returning, and he took virtually all of his things. Father is furious and vows he's going to hunt him down."

"As well he should." Kit felt her body shimmer with self-righteousness.

Cecily reached out to her. "No. In fact, that's what I want to talk to you about. If you are serious about not wanting Easton for yourself, then help me persuade my father that we—that I—am better off without him. Because I am. Truly."

"How can you say that?" Kit asked. "You ... you love him, don't you?"

Cecily frowned slightly. "I'm not so sure anymore. It's plain as day he no longer cares for me, if he ever did." When Kit started to disagree, Cecily held up her hand. "I no longer need rescuing. Despite what ... what he and I have in common, neither of us has any desire to be intimate with one another. He began seeking solace elsewhere months ago, before Henny was even born. So it's better this way."

"Better how?" Kit asked. "As long as you stay married to him you won't be able to find someone wonderful who deserves you."

The look Cecily gave her radiated the same resignation Kit had seen earlier, tinged with a bit of melancholy. "I won't be meeting anyone else, Kit. And this way, I have the perfect excuse not to get involved. I will still be legally married and therefore unavailable. If we were to part —officially, that is—then I would be hounded incessantly by friends and family to find someone new. I can't do that to anyone, Kit. Having experienced what I have, I could never do it."

"But ... but you're fine now. And Dr. Landon said it could be years before any other symptoms showed up —if they even do. You have a whole life ahead of you."

Cecily took Kit's hand in her own. It was a strange sensation, as if Cecily were consoling *her* and not the other way around. "I can't live my life always wondering, always fearful of the next rash or the next bout of the flu. I couldn't carry a child and wonder if he or she will be born—" her voice hitched, "—born with a body already broken. Once was enough, thank you." She took her hand away and pulled a small white handkerchief from the pocket of her skirt. Dabbing her eyes, she looked up again at Kit. "You and Ellie are the only people who fully understand that, the only ones, and I trust you both to keep that confidence."

*I want to kill Easton*, Kit thought, and not for the first time. She looked at her dear friend and saw the years unfolding: long and lonely, filled with substitutions for the love and family that once was all Cecily had ever wanted. And she thought of Easton who had moved on. Hopefully no one else would ever know the evil that he carried within him. She never thought she could wish such a monster well, but she did, if only for the sake of the women who might suffer if his symptoms reappeared. Cecily was right. One such victim —or two, counting Henny— was enough.

"I understand completely," Kit assured her. "Whatever I can do to persuade your father to call off the dogs, I will. Perhaps a word with my own father—" here she imitated her father's voice "' —Think of the scandal, Frank, the scandal! Far better to let it all simmer down. Follow Cecily's lead on this one; she has a much better feel for the gossip-mongers in this case, and she'll be the one to bear the brunt of it. Why put her through it?'" Kit went back to her own voice. "Something along those lines?" she asked.

Cecily broke into a smile, the first one Kit had seen in months. "I knew you'd know just what to do!"

---

Kit did. She broached the topic with her father, saying that she would be absolutely devastated if a man left her as Easton Challis had done; the last thing in the world she'd want would be the public humiliation of it all. Couldn't he talk to Cecily's father, man to man, and explain things?

And at the next charity ball—this one for the San Francisco Orphan Asylum—she cornered Franklin Anders herself, explaining over a plate of skewered shrimp and crab-filled puffs that the mess with Challis would sort itself out in time, that it was much better to keep it all under wraps. "Just make sure the cad has no legal claim on Cecily and she'll handle the rest. Your daughter is strong, and with our help she'll get through this."

Mr. Anders, his balding pate shining slightly with perspiration, patted her arm, almost dislodging her hors d'oeuvres. "I can't tell you how glad I am to hear you say that," he said. "Cecily's mother has never been hardy, and the loss of her granddaughter has just about done her in. She's of little help in the matter." He gave Kit's arm a squeeze. "Cecily's damn lucky to have a friend like you."

*If only you knew*, Kit thought.

---

In time, "The Challis Affair" did fade away. People forgot that Cecily had ever been married, and once in a while, upon noting her rare appearance at a social event, an ignorant or forgetful matron would suggest to her peers that "It's time for Cecily to find a young man," at which point another matron would remind her, *cough cough*, "Well, she's not exactly free. Her husband does seem to be away much of the time, however."

As for Kit, the idea that Easton Challis was out in the world, possibly infecting other unsuspecting women, burrowed under her skin and stayed there. It was an ever-present irritant, a reminder that men, whether they ran the biggest banks on Market Street or prowled the lowliest cat houses of Morton Street, were not to be trusted.

Kit would play the game. She would flirt and hobnob and wield the limited power of her social sphere. She would "out-Bitsy" Bitsy McFadden and put up with the emotional wasteland of debs like Beatrice Marshall. That kind of playacting she was good at; that type of behavior she knew well.

But when it came to letting someone get close, she would take her cue from Cecily and not get involved.

It was just too dangerous—and much, much too painful.

## CHAPTER FIFTEEN

*1903*

"I'm sorry, darling. I must have misunderstood you. You say you're doing what?" Josephine Firestone stood at the chinoiserie sideboard in the formal parlor of the Firestone mansion, fussing with a hothouse arrangement of flamingo flowers and birds of paradise. It was the third version that Park Presidio Florists had sent over that day; Kit's mother did have her standards.

Kit counted to five in order to keep her temper in check. "You know precisely what I said, but in case you are worried about your hearing, I'll repeat it: Will and I have assumed the guardianship of a young girl named Mandy Culpepper, whose last remaining parent recently died in a construction accident, and the three of us will be living at Will's place on Russian Hill."

Only the slightest compression of her lips betrayed Josephine's true thoughts about the matter. "Do you really think that's wise, dear? After all, what do you really know about motherhood?"

"Oh, I've had quite the teacher, wouldn't you say?" Kit tried to keep the sarcasm out of her voice but, judging by the flash of hurt that crossed her mother's countenance, she was unsuccessful. She softened her tone. "You're right, of course. But you always taught us to be kind to others, and this is indeed an act of kindness. Mandy is a bright, well-mannered girl who deserves a chance at a better life. And I feel ... I *know* I am ready to take on the challenge."

Inside, Kit did not feel quite as confident as she hoped she looked. Admittedly, assuming Mandy's guardianship had been a rather impulsive move, quite contrary to her nature. But in retrospect, she'd reasoned that it was nothing less than fate telling her it was time to take the next step toward adulthood. Accepting responsibility for something and someone other than one's next social engagement simply felt right. But being an adult also meant she shouldn't be surprised at her mother's skepticism, nor should she blame her for voicing it.

Josephine studied her daughter's face. "Was this Will's idea, or yours?"

"Oh, we ... we came to a mutual understanding," she hedged. Actually, Will had thought her crazy, and only acquiesced to her plan after Kit agreed—in a roundabout way—that he could search for any of Mandy's relatives who would be willing to take her in. He believed she'd be better off with family, not with strangers like the Firestones.

"And why, I wonder, do you feel the need to become a mother without benefit of marriage? It's usually done the other way around, as I'm sure you know." Her mother pulled some stems out of one side of the arrangement and stuck them on the other. "I fear it has something to do with that man, what was his name? Weston? Or was it Easton? That's right. Easton. Easton Challis. I don't know how long you are going to hold a torch for him, if that's what you're doing. He picked Cecily over you and look how that turned out. You were quite fortunate, I'd say."

*You have no idea, Mother.*

It had been over four years since Kit's "misadventure" with Easton Challis. Four years since Little Henny's death. Four years since Cecily had assumed the mantle of "high-strung wife" —the important word being "wife," which meant that she was never pressed to find someone new.

Kit, on the other hand, was still considered fair game. For the last four years she had played the role of highborn social butterfly, concerned only with the latest gossip and fashion, flitting from circle to circle, attracting potential partners with her gorgeous looks and witty effervescence, but never landing on any particular romantic prospect. It was a matter of the deepest concern to her mother, she knew. Josephine understood nothing of the hell Kit had narrowly skirted or the purgatory that Cecily now inhabited. She saw only that her beautiful, charming daughter could have practically any man she wanted, yet was perfectly content to reject them all. At the considerable age of twenty-three, Kit was beginning to stir up gossip, not for her scandalous behavior, but for her lack of same. It was obviously driving her mother insane, and she in turn was making Kit's life miserable. Was it any wonder Kit wanted to move out? This was a perfect opportunity to expand her horizons in a myriad of ways.

"Think of it this way, Mother. At least my moving out and becoming a parent of sorts will give you and your friends something to speculate about."

"There is that," Josephine said absently. "We'll see what your father has to say about it." She perused the arrangement a moment longer and turned to Kit. "I think it looks much better this way, don't you, dear?"

---

Kit was in heaven, and she had a most unusual fifteen-year-old girl to thank for it.

Despite her brother's reluctance, the move to his estate on Russian Hill had worked out perfectly. Once she'd settled in, Kit began to see just how stifled she'd been under her mother's blithe dominion. But caring for Mandy had become so much more than a justification for Kit's independence. To worry about another person's wellbeing over and above your own—it was humbling. She'd had a glimpse of what it was like watching Cecily with little Henny. Could she, Kit, have done what she suspected her friend had done, all for the love of her child? Possibly. She hoped she would never have to find out.

Seeing that Mandy had a safe place to live, plenty of good food, and a proper school to attend all gave meaning to Kit's life. It was far and away more satisfying than worrying about who did what to whom, or which restaurant or dress designer would be *de rigueur* that month.

Some habits were difficult to change, however. Kit had always loved dressing up, and she adored finding suitable clothing for a girl who, only months before, had been a shabbily dressed mother's helper in a bayside fishing village. Mandy herself seemed unimpressed with the material aspects of her new life but was so inherently poised that she graciously let Kit dote on her, always showing just the right amount of appreciation without sinking into obsequiousness.

Kit enrolled Mandy in Weems Academy, a highly regarded finishing school in the city. The girl's thirst for knowledge was insatiable and she showed promise as a writer. Kit couldn't have been more proud, of both Mandy and her own parental prowess.

It didn't take long for the two of them to settle into a comfortable routine with Will, largely because he ignored them much of the time. He was a twenty-seven-year-old bachelor and a talented investor with a penchant for making lots of money. Caring for children was at the bottom of his lengthy priority list. Kit did insist that they have dinner together once each week "as a family," and these occasions turned out to be a highlight of everyone's schedule.

If there was one flaw in this rosy existence, it was that Mandy felt honor-bound to take on an after-school job in order to pay the Firestones back for all they had done for her. She had no way of knowing how impossible such a task would be; nevertheless, she insisted.

"My pa—I mean my 'pa*pa*,' as my teachers say I should call him— taught me that if you don't need charity, then you shouldn't take it," she explained to Kit one afternoon. "I am able to work, and I am very happy to look for a position on my own."

Kit had implored her brother, with all his connections, to do something about it, and he'd obliged by surreptitiously funding a "historian" position at the Presbyterian Mission House in Chinatown. Will had developed contacts in that part of the city in order to market his new shipping company, and Donaldina Cameron, the mission's director, was beyond pleased to have such a well-heeled donor taking an interest in her charitable enterprise.

Knowing none of the behind-the-scenes machinations, Mandy was thrilled with her new job, which she described at their family dinner soon after she was hired.

"I have an interpreter—his name is Fung Hai— and we interview girls at the mission and find out all about them so that I can write down their stories and show other people how we are helping them. Isn't that wonderful?"

"And what are you learning about the girls?" Will inquired. (While he'd spent the first few of these dinners silently reading the paper at the table, Kit had quickly put her foot down; now he was much more engaged).

"Oh, some of their stories are so sad. Most of them are orphans like me, but they do not have wonderful people like you to take care of them. They have to be servants, and some of them are even slaves. I talked to one girl whose family was so poor that her father sold her just to buy food! And sometimes they are forced to become hundred men's wives but if they say anything about not liking it, they get beaten up."

It would have remained merely a sad topic of conversation if Mandy herself hadn't been kidnapped by the very forces she had described so forbiddingly to Kit and Will.

# CHAPTER SIXTEEN

If Kit had any doubts about her maternal instincts, they were washed away the evening in August when she and Will sat down to their weekly dinner and Mandy was nowhere to be found. As the idea sunk in that she might in danger, a feral energy took over and Kit knew without question that she would do whatever it took to get her child back safely. Luckily her brother felt the same way.

Mandy had been "on assignment" for the mission after school. A telephone call from the director confirmed that she, along with her interpreter and a servant girl named Wu Jade, had disappeared. Miss Cameron knew who had taken them and quickly organized an ad hoc posse, including Will, Kit, a Chinese government attaché, two police officers, and some extra muscle. They descended upon the headquarters of the Hip Yee *tong*, whereupon the Angry Angel (as Miss Cameron was known in some circles) marched right into the dining room where the gang leader and his minions were having dinner. He seemed amused when the feisty missionary confronted him about the kidnapping. She motioned for Kit to stand next to her.

"Tang Lin, you may have inadvertently kidnapped the ward of Miss Katherine Firestone, of the San Francisco Firestones. She and her brother William are extremely well connected, sir, up to the highest levels of the state house and beyond. I do not think you want to make trouble with them."

Kit looked directly at the leader. As their eyes locked, a strange communication flowed between them. It lasted only a moment before his gaze dropped and he assessed her physically. His expression told her he approved.

*That* was a look she understood, and she let him know with her own gaze that she accepted the compliment. He was handsome in his own right, and she let him know that, too. Under other circumstances the dance between them might have continued, but tonight only one thing mattered. And she knew precisely how to proceed.

"Amanda is like my little sister and I love her dearly," she explained in a soft, gentle voice. "Do you have a sister, Mr. Tang?"

Miss Cameron must have seen an opening in the way the leader continued to look at Kit, so she stepped in and pressed her case. The leader seemed to comprehend Miss Cameron's meaning. "I am sure we had nothing to do with the disappearance of your friends, but should we learn who the culprits were, we will pass along your message."

That was good enough for Miss Cameron. She apologized for disturbing the tong leader and herded her posse back the way they'd come.

"You were brilliant," she said to Kit once they were back on the street. "Sometimes even I must admit there are sweeter ways to catch flies."

"You knew he'd done it, but had perhaps made a mistake," Kit mused.

"Yes, and you sensed it, too. We gave him a chance to save face and he took it."

"Wait—how can you be sure?" Will asked. "The man didn't admit to anything."

"Yes, he did, in his own way," Miss Cameron said. She suggested they return to the mission immediately. Shortly after they arrived, an unmarked car pulled up in front of the building. Mandy and Wu Jade flew out of the back seat, turning around to pull out Fung Hai, who was badly beaten and could barely walk.

Kit saw that Mandy was unhurt and sighed in relief, only to feel her maternal rage kick in again at the sight of the wounded young man. "Bollocks!" she cried, running over to help him.

---

"I am all right, really, Miss Kit." Mandy sat up in bed while Kit fussed with her bed covers yet again. They had returned home a short while before and Kit was insistent her young charge lie down immediately.

Kit's insides were still roiling from the sight of that poor young man's injuries and thoughts of what might have happened to the girls. "You're absolutely certain they didn't ... harm you in any way?"

Mandy smiled faintly. "Yes. That is something I would remember. Honestly, I think I would have remained safe, but I am glad you all came to our rescue because I am pretty sure Wu Jade's fate would not have been as kind. So, thank you, especially for Fung Hai."

"Fung Hai? What did I do for him?"

"You stood in for his mother, who, if she could have been there, would have raged at the injustice done to her son and comforted him as best she could. That is what all good mothers do."

Kit looked into the strangely beautiful eyes of the young girl who was both guileless and worldly wise. If anyone from Kit's circle had been involved in such a horror, they would have no doubt collapsed in a fit of nervous apoplexy and recounted their misadventure to whomever would listen for the next decade or more. Mandy only cared about her friends' welfare and appreciated what little Kit had been able to do.

Suddenly curious, Kit asked, "Do you miss your real mother?"

Mandy paused, then nodded, her eyes welling with tears. Kit immediately took her in her arms. "I know I cannot replace her, but you can hold on to me and pretend," she whispered, and was rewarded with a child's embrace and the sigh of someone who, despite their bravery, is relieved to set their fears aside, if only for a moment.

Kit was not a religious person, but much later that night, after reassuring herself for the fourth time that Mandy was indeed back in her own bedroom, safe and sound, she offered a prayer of sorts.

*Thank you, God, for bringing Mandy back to me unharmed. Had something happened to her, I don't think I could have lived with myself. But please tell me why on earth did you have to let that poor young man get beaten up like that? I mean, what is in it for you?*

The answers to her questions weren't forthcoming.

---

In the days before she became a guardian, Kit had bemoaned any unplanned stretch of time. No matter how hard she fought the urge, she would eventually succumb to the lure of reading the society column of *The Call*, checking to see whose name might be on everyone's lips at the next soiree. Whenever there had been fewer than three engagements on her calendar for the week, she would consider (rarely go through with it, but *consider*) calling her mother to see what parties Josephine had planned. She'd been desperate to fill her days with *something*.

Since the abduction, however, weeks without incident were a joy to be savored.

Not that life was perfect, by any means. One of the most troubling news stories to haunt the city concerned the so-called Chinatown Plague. Trying to cover it up had cost California's governor his job; the new one, George Pardee, was taking an "all hands on deck" approach to stamping out the disease.

Because of the abduction debacle, Kit would have been more than happy if neither Will nor Mandy ever set foot in Chinatown again. But for some odd reason Will had taken an interest in a new sewing school there, and Mandy, despite her kidnapping (or perhaps because of it) insisted on remaining as the mission's historian. Given those facts, Kit was all for doing whatever it took to remove the threat, and apparently that meant killing rats—thousands and thousands of rats. To do that, government workers had started tearing down countless ramshackle structures throughout Chinatown where the rats found shelter.

In the beginning of the Chinatown "beautification" campaign, the entire neighborhood looked like one giant trash heap. But slowly, the trash was being carted away and the place looked better and better. She thought the people who lived there must be so very pleased.

Weeks went by without drama and Kit was lulled into a false contentment. That came to a halt in mid-November with an unexpected invitation by her mother for tea. Since it was set for the afternoon and not the evening, Kit thought it might be a perfect time to introduce Mandy to her parents. They were somewhat like grandparents, weren't they? "May I bring her?" she asked, assuming the answer would be yes.

The answer was no. "I'm sorry, darling," her mother said with what was obviously feigned regret. "It's just you I want to visit with. Can you come at four p.m.?"

Part of Kit wanted to decry the insult her mother had just dealt her. *You want me but not my child? How dare you!* But logic prevailed. Her mother had never met Mandy and probably couldn't imagine Kit playing the role of mother. Kit found it difficult to comprehend at times herself. She would give her mother the benefit of the doubt.

"So glad you made it, darling," Josephine greeted her the next day. "I always appreciate your promptness." Her mother was dressed as if she were the keynote speaker at a women's auxiliary—tasteful and *au courant*. Kit, without even realizing it, had dressed similarly.

They sat in the rear informal parlor. It was a lovely, light-filled room decorated in lush cream tones. Tall picture windows, dressed in rich damask, overlooked the Firestone gardens where a strategically placed bird feeder offered visitors a bit of visual entertainment. Kit breathed in the cloying scent of gardenias floating in a bowl across the room. She'd always preferred lilacs.

In addition to the silver tea service, her mother had ordered that an elaborate repast be laid out on the sideboard. Sampling one of each item on display would have eliminated Kit's need to eat for the next three days. Nonetheless, she dutifully filled a plate with fresh pear slices, a deviled ham sandwich (without crust), a slice of sponge cake, and a delicate lemon tart. Bertrand had outdone himself.

Kit's mother was dedicated to staying abreast of the latest social intrigue, especially when it involved the Firestone clan in any way. These days she was particularly concerned that none of her three children were anywhere close to making a match.

"I hear Buster Wainwright is looking to get closer to Beatrice Marshall," she divulged. "Will had better take care if he wishes to keep her in the running."

Kit popped a slice of pear into her mouth. It was slightly unripe and crunchy. She preferred them juicy. "Mother, I don't think Will's even thinking along those lines. You shouldn't get your hopes up."

"You're probably right." Josephine heaved a quietly dramatic sigh and paused to take a sip of tea before nibbling on a cucumber sandwich. "Well then, what about you, darling? You seem so distant lately; I've been wondering if you've been caught up in the whirlwind of a new relationship. Dare I hope as much?"

This, then, was the reason for the visit. For a moment Kit was incredulous; did her mother really not understand what Kit had been doing these past months? Then it hit her: of course she knew, but since she didn't want to acknowledge Mandy, she sought to simply ignore the fact that the girl was part of Kit's life now.

Kit would have none of it. "As a matter of fact, I *am* in a new relationship, but not the type you're hoping for. You know perfectly well that I have become the guardian for a delightful young lady—oh, wait, you wouldn't know that she's delightful, because you haven't bothered to meet her or even ask about her. Really, Mother. Where are your manners?"

Josephine's expression tightened, but she was too

skilled to betray her pique. She tried an evasive maneuver instead. "Both of your brothers are abandoning us this Thanksgiving. Jamie wrote to say he's staying in Southern California at the university, and Will tells me he'll be in New York attending Lia and Gus's wedding. I assume you'll at least be joining us."

"Just me?"

"Yes, of course. You are all that's necessary to make it a festive occasion. Although I would be more than thrilled if you brought a young man along. And have you made plans for your little charity case for over the holidays?"

Kit carefully finished her own tea, saying nothing while her mind raced to come up with an appropriate response to her mother's unforgivably rude remark. Shouting at her would serve no purpose; neither would storming out in a fit of rage, even though that's precisely what she wanted to do. No. Something else would be much more cutting, and yet fully within the bounds of propriety. She gently dabbed her lips. "Thank you so much for the invitation, Mother, but I'm afraid Mandy and I won't be able to join you and Father this year, either. You see, we ... we are going to New York as well. We'll be sure to bring your warm regards to the newlyweds. I know Lia will be happy to know how much you still enjoy the portrait of us that she painted."

Kit thought she'd feel vindicated by seeing the hurt on her mother's face. Josephine tried to hide it beneath a veneer of "Oh, isn't that nice" and "We'll certainly miss all of you," but the disappointment was there all the same.

She didn't feel vindicated, however. Disheartened? Yes. Was she really meant to be a mother? If it meant turning into someone as coldly calculating as her own parent, she didn't want to be.

Kit called a taxi before she left and decided to meet the driver at the main gate of the estate. As she walked down the hill, she realized that debating the merits of motherhood was no longer her biggest concern. Her biggest concern was finagling an invitation for both herself and Mandy to a wedding that was happening clear across the country in less than two weeks. Then she had to make sure she booked the same train as Will and hope he didn't bite her head off when she told him what she'd done. "Audacious" didn't begin to describe the telephone call she'd need to make to Lia. But if the alternative was subjecting Mandy to Josephine's cruelty, she'd damn well walk to New York.

### Josephine

"She hates me."

Josephine was sitting at her vanity table, staring at herself in the mirror. She didn't mind growing old, but she hated the thought of having worked so hard at something as important as raising her daughter, only to fail at it.

Edward stood behind his wife, attaching his cufflinks. This pair was carved from topaz, a birthday gift from Josephine years ago. They were of her birthstone, not his, because she wanted him to think of her whenever he wore them.

He put his hand on her shoulder. "I'm not going to dignify that remark with a response, darling, except to ask what led you to believe such nonsense."

Josephine turned to him and he cupped her cheek, lightly brushing a tear from it. She closed her eyes. After all these years, he could still soothe her with a touch.

"I made the monumental mistake of not taking her guardianship of the young Culpepper girl seriously," she replied. "I even went so far as to comment about her 'little charity case.' How stupid of me! I've driven her away and they're going to New York for Thanksgiving."

Edward pulled a chair close to Josephine and took both of her hands in his. "Why do you suppose you did that?"

"Because I didn't—I don't—want to think of her in those terms. She's not a mother. She's not ready to be a mother. She's still my—"

"Little girl?" He ran his hand along the back of her head with such tenderness she wanted to weep. "In some sense she will always be that, but the truth is, she's all grown up now. She's a smart, lovely young woman, inside and out, and you helped her to become that person."

Josephine nodded. It was just so damn difficult to let go. When her darling Katherine was born, so golden and perfect, all she could think was: *I will not let you down. You will be loved and cherished your whole life long.*

"You know," he added, "if Kit hadn't learned what it means to love someone and be responsible for them, I don't think she would have volunteered for the job."

"That's just it. It's so much more than just a job. Being a good mother or father is so difficult, even when there are two of you to share the load. I can't imagine doing it all alone."

"Well, she's got Will to help out."

Josephine snorted. "Our Will is a dear, but he is certainly not father material—not yet at any rate." This time she took Edward's hand. "I know I can be smothery at times—"

Edward grinned "'Smothery'? Is that a word?"

Josephine tried not to smile. "I don't know. But if it isn't, it ought to be. At any rate, you know what I mean. I care too much, I know that. I even go out of my way to pretend I don't, but it's no use. But for heaven's sake, why can't she do things in the right order? Find a man to love first, and *then* bring children into it. Lord knows she could have her pick."

"I'm not sure Kit is ready to give her heart to someone else. Even if she met her Prince Charming tomorrow, he'd probably have a difficult time with her. She needs to find out where she fits in the grand scheme of things. And let's face it —she's a very independent young woman ... like someone else I know."

Josephine turned back to the mirror and met her

husband's eyes in the reflection. An intense sadness swept over her. "You're right. When I think of how close I came ..." She shook her head to dissipate the feeling, but it remained, as stubborn as her daughter's attitude. "It's her independence that scares me more than anything."

## CHAPTER SEVENTEEN

*1903*

*O*h my God, *what* a disaster. Kit leaned back in her plush velvet seat on the Overland Limited, facing the window but seeing nothing, barely registering her brother's admonishments. Something about how rude she was not to have used the man's professional title. Had she really just made such a fool of herself?

She had.

In her defense, she'd been in the process of digesting all sorts of uncharitable thoughts about her mother while also experiencing a keen sense of guilt for having abandoned her parents on one of their favorite holidays. She told herself it was for the best; her mother was going to have to accept the fact that her children led full, interesting lives. They lived for more than simply finding suitable mates.

Such unpleasantness had been at the forefront of

her brain when her fifteen-year-old ward, Mandy, returned from exploring the rest of the train.

"Look who I found!" Mandy had cried, tugging the hand of someone behind her. Will asked Kit with his eyebrows if she knew who Mandy was referring to, and Kit answered with a slight shake of her head. *Not a clue.* The next moment, a man stepped into their compartment, ducking his head. He may as well have been holding a lightning bolt in his big hands, such were the shock waves his appearance sent through her.

Kit was used to men admiring her; she was confident that some even desired her. But this man telegraphed his primitive response to her in a way that was meant for her alone to feel, and she knew, instinctively, that she felt it because she was responding in kind. It had nothing to do with her mind and everything to do with her body. What was happening to her?

"I don't think we've had the pleasure of meeting," her brother said, extending his hand to the stranger. "Will Firestone. You're obviously a friend of Mandy's."

The man, who looked to be in his thirties, was tall with longish dark brown hair and the look of a worker about him. He was dressed in a rather shabby coat and worn trousers, and the idea that Kit might lust after such a common creature filled her with both titillation and distaste. He stared at her until Mandy nudged him, at which point he apologized and introduced himself as Tom Justice.

"And you are?" he immediately asked Kit. The arc between them snapped again.

"Katherine Firestone. I'm ... Mandy's guardian.

Will's sister." She watched his eyes grow even more intense and felt compelled to extend her hand. He took it and held it, the current flowing intensely between them. They were alone in their connection and it scared her. She pulled back.

Mandy's explanation barely registered. Something about him being a ... a *doctor*? No, it was impossible.

"I understand you are all traveling back to New York to attend a wedding." He was making small talk, as if he were just any other man.

"Yes, on Thanksgiving Day," Kit said. And what about you, Mr. Justice?" She saw her brother frown as the man mentioned something about traveling back to his home, in a buckboard, no less. He was a farmer; of course that's how he would travel.

She could not tolerate this attraction between them a moment longer; it was too much. "Ah. How ... quaint." She injected the word with a lavish dose of condescension.

It had its desired effect—the man looked at her with distaste. *Good*.

Unfortunately, well enough was not left alone. Mandy earnestly explained that she was perplexed by Kit's use of the word "quaint" because her teachers at the Weems Academy had told her it had a negative connotation.

"You didn't mean it like that, did you, Miss Kit?"

The farmer was astute—and gallant—enough to attempt to cover her rudeness. She tried to make verbal amends at the same time, resulting in a socially awkward exchange that only ended when Mandy announced she was returning to "Dr. Tom's" coach, where she'd spied more edible snacks. A moment later they were gone.

"I am mortified," Kit moaned.

"You should be. 'Quaint'? I could have sworn Josephine was sitting right next to me. When did you turn all high and mighty?"

"I don't know. I just ... I was flummoxed. I didn't know what to say. He ... he kept looking at me."

"As if that has ever made a difference to you before now. And may I add that for you to know he was looking at you meant that you had to be looking at him. 'Moon-eyed' wouldn't be too far off the mark."

Kit waved her hand to swat her brother. "Oh, stuff it. I ... I was surprised, that's all."

"Mm-m-hmm. Surprised that you've finally met someone who piques your interest."

"I'm not talking to you anymore," Kit said huffily, and turned back to watch the scenery fly by without seeing a thing.

---

She couldn't stop thinking about him. Throughout the week-long trip to New York, her friend Lia's intimate, picture-perfect wedding, and the uneventful return journey, whenever she had a moment to herself, she would unwrap images of Tom Justice like the richest cream-filled chocolate and savor them greedily. Guiltily.

How large he was, stepping into their private car,

deferential, respectful, yet filling the space with his focus wholly on her.

His dark eyes devouring her.

His rough hand engulfing hers.

He'd scared her. Shown her how easily he could tear apart the cocoon she had woven around herself. To make her *want*.

Easton Challis had done the same, hadn't he? Hadn't she fallen under his malevolent spell? Wasn't this a sign that she was weak, that greater vigilance was called for?

*Don't lie, Kit; not to yourself, at least.*

Easton Challis had been intriguing, a challenge, a sport. Only her need for social approval should their affair become public had led her to think, momentarily, that she was in love with the man. But he had not touched the core of her.

Something within her knew that Tom Justice was different, and that is why she'd ridiculed him. Subtly. Completely. And she knew she'd hit her mark by the way the fierce light in his eyes had dimmed. She could tell already that he would not pursue her as Easton had. Tom cared enough about himself to find her wanting. He did not need her.

And the thought filled her with an emptiness of spirit, the likes of which she had never felt before.

## CHAPTER EIGHTEEN

The Firestones were major patrons of St. Mary's Hospital, and as such always attended the annual charity ball for its children's ward. For the past few years Kit had been pressured into participating in one of their most popular fundraising gambits, a "raffle" of sorts in which rich young women bought expensive tickets for a chance to go out with one or more successful, ambitious, and very eligible bachelors. While embarrassing, it was somewhat entertaining to watch the men preen in front of a ballroom filled with debutantes and their mamas.

This year Kit's mother had not been able to attend because of what she termed an "annoying" intestinal ailment. It was not like Josephine to make flimsy excuses for missing a social function, and her mother's absence left Kit feeling a bit out of sorts herself. At least with her mother in tow, she had some respite from those who desperately wanted to rub shoulders with the younger generation of Firestones. Only another Firestone truly understood what it was like to be desired for your place in society above and beyond anything else.

Kit's father was no help; as always, he gravitated to the side rooms where private introductions were made, deals were discussed, and politics was never off the table.

Even Will had defected. At past galas he'd been one of the "eligibles," but this year he was a no-show. Ever since their New York trip he'd seemed preoccupied; if Kit didn't know better, she'd think her poor brother was in love. Unfortunately, that left Kit to represent the family, which she reluctantly set about to do.

The theme for this year's ball was "A *Nutcracker* Christmas," based on an obscure Russian ballet. Apparently Letitia MacIntire, chairwoman of the decorations committee, had seen a performance of Tchaikovsky's work in St. Petersburg and felt it had merit.

"The production itself isn't that memorable, but the characters lend themselves to a festive atmosphere," she proclaimed, and set about transforming the grand ballroom of the Palace Hotel into a wonderland replete with larger-than-life mice, nutcrackers, toy soldiers, sugar plum fairies, and lavishly decorated Christmas trees. According to the society reports published the next day, she'd succeeded admirably.

Kit shared a table with several of her society friends and their very suitable escorts; both the men and the women were doing what was expected of them in order to make the kinds of matches they knew their families would approve. It didn't concern Kit that she was unescorted; had she put the word out, she knew any one of the men at her table would have preferred to squire her.

Bea Marshall sat one table over, and just before dinner was served she stopped by to chastise Kit for her brother's absence.

"I thought he was going to be here tonight; I mean, he usually attends. But I heard that at the last minute he decided to back out," she complained.

Kit feigned sympathy. "Oh, that's terrible! Had he promised to escort you?"

"Well no, but still, I would think he'd want to be here, your family being such major donors and all." Bea let out a dramatic sigh, which caused her impressive décolletage to make itself known.

Kit nodded. "I couldn't agree with you more." Bea was rather tedious at times, but in this case, she did have a point. Kit made a mental note to see what was bothering her brother.

She sat through several courses of the lavish banquet, wondering how her mother would have felt about the beluga caviar and the tender *shashlyk*, the skewered kebabs that were now so popular in Moscow. A bit too much salt, perhaps? Kit frowned. *I sound just like her.* She found herself missing the family chef. Bertrand and her mother were *simpatico* when it came to understanding how delectable a dish could be if prepared properly.

The interlude between the entrée and the dessert course arrived, signaling the start of the bachelor raffle. Five outstanding young men joined Dr. Samuelson, the master of ceremonies, on the dais. Kit nearly spilled her drink when she recognized the fifth man "up for sale."

Tom Justice looked magnificent. He was wearing a custom-fit tuxedo that showed to perfection his broad shoulders and narrow waist. He did not have the soft body that so many members of her social class had. His hair was trimmed, and she wondered if a woman had done it. Yet for all that he looked extremely uncomfortable.

"And our last bachelor is also our newest. Meet Dr. Thomas Justice, who hails from Nebraska's corn country. He's a graduate of the University of Michigan, where he attended on a full athletic scholarship and as a receiver helped the Wolverines to their first-ever victory against Cornell's Big Red back in ninety-three, which I'm sure many of you in this room remember."

She had no idea what he was referring to, but several of the patrons attending the ball must have, because they cheered and raised their wine glasses in salute.

Dr. Samuelson continued. "He earned his medical degree from Johns Hopkins University Medical School, now considered the most prestigious institution of its kind in the country. He has spent the last several years as a surgical resident under the world-famous Dr. William Halsted. Ladies and gentlemen, we are most fortunate to have one of the country's up-and-coming surgeons working on our staff today."

Kit watched from across the room as dozens of debs and their mothers quickly made their way to the dais, exchanging coy looks and chirpy small talk with the bachelors. To his credit, Tom didn't appear as if this was an activity he was fond of or skilled at. Yet he valiantly put on a good face and was rewarded with quite a few tickets. Kit noticed that Bea put all of her stubs in his basket.

The ticket voting had almost ended when Kit gathered her courage and decided to approach Tom. She didn't know what she would say, and what came out of her mouth was all wrong.

"Well, now you know," she said to him.

He frowned. "Know what?"

"How the other half lives." She glanced at his clothing, wanting to touch it but not daring to. Instead, she covered her nerves with another outrageously rude remark. "If you must know, I find it surprising you have such ... suitable clothing. You don't strike me as the type who has spent much time hobnobbing with ..." She gestured around the room.

Tom sent her the faintest of smiles. "With cultured, civilized people, you mean? You're right. I was actually given this suit in trade."

"In trade? For what?"

"A tailor in Chinatown has a little boy who'd fallen from a balcony." He leaned forward. "The floor had rotted through. Broke his leg and an arm, lacerations, a mess, really. We were able to set the bones and get the boy cleaned up. His father was grateful, but he didn't have any money, so he made me this." Tom plucked his lapel. "We were both happy with the outcome."

He'd thoroughly disarmed her.

The thought ran through her head: *How petty I sound.* She knew she should apologize, but damn it, groveling was not in her nature. She grew stubborn instead. *He will not get the better of me.*

"Perhaps," she said with a tinge of boredom. "Let's hope the boy doesn't walk with a limp, and then we'll know for sure, won't we?"

That, too, was the wrong thing to say because Tom Justice turned cold. "Miss Firestone, may I ask you something?"

She was busy smoothing down her dress, hoping he wouldn't see the blush of her embarrassment. But she looked up at his request. "Certainly."

"Is it men in general you don't like or just me in particular?"

Ah. Now *that* was warranted. Cruel, but warranted. She paused to shake it off, quickly reverting back to her zone of comfort. "I don't know you, *Doctor* Justice. Why would I care about you one way or the other?" She returned to her seat, pausing only to drop her four tickets into the basket of the bachelor standing next to Tom. She didn't even notice which man it was.

That night she punched her pillow several times in an effort to make herself comfortable enough to fall asleep. She had no luck and knew her pillow had nothing to do with it.

What was wrong with her? She was drawn to the

man in every possible way, yet she challenged him with verbal broadswords whenever they crossed paths. Why was she so contrary?

*Because you are frightened to death to get close to him,* a voice said.

*Because you know he could rule your heart.*

**CHAPTER NINETEEN**

*1904*

The morning prior to Valentine's Day was dreary as usual, but the cold of the fog sank particularly deep into Kit, aided by a sense of anxiety that she was having a hard time keeping at bay. Something was amiss; she could feel it.

Christmas had been fine, more than fine, thanks to her mother's decision to invite Mandy to the family's traditional celebration. Mandy had charmed her parents as well as Kit and Will's brother, James, who was home from university. And Josephine had done her part to make Mandy feel welcome.

Surprisingly, Will was the problem. He'd been quiet throughout the festivities, and on Christmas morning, in the midst of opening presents back at their home on Russian Hill, he'd barked at Mandy in the cruelest manner possible, even though she had done nothing wrong. It was not like him at all.

The following weeks had been filled with tension; it was obvious that something was wrong with her brother, and now, inexplicably, he had not come home the night before. That fact was confirmed by his major domo, Fleming.

Adding to her concern was that Mandy herself had left that morning to meet Fung Hai at the Mission House. Kit had no reason to connect the two events, but not knowing for sure was making her jittery. When the doorbell rang, she practically jumped out of her skin.

Fleming saw to the visitor; it was Tom Justice and she could tell that it was not a social call.

"What is wrong?" she asked sharply, foregoing even the pleasantries of a greeting.

He removed his hat as he stood in the front parlor. Glancing at Fleming, he said, "I have to speak with you privately."

"You may speak in front of Fleming. He is practically a member of the family."

Tom ran a hand through his hair, obviously distressed. "Your brother ..."

In a flash Kit's heart began racing. "I knew it. What has happened to him?"

"Your brother is very sick, and Mandy is taking care of him. She wanted you to know that she would be tending him and not to worry. You won't be able to see him, but—"

Kit nodded to Fleming and he left the room. She then turned to Tom. "Dr. Justice, you must be insane if you think you can tell me something like that and not have me go to him."

"I'm sorry, but it's not safe."

He took a step toward her, but she instinctively backed away. *This nightmare cannot be happening.* "Fleming!" she called in a voice tinged with frenzy.

Fleming came back carrying Katherine's coat and his own. As she prepared to leave, it dawned on her that she had no idea where to go. "You need to tell me where he is," she ordered Tom.

"Actually, I don't," he said, his voice cloaked in the cold politeness she found infuriating. "He is most likely contagious. But out of respect for Mandy I will ride with you so that you can talk with her and see for yourself what is going on."

Kit glared at him, willing him to back down. He wouldn't budge, however, and she salvaged what she could of her dignity. "Very well. If you must tag along, I suggest we leave immediately, if not sooner. Fleming will drive us."

---

*You must hold yourself together. You must think.*

Kit sat in the back of the carriage on her way to Chinatown, where apparently her brother was holed up with a woman. Her mind was racing much faster than the horse taking her there. Tom sat next to her wearing a neutral expression, offering no further details about her brother's plight. She refused to ask him; she already felt too much like a supplicant hoping to receive an extra crust of bread.

*Will is never sick. How did this happen? How bad is he? How will I be able to help him? I should be helping him rather than Mandy. She's just a girl, for heaven's sake! What if she catches whatever he has? How is she coping? What shall I tell our parents?*

The answers weren't forthcoming and her frustration grew. She tried to focus on keeping her distance from the man sitting beside her, but it was difficult. He was so large. So *present*. Only now did she realize how physically formidable he was, how diminutive he made her feel. She wasn't used to the sensation. She didn't like it.

My God, when were they going to get there? "Fleming," she called to the front of the conveyance. "Can't you go any faster?"

Fleming turned slightly and called back over his shoulder. "Not in this traffic, miss."

Tom leaned forward. "Take Vallejo down to Grant rather than Union. Less congestion that way."

"Right you are, sir," Fleming said.

Kit stared out the window, willing the carriage to fly if possible. In truth she felt ready to fly out of her own skin. Never had she felt so afraid—she was more frightened than she'd been during the entire misadventure with Easton Challis. And sitting next to Tom Justice did nothing to soothe her rattled nerves. Surreptitiously she raised a hand to her cheek. It felt like it was cracking, as if she were Humpty Dumpty on the wall. Her face ached from maintaining a calm façade when all she wanted to do was scream. She began to smooth her skirts, a habit she had tried to break, but which re-surfaced in times of stress.

She'd known her brother was intrigued by the Chinese people. He'd fallen into Donaldina Cameron's orbit and the mission director was no doubt thrilled to have him sponsor the new sewing school she'd started up. Because of Mandy, even Kit had been drawn in; she'd already given several tours of the "new and improved" Chinatown to her friends.

But this? To find out he'd been dallying with a Chinese woman and caught some sickness, some—

The idea hit her with such force she gasped. It couldn't be. She turned to Tom. "You said my brother is contagious and he's in Chinatown. Are you saying he might have ... this plague they're talking about?"

He'd been staring out of the carriage but turned at her voice. Looking down, he saw her jittery hand and stopped its frenetic movement with his large, warm one. "The symptoms point in that direction, yes."

She stared at his hand covering hers, comforting her. Pitying her, no doubt. She withdrew her hand slowly, in counterpoint to her internal mania. Injecting her voice with authority, she looked straight ahead and said, "Well, that is unacceptable and we will simply have to do something to fix it."

"Look at me," he said in a quiet voice. When she refused, he reiterated the command, gently turning her chin toward him. "We are doing all that can be done, given the circumstances. There is nothing more that you, in particular, can add, which is why your visit will be brief."

If he thought to offer her solace, his words had the opposite effect. His self-righteousness was maddening. How dare he presume to tell her what she could or couldn't do? How on earth could she ever have been attracted to him on any level, even the most elemental? He was too big, too male, too much like the rest of them to suit her. But he was wrong and she would show him. "We'll see about that," she pronounced to the air in front of her.

He said nothing, simply returned to looking out the window until they arrived at the school.

When they entered the little shop on the ground floor, Tom turned to Fleming. "For your protection I ask that you stay downstairs, sir. Miss Firestone will only be a few moments."

Fleming looked to her for guidance. He was intensely loyal to Will, and by extension to her. If she asked him to follow, he would follow. But if it really was that dangerous, there was no point in risking his safety. "It's all right, Fleming. I'll be down to give you directions before you leave."

Kit swallowed her nerves as she followed Tom up the stairs, but try as she might, she couldn't keep her tears from overflowing their banks.

---

"This ... this quack here says that I cannot stay and take care of my own brother," she announced to Mandy, who was just stepping out of what must have been the bedroom. The door was open and she could see two shapes huddled under blankets. "That is ridiculous. How is Will doing?" She attempted to go around her ward and enter the room, but Tom stopped her with an arm across her waist. She tried to break his hold but it was rock solid. "Please!" she begged.

"No," he said. "You are not going in there."

"He is sleeping now," Mandy said, and gestured to her. "Come to the front room and talk to me."

Reluctantly, Kit followed, trying to keep herself under control as Mandy calmly recited the logic: if Will didn't make it, and Kit caught whatever he had and didn't make it either, then their parents would have lost two children, not just one.

"But why you?" Kit cried.

"Because I am perfect for the job." Mandy explained that she was protected from the disease because of shots she'd taken. Besides, she said, if anything bad did happen to her, she didn't have any family who were waiting for her to come home, who would grieve for her. "But you do," she said. "You are needed."

The absurdity of that statement lodged in Kit's throat and threatened to strangle her. Leaning in close to Mandy, she whispered, "No, I am useless."

And Mandy, with her loving heart, put her arms around Kit and whispered back, "Never say that. You have been a good mama to me."

Kit could barely respond, but was saved from further embarrassment by Tom, who broke in with a description of the supplies he'd brought and last-minute instructions for taking care of Will and the woman.

Kit wanted to do something, damn it! "Are you sure you can do this, Mandy? We can't lose him ... or you. We simply can't."

Mandy assured her she'd do her best, and with one last look, Kit grudgingly followed Tom down the stairs to where Fleming was waiting.

"We'll know if he's going to pull through in a day or so," Tom said. "As soon as Mandy gets word to me I'll pass the message on to you."

Kit blotted her face with a small lace handkerchief and busied herself pulling on her traveling gloves while inside, her self-recrimination had begun in earnest. She was helpless. Useless. Nothing more than a body taking up space. She blamed herself for her predicament, but that didn't stop her from lashing out. She looked up at her nemesis. "I will never forgive you for this," she said coldly. "You have put Mandy, me, all of us in an untenable position."

Tom's brown eyes caught hers and held them. "I didn't bring the plague, Miss Firestone, and I didn't give it to your brother. However you may think of me, this is the best way to handle the situation for all concerned ... even you."

She looked at him a moment longer, regret for her words beginning to creep in before she shut the door on it resoundingly. What might have turned into ... something, had dissolved into nothing. Worse than nothing. Before her lay only worry ... and waiting.

So be it.

"Good day, Doctor."

---

Fleming dropped Kit off at the front entrance to the mansion before taking the horse to the barn. "May I say something, miss?" he asked.

"Certainly, Fleming."

"That man, that doctor, didn't say nothin' about turning Mr. Firestone over to the authorities. I think he's going to try and keep it hush-hush. You know, make sure the Firestone name stays out of the papers and all them tattle sheets."

Kit frowned. My God, she'd been so worried about her brother that it hadn't even dawned on her what a scandal it might prove to be. And she hadn't been exactly kind to the good doctor, had she? Hell's bells. "Why would he do that? You don't think he intends to blackmail us, do you?"

Fleming gave her an incredulous look, as if he'd just watched her strip naked in the foyer. He shook his head, a sign he wasn't going to pursue it. "If you can't see it, miss, I'm sure I can't help you."

That night, once again unable to sleep, Kit's thoughts centered on one idea. It wasn't hoping her brother would live, even though she did more than anything. It wasn't hoping that Mandy would be all right—she knew her ward was a survivor.

No, the thought that lodged itself within her like a shard of glass was that she had not been able to help her brother or her ward, at all. It didn't matter how intelligent or rich or charming or pretty she was; when they needed her in a meaningful way, she was lacking.

She never wanted to feel that way again. She refused to. So, she would do something about it. Starting tomorrow.

---

It took several days, but Kit's brother slowly emerged from the nightmare, thanks to Mandy. When he awoke from his fever, however, he remained aloof; the malaise that had clung to him before he fell ill still held him in its grip.

Everyone agreed to keep Will's bout with the plague out of the public eye. Just as Fleming surmised, that included Tom Justice, who arguably had more to lose than anyone, since as a medical professional he'd been present at the death of both Will's supposed "friend" and her young daughter. Chinese mistrust of authority helped them in that regard; the bodies, Kit learned, were quarantined and eventually sent back to China for burial.

Knowing how their mother would react to the near-death of any of her children, Will and Kit agreed not to let their parents in on his misfortune. He spent the next few weeks convalescing at home while Josephine was led to believe he was traveling for business.

Kit, meanwhile, took steps that would change her life forever. She researched several nursing schools in the city, applied to all of them, and was admitted to the program associated with the Women's and Children's Hospital on California Street. It had but one drawback: it was a residential program, which meant she would no longer be able to serve as Mandy's guardian.

One afternoon in March she sat down with Will to share her news and ask for his help. She was floored by what he told her: he was leaving the country! "Where in blazes are you running off to?" she demanded.

"I wouldn't call it 'running off' as much as 'searching for,'" he replied.

She realized this is what had been haunting him. "What are you hoping to find?" she asked.

"I think perhaps myself."

While she felt deeply for her brother's plight, Kit's main concern was caring for Mandy. Josephine might be able to step in, just until Kit finished the program. That option lasted all of a second or two as she realized what an unpleasant situation she would be thrusting Mandy into.

Having her ward join the Presbyterian Mission House was a possibility; Mandy already worked part-time for Donaldina Cameron, and the director was happy to have her live and work in Chinatown. Yet turning that lovely young woman into a scripture-spouting do-gooder just didn't feel right.

To make matters worse, Will's search for Mandy's relatives had finally come to fruition. A long-lost cousin, a pastor who had been out of the country, arrived to claim Mandy as part of the family. He ran a mission trying to convert the "heathen piccaninnies" in southern Australia and was willing to take Mandy back with him. Will had stalled for time, but the man had returned, more than ready to take her away. Kit's instinctive reaction to that plan was *absolutely not.*

No, Will's departure meant that Kit would have to put her career plans on hold. *This is what being a parent is all about*, she told herself. But it was so difficult to swallow her disappointment.

The solution to everyone's problem came from an unexpected source. Amelia Wolff, the well-known artist, needed a live-in personal assistant and wanted very much to have Mandy fill that role. Already close to Lia and her husband, Gus, Mandy was over the moon about it.

Now Kit's only remaining task was to explain to her parents that she and Will were heading in new directions, that for the foreseeable future, neither of them would be as accessible as they'd always been. She dreaded the confrontation—with good reason, it turned out.

Kit invited herself over to dinner, waiting until just after the dessert was served to share her news. Her mother was anything but pleased.

"You've gotten tired of motherhood so soon?" she asked Kit. "What has it been ... barely a year?" Her tone was uncharacteristically harsh.

"I don't think it's quite like that, darling," Edward said.

"I think it's exactly like that," she said. "You took on the guardianship of that poor young girl because it seemed like fun, but now that you've found something better to do, you're foisting her off on someone else."

Kit's gut twisted into something tight and painful. The niggling guilt she felt rose to the surface, but she pushed it back down. "You're wrong, Mother."

"Am I? I don't think so."

"Yes, you are. Mandy loves Lia and Gus, and they would have asked to take her on whether I was available to care for her or not. The timing just worked out well, that's all."

Her mother reached for her crystal water glass and took a sip, placing the glass carefully back in its place. She then picked up her dessert spoon but put it down again, her lemon sorbet remaining untouched. Spearing Kit with her eyes, she said, "Well, it was convenient for you, at least."

Her blood beginning to boil, Kit's anger took control of her tongue. She would not take this! "What do you understand about it anyway, Mother? You tried college, but you only lasted two years. You couldn't even bother to graduate. Face it, you never longed to do anything but marry a rich man and lord it over society." She clapped her hands. "Well, bravo! You succeeded. But some of us want more out of life. I do, at any rate. And I'm sorry if you—"

Kit's mother said nothing, her eyes wide with shock. But Kit's father stood, an action so out of character that Kit stopped mid-tirade.

"Your ignorance and your rudeness are beyond the pale," he said, his voice deadly calm. "You will apologize to your mother this instant, or you will leave my home."

It was Kit's turn to look stunned. Never had her

father sounded so authoritative or stern. Never had she felt his censure so keenly. Swallowing back tears, she gazed at her mother, who looked equally taken aback. "I ... I am sorry," Kit said. "I apologize." She rose from the table. "I'm afraid I really must go now. Thank you for dinner."

On the way home, Kit couldn't help but continuously replay the scene in her mind. She had insulted her mother, and her father had leapt to his wife's defense like an avenging warrior. His instinct was to protect her. She at last understood that a profound and limitless love existed between her parents. She might have had that, too, but now she probably never would.

How infinitely empty she felt.

### Josephine

Although their bedroom was cool, it was warm under the covers. Other than rocking her children to sleep when they were babies, it was the one place in the world that Josephine most liked to be, as long as she was with Edward.

"You were perhaps too hard on her," she said as she lay with her head tucked against his shoulder. "And perhaps I was, too."

"Possibly. But your response was natural, given who you are, and I will not have her disparaging you, especially when she has absolutely no idea what she is talking about."

"That may be our fault as well. I sometimes feel all of our children are under the impression that you and I sprang from the earth, fully formed and connected to each other."

She could hear her husband's soft chuckle. "But we know better, don't we?"

"Oh my, yes," she said, and snuggled even closer to her mate.

# CHAPTER TWENTY

### Josephine

*1873*

"I hate men."

Maida Babcock, tall and curvaceous with deep russet hair and golden eyes, opened every meeting of the Cornell Women's Club with that pronouncement. And every time, the members responded by stomping their shoes on the floor of the back parlor of Mrs. Wingate's boarding house in downtown Ithaca.

Josephine didn't hate men ... well, maybe some men, but not men in general. In fact, one in particular was beginning to invade her thoughts in a most unnerving, yet tantalizing way. But she went along with the ritual because to have done any differently would have been to face censure from those she considered her new clan. Being ostracized from one family had been bad enough; she wasn't strong enough to endure it a second time.

Josephine had made it into Cornell University, which prided itself on being the first prestigious East Coast school to admit women. The problem was, nobody at the school knew what to do with the women they'd let in.

Located on a steep hill above the town, the university offered no women's dormitory (although an edifice was under construction for that purpose), and ladies were excluded from most school activities, including sports teams and clubs.

Josephine learned that first-hand. She'd tried to get involved with the rowing team, telling the new coach, Henry Coulter, about her Boathouse Row experience.

"I can give you references," she said. "I make a good coxswain. If you give me a chance, I can show you what I can do."

But the coach had brushed her off, telling her in a kind but firm voice, "Women just aren't strong enough to participate in rowing, especially a little thing like you."

*Then I guess it was my imagination that I called those winning races,* she thought irritably.

Despite the sprawling nature of the campus, women at Cornell didn't even have an on-campus gathering place to call their own. In fact, they were threatened with expulsion if they were caught where they shouldn't be, like Cascadilla Hall, the male student dormitory. Hence the CWC meeting occurred at Mrs.

Wingate's, where more than half of the female students resided.

While faculty members like Coach Coulter were tolerant and generally solicitous (albeit condescending) of the fairer sex, most of the male students were not. They either ignored the women completely, or, in some cases, were aggressively rude.

Maida, as usual, read aloud the latest anti-female editorial from *The Cornell Era*, the school's weekly newspaper:

"'The beings whom I was to worship beyond the shadow of the college towers—who were to make me forget for a brief time the struggles of the classroom—these fair creatures whom I had set apart as something not to be profaned by association with prosaic toil, I find with me in the classroom, their faces flushed with emulating, the spirit of rivalry gleaming from their eyes.'"

"At least he calls us 'fair creatures,'" Janice Troutman pointed out. "The last writer called us the ugliest women in creation."

Grumblings about the editorial erupted, but Maida gave the group her patented evil eye and the chatter stopped. "I for one am sick to death of being belittled and made to feel inferior by the very men we sit next to every day in class. The question is, what are we going to do about it?"

Janice had taken out her small red notebook and a fountain pen. She was an eager student, always ready to take meticulous notes or share her opinion. She raised her hand. "We can stage a protest in front of the newspaper office, or we can insist on talking to Professor White." Andrew Dickson White, the school's co-founder, still taught courses and was an advocate of co-education.

Maida was not impressed. "To what end?" she asked angrily. "We have tried that several times and nothing ever happens. No, we need to make a more dramatic stand." She looked around the room again. "Have any of you heard of the Black Veil Society"?

Josephine stiffened, but said nothing. She hadn't been active in that cabal since they'd successfully gotten Roddy Merchant kicked out of Penn. The secret group had only surfaced a time or two after that, but according to Sally, the concept had been adopted in several other cities. "You started a movement and you can't even take credit for it," Sally had written.

"Nobody?" Maida looked pleased to be sharing something no one else had heard of. "Well, they're a secret organization that seeks justice by essentially blackmailing those in power."

"Ooh. How do they do that?" a member asked.

"They dig up dirt on people and then threaten to expose them if they don't toe the line." Maida smirked. "It sounds marvelous to me."

Hearing it explained that way left Josephine feeling sour inside. It sounded so ... so malevolent. And yet, at its core, that's exactly what the Black Veil Society had done to avenge Dinah's assault. She shifted, uncomfortable with her memories. But what she heard next made her sick to her stomach.

"How do we get the dirt?" Janet asked, clearly enthusiastic about the society's methods.

*You find people who have knowledge of your target's dirty dealings, and then you*—Josephine stopped herself. She was not going to partake in this.

"Oh, we don't need to dig up any dirt," their leader said with confidence. "We're going to make it up. Now it's just a matter of determining which man will feel our wrath."

---

Everybody called him Stony, which was a variation on his last name. He was just shy of six feet, lanky, with a thick shock of golden hair that he perpetually pushed away from his lean face. He also wore spectacles. Josephine had noticed him her first week as a sophomore, and learned he was two years ahead of her at the school.

Cornell was the first university in the country to offer its students a choice of courses, called "electives," and because of that, she and Stony shared French and Eighteenth Century English Literature. Josephine had never talked to him, however, because she and her female classmates always sat together in the front of the room and left *en masse*. By some type of unwritten code, they did not acknowledge their male counterparts, and were rarely acknowledged in return. Thus, it wasn't until after the Christmas holiday (which Josephine had spent with Mrs. Wingate) that she and Stony actually met face to face.

The circumstances were less than ideal. Ithaca was in the grip of a New Year's blizzard, and she'd stumbled while trying to make it up the four-hundred-and-forty-foot "Ithaca Alps" to campus. Was it any wonder? She wore two pairs of boys' trousers underneath her skirt, a thick sweater, two pairs of woolen socks, a heavy pair of boots, and a floppy hat. She also carried a satchel full of books and papers, all of which were covered by a long woolen coat. It was a feat just to be able to walk upright, much less trudge up an icy, snow-covered incline.

She was giggling at the thought of what Dinah would think of all her fashion *faux pas* when she lost her concentration and fell. Within seconds, however, she was quickly and easily picked up by the young man in question. He'd been standing at the top of the hill looking down, and as soon as she toppled over he was gamboling down like a mountain goat. She hoped it was the warmth generated by so much clothing and not abject embarrassment that had her face heating like a flame.

"Let me help you," he said cheerfully, and without waiting for a reply, he slipped an arm around her heavily padded waist and supported her as she awkwardly made her way up the slope. When they reached the top, he steadied her and removed his arm. He was smiling and with his glasses crusted over with snow, he looked like a jovial blind man.

Without thinking, Josephine reached up and wiped the snow off his lenses. Then she stuck out her hand.

"Jo Drummond," she said. "Thank you for digging me out of the snowbank."

He had very white, straight teeth. "Stony, and you're welcome. Shall we head over to class?"

So began a relationship that built and deepened over the next several months. Even though he wasn't much of a talker, Stony seemed to know everyone, and, despite the code, he had no qualms about introducing her as his "good friend, Jo Drummond." His male classmates, who might otherwise have snubbed her, took their friend's lead and accepted her into their circle. It wasn't long before she regularly heard "Hey, Jo!" or "How's it going, Jo!" as she made her way across Cornell's campus.

In March, Stony joined Big Red's baseball team as short stop, and Josephine, though she tried not to, often wandered over to the field to watch him practice. He was all fluid and grace, reaching and catching and throwing in one smooth glide. Sometimes he'd look her way and wave. And one time, as she watched from behind a tree, she saw him scanning the bleachers where visitors usually sat. Maybe he was looking for her. And maybe she wanted him to.

They grew closer. If Jo was by herself eating lunch or reading, he would sometimes sit by her to eat his own meal or just visit. He never asked about her background, which she appreciated, and she never queried him about his. Their conversations remained light and frothy, filled with silly jokes and friendly banter, and more often than not, long stretches of companionable silence. They determined that she spoke French much better than he did, and he suggested they practice speaking it together.

She took him up on his offer one warm spring afternoon as they sat on the bank of Fall Creek, on the northern edge of the campus. Stony had laid his jacket and straw hat beside him on the grass. Rolling up his sleeves, he searched idly for small pebbles and tossed them into the rushing water. He looked strong and capable, which drew Josephine to him, yet worried her, too. She realized she wanted to know him. Really know him. "*Si tu pourrais viver n'importe où dans le monde, alors où?*" she asked.

Stony looked at her quizzically. Then he smiled, responding with, "I think you're asking me something about where I would like to live, but—"

"*Très bien!*" Jo replied. "*Mais en francais, s'il vous plaît.*"

He gazed at the creek and Josephine could tell that speaking French was the last thing on his mind. It dawned on her that he would be leaving in a few short months. The thought took all the playfulness out of her tone.

"Are you looking forward to going home?" she asked.

It took him several moments to answer; this was not the light-hearted Stony she knew. "I love my parents, and when I graduate they expect me to join the family business, along with my other relatives back in Arlington. They worry about me and want to keep me close."

"Close? Why?"

He heaved a sigh, as if he'd been down a certain road a thousand times, seen everything there was to see along the way, and longed to explore another route. "I have a problem ... with reading, you see. The words get jumbled in my head and it takes me quite a while to figure out what I'm looking at."

Josephine was shocked. She had never heard of such a thing. "And yet you're here, in college."

His voice carried a trace of pride. "I have friends who help, and a very good memory. I get it done. I always get it done. Still, they worry."

It was difficult to imagine parents who took such an interest, who cared *too* much. "Is that why you came here instead of going to school closer to home?"

"Exactly. And if I had my druthers ..." He seemed almost embarrassed to continue.

She encouraged him with a smile. "Go on."

He glanced at her and lifted a shoulder. "I'd head west. San Francisco, maybe. It's booming out there. They call it the Golden City. A man could make his mark."

"Doing what, exactly?"

Stony continued to toss the stones. "A little of this and a little of that. Business. Politics, even. I'm good with people and I'm good with numbers, too. I'm much better at math than English ... or French, for that matter." He sent her half a grin. "What about you? What will you do once you leave Cornell?"

*If only I knew!* The question frightened her to death. It had seemed a worthy goal just to go to college, but she hadn't given much thought to what she would do once she got her degree. Sad to say, there weren't many opportunities for young ladies in *any* profession besides teaching, no matter how much education they had. And right now, teaching held little appeal.

So, she hedged. "Oh, that's so far away. I have to get through college first. Then who knows, maybe I'll fly to the moon and back."

Stony wasn't fooled by her levity. "Seriously, what would you like to do ... if you could do anything?"

The answer popped out without her even thinking about it. "I'd be a chef in a grand hotel," she said. "I'd prepare incredibly delicious meals that the guests would savor, and after they finished, they'd say things like, 'Those snails were out of this world!' I'd create new flavors and maybe have a dish named after me. And then I'd—"

She stopped, mortified. All that silliness had just poured out of her, and none of it, *none* of it would ever come to pass. Feeling tears beginning to form, she tried to gather her things. "I guess we'd better—"

"No, wait," he said, gently touching her arm. "Don't. You never know. It could happen."

She leveled a look on him. "No. It's never going to happen. I could be a cook, but I'll never be a chef." Her words came out as bitter as wormwood.

"Well, maybe not in Philadelphia—"

"What?" Josephine looked at him with surprise.

"Philadelphia. That's where you're from, isn't it?"

She frowned. "Yes, but how did you know that?"

"I ... asked around." He casually took her hand in his

and said slowly, "So, maybe not in Philadelphia, but I don't know ... San Francisco, maybe?"

He gazed at her and she could feel his warm hand stroking hers. Her heart started to race and she swallowed, not wanting to misinterpret what he might be saying.

"San Francisco?"

He smiled slightly and nodded. "I was just wondering, you know, if ..."

She held his gaze and answered with a smile of her own. "I hear it's booming. A woman could make her mark."

They said nothing for several minutes, each content to gaze out at the water.

"My name is Edward Frederick Firestone, by the way."

"And I'm Josephine Rose Drummond."

---

To the world, they continued to be Stony and Jo, but in her heart, Josephine had begun to call her beau (for that's what he was, wasn't he?) Edward. And during the next few weeks, she was as happy as she'd been before her father died, perhaps even happier. She and Edward didn't spend more time together, nor were their interactions more intimate. But an undercurrent flowed between them, an understanding that their relationship had progressed beyond simple friendship.

It wasn't long before her housemates began to question her judgment.

Growing up, Josephine had felt most secure in the kitchen of the Drummond family townhome, often helping Cook prepare vegetables or roll out dough. She felt the same comfort in Mrs. Wingate's kitchen, where the middle-aged widow was happy to have her help. It was there that Maida cornered her one Sunday afternoon cutting out biscuits for that evening's supper.

"I don't trust him," Maida said. She had brought in her unmentionables to wash in the nearby utility sink. "I think he has designs on you."

Josephine did not want to have this conversation; it was best to feign ignorance. "I'm sure I don't know who you're talking about."

"Don't be silly. We all see the way Stony looks at you. I know that look, believe me."

The unwanted heat stealing its way up Josephine's neckline didn't have the decency to stop where it couldn't be seen. Oh, no, it kept right on going.

"Ha! I can tell by your blush you know *exactly* what I'm talking about." Maida squeezed the water out of her chemise with undue force. "He'll take you right where he wants to take you, and then drop you like you were yesterday's news. You wait and see."

Maida sounded unusually bitter. As pretty as she was, Josephine wondered if a man had taken advantage of her at some point. That reminded Josephine of Dinah's troubles and how her dear friend was forever committed to a life with Clarence Marshall. Because of a business opportunity, the couple had moved from Philadelphia to St. Louis, which left Dinah without nearby family or friends to make life easier. Complicating matters was the fact that she and Clarence had been trying for three years to have a baby with no success. Jo shuddered. *That will not happen to me.* Her deceptive response to Maida came so easily that she wondered later why that was so. "Stony and I are barely friends, and that's all we're ever going to be. Period."

"Of course," Maida said. "That's what they all say." She sounded like the voice of experience.

---

Another Cornell Women's Club meeting took place, and once again Maida read the paper's latest anti-female editorial out loud. As before, the group agreed that something should be done to improve their situation vis à vis the men. But this time, their leader came prepared.

"I have discovered the perfect target for our version of the Black Veil Society," she announced, looking directly at Josephine. "You all know him as 'Stony,' but his real name is Edward Firestone."

Josephine couldn't believe what she was hearing. "What are you talking about? What on earth has he done?"

Maida seemed quite pleased with herself. "Oh, he hasn't done anything; he's quite an amiable fellow—on the surface, at least. It's what we *want* him to do that's important."

"Explain," Janice Troutman said, pulling out her notebook.

"Maybe you all didn't know this, but Edward Firestone comes from one of the richest families in Virginia. They have their fingers in practically everything, and word is, he could buy and sell just about any other student at this university. In other words, he has *influence*. But he also has a problem. He can't read."

Her jaw tightening, Josephine inhaled deeply so as not to launch herself at Maida. "That is simply not true."

The club members began to murmur, many of them sending Josephine looks of envy laced with pity. Hitch your wagon to a man who can't read? All the money in the world can't make up for having a dumb husband, can it?

Maida continued unabated. "Well, maybe he can read, but not very well. I have it on good authority. So, what we're going to do is put him in a situation that forces him to do our bidding or risk being kicked out of school. Since he's about to graduate, that would be bad for him indeed."

Letty Corcoran was a very intelligent, but terribly sour young woman. Now, however, she seemed to glow. "You sound like you have it all planned out. Let's hear it."

Maida did have a plan. The first step was to procure a copy of the final English exam, which she would do. When asked how, she demurred, saying only that she had "connections." Everyone understood those connections to be with Mr. Rafferty, the married English professor with a roving eye who taught the class.

"Step two: I have one of Stony's friends plant the exam in his dormitory room."

"His friends would never agree to that," Josephine said. She was certain of it.

"You're right—not if they think it's a stolen exam. But if they think it's a love letter from *you* ..."

"That is ridiculous. I would never—"

Maida rolled her eyes. "Of course, you wouldn't. But the messenger I have in mind doesn't know that, and besides, he'll do most anything for me."

Penny Trumble, Jo's roommate, piped in. "So, you hide the exam in Stony's room. Then what?"

"Then we confront him, telling him we've learned he's trying to cheat on the final exam. He'll deny it, of course, but then he'll find the evidence of his guilt and voilà—he'll be putty in our hands. We'll be as powerful as the Black Veil Society, but we won't even have to wear black, because we'll have righteousness on our side."

Janice was still jotting notes down. "So ... what happens then? What do we want him to do in return for our silence?"

Maida's tone was predatory, a hawk circling its next meal. "With his resources, the sky's the limit. First, we'll have him write an opinion piece for the *Era* telling his fellow students that they'd better accept that we are here and we aren't going away. Then, who knows? Perhaps his family can donate a building on campus that's just for women. We have time to determine precisely the pound of flesh we want to extract from Mr. High and Mighty."

Josephine felt as if her brain had just been pounded with an anvil. Even if this trick were to be played on someone she didn't know, it was wrong—every last bit of it was wrong. She stood up and addressed the group. "I know we all have good reason to be upset by the way we're treated by most of the men here at Cornell. But inflicting such pain on someone who is innocent, who hasn't done anything to deserve it? That makes us no better than they are."

Maida directed her response to Jo. "No, you are absolutely wrong. We are fighting for a cause that is much bigger than we are. Sometimes, in war, innocent people have to pay a price. And this is war."

"Well, you can count me out," Josephine said. "I want no part of it."

Her nemesis smiled grimly. "I think you will, once I tell you a little something I've learned." With that she adjourned the meeting.

Jo waited, transfixed, while Maida chatted with a few others who wanted more details about the plan. What did Maida know that she wasn't telling everybody else?

"Let's take a walk," Maida said a few minutes later. When she slipped her arm through Josephine's as if they were bosom friends, Jo recoiled, but tamped down her revulsion. She had to know what Maida had up her sleeve.

It was late afternoon as they left their rooming house, heading down the main street of Ithaca. Maida wasted no time getting to her point.

"I did a bit of research into the Black Veil Society. Seems it's not so mysterious after all."

Cold seeped into Jo's bones. "What do you mean?"

"It turns out one of the little blackbirds chirped, you see. Bragged to a reporter they were the brainchild of a certain young woman with the initials 'J.D.' Apparently the founder of the group was off to college somewhere back east. Now who do you suppose that is?"

Josephine stared at her, not knowing precisely how to respond. Should she admit the truth or try to brave it out? She settled on the obvious question. "What do you want from me?"

"I want you to do something that you've done many times already. I want you to keep Edward Firestone occupied and away from Cascadilla Hall on the afternoon I tell you to. That's it."

"And if I don't?"

Maida shrugged. "Then a reporter for *The Philadelphia Inquirer* will receive a tip that will probably lead to a front-page story in which the Drummond name will figure prominently. I told you this was war, Jo. And sometimes, innocent people get caught up in it."

Josephine stopped and pulled her arm away. If she weren't so enraged, she might almost feel pity for the woman. "What happened to you, Maida, that twisted you up inside?"

She saw a flash of hurt cross Maida's countenance, but it was quickly banked. "Just do as you're instructed. That's all you need to know."

It was long after midnight when Jo, unable to sleep, tiptoed downstairs to Mrs. Wingate's kitchen. The landlady had banked the fire in the cast-iron stove, but Jo fed more coal to the box to build it up again. Light from a half-moon filtered through the window, casting the room in intimate shadow. She heated some milk, pulling up a chair as she waited, hoping a solution would flow into her along with the soothing liquid.

*So, this is what it feels like to be blackmailed.*

Outraged. Trapped. Powerless. Guilty.

She shuddered at the idea that she could have anything whatsoever in common with Roddy Merchant, but ironically, she did. Only *she* had created her own nightmare.

Come to think of it, no matter who caused it, how was her predicament any different in essence than her mother's, or Dinah's, or the girls of the demimonde? If she didn't play by someone else's rules, she and her family would suffer great humiliation. And even if she were willing to put her family through that, the reality was, it wouldn't make a difference. Whether she played along with Maida or not, Edward would no doubt still be caught in a compromising situation.

She could confess everything to him, of course. Warn him of what was going to happen. Expose the treachery of Maida's plan. But what would that accomplish? Every member of the Cornell Women's Club might be blamed, and the worst fears of all those editorial writers would be realized. It could cause such a ruckus that the university's board might determine that admitting women was a mistake.

There had to be another way. A way to stop the ugliness before it had a chance to fester and grow.

Josephine sipped, and thought, and eventually it came to her what she needed to do.

## CHAPTER TWENTY-ONE

It was the evening before the final exam in Eighteenth-Century English Literature, the night Maida had chosen to frame Stony Firestone. Josephine had already completed part one of her own plan, but the second half was far more difficult.

Edward had a standing poker game with several of his dorm mates, held sacrosanct even during finals week. But Maida had insisted that Josephine keep him away from the hall as long as possible so that the evidence could be planted. Then, at eight o'clock, Maida and a contingent of women would ask to speak to Edward "privately" about disturbing rumors concerning stolen exam questions. Jo had agreed to do her part only because it would enable her to do what she needed to do in order to make things right.

She had a bit of luck in that the evening was cool and warranted wearing the coat required for her plan. Unfortunately, that was the extent of her good fortune. After inviting Edward for a romantic walk along Fall

Creek ("You'll be back in plenty of time for your game"), she'd done everything she could to get him to kiss her. But he hadn't made a move and she was beginning to despair that they would ever get beyond just holding hands.

"Is there something wrong with me?" she finally asked, her voice tinged with exasperation. "Do you not find me pretty?"

Edward stopped, puzzled. "What? What are you talking about?"

"Well, you say you like me, but you never ... you know. I was just wondering if ... if there's something you don't like about me." She knew she was laying it on a bit thick, but for goodness sake! If she was going to put her own plan into action, she needed his cooperation.

Edward looked around and apparently feeling the coast was clear, gently tugged her behind a Norway maple. Taking her face in his hands, he looked into her eyes. "I think you're absolutely beautiful," he said, and kissed her full on the lips.

Josephine had never been kissed like that before. Ever. Her insides began spinning like a whirling dervish. When Edward raised his lips from hers, she said "Oh!" then reached up to pull him back to her. He smiled, inclined his head and kissed her again, more deeply than before, so that when he finally stopped, he was breathing as heavily as she.

"Take me to your room," she whispered.

He frowned. "What?"

"Let's go to your room. Now," she said. "Right now."

She reached up to kiss him again, but he took her arms down from around his neck.

"I'm not going to do that."

She almost moaned out loud, she was so frustrated. "Why not?"

"Because that's not who I am," he said. "That's not who you are. Believe me, it's not what you want."

She *hated* this. She had to get him to take her back to the hall so she could retrieve the exam. Even now it was probably being hidden in his room.

But Edward's words triggered something else in her. Something she'd never felt with him before, and it chilled her.

He was trying to control her. Attempting to tell her what to do and what not to do.

No. No, no, *no*. "How do you know what I want?" she spit out.

Edward stepped away, looking at her as if she'd peeled away a mask to reveal a gorgon underneath. He spoke carefully. "I'm not sure you know what happens between a man and a woman, but I can assure you, you do not want it to happen in hurried fashion in a room that someone else may walk into at any moment. When you and I come together, it will be under the right conditions. We will be married, and—"

She turned on him, her frustration spilling out in virulent words. "I am not some little doll you can pull out and play with only when you want to play. I do not always dance to your tune. Sometimes you must dance to mine."

"Well, not tonight," he said, straightening his coat. "I

don't know what's gotten into you, but I'm taking you home."

No, that was the last thing she needed him to do. "Oh no you're not. I am perfectly capable of getting home on my own—or do you think I'm too much of a simpleton to do even that?"

"Where is Josephine and what have you done with her?" he asked, only half in jest, it seemed.

"She is walking away from you," Jo retorted. "Go on to your precious card game, why don't you?"

"I think I will," he said gruffly and turned to walk back to the hall. Watching his determined stride, she fought the urge to run after him. Instead, after biding her time until he was out of sight, she also made her way back to the heart of the campus.

The poker game was always held in the downstairs parlor of Edward's dormitory; once he joined in, he would be easy to spot through the large picture window. She continued to wait, praying that he would not stop in his room beforehand. After a few moments her patience was rewarded. He sat down to play.

The sun had dipped below the hills by the time Jo worked her way to the back of Cascadilla Hall where, on one of their walks, Edward had pointed out his window; it looked like the third room from the rear stairwell, on the second floor.

She checked in both directions; seeing no one about, she lifted her skirts, hurried up the stairs, and let herself into the building. The second-floor hallway was deserted, but voices filtered up from the game below. She had to move quickly.

One, two, three. She turned the knob of the third room on the right. It wasn't locked. *Thank you, Lord.*

Once inside, she scanned the room to make sure she was in the right place. Both Edward and his roommate were surprisingly neat; both single beds were made up and the two small desks were also tidy. Jo looked around for anything that would identify the space as his, finally spying his dark gray woolen overcoat hanging on a hook behind the door. She also noticed a pair of eyeglasses on top of a thick book on one of the bedside tables. The novel was *Gulliver's Travels*, set in extra-large type.

*It must be here*, she thought, and rapidly ran her hands under the mattress, hoping to find the envelope containing the exam that Maida's love-struck friend had planted.

There was nothing. She went around to the other side and swiped her hands underneath but came up empty again. *Where was it?* Frantic now, she scanned the entire room until her eyes fell on a pillow that was slightly askew. She ran her hand underneath the pillowcase and there it was. Of course—Maida's friend thought he was delivering a love letter; Edward would have felt it when he laid his head down for the night.

She quickly stuffed the envelope into the inner pocket of her coat and turned to leave.

Except that she couldn't, because loud voices were coming down the hall. The game had apparently broken up early, perhaps so the students could actually study.

*This was not supposed to happen*, she thought, and did the only thing she could.

She lay down on Edward's bed and waited to be found.

---

Looking back, perhaps everything turned out the way it was meant to. Edward had no need to feign surprise because Josephine was the last person he expected to see in his room. That took the burden of guilt off him and set it squarely upon her shoulders. The news spread like wildfire across campus that Jo Drummond was a hussy and had violated university protocol in a most unseemly manner.

Her female colleagues, led by Maida, had been on their way to confront Edward about cheating, but when they heard what happened, they scuttled back to town, rather like rats leaving a sinking ship.

Retribution was unnervingly swift. Later that same evening, Josephine stood in front of Cornell's "morality" committee, comprised entirely of faculty members hastily summoned from their homes. Josephine almost laughed: the chairman of the committee was none other than Professor Rafferty, who had no doubt received quite a gift from Maida in exchange for a copy of his exam. They spent an hour listening to witnesses and conferring amongst themselves before calling her into the room.

"You know what you did is expressly against

Cornell University's rules and standards," the chairman said.

"Yes, sir."

"And you know that we cannot have women with dubious reputations and lacking such self-control corrupting our student body."

"I know that."

"Therefore, in the interest of this institution, as well as your own reputation, we respectfully ask that you withdraw from the university effective immediately. Your departure will be recorded as voluntary due to illness rather than as an expulsion. We will have your instructors base your final grades on the work you have thus far completed, so that the record will show you completed two full years before withdrawing. We will also instruct the student body how to characterize your removal, and anyone who labels it otherwise to those outside these walls will be sorely dealt with. Do you agree to these terms?"

Josephine couldn't help the tears that welled up, but she had nothing to complain about, really. It could have been much worse. "Yes, sir. I agree."

"Then goodbye, Ms. Drummond, and may you learn from the egregious mistake you made and never make it again."

Edward was waiting for Jo when she left the administration building. It was full-on dark. When the committee members wandered out a few minutes later, the chairman saw Edward walk up to her.

"I'm not sure being seen with Miss Drummond is a wise idea, Mr. Firestone."

"Sir, it is dark outside, as you can see. Unless you're willing to do so, I am going to walk Miss Drummond home."

The two men stared at each other briefly before the professor shrugged. "Do as you wish ... and by the way, you got a B on your exam."

"Thank you, sir."

Josephine said nothing, but simply headed back down the hill. At this time of year the well-worn path was covered in dirt, not snow, but it was still slippery. With so little light, she stumbled, but Edward's strong arm once again caught her and kept her steady. *The beginning and the end*, she thought.

The import of what she'd just done was slowly beginning to sink in. She had been kicked out of Cornell. She wouldn't graduate with the others in her class. She probably wouldn't graduate from anywhere. She had to return home. But home to what? A family that didn't want her, that's what.

She took in a shuddering breath and let it out.

"What happened back there?" She heard Edward's voice, but he was just a shadow.

"They asked me to withdraw from the university, which I agreed to do."

"I don't mean in front of the committee. I mean, back in my room."

She couldn't tell him. She knew Edward Firestone well enough to know he wouldn't just accept it and move on. He would try to fix it, and he would only make things worse for everyone involved. No one needed that kind of notoriety. This really was the least harmful outcome possible.

"It happened because I felt like it." She hoped she'd injected the right amount of insouciance into her response.

"But you were wearing your coat."

She shrugged. "I was cold; I was hoping you'd warm me up."

His eyes held hers, searching ... weighing. "I don't believe you."

"Believe what you will, then." She straightened her shoulders. "And count yourself lucky you found out about me now, before we took this any further."

They had reached the gate leading to Mrs. Wingate's boarding house. Edward put his hands on her shoulders. "What are you saying?"

She couldn't see his expression, but his tone told her he was in pain and didn't understand why. "Isn't it obvious?" She held out her hand, hoping he wouldn't feel it trembling. "I enjoyed knowing you, Stony. Good luck to you."

She turned to go in but remembered what the English professor had said. She had to know that, at least. "What did Professor Rafferty mean, you got a B? Don't you take the test tomorrow?"

"No, I always take my finals early. They don't want it bandied about that I get more time than anyone else, so I take a similar test before the rest of the class. Why?"

"Nothing. I just wondered, is all."

"Josephine—"

"Goodnight, Edward."

She closed the door and stood there, waiting for the anguish surging through her to subside. Several moments went by before she heard his footsteps recede.

## CHAPTER TWENTY-TWO

When she returned from campus, Josephine went directly to Mrs. Wainwright's kitchen to dispose of the exam questions she'd rescued from Edward's room. She tore the paper into pieces and fed them one by one into the firebox, watching the key to Maida's scheme flare up before crumbling away. She had to smile; all Maida's machinations had been for nothing.

The other item Jo had taken that day would not be destroyed; it was her insurance policy against any more repercussions. Once she was far away, she'd write Maida and let her know she could no longer carry out such a hateful plan without being exposed.

The hour was late and the house was quiet when she headed up to her room. A sign on her door read, "I'm sorry, but I will be staying down the hall until you move out." Penny Trumble, whom she'd considered a friend up to that point, was apparently worried that some of Jo's licentiousness would rub off on her. It hardly mattered now.

Her room looked as though it had been searched but hastily put back to rights. That, too, didn't matter. She pulled her bags out from underneath the bed and began to pack her things. There wasn't much besides her clothing, just a picture of her father, some letters from Bertie and Dinah, and a poster from Boathouse Row. She hadn't acquired much at Cornell; it would be as if she'd never attended.

At last the energy that had infused her during the night's escapade began to wane. She put her luggage on the floor and crawled into bed, still wearing her coat. It was the only thing keeping her warm, the only reminder that she was still alive.

---

"I don't care what they say, I'm going to miss you, young lady. You made the best biscuits I ever tasted."

Josephine smiled faintly as she finished the cup of tea that Mrs. Wingate had brewed. Jo had called for a buckboard to take her to the station where she hoped to catch a train to Athens, Pennsylvania. From there she wasn't sure which direction she'd travel.

*I'll miss this place,* she thought, looking around the kitchen. "I'll miss you, too, Mrs. Wingate."

"I sure do wish I could keep you on, but my agreement with the university don't allow me to rent to non-students. They're worried about morals, you know." As soon as she said it, Mrs. Wingate realized her mistake. "Oh. I didn't mean—"

Jo reached out to touch the poor landlady's hand. "It's all right, really."

The landlady bustled about the room, straightening what was already in perfect order. "Well, I'm sure I don't know what's gotten into them. I think it's disgraceful that none of your friends are here to see you off. Will you be heading home, then?—Oh, my land, I almost forgot!" She pulled an envelope out of her apron pocket. "This came for you yesterday afternoon, and I meant to give it to you when you got home, but then you didn't come, and—well, here you go."

Josephine opened the missive. It was a telegram and the message was stark:

> *Your Uncle Whitford has passed away.*
> *I need you. Please come home.*
> *Your loving mother*

"Yes, I will be going home," she said.

## CHAPTER TWENTY-THREE

It was a terribly selfish thought, she knew, but Josephine thought it anyway: Uncle Whitford could not have chosen a better time to keel over from a fatal attack of apoplexy. Like Auntie Pauline, he'd been less than mindful about what he ate, and his excesses had finally caught up with him. He left behind two very young sons and a pretty wife who was no more equipped to exist on her own than when her first husband had died. But it did give Josephine the perfect excuse for leaving Cornell.

Two weeks had passed since she'd returned home, and during that time she'd made the funeral arrangements, hosted the wake, and dealt with the family attorney, all while making sure her two half-brothers, aged two and six, were spared the worst moments of losing a father. It helped that they were so young, and that her uncle had not been an attentive parent. His pride in his offspring had focused more on who had borne his children than the children themselves. Still,

Jo knew from experience that at some point the boys would feel a great hole in their lives. When that time came, she hoped to help them come to terms with it.

She could relax in one regard, at least: Uncle Whitford had left his family in excellent financial health; there were no secret debts to deplete the family fortune and the investments he had made were sound. Still, Marrielle had no idea how to move forward as a widowed mother or woman of means. Her anxiety knew no bounds and was exacerbated by an inordinate amount of guilt. It didn't help that Uncle Whitford's physician had subtly blamed her for her amorous husband's demise.

"He told me that when a man experiences a surfeit of passion, often an apoplexy can result," she said when the tears slowed down. "I fear I may have caused his death without meaning to by indulging him too often."

"The doctor cannot know that for sure," Josephine told her, while mentally eviscerating the physician for his unhelpful remarks. "Uncle Whitford was quite overweight and they say that is a leading cause of this stroke business."

Despite Jo's counter-argument, Marrielle once more took to her bed, wanting only minimal food and her "special tea." That left her children relegated to the care of the nanny, a situation that led Carlton, the older boy, to regress in his toilet habits. Sally, who had worked for several years now as Marrielle's personal maid, shared her concerns and self-recriminations with Jo.

"Your mother has always been such a nervous type,

I thought the tea would help her relax. But I fear she relies on it too much," she said. "I'm so sorry."

"It's not your fault; you were only doing what she asked of you. How difficult would it be to wean her off it?"

Sally shook her head, letting out a whoosh of air. "The first few days would be close to hell, but it would be worth it, I think."

"Then let's do it."

The next week was indeed a horrendous one. Although they said nothing, Josephine and Sally purposefully gave Marrielle progressively weaker strains of the addictive tisane. She grew agitated and angry, and begged for more cups of the brew.

Josephine tried to ease her mother's discomfort as best she could. "You are simply going through the grieving process, Mother. You will feel better soon, I promise."

And in time Jo's mother did improve, to the point that she actually asked to see her little boys (who were really quite endearing) for more than ten minutes at a time. She started to care more about her appearance, and although she reverted to dressing in black, at least she got dressed in the first place. But her mother's dependence in other areas persisted, and Josephine, after much soul-searching, came to realize what must be done, for both her mother's sake and her own. She announced that she was moving away.

"What? You cannot leave me!" Marrielle wailed in a voice infused with panic. They were sitting in the front parlor where, had she been so inclined, her mother looked well enough to receive visitors.

"I can and I am," Josephine replied with conviction. "I've been invited to visit Dinah and her husband in St. Louis and then I ... I will let you know where I'm off to."

Her mother's face held an almost comical sense of horror. "But you'll be by yourself. What will you do?"

"I still have money left from Papa's legacy. And I will find work ... as a French teacher, perhaps. I will be fine. More importantly, *you* will be fine."

She took Marrielle's hands in her own. "Mother, you are a beautiful woman, and your entire adult life you have used that beauty to remain dependent, first with Papa, and then with Uncle Whitford. Maybe you thought it would be easier, but it wasn't right, because you brought me into this world and then you as good as let me go; you picked your protector over me."

Marrielle pulled her hands away and it was apparent from her scowl that she didn't like what she was hearing. That was too bad; it had to be said. Josephine felt a rush of love and pity toward the woman who had given her life. But she had to finish.

"I survived, but now you have two little boys who need you. They *need* you. They don't need to be shunted aside while you latch on to the next man who can manage your bills and keep you safe. You can keep yourself and your children safe. You don't need me, and you don't need a man. *You* can do that."

Josephine gazed at her mother until it seemed they turned a corner. Marrielle nodded slightly before taking Jo's hand and squeezing. "I ... I'm sorry. You always seemed like such an independent little girl. I envied that. I didn't realize ... are you sure you will be all right?"

"I'm sure," Jo said. She didn't feel sure, of course, but the alternative was to take back everything she'd just said and step reflexively into the role of temporary spouse. Until her mother found another man to take care of her, it would fall to Josephine to make the decisions, care for her siblings, run the household, and see to her mother's comfort. That could take months, or it could take years, and in the meantime, neither Josephine nor her mother would have grown one bit. No, that simply couldn't happen.

---

"You take care of her, but don't let her fall back into despair," Jo told Sally during their tear-filled farewell. She leaned forward. "And I'm so glad you have Adele." Adele, the young woman who took Sally's former post as upstairs maid, had turned out to be much more to Sally than just a fellow servant.

Sally smiled, wiping her eyes with the edge of her apron. "We'll work on getting your mum to be more independent," she promised. "You just be sure to take care of yourself."

"I'm good at that," Josephine said. "I've had a lot of practice."

Six weeks after being asked to leave Cornell, Josephine found herself at the tail end of a satisfactory visit with Dinah and Clarence Marshall in St. Louis. They lived in a small Victorian-style home in a new district on the south side of the city called Benton Park. The neighborhood was lovely, with tidy parks and tidier homes. Apparently, it was built over a series of caves that were the perfect temperature for storing beer, and the scent of hops was ever-present. "I'm going to have to learn how to drink lager from a stein," Dinah quipped. "This place is full of German brew masters."

Clarence had taken a job as the chief broker for one of the new cotton processing plants in town. Ostensibly Dinah's father hated to see his son-in-law leave the family textile business, but one evening, after two glasses of ratafia (which they had indulged in as teenagers), Dinah had confided to Jo that Clarence hadn't lived up to her father's expectations. "Clarence was all right in the beginning, but after we got married he seemed to become somewhat complacent. It was a good thing this job came along, otherwise Papa might have had to do something drastic, like letting him go."

Dinah had also confessed that her financial circumstances weren't that solid, but despite that, Jo could tell that Dinah was doing all right. It seemed her friend had been accurate in describing her marriage as "perhaps not a dream come true, but certainly no nightmare."

*Maybe that is all anyone can hope for*, Jo thought. At the very least it helped soothe the lingering guilt she'd felt for not being able to help Dinah years before. Dinah reinforced that relief by actually thanking her.

"I heard that Roddy never finished college anywhere," Dinah told her. "He married some rich girl, but she kicked him out for getting their scullery maid pregnant." She hugged Jo, her now somewhat larger figure engulfing Jo's tiny one. "I never did thank you for what you did for me."

Surprised, Jo leaned back to look at her. "I didn't want you to know."

"I know, but I found out just the same. And I thank you."

"I just wish I could have done more," Jo said, even as she thought *I wish I had done something different than destroy a man's future.*

---

"Are you sure you can't stay longer?" Dinah asked on the morning of Josephine's departure. "Clarence doesn't mind; I asked him."

"You are both very kind, but it's time for me to get out of your hair." Jo checked the clasp on her Gladstone bag. She had treated herself to new luggage before leaving Philadelphia, not knowing just how much travel she'd be undertaking. Only last night had she decided on her next destination, and that morning she'd sent Dinah's maid to the train station to purchase her ticket. It was a long way, but she was prepared to make the journey.

She straightened and checked her pendant watch. The cab driver would be there any moment to take *her* to the station, which was why she didn't hesitate to answer the front door when she heard the knock.

Standing in front of her was Edward Firestone.

---

"What are you doing here?" Josephine felt her world dip sharply, a barrel tumbling over the falls. She stepped back in shock, stumbling over her bag. As he'd done on previous occasions, Edward reached out and caught her.

"I've come to see you," he said.

"But ... but ... I've got a train to catch. I've—"

"I saw the cab driver pull up and I sent him away. I'll get you to the station. I promise."

Jo frowned. "You shouldn't have done that."

"I know. I'm sorry. I just had to talk to you."

Josephine glanced back at Dinah, who was avidly watching their interaction. Stepping onto the porch, she gently shut the door behind her. "How did you know I was here?"

"Your mother."

"My mother?"

"Yes. Mrs. Wingate told me your stepfather had died and that you'd returned home. My family was in town for my graduation and at first I thought that afterward I'd come to help you through your grief. Yet I wasn't sure how you'd receive me so I decided to wait until you got through all that. But then I couldn't stand it anymore and I came to see you, only for your mother

*Josephine's Daughter* | 239

to say you'd come here. You have some cute little brothers, by the way."

She had never heard Edward speak so fast and so long without stopping. "And my mother? How was she?"

He cocked his head, as if the answer weren't as simple as a "She's fine." "She was dressed in black, of course, and she seemed fragile, but she was perfectly cordial. She said that if I happened to catch up with you, that I was to tell you she's doing well. She seemed almost fierce about letting you know that."

Josephine nodded. That was good to know, at least. But Edward. He was *here*. "Why was it so important to talk to me?"

He gestured to the steps leading up to the porch. "Can we sit? I've been traipsing all over this neighborhood trying to find the Marshall residence."

They sat next to each other as they had so many times before, but the atmosphere between them was different, somehow. The connection was stronger than it had ever been, even when they'd had an unspoken understanding. Yet they were both feeling their way, as if they'd mixed together all the most delectable ingredients and were fearful, yet couldn't wait to take the first bite of the exciting new dish they'd made.

"You threw me for a loop back at school," he began. "I didn't understand any of it. I didn't know what you were doing."

"You weren't supposed to know."

He nodded. "I realize that now. The only reason you wanted to go to my room was to save my reputation.

Even when you were caught, I sensed there was something more to it. The next day Shorty Parnell came up to me and asked if I had gotten your love note. I didn't know what he was talking about. He said Maida had given it to him and told him to hide it under the mattress, but he thought I'd never find it, so he put it in the pillowcase instead. There was no note, because you had taken it. And it wasn't a love note, was it?"

She shook her head.

"Well, it unraveled fairly quickly. Shorty felt duped and confronted Maida, who denied everything, but then Penny Trumble—she was your roommate, wasn't she?—got upset and confessed what she knew. She said it all stemmed from a secret society—"

Josephine winced. Would she never live that down?

"—and all they wanted to do was get me to help them out." He looked at her with sadness. "All they had to do was ask."

"I should have told you," Josephine admitted. "I just thought I could make it all go away."

He took her hand. "Can we make a pact?"

"A pact?"

"Yes. From now on we talk it through. Whatever we're up against, we work it out together."

Josephine's heart began to hammer. She swallowed. "From now on?"

He didn't answer directly. Instead he asked, "Do you have a train ticket?"

She nodded.

"May I see it?"

Puzzled, she reached into her coat pocket, the same

pocket that held Janice Troutman's little red notebook, the book with all the details that she'd stolen for insurance. She handed the ticket to him.

"San Francisco, huh?"

"Yes. I hear a person can make their mark there."

"It's funny. I'm headed there, too. But first I'm going back to Arlington because I'm getting married."

*Can a person continue to live if their heart stops beating?*

Edward saw her shocked expression and grinned. "Let me rephrase that. I haven't asked her to marry me yet, because I would never presume she'd say yes. But I think she is the bravest, most clever, most beautiful woman in the world, and if she doesn't say yes, I honestly don't know what I'm going to do ... so, Josephine Rose Drummond, will you please marry me?"

*Yes, one can continue to live, if one doesn't burst from joy.*

She smiled. A test. "What if I had said I was going to Timbuktu?"

"Then I would have found the fastest way to Timbuktu. And if I can't make you a chef in the grandest hotel, then we'll find the next best thing to make you happy. Because I need to be where you are. It's as simple as that."

"Then I will give you a simple answer," she said, throwing her arms around him. "Yes."

# CHAPTER TWENTY-FOUR

### Katherine

### *1905*

"Scalpel... sponge ... retractor ... clamp ... scissors ... needle ... suture."

Kit stood at the front of the large classroom naming each instrument and item on the surgical tray. The space had been converted into a mock surgical theater, complete with a female mannequin who looked quite serene, given that she was partially covered on top of an operating table, her waxy breasts protruding unnaturally under the drape. Kit's fellow nursing students watched her recitation on a large mirror and stoically waited their turn on stage.

"*Wrong*, Miss Firestone." The instructor, Nurse Buxton, had been peering over Kit's shoulder. She seemed to find intense delight in saying those words. She was a densely compacted woman, an ex-Army nurse who, if the rules had allowed, would have no doubt commanded her current charges to stand at attention rather than sit. Behind her back, the students all called her "Sarge the Barge." Kit heard the woman had seen more than her share of war in the Philippines and only mustered out because of bad knees. She obviously missed her previous calling.

Buxton slapped her pointer against her long skirt as she paced in front of the students, finally extending the tip to a student in the second row. "Miss Winslow, what did she miss?"

"The clamp is actually a pair of blunt dissecting scissors and the scissors are straight Kocher forceps." Winnie sent Kit a rueful look.

"Precisely. Remember, ladies. You are assisting a surgeon who is quickly working his way deep into the bowels of your patient. He may be in the midst of saving a life. He doesn't have time for you to dilly-dally over which instrument is which. That's why it's critical for you to know the difference between similar instruments. You do not want to hand the surgeon a dissector when what he really needs is a hemostat." Nurse Buxton motioned for Kit to sit down and pointed to the third row. "Miss Mannon, will you please come up and identify the instruments on the table, which has been set up for a hernia repair. Perhaps you will do a better job of it."

Kit shot Roxie a warning glance as they passed. Roxie hadn't studied that much last night and their instructor seemed to be giving out extra rations of hell today.

*Josephine's Daughter* | 245

"Bowel reconstruction is a tough one," Ann Fineman whispered as Kit took her seat. "I hope I get a set-up for an 'ingrown toenail.'"

Kit snickered and smoothed her skirts, avoiding her chagrin at making a mistake by ruminating on her outfit. It seemed ridiculous that nurses' uniforms were so *white* —white shirtwaist, long white skirt, white apron, white cap, white on white on white, when any number of spills and leaks were so much a part of the average day. For heaven's sake, just a few drops of blood could ruin the whole look, not to mention require harsh bleach to remove if you didn't want it to leave a pale pink stain.

A year into her nursing program had taught Kit that handing a doctor the right instrument in the right order during surgery was only a small part of the equation. A nurse's job was to help her doctor and her patients in any way possible. If that meant sponge-washing a man's private parts, so be it. Taking a stool sample? Sometimes necessary. Lancing a pus-filled cyst? Easily done. Giving injections? Of course. She could—she would—do any of it. Gladly. And for one reason.

She was useful —at last.

---

Like most students, those in Kit's nursing program were eager for their formal schooling to be over. Yet in Kit's case, it wasn't to enjoy time off, but to finally put into practice what she'd learned. Despite the blunder she'd made in class, she was hoping to specialize in surgical assistance. Some of her fellow students were fearful of or even repelled by that aspect of nursing, but Kit found it fascinating. What could be more rewarding than opening a human body and repairing it from the inside out?

Over the next several weeks, she doubled her efforts to study every instrument and procedure until she was more than ready to put her knowledge to the test. Her opportunity to do so came sooner than she expected.

Kit and her colleagues were just sitting down to their twenty-minute dinner break one evening when Sarge Buxton walked briskly into the room, clipboard in hand. "I am looking for four volunteers to perform triage at St. Mary's, where we toured last week. Apparently, there was a gas explosion at an old apartment building on Rincon Hill. A large number of injuries, they tell me. They need our help."

Several hands went up, including Kit's. She was more than anxious to be *doing* rather than simply observing.

"All right, then. Mannon, Rogers, Firestone, Brown, be at the front of the school in five minutes, or we'll leave without you."

In the interest of saving time, the hospital had sent a car for the girls, who all piled into the back seat while Nurse Buxton rode in front. No one said much. Kit imagined an actress might feel the same kind of jitters on opening night. She mentally ran through the protocol they'd learned for situations with mass injuries and for the hundredth time, felt her pocket for her eyeglasses. She wanted to be fully prepared.

"You'll serve under my direction," Nurse Buxton commanded. "We must maintain order amidst what will surely be chaos."

They soon arrived at the hospital's Bryant Street entrance and were met by the administrator of St. Mary's, a man named Abner Huff. Huff was probably on the sunny side of forty, but too much weight and too little hair had aged him nearly a generation. He'd met all of the nursing students during the previous week's tour, and must have remembered Kit's surname, because he was particularly unctuous with her.

"Thank you, dear ladies, for coming," he said, peering at Kit and holding one of her hands in both of his. "Especially you, miss. We are honored." Kit glanced at Nurse Buxton and was met with a military-grade glower. "As you can see," Huff continued, "we have a lot to sort out."

He was right about that, at least. The foyer, which also served as a waiting room, was overflowing with wounded patients, along with relatives who must have heard about the accident and come down to check on their loved ones. The din of frenzied chatter was pierced by sharp cries and pitiful moans, and the scent of blood was everywhere. St. Mary's staff nurses scurried in all directions, a roomful of mice surprised by a blood-thirsty cat. Kit recognized a young female reporter from *The San Francisco Call* talking to victims and jotting down notes. The press certainly didn't waste time before zeroing in on bad news.

Sarge marched up to the nurse in charge, no doubt to discuss tactics now that reinforcements had arrived.

Kit's heart sped up a bit; anxiety mixed with anticipation and —dare she even think it?—a spark of joy. This was precisely where she wanted to be.

"Nate—is he all right?" A distraught, working-class woman, —a mother? A wife?—ran in, her apron soiled and her hair askew. She latched on to Kit, causing her to flinch. "He's just fifteen. He's—" She looked around the crowded, noise-filled room. "He's not here. He's not here!"

Before Kit could answer, one of the staff nurses hurried up to the woman, grasping her shoulder firmly. "Calm down, ma'am. Are you his mother? He's in surgery with Dr. Justice right now. Best place he could be. Don't you worry."

*As if*, Kit thought, before the name registered. *Justice*. Oh my God. Why was he here? Didn't he work at the Chinatown clinic? For months she'd felt uneasy about running into him. But it had never happened ... until now.

Before she could wrap her head around the possibility of facing the man, or worse yet, working with him, Nurse Buxton tapped her on the shoulder. She looked like she could chew nails and sounded as if she'd already ingested some. "Now is no time to be daydreaming, nurse. Are you willing to work here or not?"

"Yes ... yes I am." Kit resisted the urge to smooth her apron. She put on her spectacles. "Where do you need me?"

"I want you and Nurse Mannon to take that group of six patients sitting over there in the corner, interview them, find out where they hurt, patch them up, and send them on their way as soon as possible. They're low priority, but they must be dealt with." She handed Kit and Roxie three charts apiece. "Have at it, ladies."

Within twenty minutes, they had diagnosed and treated one sprained ankle, one large splinter, a deep scratch to the torso, a contusion of the hip, a possible concussion, and a case—in the absence of any other discernable symptoms—of "overwrought nerves." Not sure about the man with the concussion, they sent him to the part of the room where accident victims waited to see a doctor.

Kit was just finishing her notes when she looked up to see Dr. Justice walking quickly toward her. Heavens, not now! What should she say? She—wait, he wasn't walking specifically toward her. In fact, he didn't notice her at all. Instead he made a beeline for the head nurse. The woman pointed him in the direction of the emotional mother who had earlier accosted Kit.

"Mrs. Spellman," he said, extending his hand. "I'm Dr. Justice. We just finished a procedure on your son, Nate."

"Yes, yes, that's my baby," she said, her face ravaged by emotion. "How is he? Is he ... Is he?—"

"Your son's fine, ma'am. He's quite lucky. His shoulder was dislocated and his spleen ruptured in the explosion, but we were able to repair the damage." He gave the woman a big smile. "My guess is that boy of yours is a handful, so you'd better rest up because he's going to be right as rain in about a month or so."

The woman let out a wail of relief and wrapped her arms around the doctor, which was awkward because she was a short woman and Tom Justice was at least three inches over six feet. Still, he was a good sport about it and patted her gently on the back.

It was then that he noticed Kit. He frowned slightly, as if trying to place her, but a look of recognition soon passed over him. He pointed the boy's mother toward the head nurse and walked up to Kit. "It's the eyeglasses," he said, looking her over almost clinically. "I've never seen you in them." He cocked his head. "Or the uniform. But it suits you. Congratulations ... Nurse Firestone."

Kit was rendered momentarily mute. She found herself staring into those dark eyes of his and felt at once awkward and proud. She was a professional now, just like him. She *helped* people.

"I ... didn't know you worked here," she stammered, then mentally kicked herself for sounding so insipid. Why not graciously accept his praise and be done with it?

"I have attending privileges here and pull some—"

At that moment the doors of the hospital flew open and a group of Chinese high-binders poured in carrying a door upon which a man lay. A splint had been applied to his right leg, but it was still a mess, the broken femur sticking out from the skin at an odd angle. From across the room, the man looked to be delirious with pain.

"Where Dr. Tom?" one of the litter bearers ground out.

Abner Huff scurried up to the men. "Look here, you can't barge into a hospital like this! You need to stick to your part of town. You've got a clinic there."

One of the thugs, bigger than the rest, towered over Mr. Huff. "We have clinic, but no Dr. Tom. They say he working here. They say he the best body cutter."

Kit followed as Tom hurried over to the patient, pulling a pair of rubber gloves out of his lab coat and putting them on as he walked. He said something in Cantonese to the man who'd spoken.

The man answered in kind, then added, "Tang Lin say I speak English so barbarians understand. He say tell you he take walk and fall off roof."

Tang Lin? Kit moved closer. Yes, it was indeed the leader of the Hip Yee tong—the gang that had briefly kidnapped Kit's ward Mandy two years before. Yet he looked so different: haggard and vulnerable, no longer dangerous.

"A walk. Right." Tom Justice shook his head. He gestured to the splint and spoke again in the foreign tongue.

The man nodded. "Lee say fixing it too hard for him and you the only man for this job."

Tom probed the perimeter of the wound and Kit noticed that Tang Lin was in less pain that she'd first surmised. He was barely conscious, in fact.

"What's he taken for the pain?" Tom asked.

"A bowlful only. Just to get him here. It wear off soon."

"All right. He'll obviously need surgery to clean and set the leg—and that's if we can even save it."

"Well, you are not doing that here." Huff swept his arm across the room. "We have actual patients who need attention. We can't—"

Tom looked around the room as well. "We've already dealt with the worst of this group. I don't see anyone whose injuries are as severe as this man's." A surgical assistant had come out to the foyer to see what the ruckus was about. Tom got his attention. "John, set up OR Number Two for an orthopedic re-setting, would you?"

Abner Huff was furious. Apparently he didn't want to come across as nasty, however, so he lowered his voice and gritted out his words. "That Chinaman and his thugs do not belong here among decent people. I'm giving you ten minutes to lop that limb off and then they can carry him right back out."

Tom looked at Huff as if he'd grown two heads. His voice was low and hard. "Abner, it's hard enough for any of us to get through life with all limbs intact, so I'm going do all I can to save this man's leg. And that sure as hell is going to take me longer than ten fucking minutes." He turned to the men who'd brought Tang Lin in and spoke once more in their language. They followed his direction and moved toward the operating room.

His authority questioned, the administrator blocked their path. "Just a minute now—"

The reporter was headed their way; she obviously smelled a story. Without hesitation, Kit put her hand on the administrator's arm. "Mr. Huff, may I speak with you privately? I think there's something you should know."

Tom glanced at her, but she ignored both him and Nurse Buxton, who had walked over to observe the proceedings. She looked anything but happy; Lord knows she had warned Kit more than once not to use her notoriety to gain an advantage. In this case it just couldn't be helped.

Kit walked Mr. Huff down the hall to where they couldn't be overheard and explained that the injured man was a "secret Chinese official known to the upper echelons of the city government," warning that if word got out that St. Mary's had sent him away, those who walked the corridors of power would consider it a severe blot on the hospital's record. "So you see," she said, keeping her voice intimate and her hand on his arm, "the best idea would be for you to let Dr. Justice take the lead here and be responsible for whatever happens. I certainly wouldn't want you to have to take responsibility unnecessarily." She topped her little spiel off with a demure smile.

Abner Huff swallowed her lie whole, practically smacking his lips. "I see your point. Very well, then."

Kit watched as he strode back to the main foyer, where several of the gang leader's lackeys were now milling about as they awaited news from the OR. Judging by facial expressions and body language, the remaining patients were none too happy about it. Fortunately, thanks to the ruckus, anyone who didn't have to be in the hospital waiting area had left.

The OR assistant came out and asked Abner Huff to assign a surgical nurse. "The Chinaman says one only and no one else enters."

"I'll go," Kit said, and quickly headed down the hall before Nurse Buxton could stop her.

Tang Lin's largest enforcer stood guard by his door. Kit straightened her shoulders and sent the man a professional, "I know what I am doing" look. She paused, inhaled, and smoothed her skirt. If she was to learn, she should learn from the best, shouldn't she? And by all accounts, Tom Justice was the best.

If only she could excise the lump lodged in her throat.

---

The operating room was a small, pristine amphitheater whose viewing gallery was, for the moment at least, blessedly empty. If Dr. Justice was surprised to see her, he didn't show it. He was scrubbing his arms at the sink, so she began to scrub hers as well.

"Which would you prefer, to assist me or to administer the ether?" he asked.

Kit swallowed hard. "I ... I must admit, I've never done either in practice."

"John, if you'll do the honors with the happy gas, please?" Tom said, and John nodded, taking his place at Tang Lin's head. "The guard dog said the patient's had one bowl of opium, so I think we're all right to proceed, but monitor his vitals." While John placed the mask over Tang Lin's face, Tom put on a pair of surgical gloves, and handed another to Kit. He did the same with two surgical masks. Leaning toward her, he spoke so that only she could hear. "I'll just ask for the instrument and you hand it to me the way you were taught, all right? Don't worry if you aren't sure; I'll let you know which one I need."

He was being very considerate and by rights she should have been grateful. Instead, Kit felt like a leper at a lawn party. She longed to show him just how good she was—or would be as soon as she had some practice under her belt. She nodded stiffly.

Tom smiled as if he knew her secret. "We have no audience today, but for both of your edifications, I'll explain the procedure as we go along. How are we doing, John?"

"He's out, doc. Heartbeat steady."

"Good. Sponge, please?"

In a calm, sure voice, Tom Justice demonstrated what happens when a finely educated brain moves in tandem with a pair of highly trained, even gifted, hands. Kit watched, transfixed, as he carefully cleaned the wound and cut away the skin around the break. He examined the various parts of the leg impacted by the fracture. "The femoral artery is in good shape, but the *vastus lateralis* has been compromised and will have to be repaired. And we have a vertical break, which is trickier to screw in place, but we will do our best."

While he reconstructed the inside of Tang Lin's thigh, Tom spoke quietly to Kit, at one point asking what she'd told Abner Huff.

"I simply told him that Tang Lin was an important

person known to the upper reaches of government and that it would look bad if he were turned away."

Tom nodded at that characterization. "I suppose, in some sense, Tang Lin and the tongs are very influential in city politics, just not in the way you implied."

His acknowledgment that she lied rankled. "I also told him that it would be better for him if *you* took the responsibility for Tang Lin's survival rather than him. If something should go wrong, then it would be on your head and not his."

"Thank you for the vote of confidence." Tom's tone was just short of sarcastic.

Kit shrugged. She had always been practical, a believer in using whatever tactics worked to achieve her objective in a given situation. "He let you operate; that's the main thing."

"You're right. That is the main thing." Tom finished the internal repair, then asked Kit to grasp Tang Lin's injured leg and pull firmly when instructed to do so. The bone needed to be re-aligned. She wanted to gag, it looked so painful.

John winced. "I sure as hell wouldn't want to be awake for that."

"You and me both," Tom said. "Now, Nurse Firestone, I need you to maintain your grip while I insert the supporting screw into the medullary canal. And John, keep him completely under because the slightest movement will weaken the connection."

The next few minutes could have taken place in a carpenter's shop. Kit fancifully compared Tom to Geppetto, putting the finishing touches on his life-sized marionette. Imagine a human leg being put back together using a screw and screw-driver!

Tom must have read her thoughts. "The human body is amazing, but at its core, it is a machine. Much of surgery is simply tinkering with that machine to get it to work properly."

"Hey, you get tired of this, you can always work on cars." John capped his joke with a grin.

Tom chuckled. "I'll keep that in mind." He began to close the wound, which stretched for a good eight inches along Tang Lin's thigh.

Kit was dubious. "Will you have enough skin flap to cover it? It's awfully wide."

"It's borderline," Tom admitted. "I'm going to give it a go because it'll be difficult enough for him to keep the leg immobile without worrying about another wound from a skin graft. He may require some grafting down the road if it pulls too tight."

"What about his ability to walk?" she asked.

Tom looked down at his patient. "There'll be some impairment because of the muscle loss, but he'll have a hell of a better time hoofing it than if we had done what Mr. Huff suggested and just lopped it off."

"I'm sure Tang Lin will be very grateful ... not to mention generous. Who knows how this might help you."

Tom's face turned harsh, as if he'd just caught scent of an offensive odor. "Are you implying something here? Because I can assure you I would have done the same thing no matter who was lying on this table."

*What an odious thing to say. What was I thinking?!* Kit

felt her face turn red and was grateful for the mask. She glanced at John, who looked as though he'd rather be anywhere other than where he was. She turned back to Tom. "I ... I didn't mean to suggest—"

"Forget it." Tom was all business now; the warmth in his voice had disappeared. "In situations like this it doesn't matter who the parties are, does it? One does what one has to do."

He wasn't just talking about Tang Lin, she realized. Her old animus flared to life. "Sometimes there are other factors to consider."

"I think you're wrong," he said, and left it at that.

# CHAPTER TWENTY-FIVE

*1906*

She was always aware when he entered a room. Always. The fact had angered her at first, but after so much time, she was resigned to it.

Tom filled the arched entry of her parents' main salon dressed once again in his perfectly tailored tuxedo. He was accompanied this time by Donaldina Cameron from the Presbyterian Mission House. Miss Cameron, as usual, was garbed in a funereal shade of blue, the light of her beauty (which could have been considerable) hidden expertly beneath the bushel of her religious piety. Kit knew her well, and her presence on Tom's arm set off no internal alarms. She could be happy about that, at least. She fastened the armor of her indifference and glided over to greet them.

"I'm so glad you made it to our New Year's celebration," she said, extending her hands and directing her words to Miss Cameron.

"Oh, I wouldn't miss it—such a grand way to begin anew. I hope you don't mind that I dragged Dr. Justice along. I knew your parents wouldn't mind, and I actually consider it a good deed to tear him away from his clinic. I am all for hard work, but I swear, the man would toil twenty-four hours a day if he could." She smiled at her escort. "Besides, how often do we get to see such a gallant young man dressed so handsomely?"

Katherine made a show of regarding Tom from head to toe. "Actually, in my circles I have the privilege quite often, ma'am."

Tom said nothing, but his slow perusal, which echoed hers, had its desired effect. She felt her skin flush and tighten. She felt undressed.

"There you are, Donaldina. So glad you could ring in the new year with us." Kit's mother graciously intruded on the scene. "And Dr. Justice. How delightful that you could be here as well. What a magnificent escort you make."

"He's mine only for the evening," Donaldina said lightly. "I insisted he take a break from his important but all-consuming work."

"Indeed. Welcome, young man." Josephine's gaze briefly met Kit's while she pulled her arm through Donaldina's. "I'm sure Kit can entertain you for a bit while I take Donaldina to see one of her absolute favorite benefactors. You do ply the same trade, after all."

Donaldina's eyes lit up. "Your son has returned? My, that is wonderful news!"

The two women sailed off, leaving Kit and Tom in uncomfortable silence.

"Well, are you gasping for air?" Kit assumed a blasé demeanor as she looked about the crowded salon.

Tom sent her a puzzled look. "What do you mean? Why would I be?"

"You know. A fish out of water and all that." She glanced again at his clothing, not daring to linger as she had before. "At the rate you attend these types of soirees, your monkey suit should last you quite a few years." She took a sip from the champagne glass in her hand. It had gone flat.

Tom looked at her without responding for so long that she felt physically sick. What must he think of her? It was certainly no worse than she thought of herself. She didn't know why he brought out her inner witch.

Tom sent her the faintest of smiles. "How do you like working at St. Mary's?"

She was surprised at his question. "I ... I love it, if you must know. It is very satisfying work."

He nodded. "I could sense it in you from the beginning. The need to care for others. I have no doubt you do it very well."

"I ... well, thank you. If you don't mind my asking, why don't you work there anymore? No one on staff seems to know, and I worried that it ... that it might be on account of me."

He gazed around the room then, before sending her an amused look that said *You really do think you're the center of the universe, don't you?* "I had another altercation with Mr. Huff about the convalescence of your good friend Tang Lin, and we both agreed the hospital would run better if I weren't working there."

"Oh. I see. But you're mistaken. Tang Lin isn't exactly my friend."

"Ah, but he would like to be."

Kit sensed an edge to his words. "Oh, really? And I suppose you believe such a ... friendship ... is beyond the realm of possibility?"

"On the contrary." He paused, perusing her once more in a way that made her feel not violated, but as strange as it sounds, *admired*. "I think with you, anything is possible. And any man who could count you among his *friends*, would be fortunate indeed."

She wanted to slap him. She wanted to press her body against his. "Why do you always do that?" she asked.

"I don't know what you mean."

"You make me feel ... small."

Tom gazed at her for a moment, then leaned in and whispered, "Why haven't you forgiven me?"

"Because..." She could feel the intractable anger she'd harbored for so long wearily unsheathing its sword for yet another battle. "Because you had no right to keep me from my own flesh and blood when he needed me. No. Right."

Tom took a deep breath and looked around the room again, this time as if longing for someone to rescue him. When he turned back to Kit his eyes were apologetic yet resolute, like a government emissary who'd been given no room to negotiate. "You're no doubt right, but I would do it again in a heartbeat to keep you safe."

The words hung between them. The crux of the matter. A connection too strong to ignore but held in check by wills of equal strength. Nothing to be done.

Tom retreated first. "If you'll excuse me, I think I need a drink. Would you like another one?"

Kit shook her head and he nodded, understanding his cue to leave. "But may I just say," he added quietly, "that you look ... ravishing."

"So do you," nearly escaped her lips, but being Kit Firestone, she merely said, "Of course I do," and felt as though she'd been left alone in the wilderness, with only her sharpened tongue to keep her safe.

---

Kit had successfully avoided Josephine's well-intentioned but sticky maternal web for the past two years. While her older brother Will was off proving himself in the Far East, and her younger brother Jamie enjoyed the freedom of university life, Kit joined the ranks of working people—a feat almost unheard of amongst the women of her societal rank. Despite her mother's accusations to the contrary, Kit's only regret was giving up her role as Mandy's guardian. Luckily it had worked out perfectly for all concerned.

Mandy's letters to Kit revealed a girl who was delighted by the turn her life had taken. She loved Gus and Lia Wolff and was proud of her ability to assist the renowned painter in her endeavors. The Wolffs were building an artists' retreat up the coast, set in some redwoods overlooking the ocean; they called it "The Grove." Between Mandy's commitments at The Grove and Kit's nearly impossibly schedule, they rarely saw each other. Over time their relationship had evolved from guardian-ward to more like sisters, and that was fine with both of them. Mandy, she could tell, was growing into a fine, sensible young woman, and sometimes—secretly, selfishly—Kit took a little bit of credit for it.

Mandy's only flaw, in Kit's eyes, was her persistent wish to see Kit and Tom Justice get together. She couldn't seem to understand why Kit wouldn't give him the time of day. "He was only trying to protect you," she'd said when the issue of Will's brush with death came up.

If Mandy only knew how much the man remained part of Kit's inner life. She thought of him often, was eager to hear any news of him, second or even third-hand (although she never let on about it) and fantasized about him far more often than she knew was good for her. But she couldn't get past his self-righteousness regarding what was right and not right; she simply could not abide such moral rigidity. But 1906 was a new year, and she vowed it would be the year she'd purge Tom Justice from her system once and for all.

Which made it particularly frustrating when her mother, in mid-February, launched a two-front matchmaking offensive during a dinner party at the Firestone estate. She maneuvered Kit and Will into attending a Royal Chinese Theater performance in

Chinatown—with members of the opposite sex. Their dear mater had commandeered Will's choice by suggesting the outing in front of Beatrice Marshall, whom Will had squired off and on for years. As the daughter of one of Josephine's dearest friends, Beatrice and her patrician good looks constituted an ideal partner (in Josephine's mind, at least) for her son. Kit's mother then added insult to injury by asking Bea to set Kit up with a suitable escort. The person who came to Bea's mind was none other than Tom Justice, the man she'd "won" for an evening as a result of the hospital fundraiser.

Kit could have refused the invitation but felt a certain loyalty to her brother—he might need her help in fending off Bea. But Tom Justice? She was filled with anxiety just thinking about the upcoming event, even losing sleep over it, which further blackened her state of mind.

It was all for naught. Tom begged off, citing work as his excuse (the coward) and had sent a young intern named Anson Cotter in his place. Kit knew the young man from St. Mary's, and he was an able physician. He was also physically attractive, in the way young men with money were often as up-to-date on fashion and deportment as their female counterparts. Unfortunately, he also seemed to be aware of his attributes, which rendered him a cocky bore.

It wasn't the first time Kit or Will had attended the quirky spectacle in Chinatown. It so entertained the residents that they packed the massive theater for every show. Hundreds of men with long braids, each smoking like human stovepipes, filled wooden benches on the ground floor, while women were hidden away in their own galleries, and special guests, such as the Firestones, occupied a series of balcony boxes. Will and Kit offered the front-row seats to Anson and Bea, who had never seen Chinese theater before.

The performance took place on a stage that was nearly empty save for doors showing where an actor should enter or exit. Gongs, drums, pipes, and cymbals augmented the performance with harsh and discordant sounds. Kit watched as Anson leaned in close to Bea and said, "You call this music? I call it caterwauling." Bea giggled and tapped his arm impishly, while Kit felt embarrassed for her own similar thoughts.

The play, a morality tale like so many Chinese productions, was entertaining enough, but the real spectacle was watching Anson practice his just-shy-of-amorous moves on Bea, who lapped up his attention as though relieved that *someone* understood her true allure. Every so often Bea would catch Will's eye as if to say, *You see, other men desire me—why don't you?* Kit observed it all with amusement, but when she noted Will's pinched expression, it dawned on her that her brother might be falling for the ruse. That would never do.

Just as the play was ending, a fistfight broke out on stage between an actor and a spectator. Others joined in and it quickly escalated, spreading throughout the lower floor and threatening to rise up the stairs. Knives were pulled and cries of pain could be heard amidst the pandemonium of the shouting crowd. The head of

Chinatown's Six Companies even took the stage to try to calm the mob down, but he was nearly attacked as well, barely making it to safety.

Anson was the first to react. "Perhaps we should—"

"Yes," Kit said, standing up. "Let's go down and see if we can help."

The look on Anson's face told her that wasn't what he had in mind. She would have gone down on her own, but Will turned out to be just as stubborn. He took Kit by the arm.

"We are leaving now, dear sister, and letting the locals deal with this situation. They don't need you butting in."

Kit saw red. "You are not in charge," she growled at her brother.

But she was outvoted. "He's got a point. I think we might do more harm than good," Anson piped in, then helped Bea gather her shawl and reticule before heading for the exit. Kit could do nothing but bank her anger and follow.

On the other side of the door she was shocked to see Tang Lin, who immediately made eye contact with her.

"You are wise to leave. Come this way, please." He took her gently by the arm and led her and the others down a separate flight of stairs leading out the back of the building. She knew from his look that he remembered her and still found her attractive. Part of her responded to him at that level, as a female would to a male who sought to protect and claim her. Then she noticed the slight hitch in his gait as he negotiated each step, and a feeling swept through her that overwhelmed all others: admiration for what Tom Justice had done for this man when no one else was willing to help him, an act she knew had cost Tom his job.

Sirens could be heard in the distance. "This was not my doing," Tang Lin said. "We want to keep the peace, but sometimes the emotions of my countrymen become a bit … excessive." With a last look at Kit, the tong leader sent them on their way.

---

To get time off to attend the Chinese Opera matinee, Kit had traded shifts with a colleague; working a required number of hours each week was an aspect of her new life that her mother didn't quite understand or appreciate.

Thus, after dinner at the popular restaurant, Coppa's, Will dropped Kit off at her little house on Green Street before taking Bea and Anson Cotter home. She quickly changed into her uniform and hailed a cab to take her to St. Mary's Hospital for the overnight shift she had picked up.

Despite the inconvenience of disturbing her inner clock, Kit enjoyed the occasional nighttime schedule. (Neither she nor her colleagues ever referred to it as the "graveyard shift" because patients often succumbed in the middle of the night, and no one wanted to make light of that possibility.) She liked it because once the usual tasks were out of the way, such as prepping and distributing meds and updating charts, the ward was quiet and there was often time to visit with patients who couldn't fall asleep.

One such patient was Sean Daley, an Irish septuagenarian who had been diagnosed with inoperable lung cancer. He was entering the last stages of the disease and had been brought to the hospital by a neighbor to help manage both his breathing and his pain. A look at his chart told Kit that Mr. Daley was not long for this world.

"How are we doing tonight, Mr. Daley?" she asked as she prepared his tincture of laudanum. She gave the man her usual professionally bland smile, but the look on his face arrested her. His skin was beginning to take on the grayish look that the body exhibits as it loses oxygen and begins the process of shutting down. She took his hand. "Do you mind if I sit with you for a while?"

His eyes softened and he chuckled. "Now how could I pass up an invitation like that?"

She pulled up a chair and asked him gentle questions about his past and his family. He'd been married for thirty years, he said, but after his wife died, he couldn't see living with anybody else, so he'd stayed single for the past ten. He had a son, Paddy, who lived outside of Pittsburgh and worked the coal mines in a place called Uniontown. Paddy had a wife and five kids, with another on the way. "That's what happens when you can't afford the price of a nickelodeon," he joked.

"What brought you out west?" Kit asked.

"I followed the crowd to the Klondike in ninety-seven—thought I'd strike it rich and help my boy out. But the cold got to these old bones, so I headed back down to the states. Only made it as far as San Francisco. I guess there's no fool like an old fool."

Kit stroked his gnarled hand. The skin was nearly translucent; she could see every vein. "I'd say that was a very kind thing you tried to do for your son. When was the last time you saw him?"

"Oh, it's been three years, now. He can't afford to come out here that often and I can't afford to go there. I told him I'd let him know when to catch the next train."

Kit felt tears starting to form and discreetly tried to brush them away, but Mr. Daley was too observant.

"So, what about you?" he said by way of distraction. "You got a special fella?"

Kit thought of Tom but shook her head. "No, sir. I work a lot, and—"

He squeezed her hand with surprising strength. "Now you listen to me, young lady. I don't know much, but I do know that the most important thing you can do is find yourself a mate you can cleave to, like the Bible says. I sowed my share of wild oats when I was young, but I remembered what my pappy told me. 'Son,' he said, 'the minute you find a gal you like better than yourself, you grab on to her and don't let go. That's the kind of gal who's going to make you a happy man.' And dang if he wasn't right. My Elsie made me the happiest man—and a better man—right up until the day she died. After thirty years, I still liked her better than I do myself, and I feel the same today."

Kit didn't know how much longer she was going to be able to hold her emotions at bay, so she patted the old man's hand and stood up. "I have to get back to my duties, Mr. Daley, but I'll keep in mind what you said." She fluffed his pillow and tenderly stroked his stringy hair back from his forehead. He closed his eyes briefly and then pierced her with his gaze.

"I can't seem to get a straight answer from the docs around here," he said. "Can you tell me—is it time to get my boy out here?"

She looked at him directly, knowing he already knew the answer but wanted it confirmed. "Yes, it's time," she said.

Several hours later she checked on him again. The laudanum she'd given him had taken effect and he was sleeping, his breathing labored. He wore a frown, as if he'd incorporated his pain into a dream. It wouldn't be long before the death watch began in earnest. She checked his chart and wrote down his son's address. Whatever it took, she would have his son on the next train out of Uniontown.

## CHAPTER TWENTY-SIX

*A*n opportunity for Kit to see Mandy presented itself the following month. Her former ward was turning eighteen, and Gus and Lia had planned a surprise party for her at The Grove. Attending the event meant trading another shift or two, crossing the bay by ferry, catching a train, and traveling the rest of the way by wagon. She wasn't sure who else was going, but it was a good bet that Tom Justice would be there.

That, and only that, gave her pause.

In the way of most New Year's resolutions, her plan to excise the man from her thoughts had failed miserably. Lately, he'd even invaded her dreams. One night she was walking in a field of sunflowers and lilacs—two of her favorite blooms—and Tom was there with a sweet, sassy little girl riding on his shoulders, giggling and tugging on his hair. Kit lagged behind, big again with child. She swallowed the disappointment she felt upon waking up.

Mr. Daley had passed away, his son arriving a day

too late to say goodbye. But Paddy was overjoyed to find that his father had left him several hundred dollars over and above the cost of burial, all hidden in the room his father had rented in a Turk Street boarding house.

"I can't believe he saved enough to pay off our mortgage," Paddy said at the hospital after thanking Kit for taking care of his father. "I just wish he'd taken the money and come back to see us."

"I'm sure he wanted it all to go to you," she replied. "He mentioned your family many times, and you can rest assured he loved you very much."

Kit made a note to thank Will's major-domo, Fleming, for the successful visit he'd paid to Mr. Daley's lodgings just before Paddy's arrival. It was a small price to pay for the advice Mr. Daley had bestowed upon her.

She thought often about what he'd said. To love someone more than you love yourself— aside from loving your child that way, was it even possible? All her life she'd been self-reliant—perhaps too much so, judging by the way she'd unwittingly treated those for which she had little patience. She'd routinely dismissed her parents' advice because her mother had constantly picked on her ... or so it seemed. Thinking back, Kit realized that Josephine had rarely found fault with Kit's actions; their confrontations invariably stemmed from her mother forever telling Kit how to do something that Kit already knew how to do. Over time the challenge became figuring out how to do the opposite of what her mother expected while still doing what Kit knew was right. And the truth of it was, *Kit almost always knew what was right.*

Easton was a case in point. Kit had known enough to protect herself (thank God), and when the man failed to live up to her expectations, she had moved on. Her most vulnerable periods had come when she realized that she couldn't help Cecily with her affliction, and later, when she couldn't help Will fight his disease. Having someone like Tom Justice see her in such a state was humiliating, which was no doubt why she couldn't let go of her antipathy toward him.

But hadn't she bounced back? She'd become a nurse, and since then, her ego was reaffirmed and even augmented by the confidence that came from knowing she was indeed worth more than her beauty or her bank account. Loving yourself is healthy and good; Kit realized she'd been taught that from a young age, and if *she* ever had a child, she would teach that little boy or girl the same thing.

But, she was coming to understand, that wasn't the entire story. To live a full life, Mr. Daley believed, you had to find a mate to whom you could "cleave," someone you could put ahead of yourself. For Kit, that had to be someone extraordinary. Someone who'd give up a powerful career to help those whom most people hate.

Who'd take the time to save a man's leg, even if it cost him his job.

And who'd stop her from making a foolish mistake in a plague-ridden house, even if it drew her wrath.

Tom was that person. But was he the right person

for *her*? The idea that he might be filled her with something akin to panic. What would it feel like to care about someone else that much? She had an inkling of that kind of power during her tenure as Mandy's guardian. When her ward was kidnapped, Kit had felt a feral protectiveness, as if she would battle any predator to keep her cub safe. Kit could readily accept that kind of love.

But to say "I love you more than I love myself" to someone who might shred your emotions, or worse, ignore them? That was beyond terrifying.

She didn't know if Tom Justice was the one, and what's more, she didn't know if she had the courage to find out.

But given the way she felt about him, she might not have a choice.

And nothing was more petrifying than that.

---

"A toast to Miss Amanda Marie Culpepper, talented writer, reporter, model, artist's assistant, and all around charming young woman."

Gus Wolff lifted his glass of champagne and the rest of the two dozen or so guests followed suit, calling out "Here! Here!" and "To Mandy!" The guest of honor, who'd gone through so much heartache in her young life, had never looked happier. She seemed to be glowing.

Kit, on the other hand, was absorbing the reality of that tired but truthful cliché, "You reap what you sow."

Tom Justice had indeed shown up for the party, along with his colleague, Anson Cotter. And despite her initial resolve to try a different approach, Kit had lost her nerve and spent the bulk of the evening protecting herself by fawning over Cotter in full view of Tom and everybody else. She'd worn one of her most beautiful gowns and exuded such charm that even her mother would have been impressed.

And all the while Tom Justice, whom she knew desired her, had watched her. Quietly. Stoically. Even painfully. And she knew that because she felt the pain, too. And at last she gained enough courage to say *enough*.

Anson had soaked up her attention—and the Wolffs' finest scotch—all evening long, only excusing himself after dinner to "get some air." On his way out, he whispered something to Mandy and she accompanied him. After a few minutes, Will followed both of them. *Interesting.* She knew Will would protect Mandy, so that wasn't a worry. Still, the drunk doctor was becoming more than just a bore.

When Anson returned a short time later, he looked slightly disheveled and more than slightly angry. He tried to mask it by sloppily attempting to reclaim Kit's attention, but she was no longer vested in playing the game. Still, he persisted, and she was beginning to feel uncomfortable. Mandy, she noticed, had returned looking, well *animated*.

After opening presents, Gus approached Kit. "Your brother, for reasons known only to him, has left for Point Reyes Station. I know you were sharing his cottage with him. Will you be all right by yourself, or would you like us to switch things around a bit?"

What on earth? Will followed Mandy and Anson, Anson returned in an angry state, Mandy came back looking happy, and Will took off. Something was happening with those three, and after a few moments Kit deduced what it might be.

She smiled at Gus as she rose from the table. "No, I'll be fine, thank you. I think I'll turn in now, in fact; I have to work tomorrow evening and I'd best get my beauty sleep before heading back to the city. I think there's a noon train?"

"There is. Mrs. Coats will serve breakfast until ten or so, then we'll get you to the station in plenty of time."

Kit sought out Mandy to give her one last hug. "I do hope you like the dress I got you," she said. "It just had 'Mandy' written all over it."

Mandy laughed and hugged her back. "Can you imagine a dress like that? But I do love it. Thank you again ... for everything."

"Everything" meant a lot to both of them. Fate had brought them together, and Kit hoped they'd remain sisters in spirit for the rest of their lives. "You're welcome," she said. "Now I'm off to Brother Will's coop for the evening. He's apparently flown away, so I have the place to myself."

At the mention of Will's name, Mandy's countenance dimmed, but only briefly. "Do you know where it is?" she asked. "You follow the path to the right and keep going. His cottage is wonderful. It looks like a miniature version of the Great House, like Hansel and Gretel could live there. I can have someone—"

"No need. I'll show her." Anson Cotter came up and snaked his arm around Kit's waist, pulling her tightly to him.

Mandy frowned, slightly shaking her head. She looked at Kit. "Are you sure..."

*The time is now*, Kit thought. *Be brave*. "Actually, I've already asked Dr. Justice to walk with me," she announced. "We have business to discuss."

She removed Anson's arm and walked purposefully over to Tom, who had been conversing with Donaldina. Willing him to play along, she touched his arm and said, "I'm ready to go now, if you don't mind. You were going to walk me to my cottage, remember?"

The look of discreet confusion he gave her would have been comical if she'd been in a livelier mood. As it was, she could only raise her eyebrows. Tom looked over her shoulder and his expression cleared.

"Certainly," he said.

Anson had followed Kit and now staked his claim. "I'll walk her," he insisted, swaying a bit.

Kit turned around and pushed him gently away. "Thank you, Anson, but I'll take it from here. I think you need to go back to your room, drink a lot of water, and sleep it off. If that doesn't work, call a doctor." She smiled and turned back to Tom. "Shall we?"

Tom extended his arm and she took it. He leaned in to whisper. "I have no idea where we're going."

"Follow me," she said. She took one of the gas lanterns made available for night walks in The Grove and Tom trimmed the wick to stop the flickering. The light illuminated only a few feet of the path; everything else was lost in shadows, lending an intimacy to their walk.

Once they had moved beyond hearing range of the house guests, Kit turned to Tom. "I guess you'd like to know why I commandeered you."

"I assume you didn't want to be alone with Anson. He ... he fancies you."

Kit huffed. "No, he fancies himself. And I can handle him. No, I wanted to ... to talk with you about something that's been bothering me. It's about a certain man. You might even be acquainted with him."

"Really?"

"Yes, well, this man ... we met on a train a couple of years ago."

"Ah. Almost two and a half, actually."

"Almost two and a half years ago. And, well, we got off on the wrong foot—because of my sharp tongue, I'm afraid. And then we've had some ... disagreements. But still, I can't seem to get him out of my mind. I've tried ignoring him, being rude to him—"

"Torturing him?"

She smiled. "That, too. I'm especially good at that. But over the course of these two plus years, nothing has worked. So I realized I need to change tactics. I need to ..." She swallowed. It was harder to admit than she thought. "I need ... to forgive him."

They walked a bit farther, saying nothing. She didn't like being in the dark, especially outside. But she felt no fear.

"Do you think you can? Forgive him, that is?"

Could she? It was a question she had to know the answer to before they could move forward. "I'm not sure yet, but I thought a good first step would be to get to know him." She stopped and looked into Tom's eyes. "To get to know you. And maybe that would help."

They started walking again and Tom's voice took on a playful tone. "Well, let's see, you already know I'm a rube, a yokel from a farm in Nebraska who wouldn't know a tuxedo from a pair of overalls."

Kit could feel her face turning red; she hoped he couldn't see it in the dim light. "I ... I am sorry about that. You fluster me and I tend to use words as weapons."

"I've noticed you're talented in that regard. Well then, what else? You know I went to college, played football, and attended medical school."

How could she forget the way they'd heaped on the praise at the gala? "Yes, I'm sure you received quite a few tickets the night of the fundraiser."

"I did, no thanks to you. And I met one Beatrice Marshall, who let me take her out for coffee while she went on and on about her real swain, a certain Will Firestone."

"Oh, poor Bea," Kit murmured.

"Why do you say that?"

"Because despite our mother's best efforts, Will is never going to marry her. In fact, if my hunch is right, you already know the girl he's interested in."

"I do?"

"Yes. I'm pretty sure it's Mandy."

"Mandy? But she's too—"

"As of today, she's no longer a girl, and very much a woman whom I have a feeling loves my brother right back." She glanced at Tom. "So, what about you? Why aren't you with someone?"

"What makes you think I'm not?"

Kit stopped in her tracks. Was this all a terrible mistake? "Oh. Well. I stand corrected."

She started to remove her arm from his, but he stopped her. His hand was warm and firm. "No, you were right the first time. I have ... friends, but not that kind of relationship."

"Not ever?"

He hesitated. "In college. For three years, in fact. But I wasn't sure, and I was heading off to medical school. It didn't seem right at the time and, well, she married my cousin, actually. They have a young son and are expecting another child."

"Is she happy?"

Tom paused again. "I think so. I know *he* is. He always had a competitive streak, you see. What better contest to win?"

"Maybe you let him win."

Tom smiled at that.

"That amuses you?" she asked.

"No, you just reminded me of something my mother told me a long time ago. Maybe you're right." He waited a moment or two before adding, "So, what about you?"

They had rounded a corner and come upon the cottage. It matched Mandy's description perfectly: a

Hansel and Gretel version of the main house. Someone had lit the lamp that hung near the front door, a message of welcome. She wanted to invite Tom in but knew that would not be wise. Instead she smiled at him and staged a gentle retreat. "I think we've done enough soul-bearing for one night, don't you?" She started to open the door, but Tom put his hand on hers. She looked back at him, her pulse taking flight.

"Would you mind if I checked inside before you enter?" Tom asked. "We *are* in the woods, and that could mean big bad wolves, you know." He said it lightly, but she could tell he was serious. He was being gallant. Of course. She stepped to the side and waved him in.

While Tom checked the cottage, Kit looked into the void beyond the porch. Who knew what animals lurked out there? Deer, for certain, but what else? She wasn't used to such utter darkness; the wilderness was not her domain. She'd heard small sounds as they'd walked but felt safe with Tom. Now he was leaving, and it annoyed her that it made even the slightest difference.

"All clear," Tom said, coming back out.

"I would hope so," Kit said with a slight scoff.

Tom sent her a bemused look. "You don't like relying on anybody else, do you?"

She smoothed her skirt and balled her fists to make herself stop the nervous gesture. "I suppose not," she said, looking at him squarely. "I don't like feeling ... helpless. But I suppose you already knew that."

He leaned in and murmured, "It's nice to talk about

it, though. I guess I got you to do a little soul-bearing after all."

For a second time she felt flustered and wondered if it showed on her face. Oh, what was it about this man? She stepped back and extended her hand. "Thank you for walking me to my door, and for ... for letting me get to know you so that I can ... change my tactics."

Tom took her smaller hand in his large one and at once their eyes locked. The connection between them, as always, was undeniable. Frightening in its intensity. No one else had formed such a visceral link with her, not even Easton Challis. She made to pull her hand away, but Tom held her, indeed pulled her closer. She felt his body down the length of hers.

"I have a new tactic too," he whispered, lifting her chin and kissing her lightly on the lips. Without volition her eyes closed. She wanted this. Wanted him. His lips left hers then descended again more forcefully. He wanted her, too.

She was on the verge of lifting her arms to embrace him when he stepped back, as if he knew he'd overstepped his bounds.

He ran his tongue along his lip, a last taste. "You must lock your door when I leave," he ordered.

She tried to recover her own equilibrium with humor. "Why—are you afraid those big bad wolves might get me?"

"Yes," he said without a smile. "Especially the ones with two legs. The ones who want to devour you in every possible way. Good-night."

Kit closed the door, and only when she slid the bolt in place did she hear Tom head back down the steps.

She stood on the other side for several moments, talking herself down from the emotional precipice she'd nearly fallen over. She shouldn't be surprised to find herself here. Ever since that first encounter on the train so long ago, she'd known this man was different. And she had done all she could to keep herself from doing precisely what she'd done tonight.

But fighting it had gotten her nowhere, because at some level Tom Justice called to her, and she felt compelled to answer.

She didn't know where and she didn't know when. But it would happen. Of that she was certain.

Was it right or wrong? Was he a man she could love beyond all others ... even beyond herself?

She was afraid of the answer. But she couldn't turn back now.

## CHAPTER TWENTY-SEVEN

Like water rushing over jagged rock, time has a way of smoothing the roughest of edges. Before entering nursing school, Kit had tried her best to patch up the rift with her parents by accompanying her mother to a showing by William Keith, an artist they both adored. Kit had expressed an interest in one of his more dramatic depictions of the Northern California coast and Josephine impulsively purchased it for her.

"It's not necessary, Mother, really," Kit had protested.

"Just let me do this one little thing," Josephine said, and Kit realized her mother was trying to atone for her past misbehavior as well.

It took some time for her parents to get used to the idea, but now that Kit was a working professional, they were fully supportive of her new lifestyle—except, of course, that Josephine worried about her daughter working too hard.

"When will you ever meet someone worthy of you?" she fretted.

"I will get around to it eventually," Kit assured her, not daring to mention that she may have already done so, and that Josephine even knew him. It was much too soon for sharing something so personal.

Josephine and Edward had also come to terms with the fact that Mandy, now grown up, had guilelessly stolen their eldest son's heart. Although wary of Mandy at first, it seemed Josephine had learned enough about Kit's former ward over the past few weeks to change her mind dramatically about the girl.

And so, although her schedule was tight, Kit agreed to spend the night of April seventeenth at her parents' mansion in Pacific Heights to help plan Will's engagement party.

"I'm thrilled you're staying over, Kit, darling. We can get a head start on creating a theme. 'A Cinderella Story,' perhaps? I'm sure we can find a way to have Mandy arrive at the party in a pumpkin-like carriage. It would be such fun!"

Imagining the horror on Will's face at the notion, Kit held onto her smile. Their mother was unique—and certainly indulged by their father—but with good reason. No one could pull off a social event quite like Josephine Firestone.

But trying to push back against such a force of nature was something else entirely. If Will wanted any say whatsoever in planning his engagement party, he had better stay on his toes.

Although she'd agreed to spend the night, Kit balked at the idea of attending the opera with her parents, despite the fact that Enrico Caruso was performing the role of Don Jose in *Carmen*.

"It's the performance of the season," Josephine had gushed to her daughter. "He's come clear across the country, and simply *everyone* is going to be there. I understand Bessie Kohl's going to be sporting black lace and a two-inch-wide dog collar of diamonds and pearls. And sweet little Mary Flood's going to be simply *smothered* in jewels. How can you pass up such a spectacle?"

Kit yawned as she dropped her overnight bag in the hallway. "Because I just got off work and I'd like to relax, Mother. I'm sure you'll give me a full report tomorrow morning."

Josephine sent her the smile that had apparently captivated Kit's father so many years before. "All right, but you can be sure I'll take notes so as not to forget a thing."

"I'd expect nothing less."

Kit and her parents shared an early four-course dinner, prepared as always by Chef Bertrand, who was still in his Italian phase. It crossed Kit's mind that if she had continued to live at home instead of renting her own cottage on Green Street, her corsets would be screaming in agony. But oh, that chef could cook!

Halfway through the tiramisu, Kit was called back by St. Mary's to assist in an emergency appendectomy. In the six months she'd worked there full-time, she'd earned a reputation as an efficient operating room nurse—often requested by staff surgeons. She assured her mother she'd come back so that in the morning, when Will arrived, they could all have a lovely breakfast together "like the old days."

Kit didn't finish until after midnight and took a hansom cab back from the hospital. Her parents had already retired for the night, but a note left by her mother said that she had "oodles of gossip to share." Kit grinned at that. When her mother wasn't matchmaking or mother-henning, she was quite an entertaining storyteller. Kit realized she was looking forward to the following day. No doubt Tom Justice would be invited to the engagement party, and she found she was very much looking forward to that, too.

By rights she should have been exhausted. But operations always energized her, and she stopped by her parents' library to read for a while. It was quiet, save for the faint whinnying of horses in the stable across from the garden. She'd noticed the cab's horse was skittish, too. Could be a shift in the weather; it intrigued her that animals could sense such subtle changes.

She sat in her father's favorite leather wingback chair and picked up her copy of *Yolanda the Black Corsair's Daughter*. Just as Henry Morgan was about to rescue the pirate king's beautiful offspring, Kit finally succumbed to sleep.

It was a good thing she did.

At 5:12 in the morning, had Kit been lying in her

usual bed upstairs, a large mahogany wardrobe, carved in the Italianate style and filled with several years' worth of ball gowns, would have crashed on top of her, most likely crushing her skull.

The earth was shaking in its boots.

# CHAPTER TWENTY-EIGHT

*A* thunderous crash from upstairs jolted Kit awake. Looking up, she could see the library's glass and bronze chandelier swinging crazily, as if an altar server with a thurible had gone berserk. The lamp gathered such momentum that it finally smashed into the ceiling and shattered, its Tiffany glass showering down on Kit.

All at once, the ground began to roll, causing the mansion to groan. Everything in the room that could possibly move took flight, shifting and sliding, careening back and forth—as if an invisible bull had thundered into a china shop. Too shocked to even scream, Kit held on as her wingback chair skidded halfway across the room and abruptly stopped, nearly throwing her out of it. Books, vases, pictures—innocent objects turned into potentially deadly missiles. Plaster began to fall in chunks from above.

Kit heard a scream from upstairs and her mother's voice. "Kit! Kit! My God, where are you?!"

Kit ran into the hallway. "I'm down here, Mother! I'm all right!"

It seemed like an eternity for the shaking to stop enough that Kit could make her way to the large staircase at the end of the entry hall. She saw her mother slowly walking down the stairs, her arm around Kit's father, who seemed to be in pain. A second tremor hit, causing her parents to stumble and slide three or four steps before grabbing hold of the bannister and regaining their balance.

Kit ran up to meet them and help her father the rest of the way down. "Where are you hurt?" she asked.

"It's nothing," her father said in his typically stoic manner. "Just caught my shoulder."

"Our bed slammed into the wall," Josephine said. "I think he sprained it."

"Let me take a look," Kit said. Moments later she had fashioned a sling out of one of her mother's shawls to support the shoulder, which was in fact dislocated. "You're going to have to get that straightened out," she said.

Unlike most wealthy employers in San Francisco, Kit's mother did not like having her staff live in the main house. "They deserve their privacy and so do we," she'd once explained to Kit. Instead she offered cottages for her chef, housekeeping staff, and other servants. One by one her employees made their way to the front door "to see if the missus and the mister were all right." Josephine greeted each of them matter-of-factly and issued rapid-fire instructions, reassuring them that as the lady of the house, she was all right and in control. Yet beneath the veneer, Kit could see signs of vulnerability. Her mother's skin was very pale, and she appeared a bit unsteady on her feet. She wiped her brow several times and asked for water, no doubt to calm her nerves. At one point Kit suggested she sit down for a bit, but Josephine would have none of it.

"My lord, there's too much to do to even think of such a thing," she said, and bustled off to supervise the preparation of food for family and staff.

Will showed up at seven a.m., thankfully uninjured himself. He was clearly agitated, however; he wanted more than anything to get back to The Grove where Mandy waited.

"We saw Gus Wolff at the opera last night, but no Lia," Edward said. "Have you heard from him this morning?"

"Yes. Lia's back at The Grove, but Gus knows Caruso, so he stayed at the Palace after watching the performance. The hotel didn't suffer too badly, thank goodness. He checked out this morning and we're trying to tie up loose ends here before heading across the bay. I just wanted to make sure you were all safe before I left."

"We're doing just fine," their father said.

"I can see that," Will deadpanned then turned to Kit. "Is he all right?"

"Dislocated his shoulder. He'll be fine. You and Gus take care. Give my love to Lia and Mandy."

At that moment another aftershock struck and everyone froze, waiting to see if something structural was going to fail. "Maybe you'd better camp outside until this all settles down," Will suggested.

Josephine snorted. "I hardly think so, dear boy. This house will withstand a few rattles, don't you worry."

Will sent Kit a look that said: *I know they're a handful, especially Mother, but I need to go.*

"Go," Kit said.

An hour later she had braved the upstairs, gotten dressed, and assured herself that her parents would survive without her. She really had to get to St. Mary's; no telling what their staffing levels were like.

Her mother didn't approve. "You mustn't go," she insisted. "We need you here."

Part of Kit longed to stay; even though her mother would never admit it, she really did look shaken. But duty called. "Others need me more, Mother. Bertrand and the rest of the staff are here to help. You and Father just stay put and you'll be fine."

Josephine began to argue, but Kit's father put his good hand on his wife's arm to silence her. "Let her go," he said. "She has the skill to help many people; they need her."

Kit teared up as she hugged her parents goodbye. "I will send word when I arrive," she promised. "Watch for aftershocks."

Kit figured it would take an hour or more to walk to Rincon Hill. The morning was warm but hazy, with a strange smell in the air, as if something other than wood were burning. She gave thanks for the ugly but sensible shoes that were part of her work attire. At least her feet would survive the trek.

She hadn't traveled far on Pacific Avenue when a soldier on horseback stopped her. He dismounted, took off his riding gloves, and politely touched his cap. "Ma'am. Lieutenant George Gibbons, Troop K of the Fourteenth Cavalry. I noticed you're wearing a nursing uniform. We have orders to send medical personnel west instead of east. May I ask where you were headed?"

"St. Mary's Hospital. I work there."

"Not for long, ma'am. Sad to say there's fires in that part of town and they're shippin' patients to the East Bay before the place burns down."

What? That couldn't be right. Kit looked around at the devastation. *The damage has already been done, hasn't it? Aren't we simply picking up from here?* A coil of insecurity began to unfurl inside her. She was used to being, if not in control, at least fully informed about a given situation. But the scope of this was beyond anything she could imagine. "I ... I've seen a few small fires, but nothing ... I didn't realize it was that bad."

"Yes, ma'am. It's that bad. The Mechanics Pavilion is where you want to be. They're sending all the wounded there 'cause it's the only place big enough to hold everybody ... hundreds of them. They could use your help there for sure. You know where that is, ma'am?"

"Yes. I've gone to charity events there. It's a big barn of a place."

The soldier grinned. "That would be it. Just the other night I was off duty and saw Philadelphia Jack O'Brien knock out Bob Fitzsimmons. Took him 'til the thirteenth round. What a fight! The place was packed."

He paused, his light-hearted expression fading. "Seems so long ago, if you know what I mean."

Kit nodded. Lieutenant Gibbons was right. It seemed like an eternity.

He put his gloves back on. "If you don't mind riding, I can take you—to the Pavilion."

Kit recovered enough of her sensibilities to accept the soldier's offer. He helped her onto his horse and then re-mounted in front of her.

"We'll cut straight down Van Ness. Shouldn't take too long," he said over his shoulder.

Kit said nothing. Numbness had overtaken her. She couldn't fathom what was going on all around her—the city was literally torn to shreds. People were everywhere, many of them still dressed in their nightclothes. Some seemed to have a sense of purpose, bustling about and stacking belongings in the yards of their houses and shops. Others appeared bewildered, stopping to stare at Kit and her escort as they rode by.

One man wearing a blue dressing gown, brown socks and old-fashioned, high-buttoned shoes, called out to them. "How's it looking out there?"

"Not good," Lieutenant Gibbons called back. "Keep heading west; it's your safest bet."

As they passed California Street, Kit could hear explosions coming from the direction of Chinatown. "What's that?" she asked. "Is Chinatown all right?"

"Doubtful. They lost a lot of buildings in the quake. I think they're gonna try to build a fire-break there. They'll be damn—excuse me, ma'am—darn lucky if they can keep it under control."

*I think luck has deserted this city. Has it deserted Tom?* He lived and worked in Chinatown, and Kit left the door to her heart open just wide enough to let fear for him slide through. She wallowed in silent anxiety for a few moments before mentally chastising herself. Tom Justice was strong and resourceful. He'd probably gotten out just fine. He was no doubt operating on some of the quake victims right this very minute.

He had to be.

And she had to start being useful or she would go mad.

"How much longer until we're there?" she asked.

# CHAPTER TWENTY-NINE

Lieutenant Gibbons dropped Kit off in front of the Mechanics Pavilion and she had to muscle her way through the scores of individuals waiting to enter. Cries of "Please, nurse, can you take a look at my leg?" and "We need a doctor —tell them we need a doctor right now!" followed her.

Instinctively she tried to calm their fears with "It won't be long now, I promise" and "Just a few more minutes."

Once inside, Kit was stopped cold by the chaos. A small part of her brain recoiled at the sight of so much misery. *No one in nursing school ever said you would have to handle something like* this. For a moment she felt lightheaded, as if she might actually pass out, and she leaned against a supporting pillar near the entrance, just in case. No, she would not faint—that would be totally unacceptable. *Breathe in through the nose. Out through the mouth. In. Out.* She was a professional, damn it!

Just as she was getting her equilibrium back, a doctor hurried up.

"You're in uniform, miss; are you a nurse?"

"Yes. I work at St. Mary's."

"Good. Have you assisted in surgery before?"

At last. Something solid to hold on to. "Yes. Many times."

"Excellent. Follow me, please."

As they walked the length of the building, the man, whose name was Dr. Tillman, massaged his right hand with his left and flexed his fingers.

"How long have you been at it?" she asked.

"It's only been a few hours, but the pace is so ... well, you'll see. You'll rotate in and out, like the surgeons. We have six docs currently working hour shifts and in between they break for fifteen minutes to spell the internists and get rid of their hand cramps." He looked down at his hands and smiled gamely. "As you can see." He pointed as he spoke. "Over there is Orthopedics. Over there, Internal Injuries. In the back, Critical Care, and there..." he paused. "A makeshift morgue. It's growing, I'm afraid."

Kit began to see a kind of structure to the place. Mattresses and cots were lined up against the wall, and there were ad hoc supply stations—desks and tables—piled high with bandages, splints, and the like. It soothed her. Once she understood how a system worked, she could function in it. But she was curious. "Where did all the furnishings come from so quickly? And the supplies?"

"Department stores. Hotels. Drug-stores. You name

it. We have a lot of, shall we say, 'resourceful' volunteers."

They had made their way to the area where a handwritten sign taped to a post read "General Surgery." "You'll see a little bit of everything here," Dr. Tillman said. "You can take over for Nurse Madsen. Your name?"

"Katherine Firestone."

Dr. Tillman raised his eyebrows. Apparently he recognized her pedigree. "All right. Nurse Firestone, meet Dr. Sorenson."

The surgeon nodded to her. He had lively eyes, but she couldn't tell his true reaction because both he and the nurse she was replacing were wearing surgical masks.

Nurse Madsen spoke up, her voice slightly muffled. "I don't need a break, doctor. I—"

"Take a break, nurse. That's an order." Dr. Tillman took a mask from a nearby box and handed it to Kit. "Don't know if you've used these, but everybody will be wearing them one of these days." He rummaged around in the same box but came up empty. "Nurse Madsen, your gloves, please?"

The nurse rolled her eyes but peeled off the gloves and handed them to Kit. "I'll want them back when I return," she said.

"No time for that territorial folderol, nurse. Spend your break hunting up more gloves."

Kit donned the gloves and was surprised when Dr. Tillman poured alcohol on her covered hands. "Best we can do under the circumstances."

In short order she was assisting Dr. Sorenson in a spleen removal, followed by a bowel reattachment, a skull laceration, and a nearly severed thigh. The pace at which they worked was so rapid, she had no time to do anything but concentrate on the next patient, brought in on the heels of the last. Only once was there enough of a break to wipe her forehead with her sleeve. As she did so, she heard a familiar unmuffled voice. Her eyes welled up as she looked quickly in the direction of the sound.

And nearly crumpled with the relief of knowing Tom Justice was alive and well.

## CHAPTER THIRTY

Buoyed by the knowledge that Tom was safe, Kit was able to concentrate on assisting the doctors who rotated in and out of her area. She had never worked so fast or so hard, yet never had she felt so strong or capable. Time ceased to exist—only the next patient, instrument, and procedure mattered, handled in a rhythm born of skill and necessity.

Thus she was caught off guard when Dr. Milbank, the chief surgeon in charge of the Pavilion medical team, climbed on top of a table and shouted through a megaphone: "Attention. Attention all medical staff and patients. The Pavilion must begin evacuation procedures immediately. Doctors, please stabilize all patients, attach their records, and prepare them for transport via the Polk Street exit, following the direction of Army personnel. Conveyances will be waiting. Repeat: stabilize and prepare all patients for transport without delay."

*What?!* Hadn't they all come to the Pavilion to

escape the fire? She immediately sought out Tom and their eyes met. *Don't lose sight of me,* hers said.

*I won't.*

Word spread quickly throughout the arena and both the noise and panic levels rose. Dozens of ambulatory patients surged toward the wrong exit, and one man practically trampled an old woman in his push to get ahead of her. He was held back by an Army sergeant who pulled a gun and barked, "You get in line and stay in line, or I'm tying you to that post and you'll be the last one out of here. The same goes for anybody else who thinks they're better than the person next to them."

The chaos was increasing. Tom came over and murmured, "Stay close."

Now a team, they were quickly assigned a row of beds and told to make sure each patient was ready to be carried out with an updated chart. Tom had been given a supply of morphine to administer and Kit's only complaint was that he used it too sparingly. *Men,* she thought with irritation. *They always think they can handle pain better than anybody.* Kit had never given birth, but to hear her mother and other women tell it, *that* was no walk in the park.

Methodically they stabilized each victim and called for litter bearers to take the patient away. Eventually the Pavilion began to empty out, but just as Kit was beginning to feel a sense relief, a nurse rushed up to Tom. She looked terrified.

Kit couldn't hear the words the nurse whispered,

but she definitely registered Tom's reaction to them, one of both shock and disbelief. "Impossible," he said.

Kit touched his arm. "What is it? What's wrong?"

Before he could answer, the nurse whispered in his ear again. He frowned, looked at Kit, and put his hand over hers. "Stay here. Please. I'll be right back."

Her grip tightened; she could feel how tense his muscles were. "Whatever it is, I can help." She was trained. This time, she really *could* help.

"No," he said more firmly, a touch of desperation in his tone. "You can't help with this. I need you to stay here."

*You can't help.* It was just like before. He still considered her useless. A sharp stab of disappointment gave way to the familiar thrum of anger and she stepped back.

She watched him walk swiftly toward the far end of the hall and waited a moment before following him. *I am not going to be shut out again.*

The "critical care" section Dr. Tillman had pointed out on Kit's arrival was blocked off with blankets and sheets draped over a rope that had been strung across the room. As Tom and the nurse disappeared behind the makeshift curtain, Kit moved closer until a soldier stopped her.

"Sorry, nurse. There's a ... slight problem, and no medical personnel are allowed in at the moment."

"But I just saw a doctor and nurse enter," she protested.

"Yes. Um, we're hoping that particular doc can diffuse the situation."

"But—"

"I'm sorry, miss. Those are my orders."

Kit checked her pendant watch. Twelve forty. She looked around the vast hall; the pace of the evacuation seemed to be ramping up as soldiers, some of them nearly running, carried the last of the patients out the door. A commanding voice exhorted the soldiers to get a move on.

A few patients were also being carried out of the critical care section, but they weren't headed in the same direction. Instead, the young soldiers—some, she could see, with tears in their eyes—carried their burdens to the nearby "morgue" that Dr. Tilman had referenced. It too was shielded with a curtain.

Kit followed the litter bearers but stopped half way to turn and watch the stream of individuals still heading toward the exit. At that moment it dawned on her what was going on. What the young soldiers heading to the morgue knew. What these poor victims would never know. The magnitude of the tragedy threatened to do her in, yet the sight mesmerized her. How could such an unspeakable atrocity happen?

Caught up in the grim reality of what she saw, she barely felt the tug on her arm.

"It's time to go, nurse," Dr. Milbank said. "You don't need to see any more."

She scowled at him, hardening herself to the haunted look on his face. "Why? So I won't know what's really going on?"

He took his hand away. "What do you think is going on?"

She pointed back toward the morgue. "They aren't going to take those poor people out of here, are they?"

Dr. Milbank stared at her. "Those poor people are dead," he said quietly.

She could feel her eyes filling. "Yes, but the people who loved them aren't dead. They'd want to say goodbye, wouldn't they? Give them a proper burial? Aren't there enough wagons? Can't we find some ... some ..."

The physician shook his head. "No, we can't. We are hard-pressed to save those we can save." His voice sounded harsh and almost desperate. He scanned the hall and looked back at her. "I'm sorry, but you see what we're up against, don't you? Would you waste time and energy on them when you could help the living? Would you?"

"I suppose not. Not if I had to choose, but—"

Dr. Milbank checked his watch. "Excuse me, but I really must insist that you leave now."

Kit took one last look at the curtain hiding the deceased and wondered, *Could we have done better?* She walked back to the critical care section, but it was deserted. Where was Tom? Surely he would have waited for her. She looked toward the Polk Street exit and saw him up ahead. When she caught up to him, he was watching a soldier place an unconscious man in the back of a wagon. He stood there doing nothing, seemingly in a trance. She tapped him on the shoulder. "Tom, are you all right? Who was that? Did you know him?"

He didn't answer, except to say, "We'd better go."

All the wagons, all the patients, all the medical personnel—everyone was headed to the Presidio, the Army headquarters overlooking the ocean on the northwest side of the city. Kit had been to the base for a number of social and civic gatherings over the years; it was a self-contained fortress with its own hospital, supply depot, parade ground, barracks, and officers' quarters. Now it was transforming into a massive tent city for thousands of wounded and homeless city dwellers.

The wagon they rode in seemed to find every pothole, and while Tom held Kit's waist to keep her steady, he appeared aloof and said nothing, as if she didn't exist. That was not like him at all.

"What happened back there?" she asked. "I heard you say the word 'impossible.' Why did they need you?"

"It was nothing."

"What do you mean it was nothing? That nurse was visibly upset when she asked for your help."

"And so I helped her. There's no more to it," he insisted, and refused to say another word.

Kit didn't press him, but Tom's altered demeanor worried her. She had just witnessed him handle the enormous stress of multiple casualties without losing his composure, but now he seemed almost shell-shocked. Maybe it was a delayed reaction. Or maybe it was something else.

**CHAPTER THIRTY-ONE**

When Tom and Kit arrived at the Presidio they were immediately registered and given housing assignments. The soldier in charge handed them each a slip of paper. "This is where you'll bunk at night. Each quadrant has a nickname, but don't lose the number, because all the tents look alike and it'll be a hell of a time getting access to this list once I turn it in."

Then he directed Tom and Kit to the nearby tent hospital, where they were given their work assignments. Kit was going to assist the surgeons in the permanent base hospital, while Tom was given field duty. She couldn't believe what Tom said next.

His tone was bland, devoid of emotion. "I guess I'll see you around the camp. We'll probably run into each other, maybe at mealtimes."

It was as if they'd just met moments before, as if there was nothing between them. Stunned, she didn't know what to say, except "I'm sure we will." He turned to go, but she felt the paper in her hand and touched his arm, trying once more to connect. "So …where are you staying?"

"Oh." He paused before pulling out his housing assignment. "It says I'm in Cow Hollow."

"May I see it?"

Reluctantly he handed it over. *My God,* she realized. *He doesn't want to tell me!* After an awkward moment, she returned the slip and broke the tension with "Quite a day, wouldn't you say?"

He must have realized how cold he seemed, because he took Kit's hand. "They said he had a gun, and I couldn't ... I couldn't take the chance of you being anywhere near that. It would have killed me. I hope you understand."

Her fears dissipated a little; that was the Tom she knew. "You seem to be in the habit of protecting me," she said without heat.

He smiled then, barely. "I can't help myself."

"Well, maybe someday I can return the favor."

"I wish you could," he said, and squeezed her hand lightly before letting it go.

"I'll look for you later, then," she said, feeling slightly mollified.

---

Two days went by before she saw Tom again. She was grabbing a bite of lunch when she spied him at one of the tables in the cafeteria tent. As she walked up to him, she could see that he was very tired. She wanted to wrap her arms around him.

"How are you doing?" she asked.

"Fine ... busy... you know." He tried to look nonchalant, with a hand in his pocket. "How about you?"

"Oh, the same. We've been very busy. Almost nonstop surgeries. We could use your expertise in there." She sent him a smile. "After all, we work pretty well together." *Agree with me, damn you. Say something. Something about us.*

But he didn't. After a "Got to run. See you soon," he practically raced out of the tent.

Something was definitely wrong ... and it seemed to run deeper than the tragedy they found themselves embroiled in. She tried to summon her usual indignation, but only despondency raised its weary head.

---

When more time passed without seeing Tom, it slowly began to drive Kit mad. Where in damnation could he be? The day of the earthquake, she'd felt as close to him as she'd ever had to any human being. What they'd been through at the Mechanics' Pavilion had somehow bonded them—or so it seemed to her. Even though they'd been assigned different duties at the base, she'd assumed they would find time for one another. A look, a quiet conversation, the touch of hands. A promise to be kept when the world around them righted itself. She'd been filled with the sense that this man, despite everything, was her destiny.

But it hadn't worked out that way at all. Other than their chance meeting during lunch, which had been awkward at best, it was as if he'd fallen off the face of the earth—or worse, that he didn't want to be found.

Thankfully there'd been no gossip about him (The grapevine amongst medical personnel was every bit as pernicious as that in Kit's old social circle). Had she said something to offend him or give him the wrong impression? She searched her memory. No, she hadn't. For once, she wasn't at fault.

Tom's distance bothered Kit so much that after dinner one night she walked halfway across the compound to Cow Hollow, his section of tents. She found his cabin and stood outside, calling softly, "Is anybody home?"

When there was no response, curiosity got the better of her. Looking both ways to make sure she wasn't seen, she slipped inside. To her surprise, the tent wasn't empty, but housed the very man she'd been looking for.

Tom was stretched out on his cot, lying on his stomach, still wearing trousers, but without his shirt. His back was broad, and even in repose, she could see the muscles beneath the skin. One well-defined arm was extended above his head, but the other one was tucked in close to his side.

She wanted to crawl in next to him. She wanted to feel the warmth of his body against hers and feel safe from all the mayhem that surrounded them. It would be scandalous to do so, but she wanted it just the same.

Knowing that it would reflect badly on him was the only thing that kept her standing.

The night air was growing chilly, so she drew closer, intending to pull the blanket over him. As she did so, she saw a small bottle of laudanum perched on the overturned box being used as a bedside table. "Poor man. You probably haven't slept well for days," she murmured. She picked up the bottle and sniffed the contents; it smelled sour and she shivered. She'd never tried the opiate, but it was good to know it worked for something.

After arranging the blanket over him, she left the cabin and sought her own sleep back in Forest Knolls. Dreams of being wrapped in Tom's arms, responding to his touch, left her fitful and she woke, breathless and perspiring, in the middle of the night. Tom Justice had a hold on her.

She feared such power.

And she craved it.

# CHAPTER THIRTY-TWO

## Josephine

Josephine had been right about the sturdiness of their Pacific Heights home. Despite several aftershocks, the structure held and she was soon able to begin the process of setting things to rights again.

Others weren't so fortunate.

At first they came gingerly, one or two families at a time, hats in hand, knocking on the estate's massive front door. With the rest of her staff engaged in clean-up efforts, Josephine herself answered the bell.

"Beg pardon, ma'am," the first man said, "but our place is nothin' but rubble and we got no place to pitch our tent. Would you mind if we took up a bit of your lawn? We promise not to burden you none."

Of course, Josephine said yes, and of course that opened the floodgates. Soon the entire front and back lawns began to fill up with refugees carrying little more than the clothes on their backs and whatever materials they'd found to build a shelter against the elements.

Edward was helping out as best he could, with a shoulder she knew ached like the devil. He was taking a break in their kitchen, applying a small bag of chipped ice to the sore area, when Josephine swept in to find something to eat and drink. She pulled out a basket of Bertrand's yeast rolls and reached into the ice-box to pour a glass of milk, offering some of each to her husband.

"You really must have that shoulder looked at," she admonished him. "You're not doing anyone any good by being heroic about it."

Edward smiled, but it was more of a grimace. "Believe me, if I could easily straighten my wing, I would, but it can wait." He pulled his wife down next to him with his good arm. "It can wait until you agree to see Dr. Gage about what's ailing *you*."

"Nonsense," she countered. "There's nothing wrong with me that a little rest and relaxation won't cure—and we both know that will be in short supply for a while. What we really need is some way to help these poor folks who are camping on our lawn. I was thinking ..."

"What now, darling?" Edward sounded dubious, which was fair; sometimes, she knew, her ideas showed more imagination than practicality. This one was sound, however.

"I thought we might get word to Lionel Aldrich over at the Presidio. I just spoke with a gentleman with a large gash on his arm who said he'd heard that was the place to go for medical care. Perhaps we can have Lionel send over a doctor and a nurse to see to our little population. Maybe bring supplies as well."

"And the nurse, I take it, would be Kit?"

Josephine smiled. "You are such a clever man."

The day unfolded in such a manner until the late evening, when there was yet another knock on the door. Weary from the day's exertions, Josephine nevertheless donned a robe to see who it was.

Dinah, her dear childhood friend, and Dinah's daughter Bea stood on the front terrace. They were dressed in fine clothes yet carried nothing and appeared even more weary than Josephine.

"My word, are you all right?" she asked, ushering them inside. Her gaze swept the front veranda. "Where's Clarence?"

"We have no idea," Dinah said. "He's up and disappeared."

---

"I wager you regret moving to the Golden City now, dear friend."

Josephine and Dinah were sitting in the upstairs parlor, cups of tea in hand, having sent Dinah's daughter off to bed. It felt much like old times, except that Jo was terribly tired and her feet tingled.

"Surviving an earthquake certainly wasn't on my wish list, but I daresay I would have had these particular problems wherever we'd moved."

The problems she referenced were with Clarence, her spouse of more than a quarter century. His position in St. Louis had lasted barely a year, and when Josephine told her she was moving to San Francisco with Edward Firestone, Dinah had begged her to see if Edward could find Clarence a position.

"He's a good sales person," she said. "He just needs to find the right fit."

Josephine had prevailed upon her adoring groom, whose family contacts stretched clear across the continent. He indeed found Clarence Marshall a job, and a good one, with an import company who traded with the Far East.

Josephine had been thrilled to have her childhood companion nearby, especially as she began both her marriage and her conquest of an entirely new city. She'd given up her pipe dream of becoming a renowned chef, but that didn't mean she couldn't use food in some other important way. With her husband's support and delight, she began to entertain.

More friendships followed. The two couples joined a social circle of elites that included Franklin Anders, a prominent banker, and his timid wife, Hazel. They were beginning to forge the relationships that would last a lifetime.

In the beginning, none of the young marrieds had children, but that soon changed. Josephine and Edward led the way with Will, who was born barely ten months after they exchanged vows; Katherine came along a few years later.

Dinah joked that she hoped Josephine's fertility

would rub off on her and Hazel, who had been trying to conceive for some time.

It did. The year after Katherine's birth, Hazel and Franklin became parents to sweet, adorable Cecily, and two years after that, Dinah and Clarence at last welcomed little Beatrice into the world. For a while, all seemed well as the three little girls (and by now two Firestone boys) grew up in an atmosphere of doting parenthood.

But unbeknownst to any of them, Clarence Marshall was leading a not-so-reputable life on the side. While he held onto his position with the trading company, he apparently felt it necessary to try to increase his income to match that of his friends. He'd started to gamble, and having some success, he gambled even more, but with less fortunate results. He also began a series of trysts with less than stellar women.

As Dinah related all of this, Josephine's heart nearly broke for her friend. Although they'd never talked specifically about Clarence's infidelity, Josephine had heard rumors. She'd also suspected Cecily's true parentage but had chosen never to bring it up. If Dinah could live with such a possibility, who was Josephine to stir the pot? Remnants of her old guilt resurfaced: *Why couldn't I have fixed things?*

Now, sipping a soothing cup of hot chamomile, Dinah was calm, even fatalistic. "When the quake hit this morning, Clarence hadn't even been home; he's been gone for three days."

"A business trip?"

"No. I'm fairly certain he's in the city, but I have no idea where he's been staying, or which wagtail he's been staying with. Bea is worried about him, but honestly, I am beyond caring at this point."

"What about your house?" Josephine asked.

"Utterly destroyed. We are quite homeless at the moment." She smiled gamely. "You don't happen to have an extra tent to spare, do you?"

"Don't be silly. You and Bea will stay here as long as you need to. I'm not so sure how thrilled I would be to take in Clarence, but if we must..."

Dinah shook her head. "I don't think he's coming back. But we have a lifeline. This afternoon we found a telegraph office that was still operational and I sent word to my cousin in Baltimore; we will be out of your hair as soon as possible."

Josephine leaned over to hug her friend. "Never feel that way, Dinah. You are not a burden. I love you, and always will." She paused and decided to air one of her worries.

"Is Bea ... Are you ... all right with what happened, or rather didn't happen, between your daughter and Will? I feel terrible about how he must have led her on for so many years. I truly wanted the two of them to make a match of it."

Now it was Dinah's turn to ease Josephine's mind. "May I tell you? I never felt that Bea and Will were meant for each other. I know *you* wanted it, but I fear that was more for my sake than hers. I always felt they were both marking time. Now it seems that Will has found a woman he adores; let's hope Bea find a young man who makes her feel as special."

"I wish that for Kit as well." As the two women embraced once more, Josephine said, "Have I told you lately how very blessed I was to have you and your family move to Delancy Place so many years ago?"

"So many years that we dare not count," Dinah quipped. At that moment the house trembled slightly with another aftershock. There had been dozens, and by now they caused no concern.

"Even the house shudders at how long it's been," Josephine said, and they laughed as if they were once more teenagers with few cares in the world beyond their next cotillion ball.

### Katherine

"I'd like to get a message to my mother and father," Kit told the sergeant in charge of the camp's "Grand Central Station." The day after visiting Tom's cabin, she'd finally gotten enough of a break to let her parents know that all was well. She also wanted to remind her father that he should have a doctor look at his injured shoulder as soon as possible. She hoped she could have a note delivered by someone who had business near Pacific Heights.

"Nurse Firestone, you must be telepathic," the sergeant said. "I just got orders to round you up and send you over to your parents' place. They've requested a doctor, too. Apparently they need some medical attention."

Kit felt the earth tilting beneath her, and it wasn't an aftershock. "What? What's happened? Are my parents—"

The sergeant held up his hand. "Whoa. Hold on. Don't you fret. Word is they don't need it for themselves, but for some people staying with them." He looked again at the written orders he'd received. "Says here you're to go with Dr. Tom Justice."

That couldn't be. Her parents had only met him once or twice, hadn't they? And they certainly didn't know that she and he ... "Why Dr. Justice?"

The sergeant shrugged. "I dunno, ma'am. I only know the order was signed by Dr. Aldrich, and he's the chief medical officer. I was just getting ready to fetch the both of you when you walked up. You wouldn't happen to know where he's working this morning, would you?"

"I have no idea," she said. She felt a moment's unease. It was after two o'clock and she still hadn't seen him around the camp. Why was someone pushing them together? It didn't make sense. And why did it inspire a feeling of dread?

---

*I will not cry*, Kit told herself. *Crying is for weaklings.* During the ride to her parents' home, Tom sat upright, the hand nearest her deep in his pocket instead of around her waist as it had been during their last ride together. He said nothing, and neither did she. What more was there to say?

He had launched his verbal attack the moment he saw her standing next to the wagon. "What are you doing here?" he ground out.

"I was told I was needed at a location in Pacific Heights." She straightened the cape of her uniform, reluctant to look at him.

"What location?"

She hesitated. Swallowed. "My parents' estate."

"What? Why in the hell—"

"I am as much in the dark as you are about this! It was probably my mother's doing. I can see why she'd use her influence to get me to come, but you, I don't understand. I've never said anything to her about you or our ... friendship ... and she only met you briefly at their New Year's gathering, do you remember?"

"Of course I remember, and it was twice—once while you were shopping, too. But I find it hard to believe you had nothing to do with this. People like you are used to getting their way."

He may as well have slapped her in the face. That's certainly what she wanted to do to him. But she didn't; instead she fell back on her usual linguistic swordplay. "People like me?" she asked. "Do you mean rich people? Privileged people? Perhaps you're right. We do get our way. But why on earth would getting my way involve you?" She hadn't let him respond, turning quickly to climb aboard the wagon. Tom had made it clear what his true feelings were. It was apparent that he'd decided not to pursue a relationship with her.

Hence the silence.

She thought of the mistake in judgment she'd made with Easton Challis and wondered, *How could I have been so stupid a second time? Didn't I learn anything?*

At least this time she hadn't taken it beyond a kiss. But just imagining what pleasures they might have found together sent her spirits lower that she thought they could go. Whatever the problems between them, Kit knew inside how exceptional Tom Justice was, and she already mourned the loss of what had always seemed just beyond her reach.

Wallowing in a hefty sludge of self-pity, she didn't pay attention to their surroundings until just before they reached her parents' estate.

"Oh my Lord," Kit said.

The gate was open, and as they turned off the main street they were greeted by an army of squatters who had taken up residence on Firestone land. Whatever could serve as a shelter did so, from tents and wooden structures to slapdash lean-tos and large shipping cartons. She could tell many of the latter were comprised of that new heavy paper made by a company Will had told her to invest in. "They make what's called 'corrugated cardboard,'" he'd said. "I'm telling you, it's going to take the shipping industry by storm."

But right now the containers were being used as tiny houses; along with the more familiar structures, they had taken up nearly every inch of open space on the grounds.

In the ramshackle village, people were going about

their business as if they'd lived there all their lives. Some tended fires; some cooked in iron pots hanging from makeshift racks; and some scrubbed clothes in tubs filled with soapy water before laying them on tree branches to dry. And throughout the community, children were running, seemingly oblivious to their pitiful surroundings. To them it must be an adventure, while their parents were likely just relieved to have something covering their families while they slept.

The closer Kit and Tom got to the house, the more campers they encountered. The only barrier between the masses and the mansion itself was a rope.

Tom finally spoke up. "Your parents' home looks to be under siege."

"I can't imagine my mother's reaction to all this. She must be livid." That's all Kit needed: a Josephine on the warpath.

Pointing toward the house, Tom said, "I don't know. She looks pretty jovial to me."

Kit followed his gaze to see her mother waving wildly at them. She was even more shocked when, minutes later she hopped off the wagon and her mother swept her up in a hug. "Isn't it marvelous, darling? Welcome to Firestone Camp."

## CHAPTER THIRTY-THREE

### Katherine

The setting was straight out of an absurdist theater production. Kit's mother, Josephine Rose Drummond Firestone, one of the *grandes dames* of San Francisco society, had become the commanding officer of a rag tag refugee camp and appeared to be having the time of her life. She looked as pale as the last time Kit had seen her, but now she was radiating a fierce kind of energy.

As they reached the entry hall, Josephine put her arm through Kit's and looked up at Tom. "We're so glad you could make it. And when I asked dear Lionel to add a physician to the mix, I never dreamed he'd send me a familiar face. You're Dr. —?"

"Justice," Tom said.

"Yes, that's it. I believe we met around the holidays, once out shopping, and you were Miss Cameron's escort for the evening. I remember you filled out your tuxedo rather well."

"Mother. That is hardly—"

"Oh come now, Kit, this is no time to worry about offending someone's sensibilities when so much else is going on. Isn't that right, doctor? May I call you Tom?"

"Yes, of course," he said, falling under her mother's spell as everyone did.

"Splendid. And do call me Josephine. Come, let's take a tour and I'll fill you in on what we're about."

Kit's mother proceeded to walk the camp, which now encircled the mansion, as if she'd founded it herself. Greeting one family after another, she was hailed in turn with calls of "Halloo Miz Firestone," and "Afternoon, ma'am. Nice day for a stroll."

"It's really quite remarkable how well our little camp runs, given that it's less than a week old. We supply water from our two wells, enough for drinking and cooking, at least. A lovely supply sergeant from the Army brings us basic food supplies and linens, and we distribute them as needed in an orderly fashion. And naturally I have Bertrand making scones and tarts and cream puffs all day long so that each afternoon we can pass out a bit of a treat to the children." She looked around and paused as if to soak it all in. "They have so little, after all."

"And health-wise, how are things?" Tom asked.

"Ah, that is where you and Kit come in. I've been told that living in these types of conditions can lead to dreadful illnesses, and I want to make sure we forestall such a calamity. We have set up hand-washing stations throughout the camp, which they tell me helps to keep those nasty germs from spreading. But there are still residents with wounds from the quake and the fires who need medical attention."

They'd reached the large Queen Anne-style gazebo in the Firestone's lower garden. "I thought this might provide a central location for your little clinic. It's big enough to house a table or two, and we can string a curtain across for privacy, if you like. Plus, there is plenty of storage in the benches."

Kit knew the gazebo well. Growing up, they'd called it "The Ruby" because it was round and painted red. It had always been the base for hide-and-seek, and she'd received her share of stolen kisses there. Now, apparently, it would serve a nobler purpose. Kit felt a surge of familial pride; her mother was making this happen!

"I think this will work fine." Kit turned to Tom. "Don't you think?"

Tom walked around the space looking skeptical. But then he turned to them, and though his smile seemed a bit forced, he nodded. "Let's give it a whirl."

Josephine clapped her hands. "Wonderful! Just tell me what you need and I'm sure we can scrounge it up."

In short order the Ruby was furnished with tables, basic medical supplies, and a curtain that bisected the space. Tom suggested that in the interest of efficiency, Kit should handle triage, and send Tom the patients she couldn't handle on her own.

One of the first to show up was Kit's father, apparently at his wife's insistence. He was still wearing a version of the sling Kit had made.

"I told him I wouldn't open the clinic to others until he got some relief besides just ice and whiskey," her mother said. "He's been putting it off and I told him it's just going to get worse if he doesn't deal with it."

Kit couldn't help but tsk. "She's right, Dad. I told you to have it looked at." Lord, she sounded just like her mother!

"May I?" Tom asked him. At her father's nod, Tom palpitated the shoulder, talking quietly the whole time. "You don't have much bruising, which is good. Have you felt tingling or numbness at all?"

Her father nodded.

"And you've been icing it?"

"As often as I can get him to sit still," Josephine said.

Tom finished the exam and gestured to the table behind the curtain. "I don't feel any broken bones, so I think we may be able to re-align it without too much trouble. I'm going to have you lie on your back while I maneuver your arm back in place. Mrs. Firestone, could you please go back to the house and find your husband's favorite libation?" He glanced at Kit's father. "He's going to need it. And Katherine? You should go with her."

"What? Why?"

"Please, Kitty Kat. Do as he says."

Kit's father hadn't called her that in years. He looked ashen and was beginning to sweat.

"Come along, darling." Josephine blew a kiss to her husband and hustled Kit toward the house.

Accompanying Josephine across the grounds, Kit noticed her mother walking without her usual vigor. Several campers called out to her, and though she waved to them, she said little. When they reached the front door of the mansion, it was unlocked.

"It's amazing how honest everyone is," Josephine commented as they entered, echoing Kit's thoughts. "We have had no issues regarding pilfering of any kind. Everyone realizes we're all in this together."

"I must confess, I'm surprised that you would take on a project like this, even under these circumstances."

"Are you?" Josephine looked back. "Well, I'd heard what Alma de Bretteville was doing with the tent city in Golden Gate Park. What a dynamo she is! So, I thought we could do the same thing here, and of course, I was right."

Katherine couldn't believe the expression on her mother's face. She was glowing with pride.

They went to Kit's father's office, which had been set to rights after the quake dislodged nearly all the books from their shelves. Opening the small liquor cabinet near the window, Josephine pulled out a bottle of Glen Fiddich and two glasses. As she straightened, Kit noticed her mother wince.

"What's wrong, mother? You look pale, and you seem to be in a bit of pain."

Josephine shrugged. "It's nothing a nice long nap won't take care of. Now, what can I get you to drink while I'm here?"

"Shouldn't we get back to the Ruby?"

Josephine gestured to a pair of upholstered chairs

placed to take advantage of the garden view. "I think your father would like us to take our time. Please, have a seat so that I can do the same."

Without repeating her request, Josephine poured a jigger's worth of the scotch into each glass and handed one to Kit. "The other night Dinah and I shared a pot of tea; we should have added some of this."

"Oh, Dinah was here?"

"And Bea, too. They left this morning. Their home was destroyed and Clarence, that no good scoundrel, has taken off for parts unknown."

"Scoundrel" was too good a word for that reprobate. If only her mother knew what Kit had learned so long ago. "That's terrible," Kit said. "I bet you wished you hadn't insisted she and Clarence move here—at least they would have been spared this nightmare."

Josephine sent Kit a puzzled look. "I never insisted the Marshalls move here, darling. It was Dinah who wanted desperately to come."

"What? I thought—"

"No. Clarence had lost another job, you see, and Dinah was hoping your father could put in a good word for him with one of the executives he knew here in town. To save face, we told everyone that I begged them to come. I will say I was glad it worked out, however. Dinah is my closest friend and it has been wonderful having her here all these years ... even if it's been less than idyllic for her."

Her mother had said those last words under her breath; perhaps she knew more about Clarence Marshall's proclivities than she'd let on. Kit tested the water. "I wonder how the Anders family fared," she asked. "Have you heard from them?"

Her mother sent Kit a look that spoke volumes, and Kit realized Josephine knew perfectly well the illicit connection between those two families. Apparently, however, she wasn't going to confirm or deny anything.

"Not a word," Josephine said. "I've been very concerned about poor Hazel these past few years. She's become ever more frail since her granddaughter's death. But you would probably know more about that whole sorry episode."

Now they were in territory of which *Kit* wished to steer clear. How alike she and her mother were—soon they would be reduced to talking about the weather! She chose to ignore the comment.

"Well, I still think you should take it easy; you don't seem to be quite yourself."

Josephine finished her drink and rose from the chair. "I'm enough myself to know your father could use his drink by now. Shall we go?"

Katherine and Josephine returned to The Ruby with the bottle of Glenfiddich and two fresh glasses. Josephine poured a shot for her husband and offered another to Tom.

"No thank you, ma'am, but perhaps later tonight I'll indulge."

"Fair enough," she said. "By the way, we've made up a guest room for you. It's two doors down from Kit's old room. I've put spare towels in there for you. Kit can show you where it is when you're ready to retire.

Oh, and Dr. Justice? Thank you for sparing me the pain."

"The pain?"

"The pain of watching Edward deal with *his* pain. Don't think I didn't know what you were doing, young man."

Tom smiled. "I don't think I could put much past you, Mrs. Fire ... Josephine."

Patients had begun to line up outside the Ruby, so Kit and Tom fell easily into a routine. They worked well together, treating a variety of injuries and ailments, from cuts and puncture wounds to headaches and insomnia.

Tom let Katherine handle any injections, and surprisingly, he encouraged her to stitch up a gash in an older man's arm. "I know you can do it, and this is the perfect time to practice."

*Why is he being so accommodating?* she wondered, even though she had to admit she was rather pleased to be able to practice her suturing skills on something other than a linen-draped doll.

Late in the afternoon, a skinny, distraught young mother came in with her newborn, who was listless and suffering from diarrhea. The baby could barely cry, much less wail.

Kit's first reaction was fear that the infant was suffering from the scourge that had killed Henny, but she soon realized the baby simply wasn't getting any nourishment.

"Do you have a caked breast, ma'am? That's when

your milk ducts clog up. If so, your breast would feel overly full and even hard."

"No, it's just the opposite," the woman cried. "I don't have any more milk. It dried up and I've been giving her regular milk, but she spits it out. I tried apple juice, but nothing's working."

Tom had heard the commotion and stepped from behind the curtain. "May I?" he asked, taking the little baby in his arms. He cooed to the infant for a bit. "My guess is that your little girl—what is her name?"

"Amy."

"My guess is little Amy here isn't quite ready for what you've been giving her. You were smart to bring her in, because babies can get dehydrated very quickly and that's not good. Our first goal is to get her suckling again, so if you've no objection, I'd like to find you a wet nurse, someone here in the camp who can help you out for a few days."

The mother started to blush. "Who would do such a thing for me?"

"You'd be surprised. You'd do the same for someone else, wouldn't you?" Tom handed the baby back to its mother and spoke with Kit privately. "Any chance you could send your mother on a mission? We need a woman who is currently nursing to come and see me, and Mrs. Firestone probably knows everyone in the camp by now, so ..."

Kit couldn't help smiling. This was the Tom Justice she had fallen in love with! "She would love that mission!"

Surprisingly, he frowned as if she had crossed a line, as if she'd broken a rule and been happy, if even for a moment. His countenance sober, he added, "We need some white grape juice as well. Maybe her chef keeps some in stock, but it needs to be white, not purple."

Katherine nodded, not willing to show him he'd affected her yet again. "I'll see what I can do."

That evening, Tom begged off dinner. "I need my beauty rest," he'd quipped on his way upstairs. Josephine's father, obviously feeling much better, thanked Tom for "setting him straight."

"I'll have a tray sent up to you, dear boy," Josephine said as he left the room. "You must keep your strength up for these trying times."

Kit said nothing, fearing her tongue might get her in trouble once again. She went to sleep wondering what had happened to the man whom she'd glimpsed so briefly that afternoon.

# CHAPTER THIRTY-FOUR

The next day's work was almost pleasant in that the patients Kit treated were only slightly hurt, and most seemed to be in a good mood. Kit's mother had found an agreeable wet nurse for the poor little baby, and the father stopped by to thank them for setting it up. He was a humble-looking man, as thin as his wife, dressed in a dusty jacket that smelled of smoke.

"Just wanted to let you know it's working out good, doc. The lady Miz Firestone found is nursing Amy right alongside her own little boy. Says she's got plenty of milk and is glad to do it. Turns out her family tent is on the same side of the Big House as ours, so it's real convenient, too. We can't thank you enough."

He extended his hand, and Tom glanced at Kit before extending his own to quickly complete the shake. Something about it struck her as odd.

That evening, over a dinner of Bertrand's delicious

French onion soup and some frankly boring cucumber sandwiches, Tom announced to Kit and her parents that he would be leaving the next morning. Kit's heart took a tumble, but she focused on keeping her reaction hidden.

"That's probably a good idea," she said with what she hoped was the right amount of indifference. "I was planning on heading back myself. I'm sure there's much left to do at the Presidio."

"Oh, must you go so soon?" her mother asked. "I'm sure Sergeant Watkins could give you both a ride back to the Presidio once he brings supplies tomorrow afternoon. Isn't that right, Edward?"

Edward looked at Tom. They seemed to be communicating something. "I'm sure the good doctor can find his own way back, darling."

"Ah. Yes," Tom answered. "I've got to stop somewhere on the way. But thank you so much for your hospitality ... all of you." He gazed at Kit as he finished.

---

A little after nine that evening, Kit lay awake stewing about the mysterious, calamitous change in her and Tom's relationship. When she heard him head down the hall toward the stairs, she impetuously threw on a dress and grabbed a lantern so that she could follow. She didn't know what she hoped to accomplish, but maybe she would learn something by simple observation.

Keeping the wick low so that he didn't notice her presence, she followed him down to the camp, coming upon him just as he was being introduced to the woman who was breastfeeding the baby they'd treated. The women were insisting that he hold the infant, and as he took it from them, he said, "She looks much more relaxed. She's a beautiful little girl, ma'am."

But it wasn't what Tom said that had Kit staring in shock. It's what she saw.

Because when Tom took the little girl, his hand shook terribly, like he had the palsy.

She couldn't help stepping forward. "Yes, she is, isn't she?"

The painful look on Tom's face told her he realized he'd been caught.

"I'm the nurse who's been working here today," Kit said to the women. "I wanted to let you know the doctor and I will be leaving tomorrow, but if you need any help in the next few days, just let Mrs. Firestone know and she'll get you what you need."

Tom handed the baby back to its mother. "Well, good luck to you, ladies. And goodnight."

He tried to walk away, but Kit caught up with him. "We need to talk. Will you come with me?"

He hesitated, then nodded and followed her as she headed toward the far side of the lower garden, where stairs led down to a path running alongside a brook. The water level was low but even in the near dark Kit could hear the soothing sound of the trickling rivulet. "Almost there."

"There" was her beloved nannybone tree, which she hadn't climbed in years, but which remained in her memory as a safe and peaceful retreat. Only once, when she'd learned how deceitful adults can be, had it failed in its purpose.

She hopped onto the tree's massive lower branch. "This used to be my favorite refuge against being Katherine Madeline Mariah Firestone."

"You found that a tough assignment?" He stood near her, but on the ground, which put her slightly above him. Everything about him was dark: his clothes, his hair, his countenance. She wanted to change that more than anything.

"You've met my mother; no doubt you can imagine what it was like," she said. "It took me a long time to get out from under her shadow and find my own way."

"And now you have."

"And now I have. But that way led me to you."

"No, we just happened to cross paths for a time, that's all."

She held her temper in check. Barely. "That's not all, and you know it. Less than a week ago we were ... connecting. I felt it. You felt it. I know you did. We have danced around it for so long, but I felt ... I felt things were changing. And now..."

"And now you see that I'm like all the rest."

Frustrated, Kit hopped down from the branch. Despite their height difference, she stood up to him. "You are not like all the rest. But you've changed." She pointed to the hand in his pocket. "Let me see it."

He stiffened, saying nothing.

"Let me see it," she said, tugging on his arm.

Slowly he drew his hand out, and in the meager light of the lantern they could both see that it trembled.

"This happened five days ago, didn't it?"

"Yes."

"And you said nothing, thinking I wouldn't notice, thinking that you could just slink away from me. Was that your plan?"

He winced. "Yes. So what?"

"So you could be overreacting. It's been less than a week. Maybe it's some kind of muscle spasm. Maybe you've been working too hard."

Tom's laugh was bitter. "Maybe I need sleep. Maybe I need to eat better. Maybe I need drugs. Maybe I need more sex. Who knows what the hell is going to fix it? All I know is, it isn't getting better."

She reached for him. "We can figure it out. There must be someone who can help you. We can—"

He stepped back. "No. *We* aren't going to do anything. I don't want you to be any part of this. Whatever *this* is."

The words were designed to inflict pain, and she felt each of them, a thousand piercing cuts.

Inhaling sharply, she drew on her simmering anger, one of her few remaining weapons. "There you go again, deciding what's best for me."

He shrugged, infuriating her. "Not very modern, I know. But in this case, you know I'm right."

"I know nothing of the kind."

"Regardless. I'll be leaving in the morning."

"Where? Back to the Presidio?"

"To tie up loose ends, yes. Beyond that I have to find some answers." He held up his quivering hand. "I have to see what my new friend has in store for me."

Kit waived her own hand dismissively, trying and failing to sound unconcerned. "That's insignificant. You are so much more than your silly hand."

"It's part and parcel of who I am." He touched her cheek, so tenderly. "You should be with someone whole and healthy. Someone who doesn't feel like some kind of creature stuck in a body that doesn't obey him."

How could she make him understand? She took his hand in both of hers. "Listen, what is the worst that can happen? If you can no longer perform surgery, there are other forms of medicine. You were wonderful with that poor young mother yesterday, and see how grateful she was? You can consult. You can—"

He pulled his hand away. "Katherine. You're not listening to me. I will never be happy the way I am right now. And if I'm so caught up in my misery, I will never be able to make *you* happy, to give you everything you deserve." He ran his good hand down the back of her head in one last intimate gesture. "And you deserve everything. You surely do."

She looked down so that he couldn't see the turmoil within. When she faced him again, it was with renewed purpose. "I don't accept your premise."

"Well, you're going to have to, because you can't help me. And even if you could, I wouldn't want you to.

Let's just leave it at that, all right? Now I really need to get some sleep."

A memory flashed: Kit as a toddler, demanding fealty from her brothers, kicking and hollering until they acquiesced to her demands. She felt the same unbridled anger now but knew she could no longer fix it with a simple tantrum.

While others around them had met adversity by banding together, Tom had closed himself to her completely, determined to go it alone out of some distorted sense of self-sacrifice. She wanted to throttle him.

As they headed back to the house, Kit kept the lamp low so as not to disturb the sleeping refugees.

"We always seem to be finding our way through the dark," he said, once they were inside the mansion.

"We don't always find our way." She turned off the lamp and they walked upstairs together. Just before entering her room, she wished him good night. It felt like goodbye.

---

Kit paced the Aubusson rug of her old bedroom, thinking of the man sleeping two doors down. She loved Tom Justice. More than herself. It was a most inconvenient time to come to that realization, but there it was. What she didn't know was how to help him. He was hurting, so affected by what had transpired since the earthquake that he no longer felt whole. And he was ready to leave her because he didn't want to drag her into his own private hell. By that admission she knew he loved her, too.

She could not budge him through arguments or entreaties; she could not charm him or force him to act a certain way.

She was back to feeling powerless.

So, what was there to do?

Only one thing, she realized. Show him what he meant to her. What they could be. What belonged to him by virtue of her love.

She reached into the nightstand drawer and pulled out the three wrapped prophylactics she had collected from occasional forays into her brother's domain. She dropped them into the pocket of her dressing gown before leaving her room and tapping softly on his door.

Tom's growl rumbled through the wall. "Come in."

Opening the door, Kit knew that the dim light of the hallway put her in silhouette. Her gown, made of silk, caressed her body. She felt agitated, her body humming. "I've come to see how you're doing," she said.

He was laying nonchalantly on the bed, wearing pants but no shirt again. His chest was wide and muscular and she longed to touch it.

"What a good little nurse you are." He opened his arms wide. "As you can see, all is well." He waved his hand wildly. "Except for a traitorous hand that won't stop shaking, life is glorious."

She noticed the half-full bottle of Scotch on the nightstand. A typical male. Apparently he hadn't been able to sleep either. *Good.*

Shutting the door quietly, she moved closer to the bed and took a deep breath of courage. "I'd like to give you something."

"A going-away present? Let me guess. Another pep talk? A piece of your mind? A kick in the ass?" The alcohol hadn't improved his mood.

"No," she said. "Just me."

"Just you."

She moved even closer. "That's right. Just me. Tonight I want to be with you. It's as simple as that."

He laughed, a short cynical burst. "It's never that simple."

She was next to the bed now and she paused. "Tonight it is." She slowly untied the belt to her gown and let the garment drop.

Underneath she was naked.

"You ... don't know what the hell you're doing," he stammered.

She leaned over and whispered in his ear. "You aren't the first. Does that matter?" Then she nuzzled him.

He slowly shook his head. "You ... you have to stop now, because—"

She climbed on the bed and straddled him, feeling him straining against his trousers. Leaning forward, she pressed herself against him. "Because you won't be able to stop yourself if I continue? I'm counting on that, Tom." She kissed him deeply before adding, "I'm counting on that very much."

"Ah, Katherine," he sighed. A decision made, he took

her face in his hands and kissed her back tenfold. And the joining began.

---

*He's going to leave and I have to let him*, she thought. It was early; dawn had barely arrived.

Naked from their last tumble, she lay on her stomach, her face turned away from his side of the bed. Tom had gotten dressed, she knew, and was now sitting beside her, running his hand softly down her back.

"You are more beautiful than I ever imagined, and I imagined you just like this so many times," he murmured.

"If you think me beautiful, then stay with me." She turned onto her back and gazed at him, melancholy seeping into her; she already knew his answer.

His expression was equally sad. He held up his hand, which still shook. "I wouldn't make you live with this for all the tea in China."

"That's a prodigious amount of tea." She sat up and let the covers fall, revealing her breasts. As she hoped, his eyes went straight to them. "Think what you'll be missing."

He chuckled softly. "You are a very cruel woman, Miss Firestone. But so lovely ... in every way."

"Will you write to me?"

"No."

Do you ... need any money?"

He frowned with a quick shake of the head; she realized it was a stupid thing to ask.

"One other thing," he said.

"What? Anything."

"Don't have me followed. Do you understand? You will not use your money and influence to control me. I am not some sort of ... family pet who's run away from home."

Kit sensed the familiar anger about to burst before admitting she would likely have done just what he warned her not to do. Even so, she couldn't let him off the hook so easily. "Don't you think that's a bit extreme?"

"You're probably right. But promise me anyway."

She felt deflated, a balloon gone flat. "All right. I promise I won't have you followed."

Tom lifted her chin. "Thank you for that."

Time was running out and she felt a jolt of panic. Once again, options ran through her head: begging, crying, reasoning, demanding.

No. She knew Tom Justice well enough to know none of that would make a difference. If nothing else, he was consistent in his need to protect her, even though in this case, the danger existed only in his imagination.

Instead, she merely said, "What would you like me to tell everyone?"

He gestured to the writing desk in the corner. "I left your parents a thank-you note, and I'll inform Dr. Aldrich. He'll make sure someone good comes to take my place."

Tears welled up. "No one can take your place, Tom."

"They'll have to," he answered, his voice sounding as

desolate as she felt. He leaned down to kiss her tenderly. "They'll have to."

A moment later he was gone, and Kit lay there, thinking of the night they'd just shared. If his hand had trembled, she hadn't noticed; she'd only felt his sure and loving touch.

## CHAPTER THIRTY-FIVE

*Is* there anything more difficult than letting go of someone you adore? Kit now knew for certain that she had never loved Easton Challis, because losing him felt like child's play compared to the void that now threatened to swallow her.

After Tom left, Kit rose and spent the morning with her parents before catching a ride back to the Presidio with the quartermaster who delivered supplies to Firestone Camp. Her mother, as usual, had gone on and on about Tom, extolling his virtues, remarking on "what a lovely, thoughtful young man he is." Her father, normally taciturn, heartily agreed, capping his compliment with a demonstration of the range of motion he could now indulge in without pain. "He's a good, solid citizen," Edward said, a true compliment coming from him.

Before she left, her father took her aside and reiterated his desire for her to return sooner rather than later. "I'd like you to talk to your mother about some issues," he said cryptically.

Kit frowned. "Why? What's wrong?"

"Oh, it's probably nothing. She says it's nothing. But she's been ... sluggish of late. I think she should get it checked out."

"I noticed a change as well. But Father, she's fifty, not twenty, and you have both been through quite a lot. I'd say she's entitled to feel a bit tired."

"You're right, of course. But still, I'd like you to talk to her anyway."

Kit patted his hand. "She will probably bite my head off, but I will do it, for you. I'll be back next week. I promise."

She returned to the Presidio and her parents were all but forgotten as she was met with a barrage of questions from the medical staff about Tom's disappearance. The grapevine had worked amazingly well; they'd heard he wasn't coming back.

"You just worked with him, right? I heard he walked off the job—couldn't take it anymore."

"Did you hear about Tom Justice? He's got a drug problem and left to try and get help."

"They say Tom's heartbroken because his mistress died in the Chinatown fire. You know anything about it?"

Kit would have laughed if she hadn't been worried about bursting into tears. She told each gossipmonger the same thing: "Dr. Justice just worked himself to the bone and told me he's taking some time off to visit his family and get his stamina back." Colonel Aldrich told essentially the same story, and by week's end, Tom's departure had been forgotten by everyone.

Everyone except Kit.

She tried to accept the unfamiliar reality of losing, but questions kept swirling. Could she have done more to keep him from leaving her? Did she even want a man who let something as trivial as a hand tremor get in the way of their future? Did he care anything at all about her?

And on the heels of those self-serving thoughts came the bitter acknowledgment that she really had no understanding of what it meant to lose something that defined who you were. What would be the equivalent for her? Losing her looks, her nursing skills, or, God forbid, her fortune? How would she react if the situation were reversed? "Oh, my face is terribly scarred, but you'll still be attracted to me, won't you, Tom?" Honestly, would she expect such a sacrifice from him? The answer was no.

Tom cared for her, she was sure of it; he just didn't feel as if he could stay with her as long as he carried such a burden. He'd left, and she had to move on with her life. But what did "moving on" mean, precisely? She couldn't simply put her feelings for the man on a back shelf and expect them to stay there and not cause trouble. They wouldn't obey, no matter how much she tried to reason with them.

And she did try to reason with them.

*You cannot pine for someone who doesn't feel as deeply as you. You have to re-engage with the world. You have to put one foot in front of the other and be open to new experiences.*

The first of those experiences was finding a new place to live.

The refugee camps at the Presidio, Golden Gate Park, and several other locations crested with a population in the tens of thousands. Over several weeks, the numbers began to recede as victims found places to live whose walls weren't made of canvas or shipping cartons. Some were able to return to their damaged homes. Others moved in with relatives or left the city altogether. And some, like Kit, found new places.

Yes, she could have easily moved back in with her parents (wouldn't her mother have loved that!), but Kit cherished her privacy and counted herself lucky to find a tiny one-bedroom apartment to rent near Mission Dolores.

St. Mary's Hospital had been destroyed by fire, but plans were already underway to rebuild it. In the meantime, a tent hospital had been set up near Golden Gate Park; after that, the medical staff, including Kit, would move to a temporary facility at the Maudsley Sanitarium.

The city itself was moving forward. Immediately after the quake, a "Committee of Fifty," made up of the city's most prominent business, financial, and government leaders (including Edward Firestone) met to help the homeless and start making plans to rebuild San Francisco. City Hall, the Palace Hotel, the Mechanics Pavilion, and even Chinatown were destined to rise again, more impressive than ever before. Those stern

Presbyterians who'd said that San Francisco was "so wicked that God had to punish it" could only hope the modern-day Sodom and Gomorrah had learned its lesson.

Capping the positive news on a personal level was the fact that Will and Mandy were able to tie the matrimonial knot. It wasn't the social event of the season, as Josephine might have wanted, but something better: a small celebration of family and friends at The Grove. And it took place just three weeks after the quake.

Kit hadn't been to the artists' retreat since Mandy's eighteenth birthday, the night Tom had first kissed her. She knew she would miss him more in that setting but missing him had become part of her emotional wardrobe. Like a corset, she put up with its familiar discomfort, not daring to imagine life without it.

The simple ceremony, conducted by a pastor from the nearby village of Little Eden, was held on a bluff overlooking the ocean. Surrounded by those, and only those who loved her, Mandy moved nearly everyone to tears in a simple white cotton dress that let her innate loveliness shine through. And Will—had he ever looked so happy? He was full to bursting with love for his bride, and Kit considered it a victory of sorts that she felt no need to lessen his joy by sharing her lack of same. She had always been a good actress, and Will's wedding provided a worthy stage for her performance.

Josephine was surprisingly charitable. She didn't disparage the venue or the dress or the flowers. She merely held on to their father's good arm as she watched her first-born pledge his life to a very special girl. *This is how life should be*, Kit thought. *This is how it can be.*

"It's such a shame that Dr. Justice had to leave town," her mother remarked at the picnic-style reception. "I enjoyed him very much."

"Well, duty called him in another direction," Kit managed, and quickly pointed out the apple fritters gracing the checkered cloth covering the buffet table. "I wonder how they compare to Bertrand's *torta di miele*," she offered. Her mother sent her a knowing and surprisingly sympathetic look; she obviously saw right through Kit's attempts at re-direction. Perhaps her acting skills weren't so exceptional after all.

Only after she'd returned to the city the next day did Kit remember that she'd promised to look into her mother's health. Josephine had seemed fine at the wedding, hadn't she? Or was Kit so self-absorbed that she hadn't even noticed? She moved "talk to Mother" farther up on her list of things to do.

---

A week after the nuptials, Kit was reminded that even the happiest of endings sometimes have residual pain attached. In Will's case, two individuals were profoundly affected by his love for Mandy, and both drew Kit into their tortured orbit.

It would be romantic to blame it on unrequited love, but that was not the case. It seemed the earthquake and fire had destroyed more than just buildings and grounds. Society's apple cart had tipped over, too.

For families that had been surviving on their name and connections for quite a while, the earthquake wiped out whatever assets, hopes, and plans they'd been subsisting on.

Bea Marshall was such a casualty. She had no doubt hoped to make an advantageous match with Will, but it didn't happen. After the quake, rumors swirled that her father had run from creditors, leaving Bea and her mother stranded. After spending a night at Kit's parents' home, they had not been seen in social gatherings, minimal as they were.

It was a surprise, then, when Kit arrived at her apartment on Church Street after work one evening to find Bea waiting for her. Her friend wore a forest-green wool coat with a rather sad-looking fur collar, and no hat. And most provocative of all, she was smoking a cigarette.

"Bea, what are you doing here?" Kit pulled her nurse's cape closed to guard against the chill in the air.

"Oh. Oh, Kit. I've been waiting for you to get off work. I need to talk to you about something. Do you mind?"

"No, of course not. Have you eaten?"

Bea shook her head. "I haven't been too hungry lately."

"Well, you can watch me eat, then," Kit teased.

In the light of her small parlor, Kit could tell that Bea wasn't feeling well. Her skin, usually of the "peaches and cream" variety, was ghostly pale, and her eyes held the shadows that too little sleep brings. Kit had started to put on the tea kettle, but seeing Bea's condition, she opted for brandy instead. Bea was grateful for the snifter. She heaved a deep, shuddering breath, took a hefty sip, and set the glass down. By then tears were rolling down her face.

"Oh, Bea. Is it ... is it about Will? Did you hear that he …"

Bea looked at her, puzzled, before understanding what Kit was trying to say. She smiled slightly and shook her head. "I knew I wasn't the one for him years ago."

"What? Then why— "

"Because he was rich and handsome and well-connected. And I thought maybe your mother would push him to make it happen. He was worth the investment."

The unabashed cynicism of that remark shocked even Kit. "That seems harsh, Bea; is that really what you thought of him?"

Rather than answer directly, Bea paused to take another sip of the spirits. "You've heard about my father, no doubt."

"Not really. Or maybe something about some 'reversals.' You know how the grapevine is."

"Yes, I know how it is," she said dryly. "But the truth is, my dear old papa has hung Mother and me out to dry. He took everything that wasn't nailed down, including his latest mistress, and left for parts unknown."

"Oh my God. That's despicable."

She chuckled without humor. "On a good day we call it that. My mother's cousin wired us some money and we found a room to rent just south of here, in Noe Valley. But that's not why I'm here."

Kit waited for Bea to gather a little more courage from the glass.

"You remember Anson Cotter, don't you?" Bea asked.

"Yes, of course. I occasionally work with him. And we all went out to the theater that night. It seems so long ago, now."

Bea nodded. "Yes, well, Anson and I found we had something in common: he held a torch for Mandy and I had been passed over for her. We became ... close, and he's going to handle something for me, but I don't want to be alone with just him when it happens. I thought ... I thought, since you and I are friends, and you're a nurse and all, that maybe—" Bea took another fortifying breath. "Maybe you could be there with me."

It took but a moment for Kit to fully grasp what Bea was asking. Her voice, so hesitant, so deferential, struck at Kit's heart. She knew instinctively that Will wasn't the father, and her respect for Bea rose as she realized the girl could have blamed him and very likely gotten away with it. Maybe she wasn't quite so cynical after all. But was abortion the right decision?

"Have you ... have you talked to the father about possibly getting married and making it work for the sake of the baby?"

A look of profound sadness stole over her features. *Yes*, her expression said. *I have tried.* "I guess I'm no more his type than I was Will's."

"If you don't mind my asking, who is the father?"

Bea looked surprised. "Isn't it obvious? It's Anson's."

---

It was Kit's turn to lie in wait. She'd agreed to be there for Bea during the procedure, which was set to take place in Bea's room the following week. But in the meantime, why not talk to Anson? Maybe he could be persuaded to change his mind. Bea was a nice young woman, and pretty. Obviously he'd been physically attracted to her. And it was apparent that she quite desperately wanted something to happen. Could anyone blame her? Perhaps she and Anson didn't love each other deeply, but hadn't a lot of marriages started with less and succeeded? None immediately came to mind, but surely there were *some*.

Kit checked Anson's schedule and found a time that worked for her to waylay him after his shift.

"Anson," she said as he left the tent hospital two days later. It was eight in the morning and he'd just finished working a nighttime shift.

He looked at her with suspicion. "Something I can do for you?"

She really did not care for the man. Time for another performance. "You can let me buy you a cup of coffee. Patty's is just up the street."

She could tell he was ambivalent, but perhaps his curiosity won out. Or perhaps he thought she'd changed her tune about getting closer to him. "Sure. Why not."

Ten minutes later they'd put in their orders for

Patty's renowned sourdough pancakes and Kit got right to the point. "I talked to Bea."

He nodded, took a sip of coffee. Looked out the window. "I figured."

"Yes, well, she's asked me to be there and I said I would, but I felt I had to talk to you about it first."

"Why? What's to talk about?"

She hesitated, wondering if she should appeal to his professional or personal side. "You know the oath you took when you became a doctor?"

"*Primum non nocere*, you mean?"

"Yes. 'First do no harm.'"

"I'm not doing any harm. Bea's going to be fine. She'll still be able to have children down the road."

Was Anson being obtuse on purpose? "It's not Bea I'm talking about."

Anson sent her a look filled with disdain. "Ah, you're one of those." He leaned forward. "I've got news for you, sweetheart: at this stage it's nothing but a bunch of bloody, pulpy cells."

"Cells that if left alone will grow into a little girl or a little boy. Maybe someone who looks just like you." Kit gazed at him. "Doesn't it bother you just a little bit to know you're going to destroy that?"

She could tell by his flinch, slight though it was, that her words had struck a chord. Still, he was like most men; he could put inconvenient feelings in their own little drawer and shut it tight. She tried another tactic. "If not for what you're giving up, then what about Bea? She stands to lose something, too."

"She doesn't want it any more than I do. My God,

it's just about the quickest and easiest procedure there is, short of draining an abscess or removing a hangnail."

Kit swallowed a barrage of sarcasm along the lines of "Then let's just snip the head of your penis off while we're at it and whack off one of your gonads like ranchers do to a steer! It's quick as you please, and we'll even leave one hanging so you can pass yourself on to the next generation when you feel the timing's right." Of course, in the interest of keeping it professional, she said none of those things, instead offering to work with Bea ahead of time to keep her calm, and at least put her in twilight with some ether to make it as painless as possible.

"Not necessary, but if it makes you feel better, be my guest. Only I won't risk my reputation procuring the drug. That's strictly on you."

Kit did bring herself to ask Anson one more question. "Why did you become a doctor, anyway?"

He held up his palms. "Because I'm damn good with my hands, that's why."

*But what about your head and your heart? Aren't they just as important?* And that thought led to Tom, and Kit realized how many ways in which men, both good and bad, could be stupid.

---

The procedure known as dilation and curettage is relatively safe and simple, especially if performed by a trained physician instead of a seedy-looking stranger armed with knitting needles in a dirty room off a dank alley. At the hospital, Kit had assisted on several cases where the female patient needed a "D&C." In some situations the pregnancy hadn't taken hold from the beginning; it was dealt with early and the fetus was not quite human-looking. Other procedures took place much later in the gestation, when something had gone wrong with the placenta and one could look at the dead, unborn child and say, yes, that is a baby.

No matter how far along the mother had been, when it came time to scrape the walls of her uterus clean of the life she'd been trying to grow there, she had invariably wept and clutched the doctor's arm, or even Kit's. Many, before succumbing to the ether, asked, "Will I be able to conceive again?"

And every time, the doctor, or Kit herself, would say, "Of course," even when conditions might never be right for another pregnancy to take hold.

If Bea felt as all those other mothers did, she had yet to express it. "I'd just like to get this behind me," she'd told Kit.

And Kit could see why. Apparently disgusted by the chain of events that led to Bea's predicament, Dinah Marshall had moved to Baltimore to live with her cousin and his family.

Kit was frankly surprised by Mrs. Marshall's lack of support; no doubt she was embarrassed by the affair, but Bea was her daughter, for heaven's sake! At least she'd been kind enough to leave her with rent paid through the month of June. The story for public consumption was that Bea had found a job as a "relief worker" and would follow her mother when her job dried up.

The day before the procedure, Kit went over to Bea's room and the two of them scrubbed the walls and the floor and the bed frames in order to make it as sterile an environment as possible. Kit had brought fresh linens and towels and set up the room to resemble a clinical setting as much as she could. She'd also managed to get some ether from her old friend Ellie James, the nurse who had helped out with Cecily. Ellie was now a student at the California College of Pharmacy, which luckily had sustained only minor damage from the earthquake. She purloined some of the drug from the supply that students used on themselves to understand the drug's effects. "I'm glad to help," she told Kit.

Kit had also brought some sticks of laminaria, a type of sterilized seaweed from Japan that had been used for centuries to soften a woman's cervix. The matchstick-sized dilators, called "tents," were inserted through the vagina to the cervix, and as they moistened overnight, they expanded into a gel that gently opened the gateway to the womb. At least Bea wouldn't have to be pried apart like a stubborn clam shell.

Anson Cotter, for all his callousness, was punctual, arriving with his medical bag and a neutral expression. Kit thought perhaps he and Bea might want to be alone for a few minutes in order to come to terms with what they were about to do, but when she offered, neither of them seemed to feel the need. Anson was all business, and Bea was simply too anxious to do anything besides follow simple instructions.

Fortunately, the room had twin beds, and Kit had arranged the furniture to enable Bea to bend her knees and open her legs so that Anson had room to work from the end of the frame.

"Are you ready?" she asked her visibly shaking friend.

Bea nodded, and looked at Anson one last time with what seemed to be both hope and dread. He avoided her eyes, busying himself with laying out his instruments and wiping them off with a small towel. *My God, had he even sterilized them?*

Kit couldn't help asking. "Are they—"

"They're fine," he said brusquely. "Let's get this done." She could tell by his tone that he wasn't entirely immune to the situation.

Kit lowered the ether-soaked cloth to cover Bea's nose and mouth, and she quickly dropped into a light sleep. True to his word, Anson was good with his hands. He worked quickly, examining Bea's pelvis to determine the size and location of the uterus. He used a speculum to open the vagina and a tenaculum to keep the dilated cervix open, giving him room to use a curette to scrape away the contents of her womb. The endometrium was indeed a "bloody, pulpy mess," but it also contained a fetus that, at three inches, was large enough to be identified as the beginnings of a human. Kit swallowed her sadness and wrapped the tissue up before putting it into a sack to be disposed of. That was nothing Bea should have to see.

"That's it," Anson said at last, removing the instruments and wiping away the blood from between Bea's legs. "You know the drill. Tell her some cramps are normal and to keep it clean down there." He packed up his bag and put his coat on.

"That's it? You're not going to ... to stay and, well, maybe have a cup of tea or something?"

Anson looked at Kit as if she'd said something ridiculous, which, she realized, she had. "This wasn't a social call," he said. "Tell her ... tell her she'll be fine. That's all I can say." Then he donned his hat and left the room.

Kit heard a slight moan and saw that Bea was coming out of the anesthesia. *Don't be judge and jury*, she thought, understanding that her goals now were to be a good nurse and an even better friend. She set about accomplishing both.

# CHAPTER THIRTY-SIX

Melancholy can take many forms. Kit dealt with her own by staying active, while others become paralyzed by sadness. And some, it turned out, fit in a category all their own.

While Bea was recovering in seclusion from her "medical procedure," as she called it, Kit paid a visit to her old friend Cecily, who had moved back into her family home not long after the syphilis had entered its dormant stage. It was the price Cecily paid for choosing to remain apart from society.

Her mother, Hazel, always a frail woman, had doted on her, no doubt worried that she'd passed on her own weakness to her daughter. Apparently the stress was too much for the woman because Hazel suffered a fatal heart attack during the quake and the family was now in mourning. Cecily's father, Frank, answered the door dressed somberly and wearing a black crepe armband. He was a tall, thin, reserved man who seemed accustomed to a lack of joy in his life.

"It's very kind of you to call," he said to Kit, engulfing her hand in his. "Cecily has been more dispirited than usual, I'm afraid. Your visit is sure to cheer her up."

Kit found Cecily lying on a settee in an upstairs parlor that her friend had apparently taken over as her sanctuary. A tray laden with breakfast pastries looked untouched, as did the tea service next to a small stack of books on the adjacent table. Cecily was wearing a lacy bed jacket and her legs were covered with an intricately knitted afghan. The thought ran through Kit's mind that the loss of her friend's mother might have triggered a relapse of the syphilis. "Oh, Cecily, are you all right? Are you ... that is ..."

"No, no, nothing like that," Cecily assured her, swinging her legs off the couch and pushing the blanket away. "I'm so glad it's you and not another friend of the family come to weep over Mama."

"Oh, but—"

"No, I didn't mean to insult you. I know you are paying your respects, and I appreciate it. But you know what I mean. It's this damn playacting—it's driving me round the bend." She got up to pour Kit a cup of tea and offered her a hot cross bun. She seemed in perfect health.

"I'm afraid you're confounding me," Kit said.

Cecily sent her a crooked smile and sat down again. "I have dug my own grave." She looked heavenward. "Sorry, Mama."

Kit took a sip of the lukewarm tea and put it down. "From the beginning, please."

"It's just that in order to keep questions about the ... you know ... to a minimum, I latched on to the diagnosis of 'nervous disorder.' Mama suffered from it, felt perfectly at ease with it, as did Papa, who's been dealing with it for years and probably figured I'd inherited it. Well, the so-called cure for such a thing—not that it helped poor Mother any— really and truly is to do practically nothing. I mean it. *Nothing.* No stimulus of any kind. No exercise, no social activities, no creative outlets, and certainly no mental taxation." She pointed to the stack of books on the table. "I have to bribe Gladys, my maid, to get me reading material. Have you read 'The Yellow Wallpaper'?" She pulled out a slim volume and handed it to Kit. It contained a short story called "The Yellow Wallpaper" by Charlotte Perkins Gillman. Kit had read one of the author's essays about the economic plight of women years earlier.

"You have to read it," Cecily said. "The woman is in a situation like mine and it literally drives her insane."

Kit took the little book and put it in her reticule. "That seems so extreme."

"Yes, but those are Dr. Riggin's orders. And what can I say? 'Oh thank you, doctor, I'm cured now.' Because then my parents would expect me to be out and about again. As far as society knows, I'm still married to Easton, who has 'gone away to deal with family business.' It's his absence, along with the ... the death of Henny, that has ruined my nerves. It's even worse now that my mother has gone. While she's no doubt in a happier place, my father has transferred all his doting onto me. It's quite smothering, actually. I've become a prisoner of my own making."

*My God, what messes we get ourselves into.* "Speaking of Easton, have you heard anything about him?"

Cecily sat down again and leaned toward Kit. Her voice dropped in volume. "As a matter of fact, I have." She pulled a letter from her pocket and handed over. "He says ... he says he's had a change of heart and would like to come home. He swears he thanks God every day that I didn't divorce him, and that he would like to try it again, despite everything."

Kit scanned the letter. It seemed legitimate, but ... "Are you considering taking him back?" she asked, glancing up at Cecily.

Her friend leaned back with an air of exasperation. "I don't know. I feel as though I'm in limbo. To rid myself of him publicly is to risk connecting with someone else. I know that wouldn't be good for my body, and I fear it would be fatal to my heart. Yet as long as he is in the picture, even in name only, I have to pretend that I'm indisposed. If he were to return, we could at least put on a front for society's sake and go back to some degree of normalcy."

Kit tried to put herself in Cecily's place. "But what about ... about his proclivities. How could you stand by while he dallied elsewhere?"

"I wouldn't. That would not be part of the arrangement."

"Then ... what if he wants *you?*"

Cecily shrugged. "I have already been in touch with Dr. Landon about it. She says that since I am infected already, there's no harm in it. There is just ... just the possibility of harm to a child. But I will never let that happen again." She squared her jaw. "Never."

"Oh, Cecily, these are such difficult choices you have to make," Kit said, taking her hand. "I wish I knew the right advice to give."

Cecily pressed her hand. "Just having someone to talk to about it makes a big difference." Her eyes were moist with emotion. "Believe me."

True to form, Kit considered all possible remedies to the situation. None were readily apparent, but she did hit upon an idea that would relieve some of Cecily's boredom in the meantime. "I wonder if you might do me a favor," she said.

"What? I'd give anything to be useful for a change."

"I know you haven't spent much time with Bea Marshall since ... well, since we learned what we learned as children. Perhaps you feel uncomfortable knowing the heritage you share. But even though she's a bit flighty, she is a good person at heart, and, well, her family is going through some difficult times, plus my brother did recently marry another, and ..."

"And she's heartbroken about that?"

"I'm not sure I would use that term, but something like it," Kit hedged. She felt a bit underhanded by not divulging all she knew. Still, everyone had secrets, didn't they? Cecily certainly did. So did Kit. And it was up to friends to keep them when they could. "At any rate, she has been feeling poorly and I thought perhaps you and she might cheer one another up."

"By all means, ask her to call on me. Tell her I would

love the company." Cecily leaned forward again. "Truth be told, my father could use some company, too. Then perhaps he wouldn't hover over me as much. Do you know any eligible matrons who could use some distraction of their own?" The two women laughed at the jest and Kit left feeling slightly less blue than she had before she came.

When she returned home, however, those warm feelings vanished as she read the note waiting for her. It was from her father.

*Your mother collapsed this morning. She is very ill.*

# CHAPTER THIRTY-SEVEN

## Josephine

*So this is what it feels like to fly above the clouds. I like it.*

Josephine hovered between wakefulness and sleep, her limbs heavy, her eyes too weary to open. She felt warm and languid and happy, until voices intruded from a distance.

Familiar.

Who were they?

Someone was angry.

"Bright's disease."

How can a disease be bright?

"Incurable."

Who was ill? She would ask Edward. Was he there? He would know.

She would send flowers.

In just a little while,

After she ...

## Katherine

"Please, let me see to my mother's comfort and ... and necessities, and I'll join you shortly." Kit shooed her brother, father, and Dr. Gage out, knowing they'd assume she was handling female-related matters. Once she made sure her sleeping mother was clean and decent, she began her true mission, which was to check every shelf and every cupboard in the room to make sure Josephine wasn't hiding something from all of them. Was she taking pills or elixirs she shouldn't be? Kit wouldn't put it past her to think she knew how to treat herself better than a physician would.

She found nothing. Not even a bottle of acetylsalicylic acid powder.

Just to make sure, she checked every compartment in her mother's dresser. Again, nothing.

Finally, she went through the clothing in her mother's armoire, noticing an old hatbox at the bottom of the cabinet. It was faded and didn't match her mother's other storage boxes. Opening it, Kit found nothing medicinal in nature, but something odd nonetheless. It was an old-fashioned mourning hat with veil, and beneath it was a small red journal. She opened the little book and was shocked by what she read. Josephine? Her mother? Part of some ... some...

Her mother stirred, moaning slightly, and Kit quickly replaced the journal, closing the box and shutting the armoire. Whatever story the journal told would have to wait. For now, it was just a relief to know her mother hadn't used any quack remedies to inadvertently cause herself harm.

Kit checked on her mother once more before joining the men in the upstairs parlor.

Dr. Gage was in the midst of explaining Bright's disease. Her father and brother looked glum, and Kit began to pace the room while he spoke. When he finished, she shook her head.

"I do not accept your diagnosis," she announced.

"Now Kitty Kat—"

"Don't Kitty Kat me, Father. I'm no longer a little girl who needs to be protected. I'm a medical professional—"

"And as such, *Nurse* Firestone, you should know that of all the people in this room, I am the one with the most education and experience to be able to diagnose my patient based on her symptoms," Dr. Gage said.

She wanted to wipe that smug expression right off his face. "You haven't even given her a blood test! You haven't even—"

"I don't have to, I know her albumin levels will be high." Dr. Gage turned to Kit's father, who was obviously more receptive. "I'm sorry, Edward. Based on her visits to me over the past few years, all the signs point to advanced kidney disease."

"What can be done about it?" Her father sounded frantic.

"Very little, I'm afraid. It's more a case of treating the symptoms rather than the underlying disease.

Warm baths, diuretics, bloodletting when appropriate. Opium as the pain increases, mercuric compounds —"

"Wait a minute," Will said. "That all sounds pretty drastic."

"That's because it *is* drastic," Kit shot back. "No to the bloodletting – that's barbaric and serves no useful purpose. No to the diuretics, no to the opium and an *absolute* no to any treatment using mercuric compounds. Those ameliorants are treacherous—they're worse than the disease itself." Kit turned to her father. "There's only one thing Mother needs, and she needs it as soon as possible."

"What?" Edward cried. "What it is?"

Kit glared at Dr. Gage. "A second opinion."

---

Kit didn't wait until the next day to make an appointment. She didn't even call to see if she would be received. Close on the heels of Dr. Gage's departure, she took a cab to Dr. Alice Landon's home office in Presidio Heights. It was just past the dinner hour.

A tall, gentle-looking man dressed in a cotton shirt, trousers, and suspenders answered her knock. He looked to be in his forties. Standing just to the side of him was a young girl who must have been around fifteen. Kit remembered her from the photograph she'd noticed in Dr. Landon's office years earlier.

"May I help you?" the man asked.

"Mr. Landon? Hello. I'm sorry to bother you at such an hour. I know it's inconvenient, but I'm ... I'm a friend of your wife's and I really must speak to her this evening."

Such occurrences must have been common, because Mr. Landon opened the door wider and motioned Kit inside. "My wife is working in her lab. Please come in."

Sure enough, Alice Landon was sitting at the long table Kit had noticed during their last visit. She was peering through a microscope and paused to write something in a notebook.

"Darling, you have a visitor."

"Miss Firestone!" Alice rose and held out her hand. "How nice to see you. Come in."

Kit glanced at Mr. Landon, who smiled and backed out of the room. "I'll leave you ladies to it."

Alice grew serious. "This isn't about your friend, is it? She hasn't—"

"No, Cecily is fine. She has appreciated all your counsel by the way."

"That's good to hear."

Now that she was there, Kit felt strangely reluctant to explain the reason for her intrusion. It was as if stating her mother's illness out loud would make it a reality. To postpone the moment, she walked over to Alice's work table. "What are you working on?"

The doctor broke into a smile. "Oh, it's the most marvelous thing! Do you remember when you first came to see me and I told you that there was no cure for syphilis? Well, there still is no cure, but two years ago researchers in Germany isolated *Treponema pallidum*, the nasty little bacteria that causes the disease. And earlier this year, Dr. Wasserman created a complement fixation test to check for the presence of antibodies."

"A blood test?"

"Yes, which means that now patients can be tested early, even before there are signs of the disease, to make sure they don't pass it on."

Kit was fairly confident that she'd contracted nothing with Easton Challis, and the few times she'd been with Tom, he'd worn protection. Still, it would good to finally *know*. Their eyes locked. "Would it be possible for me to take the test?"

"Yes, it would." To smooth over the awkwardness, Alice added, "And it's useful for detecting the presence of other illnesses as well, such as malaria and tuberculosis. But that's just the beginning."

Kit had to smile at the physician's enthusiasm. "What? There's more?"

Alice laughed. "Yes, especially when it comes to my practice. It has always frustrated me that one in a hundred women die in childbirth, many due to obstetric hemorrhage."

"They bleed to death," Kit said.

"That's right. Cecily said you had become a nurse. Good for you! Then you're no doubt familiar with many cases where blood was desperately needed but couldn't be provided because of the risk of rejection."

Kit did indeed know about it, assailed by memories of cases in which surgical patients desperately needed blood but couldn't get it. In some cases, the bleeding could be stopped internally with quick and accurate suturing techniques—Kit had seen Tom perform those procedures several times. But there were other times when a patient wasn't so lucky and died from excessive blood loss. "Yes, I'm aware."

"Well, all that is changing because researchers have discovered a way to identify each person's blood so that those with compatible blood types can share it. Imagine that!"

Kit shuddered at the thought; it reminded her of the bloodletting that Dr. Gage had suggested for her mother. "Do you really think people will want to do that? It reminds me of that book a few years' back. *Dracula*, I think it was called."

"We can only hope they see the positive sides of it, because it truly will change everything." Alice knelt down and poked the embers in the fireplace before adding a log. Then she gestured to a chair. "I know you didn't come here at this hour to ask about my research. Why don't you tell me what's going on?"

Kit took a breath. Time to face it. "Dr. Gage has just given my mother a death sentence. He says she has Bright's disease and that there's nothing to be done about it. My father is devastated. He can't lose my mother." Kit could barely continue past the lump in her throat. "*I* can't lose my mother. We don't always see eye to eye, but she ... she is too young for this to happen. I won't let this happen, and I need your help."

Alice stared into the fire for a moment. "Bright's disease is quite serious. How are her albumin levels?"

"He hasn't checked her blood but is confident the levels will confirm his diagnosis."

"Tell me, what other symptoms? I mean, what led him to specifically determine it was Bright's?"

"She has some edema, and often complains of thirst. Even though she eats quite a bit, she seems to have lost some weight. But the most telling symptom is her lack of energy. My mother is normally a whirlwind who puts the rest of us to shame. But yesterday she actually fainted and has felt weak ever since."

Alice reached over and took Kit's hand. "You know I can't promise you anything. Kidney disease is not my specialty. But your mother's symptoms suggest perhaps something else is going on."

Kit perked up. "What? You mean something other than Bright's disease?" Oh, she would be so delighted to prove Dr. Gage wrong.

"No, but possibly in tandem with it. We'll just have to see. If you like, I will run some tests, examine your mother, and we'll take it from there, all right?"

Kit swallowed her disappointment. The most important thing to have was knowledge, no matter where it led. "When can I bring her in?"

"It just so happens I have a one o'clock appointment tomorrow with your mother's name on it."

## Josephine

"There is nothing wrong with me."

Josephine sat serenely on the sofa in the upstairs parlor with a brightly colored afghan covering her lap, sipping her tea and trying to mask the anxiety that coursed throughout her body. She had been feeling out of sorts for some time, and then to have fainted—*that* had her worried. But that didn't mean the rest of her family needed to be.

Edward and Will sat nearby looking like death warmed over, and Kit paced the room like a jungle cat, her skirts swishing every time she made a turn.

"Josephine, darling, please. You know that's not true," Edward said, leaning forward in his earnestness.

She hated to see her husband in any kind of pain, especially if she had caused it. "I know nothing of the sort," she shot back. "It's ... it's just a touch of flu, that's all, it's—"

"Mother, Dr. Gage told us you've been seeing him off and on for some time," Will chimed in. "He said your symptoms all point to kidney disease. He has—"

"He has a big mouth, is what Dr. Gage has. I'm telling you—"

"Mother, will you please *stop*?!" Kit's voice fairly shook the rafters. "Stop pretending that nothing is wrong, and you—" She pointed a finger at her father —"*You* stop acting as though she's at death's door. We are going to get to the bottom of this, starting today."

"Today?" Will asked.

"Yes, today. I made an appointment with Dr. Landon at one o'clock."

"Do you mean Alice Lan?—" Josephine caught herself, but not in time.

Kit narrowed her eyes. "How do you know Alice Landon?"

Josephine squirmed. "Oh, well, it's been quite a few years now, but—" Kit held up her hand; by her expression, Josephine could tell she'd figured it out.

"You're right about one thing: Dr. Gage does have a big mouth. Regardless, at least you know that Dr. Landon is wise and reasoned and will give you an honest, thoughtful opinion."

"Well, perhaps I'll think about it."

"Not good enough." Kit leaned over and put her face right next to Josephine's. "Not good enough. You. Are. Going. I am taking you. And that's final."

*When did you turn into such a harridan?* Josephine thought as she matched eyes with her daughter. And in that moment she was struck by the truth. Kit wasn't so much a harridan as she was a warrior. And a warrior, Josephine realized, was just what she needed.

She swallowed. Tilted her chin up. "Well. If it will make you feel better," she said. "I suppose it will be all right."

### Katherine

"The results are mixed," Alice Landon said to Kit and her mother, who were once again seated in her office. Kit was beside herself with anticipation. Three days earlier the physician had taken blood and urine samples from Josephine, given her mother a physical examination, and listened as Josephine recounted, at

Kit's insistence, the various health issues she'd been dealing with over the past few years.

"Let's have the bad news first," Kit said. She felt rather than saw her mother stiffen and reached for her hand. *We will get through this together*, she vowed silently.

Alice looked to Josephine, who nodded. "All right, then. The albumin level in your blood is high; Dr. Gage was correct about that. Then there's your slightly elevated blood pressure and your edema."

"Both of which I had through all three of my pregnancies," Josephine muttered.

Kit rolled her eyes. "Well, unless you and Father have some unusual news to share with us, we can't attribute your symptoms to that."

"She's right," Dr. Landon said. "In the absence of other factors, those are clear signs of kidney impairment. But something else is going on that involves your pancreas, I'm afraid."

Oh no. Kit had covered it in nursing school. "Diabetes." *Not good.*

"That's right." Alice got up and pointed to a large poster next to her desk, showing a life-size female body from the inside out. The illustration showed all of the internal organs as well as muscles and the circulatory system. "Think of it this way: your cells, the building blocks of your body, need food, which they get in the form of a type of sugar called 'glucose.'"

"I certainly know about food," Josephine murmured.

Alice smiled. "Then you know how important it is

that the food is prepared properly. Your pancreas makes a hormone called insulin that helps prep the glucose so that it can be absorbed by the cells. When the pancreas isn't working properly, the glucose builds up in the bloodstream, which causes fluid to be pulled from your tissues. You need to replace it—"

"By drinking! That's why I've been so thirsty all the time."

"Exactly. And when there isn't enough sugar feeding your cells, every part of your body starts to lose energy, which is why you're always hungry as well as tired. Your body keeps trying to feed itself, but the nutrients aren't getting where they need to go."

"So what does this have to do with my mother's kidneys and the high albumin levels?"

"It's all connected, which in some ways is a good thing."

Kit's mother looked lost and wasn't afraid to admit it. "First you tell me I have two diseases, not one, and now you tell me that's a good thing? I'm afraid I don't follow."

Alice pointed to the kidneys on the poster. "All right. When your insulin is compromised and you have too much glucose in your blood, it begins to erode some of your smaller blood vessels, like those in your feet—you mentioned a tingling sensation, correct?"

Josephine nodded. "Like little pins and needles."

"Well, the same thing happens in your kidneys, whose job it is, among other things, to process protein. Albumin is a protein, and when your kidneys can't deal with it, it ends up in your bloodstream along with the sugar, and that's why we can test for it."

Kit hadn't heard of that. "So you can test for both albumin and sugar through the blood now?"

"Albumin, yes, but blood glucose tests are still too cumbersome. So we have to rely on a centuries-old technique to test for excess sugar." She looked at Josephine. "Any idea what that is?"

Kit wrinkled her nose; she knew all too well.

Josephine shook her head. "I have no idea."

"Well, how would you test a fine wine?"

It took Josephine a moment, then her eyes grew wide. "You're joking."

"No ma'am. The urine of a diabetic tastes quite sweet."

"That's repellant!"

"But effective."

Kit was growing tired of theory; she wanted to take action. "So how do we go about curing these various problems?"

Alice sat down again and picked up the medical journal on her desk. "There is no commonly accepted cure for diabetes or the kidney damage that may stem from it."

Kit felt an enormous loss of energy, as if this had all been nothing more than a mental exercise. "Then Dr. Gage was right after all." She gazed at her mother, who was sitting stoically, keeping whatever feelings she had to herself.

"Dr. Gage is of the old school, which rarely connects kidney disease with diabetes. But in your case, I truly believe the two are linked. And I say that's a good thing because if you can alter the course of your diabetes, then you can possibly improve the state of your kidneys." She handed the journal to Josephine. A page had been marked.

"I told you there was no common cure. But that article, written by a dietician, tells the story of a German educator by the name of Arnold Ehret, who at the age of thirty-one was diagnosed with Bright's disease. No fewer than twenty-four doctors pronounced him incurable. But he wouldn't accept the diagnosis and set about finding a cure on his own. And guess what? He did! He made an amazing recovery. His theory is that illness in the body stems from too much mucus. It's an unsavory approach, to be sure, but still…"

Kit heard only one word. "He found a cure?"

"Well, if not a cure, then a way to control his condition. He believed in cleansing the body and restocking it with what he considered healthy foods. I think you'll find it fascinating, Mrs. Firestone."

Kit's mother turned to the flagged page and began reading it. After a moment she looked up, her eyebrows raised. "What? Fasting for days on end? Living on nothing but fruits and vegetables? That is sacrilege!" She tossed the magazine back on the table, but Kit picked it up immediately.

It was a lifeline.

Moments later Kit and her mother said their goodbyes, promising to check in with Dr. Landon in a week's time. They were settling into the Winton, ready to have the family chauffeur take them home, when Alice ran up and tapped on the window.

"I forgot to thank you both for having your blood identified and added to my list," she said. "I am trying to determine if there is any special nature to the blood of the females in this area, if there are more O's—like you, Mrs. Firestone—or AB's or what-not, and I need as many samples as possible." She reached into the pocket of her apron and handed a folded note to Kit. "And here's the answer to the question you posed some time ago," she added.

Kit slipped the note into her reticule and held up the journal. "Are you sure this story is legitimate? This Professor Ehret really did recover?"

Alice sent her a knowing smile. "He really did. I told you there is always hope."

---

They'd barely left the Landon residence when Josephine said, "I didn't notice you giving a blood sample to Dr. Landon. When did you do that?"

*Of course she would pick up on that.* "Ah, I did so when I first went to see her about you. She was so enthusiastic about her research project that I ... I thought I might help her out."

"I see." Josephine looked out the window for few moments before turning back. "It's impossible, you know."

"What's impossible?"

"This notion of being able to turn this all around

through diet and, God forbid, exercise. I can't do it. Bertrand would never stand for it, and neither would Edward. I simply won't do it."

Kit said nothing, knowing her mother wanted to fight about it, wanted to throw up any roadblocks she could imagine. It reminded Kit of when she'd first met Tom, and how she'd fought against her feelings for so very long. And why had she done that? Out of fear, plain and simple. Fear that he would cause her to lose control of her emotions, fear that she'd make the same mistake she'd made with Easton Challis.

She thought of the note in her reticule and hoped its contents would put her deepest fears to rest at last.

There it was again, fear. Perhaps her mother was feeling it, too. Fear that she was losing control, that she would have to try something completely different from what she was used to. Fear that she wouldn't be able to do it. Fear that even if she did every possible thing right, it still might not work.

Kit watched her mother's profile and saw the hint of a tear on her cheek. Quietly Josephine took out a dainty handkerchief and discreetly wiped it away. "Such dust still on the roadway," she murmured.

Kit held on to the journal she'd taken. *I will make this happen for you*, she vowed, *whether you want it or not*. And she spent the rest of the drive deep in thought.

## CHAPTER THIRTY-EIGHT

Kit decided to move back into her parents' home until her mother fully recovered from what Josephine was now calling "the little incident." Kit's father was grateful beyond measure, and it was partly for his sake that she'd suggested a temporary stay. A strong man in many ways, Edward was a puddle when it came to his beloved wife.

After her shift at the hospital each day, Kit searched for more information about Professor Ehret and his unlikely but apparently effective "cure." Fasting, she learned, was an ancient practice followed by every major religion. There were several ways to do it, and she looked for methods that wouldn't harm a person as petite as her mother.

Food—the right kind—was key to Ehret's success, which meant that Bertrand, the family chef, would have to be part of any solution. Before approaching him, however, she learned as much as she could about the pros and cons of what they currently ate. She almost wished she hadn't. It was disconcerting to know, for example, that a delicious steak, perfectly seasoned and grilled, could produce much of the dreaded "mucus" Ehret felt was so detrimental to one's health.

To keep focused, Kit's mantra became "He recovered." She repeated it often as she drew up two lists: one containing the foods that should be avoided at all costs, and one containing the foods that had turned a sickly young man into a pillar of health.

"Mother is not going to be happy about this," she muttered as the list of foods to eliminate grew. Gone were those luscious steaks along with all other red meat. Gone were the butter, milk, sugar, and eggs that made up so many of Bertrand's finest creations. Gone were alcohol, caffeine, and all teas besides herbal brews. Gone were fried foods and corn and wheat and even the innocuous little jams and jellies that made a piece of toast worth eating.

The list of acceptable foods, primarily fruits and vegetables, with limited amounts of fish and chicken, was much less inviting.

Ever a planner, Kit had mulled over several courses of action while gathering her facts. She decided upon one rather outlandish scheme that involved both Bertrand and Will. One afternoon she caught her brother as he was leaving his office and presented the plan to him over coffee. He was skeptical, but more than willing to participate.

"Our mother invented the word 'stubborn,'" he

warned.

"She did, which is why we have to resort to such extremes."

"Well, you have my full complicity. Good luck."

Bertrand, she knew, would be a more difficult sell. While her mother was napping one Sunday, she found the portly chef in his domain, putting the finishing touches on a perfectly lovely peach tart. She knew from experience that it would taste even more luscious than it looked.

"May I be of assistance, mademoiselle?" he asked.

"I hope so, Bertrand. My mother desperately needs your help."

As she explained the basics of her mother's illness, the possible cure for it, and the role he could play, Bertrand grew more and more morose. "I had no idea that the foods I prepared would be *tellement dangereuses*."

Kit reached for him. "No, no, no, Bertrand. It's certainly not your fault! You have kept us healthy and happy all these years, and now is your chance to do so with the one person you love best."

She handed him the lists, which he perused, shaking his head and mumbling "*Sacre bleu!*" several times. *He can't do it*, she thought with disappointment. *It's too much*.

Finally, the chef looked up at Kit and spoke. "You have just offered me the greatest challenge of my career. I accept."

## Josephine

*I cannot believe this is anything more than a stubborn cold. How can I be so sick? It's unacceptable.*

Josephine sat once more on the sofa in her upstairs parlor drinking tea. She'd wanted to read the journal article Dr. Landon had given her, but Kit had apparently absconded with it.

Her condition reminded her eerily of her own mother. Marrielle had improved slightly over the years, it's true. She hadn't rushed into marriage again after Uncle Whitford's death and had learned to run her household and take care of Josephine's half-brothers tolerably well. But once they'd moved out and started families of their own, she regressed to her complacent, passive state. She had not watched her eating habits, nor had she deigned to move much. As a result, she fell prey to the same malady her second husband had and died from apoplexy when she was but sixty-four years old. Josephine did not want to follow in those footsteps.

She considered what she could do about her situation: drink more water, rest more, eat a few more vegetables, perhaps walk the grounds more often. But would it be enough? Will had announced that he and Mandy were already expecting. She had every intention of seeing that child grow up, as well as any others who might follow. She would do whatever it took to make that happen, if only she could be sure it would work.

She was pondering how her chef would take to

making a few changes in his menu when the subject of her thoughts appeared in the doorway.

"*Excusez-moi*, madam. May I enter?"

"Of course, Bertrand." She pulled the afghan away, intending to rise. "Is anything wrong? Should I—"

He stayed her with his hand. "No, madam. I have come to discuss a very important matter with you." He paused, fidgeting with his apron.

Bertrand was normally a man of few words, unless it came to food. She waited for a moment, then prompted, "Well?"

"I ... I have come to tender my resignation," he said. "I have been given an excellent opportunity to challenge my creativity and I want to take it."

Josephine was incensed. "What? Who would do such a thing as to steal you from me? Everyone knows you are irreplaceable. Well, I won't allow it. You belong to me."

Bertrand's eyes bespoke a deep sadness. "No, madam, I do not. And ... well, this is quite important to me."

"Who is this thief, may I ask?"

More fidgeting. "It's ... your son. He has decided that he and his wife wish to lead a healthier life, and he wishes to improve his palate with an entirely new approach. I find the notion intrigues me, very much."

Josephine stared at her chef and watched him nearly tremble from her scrutiny. "Might this new palate include fewer fatty foods and many more fruits and vegetables?"

Bertrand swallowed. "*Oui*." He patted his stomach.

"*Du reste, je suis trop gros.*"

"That is silly. You are not too fat." She continued to gaze at him as the tumblers clicked into place. "Have you been talking to Katherine about this, per chance?"

Shrugging, Bertrand gave no other answer. He really was a terrible dissembler, which was one of the things she loved about him.

It was clear to her now what was going on. She could call their bluffs, of course, but what would be the purpose of that? Bertrand really would leave—she could tell he was desperate to help her, which meant, if she *wouldn't* accept his help, he would probably not want to be around to see her decline.

She thought of the energy being put forth by Kit and Will and Bertrand and no doubt Edward—how they were all doing their best to help her get better. The love she felt for all of them rose up in a tidal wave of joy. It humbled her, and it reminded her of who she was. She knew then what she must do.

"Tell me, if I paid you more, would you consider staying on and creating your fancy new cuisine here, for us? Far be it from me to stifle your creativity."

His eyes lit up. "Oh, madam, I do not need a raise. I —" He stopped, no doubt seeing the gleam in her eye.

*Yes, I see right through you*, she thought. *And I love you for it. If you are willing to fight so hard for me, then so am I.*

"I have already begun to experiment, madam. Would you care to see? I could use your expert advice."

"I would be delighted." She rose and took his arm, and together the two friends went downstairs to one of her three most favorite places in all the world.

## CHAPTER THIRTY-NINE

*How is it possible to be both elated and sad at the same time?* Kit pondered that conundrum as she rode the taxi to her parents' estate. She'd been back at her own apartment for some time now and her mother had invited her over for a small supper to showcase Bertrand's "revolutionary" cuisine. Kit was beyond thrilled that Josephine and her chef had embraced the new dietary guidelines. They weren't quite as draconian as Arnold Ehret's, but they reflected a much greater understanding of how different types of food impact the body than Josephine's diet had before.

"She's feeling much better," Kit's father had reported. More comfortable with numbers, he was also pleased to share that his wife's albumin levels had begun to drop. "She and I traverse the grounds every afternoon as well," he said proudly. "Sometimes I must jog to keep up with her."

She should have known that moss never grew

beneath her mother's feet. As refugees found other housing and eventually left the impromptu Firestone Camp, Josephine had lost no time—even beset by illness— in having the estate buildings fully repaired. Now their residence was once again a hub of activity for the city's power brokers. Over cocktails and Chef Bertrand's "new and improved" cuisine, more deals were being struck to rebuild banks, investment houses, hotels, department stores, and hospitals, along with the civic infrastructure needed to make the Golden City more desirable than ever.

When Kit arrived at her parents' home, she began to question the "small supper" her mother had advertised. It was small in terms of attendees, perhaps, but not in terms of consequence. One of the guests was a young attorney named Jonathan Perris. Single and "quite manly" (to hear her mother tell it), he'd come highly recommended from London and had recently been hired by the "Committee of Fifty" to help with legal matters. As much as her mother approved of Tom Justice, it was obviously a case of "out of sight, out of mind."

"Jonathan's an exceptional young man, quite intelligent and thoroughly charming," Josephine gushed moments before the new suitor arrived. "And he seems to have a moral backbone as well. Why, during a rather contentious meeting with Bill Bunker from the Chamber of Commerce, Jonathan spoke adamantly against moving the Chinese out of the city. 'They've earned the right to rebuild where they are along with everybody else,' he said. He even pointed out that over time they would provide an economic draw for the city. Your father was quite impressed."

*Some things never change,* Kit thought, *and my mother's penchant for matchmaking is one of them.*

As the evening progressed, she had to admit that Jonathan Perris exhibited all of the virtues Josephine had lauded, and more. Such a pity that her passions lay elsewhere. Instead of being fully engaged with her dinner companion, Kit was ruminating on the fact that Tom would have understood the science behind Josephine's new dietary regimen. She missed being able to share this little victory with him. It had been nearly four months and she longed for him more than ever.

What's worse, she was losing her ability to mask her emotions. Remembering how she'd treated Tom the first time they'd met, Kit had vowed to no longer hide behind an acerbic tongue, especially with those, like Jonathan, who didn't deserve it. Yet she couldn't quite summon the effervescence she'd wanted. During the salad course Jonathan leaned over and murmured, "Miss Firestone, you look like a woman who hasn't quite reached her happy ending and is perplexed as to how to achieve it."

Kit's shocked reaction had him chuckling. "A decent attorney must have at least some skill in the art of intuition," he said. "Besides, I know a kindred spirit when I see one. I too suffer from a bout of unrequited love. Alas, in my case the young lady has gone to the far ends of the earth, vowing never to return."

Kit looked into Jonathan's eyes and saw a kind of poignant resignation, an acceptance that this particular happily ever after was beyond his grasp. Tears unexpectedly welled up. She liked this man. He could be a good friend.

"You are far too perceptive, Mr. Perris," she said lightly, dabbing her eyes discreetly with her napkin. "I would hate to have to hide my true motives in a criminal matter. I'll wager you can establish the guilt or innocence of your clients in your first interview."

"Which is why, after representing criminal defendants for a decade, I have recently branched out to contract law. Too many guilty souls expected me to secure them an acquittal, which indeed was my role."

"That must have been difficult," she said, all levity gone. "I imagine one would begin to lose faith in the viability of the justice system."

"I couldn't have said it better." He took a sip of his wine. "Those were trying times, for me, at least. No pun intended."

As the rest of the evening floated by on a cloud of easy conversation, Kit had to admire her mother's own considerable powers of intuition. At the end of the soiree, Jonathan asked if Kit would like to have lunch in the near future.

"It will appease your matchmaking mama, perhaps giving you some relief on that front, and I must confess that even after one evening, I sense that you are a person with whom one may share matters of the heart with impunity."

Kit smiled and held out her hand. "I feel the same about you, Mr. Perris. I would be delighted to further our acquaintance."

Thus Kit made a new friend, and over the next several weeks she discovered that Jonathan (they had quickly dispensed with surnames when in private) possessed a quick wit, a sharp intellect, and a kind heart. In those aspects, if not others, he reminded her of Tom.

---

As life in the Golden City began to normalize, so did Kit's routine. She now worked full-time at the Maudsley Sanitarium on Pine Street, which the owners of St. Mary's had converted into a temporary hospital. More than once she endured jests along the lines of "What lunatic did you restrain today?" to which she invariably replied, "The one you saw in the mirror this morning."

As a Firestone, even a working Firestone, she continued to socialize, although many of her lifelong friends had taken distinctly different paths.

Her old acolyte Ellen, for instance, was now married to a real estate developer and was the mother of two. They met for lunch at their favorite place on the Wharf, Castello's, and she enjoyed a spicy *spaghetti al pomodoro* while Ellen pontificated about the best dress designers and shoemakers and where they'd relocated after the quake. Apparently, her husband insisted she always look top-notch.

"You can't imagine how much more difficult it is now to have a ball gown made on short notice," her friend complained. "And finding the right color of periwinkle? Impossible."

Toward the end of the conversation, Ellen actually brought up Kit's nursing position and asked if she'd met anyone special. When Kit replied that she hadn't, Ellen was effusive in her sympathy—tinged, Kit thought, with a bit of satisfaction that the once-vaunted Katherine Firestone was undeniably one of the last spinsters in their group.

Kit's visit with Cecily was more rewarding, yet more disturbing at the same time. On one of her days off she dropped by to enjoy afternoon tea. They had just settled themselves at a table in the Anders' garden when Cecily imparted some startling news. Easton had returned, not only to Cecily's father's bank, but to the residence, and more importantly, to her bed.

"He's promised not to stray," Cecily said, handing Kit a cup.

Kit couldn't hide her shock. "Do you really believe that?"

"Not entirely, but I am encouraged by the fact that by his own admission he's become persona non grata in the city's demimonde." Cecily shrugged. "He can do me no more harm physically, and when we are without symptoms, marital relations can be quite pleasurable." She sighed over her cup of Darjeeling. "For now, the titter is all about 'poor Mrs. Challis, who can no longer have children,' a rumor we ourselves have circulated. Soon enough, when one or both of us begins to deteriorate, the gossip will erode as well."

"But that may never happen." Kit tried to sound positive. "One or both of you could escape the worst outcome. You could."

"I doubt it. It's unlikely that both of us will be spared. In fact, I think one of Easton's prime motivations for returning is not wanting to be alone when it happens. I don't blame him." Cecily paused before sending Kit a look of sad resignation. "In the end, this may be the way God meant for things to turn out. I don't come from the holiest of unions, as you recall."

"Nonsense," Kit said, but left it at that. As she had so many times before, she thanked her good fortune for not being forced to walk down Cecily's path. The note Dr. Landon had slipped to her after the appointment with her mother did indeed state that she had no trace of *Treponema pallidum* in her blood. But there were those who'd consider Kit's predicament almost as bad as that of her friends. To remain alone and unloved, her only solace found in changing bed-pans and cleaning up patients' vomit? She shuddered at the prospect and tried to lighten the mood. "So, will you two be residing here permanently with your father? It's such a large house, it seems as though there's plenty of room."

"Gracious, no. I suppose you haven't heard yet, but Father, for all his devotion to my mother, has scandalously decided to remarry. Two ladies of the house will make this place, cavernous though it is, a bit too crowded."

"Who's the fortunate lady?"

Cecily smiled gamely. "Why, Bea Marshall, of course. She's been sharing my father's bed for weeks now. He calls her 'my beautiful Beatrice.' He's head over heels."

"What?!"

"You heard right. Bea and I became close, and then she and my father became even closer. At one point she even confided that my father was a 'most insatiable lover' and that she thinks she might already be pregnant, which is why the nuptials have been moved up to the end of this month. She was giddy when she told me all this, so I take her at her word that she is happy. More to the point, she makes my father happy, which means he is much less worried about me. Do you know something? I don't think Bea even remembers that we are half-sisters and I am certainly not going to remind her. What would be the point? We do get along well; I just wish she would keep certain details to herself. I really do not need to know that my father has a fondness for large breasts."

Cecily chuckled selfconsciously and Kit joined in, if only to give herself a moment to take it all in. Bea? With a man almost thirty years her senior? But why should she be shocked? Like Cecily, Bea was doing what she had to do to survive, to find a modicum of happiness. Shouldn't everyone be looking for that? Shouldn't she?

Instead she was waiting. For what, she didn't know.

---

It was five o'clock on a Monday afternoon in mid-December, beyond dusk, when Kit left Maudsley's for home. She'd been chatting with a co-worker, Dale Bettis, when Tang Lin stepped out from the shadow of the building. He ignored the man standing next to her.

"I need to speak with you," Tang Lin said.

Misreading the situation, her colleague came to what he assumed was her rescue. "Wait just a minute. You can't—"

Kit put her hand on Dale's arm. "It's quite all right, Dr. Bettis. Tang Lin is a ... a childhood friend of mine."

The two men glared at each other.

"You're sure," Dr. Bettis said, his eyes on the Chinaman, as if that alone would hold him in check.

"I'm sure," Kit said, and purposefully slipped her arm through Tang Lin's. She addressed her new escort. "It's so good to see you. Shall we go?"

As they walked away, Tang Lin couldn't help but snort. "The man's expression—so protective and fierce. I feel as though a hole is being burned into my back."

Kit laughed lightly. "If he knew who you were, I think he'd be singing a different tune. Slightly more circumspect, at least." When they had walked halfway down the block, she stopped briefly to study him. He was as handsome as ever, but still mysterious and somewhat forbidding. His limp, she noticed, was ever so slight.

"To what do I owe the honor?" she asked.

"I wanted to deliver a message to you, so I asked your brother where you worked and he gave me your direction."

Kit nodded as they resumed their stroll. "How is my dear brother holding up?"

"Not well, I'm afraid." Tang Lin chuckled. "He is on the very edge of composure as he waits for Mandy to tell him to call the midwife. He is bursting to do something, but knows it is completely out of his hands."

"That's Will, all right. I have a feeling he'll be going through this a lot in the next few years."

"I hope so. He is an honorable man and should have many children to carry on his name."

The idea of children invariably brought up memories of Tom, which Kit tried to keep at bay. She had begun to realize it was folly to keep pining away for a man who apparently did not want her.

"Why have you come to see me?" she asked.

"I need to reach your friend, Tom Justice."

Kit felt her heart speeding up. "I'm afraid I can't help you there. Tom left the city months ago."

"I know he left the city. I helped him do it. Although why he would want to leave town when he has the love of a woman like you is beyond understanding."

They stared at each other for several moments, a thread of the finest silk between them, communicating what might have been between them in another time and place.

Kit broke the spell. "Why must you find him?"

"To warn him."

"Warn him? About what?"

"There has been an inquiry into what happened after the earthquake and fire last April. Everything from how the victims were evacuated to how the fire was fought. Fingers are starting to point. Scapegoats are being sought. Something known as "The Pavilion Protocol" is being whispered about and Dr. Tom's name has been included in the chatter. Apparently, a doctor has come forward and accused him of improper conduct, of taking matters into his own hands."

"What? What is this 'protocol'?"

"I'm not certain myself, but some are saying it involves willful murder."

"You've got to be joking."

"I wish I were. My sources tell me that funds are about to be expended to find certain individuals who were there that day. It does not look good that Dr. Tom has left the Golden City. I wanted to check with you before tracking him down."

"No! You can't do that. I mean, I promised him I would not use any resources to have him followed."

"It would not be you, it would be me looking for him."

"Still, he would believe I had a hand in it." They had come to a small park and Kit gestured for Tang Lin to sit with her on a nearby bench. Images of that horrifying day assaulted her. Tom, acting strangely. Clamming up. What if? ... No. Impossible. Her thoughts coalesced around one: She had promised not to send anyone to spy on Tom, but she hadn't said *she* wouldn't follow him.

At once it became clear: Tom Justice needed to know what was happening here in the city. She would find him and let him know he must address whatever fraudulent charges were being cooked up against him. He hadn't done anything wrong and if his presence would clarify matters, so much the better. And, once they saw each other, she would know—using some of that intuition she and Jonathan Perris had talked about

—whether he truly wanted to be part of her life. She was ready to accept whatever interest he might show, even if that meant there was no interest left.

She turned to Tang Lin. "I will find him and bring him back. You said you helped him leave. Tell me what you know."

**CHAPTER FORTY**

Tang Lin knew only that Tom had gone to see a doctor in Oakland who specialized in nervous disorders. Kit had her brother use his contacts to determine that the doctor in question was Wendell Sussman, a good friend, it turned out, of Colonel Aldrich at the Presidio. In the manner of wealthy, connected families everywhere, Will prevailed upon the colonel to ask his friend Wendell "off the record" about the referral he'd sent to him back in April, the doctor named Tom Justice.

The answer came back within a day: Yes, Dr. Justice had come to see him, and Dr. Sussman could find no physiological reason for the man's tremor. Suspecting he suffered from neurasthenia, he'd put Dr. Justice in touch with William Muldoon of the Muldoon Hygienic Institute of New York. That was the last he'd heard.

Upon hearing Will's report, Kit put in a call to the Institute, only to be informed by a woman that "neither Professor Muldoon nor members of the Institute comment on inquiries about gentlemen who may or may not be clients of the establishment." Kit then asked in her most imperious voice to speak to Mr. Muldoon himself, but the woman, apparently used to such high-handedness, refused to surrender the gate. "I'm sorry, but I have no more information for you, ma'am," she said, and severed their connection.

Undaunted, Kit immediately booked a ticket for one of the first-class sleeper cars on Saturday's Overland Limited, leaving San Francisco for New York. She'd asked for time off "to visit a dear friend back east," and because of her stellar work record, she'd been given permission along with a promise that her position would be held for her return.

She spent the night with her parents, who offered to take her to the station the following day. She told them she'd been invited to visit Lia's sister, Emma, in New York, leaving out the real reason for her journey. It was a partial truth. Three years before, Kit had invited herself and Mandy to Emma's home for Thanksgiving, mainly to avoid her mother's hurtful indifference toward her ward. How much had changed since then! This time she was on a more proactive mission. Fortunately, Emma was delighted to have her visit under any circumstances.

Surprisingly, Josephine hadn't put up any kind of fuss, even knowing that her daughter might not be back in time for Christmas. She was no doubt consumed with regaining her strength and getting ready for her first-ever grandchild.

"Give our love to the family," Josephine said as she and Kit's father said their goodbyes.

Now settled in her private compartment, Kit gazed out at the rapidly receding California foothills and wondered just what lay in store for her. The thought of seeing Tom again filled her with a sharp sense of both anticipation and dread. She'd been traveling on the same train when she'd met him three years earlier and had treated him abominably. This time she was chasing after him. How would he react when he saw her? She was prepared for anger, even ambivalence; as usual, it was the not knowing that set her heart beating rapidly against her chest.

---

Snow had been falling for nearly an hour when Kit's New York taxi turned at last through the gate of the rural property known as "The Olympia." Kit pulled her coat more closely around her and wished she'd brought a fur muff and woolen hat. "What was I thinking?" she murmured.

"What's that, ma'am?" the driver called over his shoulder. "Are you warm enough back there?"

"It's nothing, really. I'm fine. Just anxious to be there."

"Well, you cut it just about as close as you could. The season's over at the farm and the Professor—that's Mr. Muldoon—always closes her up right around Christmas. A few more days and you'd probably have missed him."

Minutes later they pulled up in front of an impressive mansion designed to resemble a country lodge. "I really don't plan to stay long, so if you wouldn't mind waiting?"

The driver checked the sky and Kit followed his gaze; the snow showed no signs of letting up.

"Well, not too long, ma'am. Don't want to get stuck out here."

"I understand; I'll be brief."

The young woman who answered the door was trim and pretty but buttoned-up. She looked wary and not at all accommodating. "May I help you?" Her tone implied she would prefer not to.

"I am here to see Dr. Tom Justice," Kit announced. "I'm a friend of his and I understand he was a guest here. I have an important message to give to him."

Kit waited patiently; she could practically see the wheels turning in the woman's head. "You're the person who called several days ago," she guessed. "You must really want to see him." She perused Kit a bit longer, but her loyalty and training prevailed. She did throw Kit a bone, however. "I'm sorry. Dr. Justice was a member of our staff but is no longer employed by the Institute. He's been gone for several weeks now."

Kit paused to absorb the punch of disappointment and the flare of unease. "I see. Well, can you tell me where I might find him now?"

"I ... I'm not at liberty to ..." The woman stopped and looked over Kit's shoulder, where a robust, middle-aged man dressed in a white overcoat was striding up with a panting St. Bernard in tow. Handing the dog over to the young woman, he extended his hand to Kit.

"William Muldoon, at your service. And you are?"

Kit sensed honesty was needed. "Katherine Firestone, of San Francisco. I ... I am a friend of Tom's." She felt herself blush.

Muldoon didn't bother to feign ignorance. "A very good friend, I'll wager. Now I know why he didn't seem all that interested in our local misses. I take it he hasn't seen you in a while?"

Kit shook her head. "No. But something has come up and I ... I really must see him, Mr. Muldoon."

Muldoon considered her for a moment. "Tell you what. You join Miss Farrell and me for dinner, and afterward I'll decide whether you are worth breaking my buttoned-lip policy. All right?"

Kit forced a smile. Whatever it took, she would do it. "I'd be delighted."

After taking her bag and dismissing the taxi driver, Kit joined Muldoon and his secretary, along with his housekeeper, an older, capable-looking woman named Mrs. Lutringer, for steaming bowls of vegetable soup and sliced beef sandwiches. The banter was light and courteous; it was obvious Muldoon cared for these two women and they him. He soon launched into what was apparently a favorite topic: the benefits of physical culture.

"President Roosevelt sums up civilization nicely. He says that man's mission is to work, fight, and breed. It's that simple. And the poorest people know it, believe it, and live it, which is why they don't need my services."

"Besides, which, they can't afford your services," Miss Farrell pointed out.

Muldoon grinned. "That, too. But there's a whole group of men nowadays gettin' fat and losin' sleep because they're too worried about this, that, and the other thing—most of which they can't even control." He ticked items off his fingers. "You take your headaches, your bellyaches, your itchy skin"—he looked pointedly at Kit before gently shaking his right hand—"your shakes. All ways your body's telling you you're off-kilter. You're not in balance."

"And you can restore that balance?" Kit didn't mask her disbelief.

"No, ma'am, I can't. But I can teach men how to find their own balance by eating, sleeping, and exercising the right way. Once they do that, ninety percent of that bilious energy just fades away." The ferocity of his beliefs propelled him forward in his chair. "I tell you, it would be worth losing my business if the whole damn country figured that out."

Mrs. Lutringer sniffed and rose to clear the plates. "Lucky for you there are plenty who suffer such maladies, and they're well-heeled."

Muldoon smiled at her. "Lucky for all of us."

"But what about women?" Kit said, playing devil's advocate as Mrs. Lutringer sat back down. "A close friend of mine who lost a child was diagnosed with the nervousness you describe but the doctor prescribed the opposite. She wasn't allowed to do *anything*."

Muldoon looked sheepishly at the two women he obviously relied on. "I can't exactly say women are the weaker sex, leastwise not in this household. But I'm not sure women's concerns rise to the level of ... of ..." Kit, Miss Farrell, and the housekeeper sent him a trio of glares. He swallowed. "Well, what I mean is ... women have other things to worry about."

"Like running households and holding down jobs and having children and rearing them properly, since children *are* the future of the human race." Mrs. Lutringer matched her employer in passion.

Muldoon shrugged. "Honestly, the rest cure for women has me baffled, too. Nellie Bly—have you heard of her, Miss Firestone? She's a reporter for *The New York World*. Well, she's a little slip of a thing and a few years back she sailed through my program with flying colors. I've half a mind to open an institute just for females."

"A capital idea," Miss Farrell said. She raised her glass of wine. "I'll drink to that."

Kit hesitated before asking, "So ... about Tom. Do you think his ... nervousness ... dissipated while he was here?"

"Tom was in good physical shape when he arrived, but when he left, he had definitely improved his game. The man's solid muscle now. His hand was doing better, too."

"It was?" Kit was greedy for any and all information about Tom. Maybe things had changed. Maybe he was ready to go back and—

"There's something weighing heavy on that boy," Mrs. Lutringer said. She tapped the side of her head. "He needs to lighten the load up in his noggin."

"Leonie's right," Miss Farrell added. "Dr. Tom was looking for answers; apparently he didn't find them here."

Kit couldn't suppress the sadness she felt, both for Tom's predicament and her own. "Where has he gone to look now?" she asked, her tone wistful.

Muldoon covered her hand with one of his. "He's flown south for the winter, my dear. You'll find him down in Texas, near the border of Mexico."

## CHAPTER FORTY-ONE

Kit couldn't bear to think that Tom might actually leave the country altogether. If he did, would she ever see him again? The idea filled her with such misery that it took all of her will power to maintain a façade of equanimity. Muldoon invited her to stay until they buttoned up the farm, but she demurred, explaining that she had plans with friends in New York City.

"At least spend the night, then. Storm's clearing out later tonight and I'll drive you to the station in the morning."

"That's very kind of you," Kit said. "I accept."

Mrs. Lutringer showed Kit her accommodations upstairs. "This was Tom's room during his stay. Maybe you'll feel his spirit here."

Her words brought forth unexpected tears. Hastily wiping her eyes, Kit choked out a laugh. "I'm sorry. It's …"

"Complicated. I sense that. So's the man. I hope it works out for you."

That night Kit lay awake, imagining Tom next to her. She rarely allowed herself such indulgence, but the fact that he'd been in this very bed gave flight to her imagination. His powerful body, moving over her, pouring himself into her. The memories nearly overwhelmed her. *Please come back to me. Please.*

The next morning, as promised, William Muldoon drove her to the station in the village of Purchase, where she caught a train to New York City. She was met by George Powell, Lia's brother-in-law, who took her bag and settled her into his car. "We're glad you could join us, although I must warn you, it's a bit chaotic at times with four children wreaking havoc. But I expect you've had more than your share of chaos, too, and not of the good kind."

"Yes. It's been quite a year."

The time spent with Emma, George and their growing family was a lovely distraction, filled with all of the holiday traditions she'd had growing up, and some she hadn't. She helped Little George (who was now nine) string the new electric holiday lights; she joined the family's quest to cut down the perfect Christmas tree; and she lent her voice to more than a few Christmas carols sung around a crackling fire, eggnog at the ready. She'd even tried ice skating for the first time, although not with much success. They convinced her to stay and ring in the new year, which she did because she wanted the holidays behind her in case bad news lay ahead.

All in all Kit had a wonderful visit, but throughout her stay she was infused with a current of restlessness, a thrum of energy that kept her anxious, though she tried to suppress it. She had explained her mission in broad outline, and George, whose family was as well-connected on the East Coast as the Firestones were now on the West, had generously offered to use his high-level contacts to further track down Tom.

Kit thanked him but declined, making light of the situation. "I know he's working for the railroad down in Brazoria, Texas. I'm afraid if I warn him of my arrival, he may flee the country entirely." Both George and Emma laughed, but the looks in their eyes told her they understood her underlying fear of the unknown.

"If there's anything we can do, *anything*, you will let us know, all right?" Emma said as she hugged Kit goodbye.

"Thank you for understanding," she whispered back. "I am so glad I foisted myself upon you."

The train arrived and after boarding, Kit was once again on the move. Despite the lines that now crisscrossed the country, the most efficient way to reach her destination was to backtrack to Chicago and head south. At that point, the railroad agent assured her, the frigid January weather would improve along with travel times.

Her plan was to pick up the St. Louis, Brownsville, and Mexico Railway at Robstown, Texas, and take "The Brownie" east to Brazoria. But even if she caught every connection on time, it was going to take several days to get where she needed to go. She would be lucky to make it back to San Francisco by the end of the month.

Kit settled in for the next leg of her adventure.

---

Despite the new railroad depot a scant mile away, it didn't sound like Refugio, Texas was much to look at, especially on a rainy evening. Set on the north bank of the Mission River, the little town had seen a lot of turmoil during the Texas Revolution, including the tragic "Battle of Refugio" in which several brave Texans lost their lives at the hands of Mexican troops.

According to a brochure handed out to first-class passengers, travelers could now visit the old Spanish convent, get a drink in one of two saloons, and stay at the lone hotel. Kit checked the schedule. The train stopped for twenty minutes to take on water and she thought perhaps she'd get off just to stretch her legs; pacing back and forth through the cars had lost its allure days ago.

The truth was, she needed to walk off some nerves. Early tomorrow morning she'd get off in Brazoria, the town Tom supposedly lived and worked in now. How was he going to react when he saw her?

She glanced over at the couple who'd sat across from her for the past two days. Mrs. Carmichael was heavyset and dressed in plum-colored bombazine from head to toe. From the moment they'd entered the car she'd directed a nearly nonstop diatribe toward her husband. Today the chicken at lunch was too spicy, the beans too crisp. The air was too stuffy, the seats too lumpy.

Her husband, so thin compared to his wife that Kit had mentally nicknamed him "Jack Spratt," sat placidly, nodding occasionally but saying virtually nothing. Was he even listening to her? Kit couldn't stand being in a relationship like that. She would tell Tom—

Wait. That was not how she wanted to approach the situation. She went back to her original plan: she would tell Tom about Tang Lin's warning and let him make the next move regarding their relationship.

Kit's plan was a sound one, but it was incomplete. It didn't account for the series of storms that had turned the feeder creeks Blanco and Medio into their own raging waterways. Together they'd overwhelmed the larger Mission River which in turn washed out a critical section of track a few miles before Refugio. Day was heading into a rain-soaked dusk when the engineer finally rounded the last bend and realized the gaping hole that lay just ahead.

He didn't have time to stop the train.

## CHAPTER FORTY-TWO

The ear-splitting screech of brakes ripped through the quiet rumbling of the train. At once, Kit's parlor car began to rock wildly, a carnival ride gone haywire. With no time to consider her options, she dropped down between her seat and the one in front, clutching the wooden frame to keep from flying across the aisle.

There was no stopping the nightmare. In the space of mere seconds, Kit sensed nothing but air beneath her, followed by a sickening roll, shattering glass, and the deadly crunch of metal and wood. Luggage and people flew overhead, smashing into her side of the crumpled car and then dropping back with a horrifying thud.

Then the screaming began.

"Wendy! Oh my God, Wendy!" Kit caught a glimpse of Mr. Carmichael crawling over a pile of debris to his wife. "Wendy!" he cried again.

Kit, on the bottom of the tilted car, was pinned by

several bags that had landed by her seat, blocking the aisle.

"Mr. Carmichael!" she called out. "Can you help me, sir? I'm a nurse, but I'm stuck behind these bags."

It took a few entreaties, but at last he emerged long enough to crawl over and remove the obstruction. "Can you help my Wendy?" he asked, desperation lacing his voice. "Can you help her? Please!"

Kit followed the anguished husband who had returned to his wife and now cradled her head in his lap. Mrs. Carmichael's eyes were open, but it was obvious by the angle of her neck that it was broken. In that moment Kit wanted nothing more than to hear the lady's nonstop complaints. But she was silent and forever would be.

That didn't mean there weren't others to help. Kit murmured "I'm sorry" to Mr. Carmichael, then worked her way to the next victim.

***

"Pull this tight for me, will you, Francis?" Kit had enlisted the aid of the porter to help her tighten the tourniquet on the leg of a man whose thigh had been pierced with a nasty-looking piece of jagged metal. He lay on what was now the floor of the car, his teenage daughter holding onto his hand for dear life.

"You're not going to cut my daddy's leg off, are you?"

"Shh," she told the girl in a soft voice. "Nobody's going to do anything like that, honey." *For the time being, at least.* "We have to wait for the doctor to get here because your papa might lose too much blood if we try to move him right now."

Shortly after the accident, they'd learned that a special hospital car was on its way from Houston, but in the meantime, several of the three dozen or so accident victims had to be stabilized. Francis, with nothing more than a sprained thumb, was more than happy to help. He'd immediately salvaged a box of medical supplies stored in the front of the car which Kit used to clean and bind wounds, including those of a young man with a broken arm and his very pregnant wife, who suffered a severely cut lip.

Although the two passenger cars behind hers hadn't tipped over completely, they had still sustained major damage, resulting in more injuries. Having done all they could in their own car, Kit and Francis went in search of other victims to help. Outside, the rain continued to fall, causing leaks everywhere. Kit's dress was already damp from interior puddles and drips.

"I sure don't mind the rain as long as it stops the fires," Francis said. "Ain't nothin' worse than a burnin' train."

Sometime later, Kit was in the midst of stitching a little girl's forearm when she heard the rhythmic chug of a slowing train engine and the whistle announcing its arrival. By now it was long past dark, and she'd been working by the light of an emergency lantern commandeered by the porter.

"You're such a brave girl, Ginny," she crooned to the

tearful child as her anxious mother looked on. "You're going to be just fine."

Kit was kneeling at the back end of the car and heard male voices in the front. *The cavalry has arrived,* she thought, relief wafting through her. "I told you help was coming," she said to the mother. "He'll have a look at both of you to make sure everything else is in working order." She turned to call out through the gloom. "Are you a doctor?"

"I am."

Kit stopped short. She knew that voice.

Using the back of the seat as leverage, she stood up and watched Tom working his way toward her. He looked shocked, but gave nothing away, choosing instead to kneel down and speak directly to Kit's patient. Kit did the same.

"And whom do I have the pleasure of meeting?" he asked.

"This is Ginny, and she is a very brave young lady." Kit brushed the child's curls back from her cheek, hoping it would calm her.

Ginny couldn't speak, her breath coming in little gasps. Tom got her to look at him and said, "Ginny, you are very lucky to have met Nurse Firestone. She is one of the best." He took carbolic acid from the bag he'd brought and dabbed it on the girl's six-inch suture.

Tom glanced at Kit before unpacking a roll of gauze to wrap around the child's arm. "So, you got my letter?" he asked quietly.

Kit frowned. "Letter? No, I—there was no letter."

He met her frown with his own scowl. "Then what the hell are you doing here?"

She wanted to slap him, but that would accomplish nothing. Instead she rose and wiped her hands on her skirt. "Does it matter? You have work to do, Dr. Justice." She leaned over to speak to Ginny's mother. "You see? Everything's going to be all right now." She'd heard another doctor enter the car and moved on to help him.

<hr />

Inside of two hours, every victim of the train wreck had been stabilized and triaged for removal to the hospital train or to the hotel in Refugio to await transport once their less serious wounds permitted. Silas Hall, the man with the metal imbedded in his leg, was the last to be evacuated, primarily because it was difficult to get him through the window. Kit offered to take his daughter, Cassie, to where the other uninjured passengers waited. Cassie hadn't wanted to leave her father but Kit remembered the time Tom had asked her to leave while he straightened her father's shoulder, so she whispered, "Your papa will probably need to yell when they move him and I think he might be embarrassed to show he's in pain in front of you."

Cassie understood. "I'll see you soon, Daddy," she said before leaving.

By the time Kit returned, Mr. Hall had been moved to the hospital train and the two other railway surgeons were discussing his case with Tom.

"Here's how I see it," Dr. Sumner said. "The leg's got to go. We try pulling that spike out and no telling what we'll find. It may be blocking an artery, and by the time we get him plugged up he could bleed out. On the other hand, we do a normal transtibial amputation, leave him six inches, as much as we can, and he's got enough for a prosthesis."

"Can't we at least try?" Tom argued. "The metal might have missed the artery entirely."

"You'd take the chance on that?" Dr. Calhoun spit out. "And let's say you're right. Are you going to sew him back together, layer by layer, nerve by nerve, just to save that mess of his? Because I'll tell you"—he pointed to Dr. Sumner and himself—"despite what they call us, neither of us has the skill for that kind of surgery. Meanwhile the rest of the patients need to get to a hospital, but we can't leave because Dr. Justice is still at it. And what if you lose him? What are you going to tell that little girl of his?"

Dr. Sumner concurred. "Whether you rebuild his leg or we amputate, he's still going to have a limp."

Katherine turned to Tom and spoke softly. "I saw the wound, and I think the lower leg needs to go," she said. "This is not Tang Lin and you are not who you were."

"Do you two know each other?" Dr. Sumner said.

Katherine looked at Tom. "We used to work together. It was a while ago."

"Well, I vote to amputate," Dr. Calhoun said, "and if that's going to happen, I think we need to get it done now."

Kit watched as Tom processed the situation, including the remarks she'd made about Tang Lin. "All right," he finally said. "I would be happy to assist."

---

The St. Louis, Brownsville, and Mexico Railway offered to pay the hotel bills for every accident victim who needed to recuperate before heading off to their final destination. Kit volunteered to stay behind and look after them, as did Tom. That left Sumner and Calhoun to accompany those who had been more seriously wounded, like Silas Hall, back to Houston.

After spending half the morning attending patients, Kit and Tom went to their respective rooms to wash and change clothes. By some unspoken agreement they returned to the hotel's empty dining room to catch a bite to eat. Knowing she'd need energy for the talk they were about to have, Kit ordered toast and coffee. Tom, on the other hand, went straight for a shot of whiskey.

"Why in heaven's name were you on that train?"

His tone was much less angry than before, but she was still on guard.

"Isn't it obvious? I was looking for you."

"But you promised. I'm surprised, is all. I didn't think you'd go back on it."

"I kept my word. You made me swear not to have you followed, and I didn't. You never said I couldn't follow you myself."

"Now you are splitting hairs."

"Perhaps." She couldn't bear to go into the real reason for her trip. Not yet. "How have you been?"

Tom looked into his whiskey glass and Kit wondered what he was hoping to find there. When he gazed back up at her, her said, "Not great, but you are a sight for sore eyes, and that's a fact."

She hated meaningless flattery, especially at a time like this. "Stop that. You cannot say things like that and be fine with leaving me for no good reason."

"I have every reason," he said, holding up his hand. "This ... whatever it is, is *maddening*. I have tried everything. It's fine and then"—he shook it—"it's useless. I cannot trust it."

"Then don't. Be someone who doesn't need that hand. I can love you without that hand. Why can't *you*?"

"You make it sound so simple, but it's not. It's like asking that poor fellow to give up his leg. As if he would ever willingly agree to such a thing."

"So what, then? You just give up? You say, 'The hell with being happy if I have to do something different with my life'?"

"No! God, no. I want to make it work. More than anything. But—"

At that moment the young father-to-be with the broken arm rushed into the dining room. "Doc? My wife's going to have our baby now and we need your help."

"But I just saw her two hours ago," Kit said.

"I dunno. Everything was fine, but now she's got pain somethin' fierce."

Kit glanced at Tom; she knew they were thinking

the same thing. It was likely premature labor, brought on by the accident.

They all headed upstairs where they could hear his wife's moans from the hallway.

"Carl—that's you name, isn't it?" Tom asked the man. "I need you to go downstairs and ask the clerk to round up the local midwife. Have her come right away and bring a tincture of red raspberry and cramp bark if she's got it. She'll know what that is. Can you remember that?"

"Red raspberry and cramp bark. Yes, sir." Carl headed back down to the lobby while Kit entered the room and started to prep the young woman for labor. Her name was Maggie and she was trying to be brave amidst what appeared to be very painful contractions. Tom examined her and explained that they were going to try to "slow her down" a bit. Then he motioned for Kit to join him in the hall. He was about to speak when Carl returned with the midwife. Mrs. Mabel Washington looked about as old as the hills, but she had come prepared.

"Ma'am, we need to stop the contractions as soon as possible, because Mrs. Lawson's baby is presenting breech."

Breech? Oh my God. Kit knew the danger inherent to breech delivery; the baby could lose oxygen while trying to make its way down the birth canal feel first.

"Breech, you say?" Mrs. Washington's attributes didn't include hearing well.

Tom raised his voice. "That's right. We need to slow her contractions down right away."

The old woman pulled a bottle from the satchel she carried. "This should put the brakes on a mite. I mix it with a little St. John's Wort. We got to move the babe back into place before the birthin' starts, though. Otherwise the mama's in for a world of hurt."

"Precisely, ma'am." Tom remained remarkably calm. "If you would give her the tincture, we'll follow in a moment."

When the midwife entered the room, Kit suggested they prep for a cesarean, but Tom was adamantly against it. "With this hand, I can't take the chance. The good news is that she hasn't dilated much, nor has her water broken. Once we get her calmed down, I want to try an external cephalic version. Have you ever done one?"

"Flipping the baby while it's still in the womb? No. I've never even seen it done."

"Well if we can get Mrs. Lawson's contractions to subside, you may get the opportunity."

Over the next several hours, Kit and Tom stood by as the wizened midwife eased Maggie's contractions with special concoctions until they had almost completely stopped. Tom arranged for Mrs. Washington to return the next morning and checked once more on his patient.

"What's in that tea the lady gave me, anyway?" Maggie asked. Tom told her, but halfway through his explanation her lids began to droop. She was obviously worn out, but Kit knew the worst was yet to come.

"I think I'll turn in now," Kit said, realizing that she herself was tired, having checked on all the patients in the hotel throughout the day. "I'll see you in the morning."

She'd intended to sleep all night, but of course, sleep did not come. Sometime after midnight she pulled her robe from the bag she'd salvaged from the wreck. She thought to make herself some warm milk, but when she entered the hall, she saw a light underneath Tom's door. She knocked but got no answer. Slipping inside, she saw him sprawled on the bed, much like she'd seen him at the Presidio. She tip-toed closer and was relieved to find no bottle of laudanum on the bedside table. He was apparently just exhausted. After untying his shoes and placing them under the bed, she covered him with a quilt and returned to her room, where, surprisingly, she drifted off into her own deep sleep.

The next morning she awoke early and checked on Maggie before heading down to the dining room. She'd hoped to see Tom for a few minutes before their day started, but he wasn't there; the waiter said he hadn't seen him come down yet.

Finding him still asleep, she gently shook him awake. "I've seen Mrs. Lawson already and she said she was able to get some rest. Her husband and Mrs. Washington are with her now. I don't know how much of a window we have, but if we're going to attempt the version, now might be the time."

Tom agreed and shortly thereafter he explained to the young mother-to-be what he was going to do. "You're going to feel a lot of pressure, and you need to tell me if it's too much, all right?"

"Don't you worry none, honey," Mrs. Washington said. "It may feel a bit tight, but it'll be well worth it when the baby's time comes."

What followed was another small miracle, as Kit watched Tom use his hands—and Kit's—to move Maggie's unborn child while it was still inside her body. It wasn't fun for Maggie at all, however; she let them know how painful it was.

But when the baby flipped into the vertex position, Kit felt it and so did Tom. Their eyes locked in mutual delight.

They had no time to crow, however, because almost immediately Maggie's water broke and her delivery started in earnest. It took another twelve hours, but finally they helped bring Evan Carl Lawson into the world.

After seeing to the newborn and sending Mrs. Washington on her way, both Kit and Tom headed for his room and collapsed on the bed.

She turned to look at him. "You see? You didn't need your hand."

"This time," he said, and held it up. She watched it tremble ever so slightly and knew the next moment was critical.

"I think you need it now," she said, and placed it on her breast. "What do you want, Tom Justice?"

He didn't hesitate. "I want you. I've wanted you since I met you, and God help me, I don't think that's ever going to change."

That was what she wanted to hear. That was enough. She sat up and smiled at him and untied her apron before starting on her shirtwaist. "I am very glad to hear it, because I have missed feeling you next to me."

---

They came together as they had before, passionately, powerfully. But this time it was different. Deeper. More committed. Kit didn't bring up protection and Tom didn't offer any, as if they both knew and accepted, perhaps even welcomed, what might come of their joining.

Afterward they made rounds of the patients remaining in the hotel, but later returned to the room and continued where they'd left off, at last falling asleep enveloped in each other, sated and at peace.

Kit was sleeping, surrounded by Tom's muscular body, when she felt the lightest kiss on her neck. "Mmm," she said.

"Why did you come here?" he asked in a gentle voice. "Why did you need to find me now?"

She turned over to face him, understanding she couldn't put it off any longer. She stroked his bristly cheek and sat up, wrapping the covers around her. "It was because of Tang Lin."

"Tang Lin? Is he all right?"

"Yes. Everyone is fine. But Tang Lin came to see me. He wanted help in locating you. So that he could warn you."

"Warn me? About what?"

She told him about the aftermath of the tragedy in

San Francisco, how factions were starting to point fingers at one another for mistakes that had been made. "Tang Lin learned that a doctor had gone to the district attorney alleging that a crime took place at the Mechanics Pavilion. They're saying it was murder."

*Oh, this was difficult to say.* She took a deep breath. "And they're saying you're to blame. It's ridiculous, I know, but they're recalling everyone who was there to testify and Tang Lin says they have a warrant out for your arrest. It looks bad that you left the city, so I said I would find you and bring you back to clear it up."

Kit saw the arrested look on Tom's face and it filled her with a sense of dread. Her disturbing memories of that day returned. The abrupt change in him. The distance. "You know what they're talking about, don't you?"

A sigh escaped him. "I do."

She paused and reached for his right hand. "And this has something to do with it."

"I think it does," he whispered.

She had a million questions, but only one goal: to let him know how much she believed in him. So she wrapped her arms around him and held him tight.

---

They decided to wait until the last injured passengers in their care were ready to travel before returning to San Francisco. When they had time to spare, Kit tried gently to get Tom to share what had happened the day of the fire, but he would not confide in her. Once again, he sought to protect her; still, it rankled. He told her that eventually all would come to light and that she should trust him. What else could she do but agree?

If only they had left a day earlier.

They were finishing dinner in the hotel dining room two nights later when two men approached their table, one a uniformed police officer and the other dressed in civilian clothes.

"Dr. Thomas Aaron Justice?" the second man said. "I am Mr. Beauregard Hanley and I have been authorized to serve you with this arrest warrant and escort you to the city of San Francisco for prosecution."

Kit was incensed at the man's nerve. "Couldn't this have waited until after dinner?" "You are drinking coffee, ma'am. I'm assuming you already ate."

Tom took the news calmly, asking what crime he was being charged with and then proclaiming his innocence. That made no different to Mr. Hanley. He gestured for Tom to come with him, but Kit cried "Wait! He has patients to attend to!"

Tom rose from the table. "You will handle them just fine, Nurse Stone."

Nurse Stone? He was already protecting her from any association with him. "But—"

"Please contact my colleague, Dr. Herzog, in Brazoria, for your wages. You've been a great help to the company." With that, Tom and the two men left her standing there.

She had never felt so alone.

## CHAPTER FORTY-THREE

As she watched Jonathan Perris walk into the private dining room she'd reserved, Kit was aware of two things: one was that if she weren't already in love with Tom Justice, she very well could have fallen in love with the handsome attorney heading toward her. The other was that her instincts were holding true: Jonathan was absolutely the right choice to defend Tom against the charge of murder. "I'm so glad you could make it," she said as he drew near.

Being English and rather old-fashioned in some respects, Jonathan kissed rather than shook her proffered hand. "Your servant, Miss Firestone."

Kit smiled to hide her nervousness. "You're not my servant, but I'm certainly hoping to employ you."

"As what? A chimney sweep? Carriage driver? Body guard?" He waggled his eyebrows at the last suggestion. At that moment the waiter approached and offered to take Jonathan's coat and hat, which he placed on a stand by the door.

"I could have done that myself," Jonathan muttered.

"Yes, but this is the Cliff House, and you are my guest." She turned to the waiter. "Samuel, would you please bring the Inglenook zinfandel I selected?" She turned back to Jonathan. "I hope that's all right. I know you love ale like all your countrymen, but ..."

"I'll adjust," he said with a grin, settling into his seat. "I'm deliriously glad you are back in town and that you thought to invite me to lunch. So tell me, how can I be of service?"

He was in a lighthearted mood, she could tell, and obviously happy to see her. He probably wouldn't feel as sanguine by the end of their meeting, but it couldn't be helped. "I told you I was visiting friends on the East Coast over the holidays, and I did, but the primary purpose of my trip was to find another person I am very close to, Tom Justice. Have you heard the name?"

"It sounds vaguely familiar, yes."

"That's because he's been arrested for murder. He didn't do it, and I need you to defend him."

She waited while Jonathan absorbed the information. When he spoke, his voice was tender. "Katherine, I only recently passed the bar in order to practice in this state. There are litigators far more experienced than I in this matter."

"I know that you are new here, and I know that your preference now is to practice contract law. But I also know you have years of experience as a defense counsel in London, and it is precisely your newness that makes you perfect for the job."

Jonathan fiddled with his cutlery and was about to

speak when Samuel came back with the wine, which Kit tested before giving him permission to pour. Dr. Landon's joke about "testing fine wine" came to mind. The jest was not worth sharing.

The waiter handed out menus and they made their selections. Kit looked longingly at the *filet de boeuf* but chose a chicken curry, while Jonathan opted for the shepherd's pie.

Once Samuel had taken their order, Jonathan leaned forward and spoke in a low voice. "Perfect for the job because I'm new? I'm afraid that makes no sense."

Kit tried to keep her voice down as well. "Listen, I know the powerful members of this city, the movers and shakers, if you will. They have been visiting my family home since I was a child. I practically grew up with them. You've been there; you know what I am talking about.

"Most of those people are solid; they care about what happens to The Golden City. But some are not. This entire case against Tom is an effort to distract from matters that are not above board. The reconstruction money swirling around this city is astronomical and it is not always landing where it should. I am telling you, Tom is a scapegoat for mistakes that were made, and he is as innocent of murder as you and I are. I know him ... very well. He is a healer. He did not commit this crime."

"Are you an eyewitness?" he asked.

She shook her head; if only she'd followed Tom

behind that curtain! "I so wish I had been. It was ... chaotic. But I know—"

"You believe," he corrected her gently. After a pause he ventured into the dangerous territory of her emotions. "You seem to care for this man a lot," he said carefully. "I think perhaps he is the reason you seemed sad the night we met."

She nodded, tears threatening.

"Then why in God's name pick me?"

It was a reproach, albeit a subtle one. It told her that he cared for her, more than he'd admitted and perhaps more than he should. She saw the irony inherent in the two men working together, but she also knew why it must be so. "It's a fair question. I'm sure you know I could hire just about any defense attorney in this town. Some of them are superb trial lawyers. But they all know each other. They all scratch one another's backs from time to time. And this would be one of those times, I'm sure of it.

"So I choose you because you are not only intelligent, but wise. You have integrity and will not succumb to the machinations of those in power, as every other high-level attorney in this city is so often tempted to do. I know you can focus on the facts, not the politics, and prove his innocence."

"You think you know me so well," he said in a way that implied she knew nothing at all about him.

She observed him for a moment. His gaze was clear and intense. She could tell he was analyzing the situation. Analyzing her. He was a realist and didn't want to promise what he couldn't deliver. But he was more than that.

"I have been wrong about people in the past," she said. "I suppose I could be wrong about you." She reached for his hand across the table. "But I don't think so. I think in your heart you are a protector. You will work as hard as you possibly can, do as much as you possibly can, to see that an innocent man goes free. No matter who he is. No matter what it may mean for you. I believe that about you, Jonathan Perris. I believe in you."

---

Jonathan Perris agreed to take the case and Kit enjoyed what she'd been lacking for some time: a good night's rest. The following day she met him at his office, paid him a sizable retainer, and told him to spare no expense in tracking down any and all witnesses who might help frame the case in the proper way.

"He'll tell you to send him the bill," she cautioned, "but that is poppycock. I don't want you to pinch pennies because your client has no money. I think you should—"

"I think I can take it from here, Katherine," Jonathan said. "I will spend what I need to spend and no more. All right?"

She nodded, more assured than ever that she had done the right thing but anxious to help out in any other way she could, even if it was no more than visiting Tom in jail.

But Tom wanted no part of her. Ever since the U.S. Marshall had extradited him to California, he'd distanced himself. He no doubt felt tainted, and once again wanted to shield Kit from harm, even the harm of being publicly associated with him. Although it seemed that Tom had taken to Jonathan well enough, he'd instructed the attorney to tell Kit to stay away.

She would throttle both of them if she could.

Only the letter kept her calm. Tom had in fact sent her one, which had arrived after she'd left to find him. And though it was short, it told her everything she needed to know about where she stood with him.

So she waited.

And more weeks went by.

Two months into the investigation, Cordelia Hammersmith, one of the law clerks Jonathan had hired, contacted Kit regarding an interview.

"With me?" she asked.

"Yes, ma'am. Because he knows you personally, Mr. Perris felt I would be more objective in getting to the heart of your relationship with our client. May I meet you for lunch?"

They agreed on the Café Majestic, located in the hotel of the same name up on Sutter. The hotel had survived both the earthquake and fires, and now ran full every night.

Based on her telephone voice, Kit had assumed Miss Hammersmith was much more substantial than she appeared in person. The woman who greeted Kit was as petite as Kit's mother, but with rich, dark hair. Once she began to speak, however, Kit understood why Jonathan had hired her. She was a force to be reckoned with.

"I have interviewed nearly all of the female witnesses associated with our client," she said. "Yours is one of the few remaining."

Kit couldn't help herself. "Were there ... many?"

Cordelia offered up a crooked smile. "Although I can't attest to it, my guess is that Tom Justice cleans up pretty well. Let's just say that he has not lacked for female companionship over the years."

"Ah." Kit was sorry she'd asked. "Well, what would you like to know?"

Cordelia pulled out her notebook and pen. "For the record, just how intimate are you with Dr. Justice?"

Kit frowned. "For the record, I don't think that's any of your business."

Cordelia put down her pen and sighed. "I apologize. Sometimes I am a bit of a bulldog when it comes to gathering facts. I have been told more than once that I need to be more subtle. Look, under normal circumstances, I would not share our defense strategy with anyone outside our team, but seeing as how you are paying our client's legal fees, I am going to assume you will not run and tattle to the other side."

"Certainly not."

Cordelia took a drink of the iced tea she'd ordered. "The prosecution is trying to build a case that Dr. Justice killed his cousin—"

"His *cousin?*"

"You didn't know?"

"No. I knew at one point he dealt with a ... a difficult patient at the Pavilion, but he never said he was related to the man."

"Well, it was his cousin, and the prosecution's theory is that Tom took Mr. Porter's life because he was jealous that Eli Porter had married Tom's old flame."

"That's right. He mentioned that to me a long time ago, the marriage, I mean."

"Good. Then you might be able to describe his state of mind when he told you—if he seemed agitated about it, for instance, or heartbroken. I hope he wasn't, because the point we are trying to refute is this notion of Tom, so despondent he'd lost his girl that he sought to kill the man who took her away. The facts we've gathered so far indicate that Dr. Justice did not hold a torch. Far from it, in fact. Rather he had ... um ... what I would characterize as a healthy series of encounters. At least I have recorded no complaints from any female witnesses so far. Now if you'd like to add something...."

Kit felt a blush begin at her neckline and work its way to the top of her head. She wanted to fan herself, but dare not. "Ah, no. I certainly have nothing to add along those lines."

Cordelia gazed at her, mild skepticism etched on her face.

*Well, she will just have to wonder*, Kit thought.

"Well then, how would you describe your relationship with him?"

*The love of my life. The man I'm not sure I can live without.* "I'd say ... friends. Good friends. Close friends.

We have worked together professionally, of course. He is an exceptional surgeon. I am proud to know him."

"And that's it?" Cordelia was obviously waiting for more.

"Yes. That's it ... except that he didn't seem distraught when he told me about his former sweetheart's marriage. Indeed, he genuinely hoped she was happy in it."

The attorney nodded and put her notebook away. They then spent the rest of the lunch hour chatting about things that women chat about—like the difficulties of working with headstrong men, such as attorneys and doctors, and the problems of balancing a social life with work duties.

As they prepared to part company, Cordelia spoke up. "I want you to know I greatly admire you, Miss Firestone. You obviously have more money than God —" She paused. "— That came out wrong, I'm sorry. What I mean is, you are quite well off and have no need to work, yet you do, in a profession that is quite difficult and often less than rewarding. I applaud you. That's all I want to say."

Kit felt a rush of happiness for the first time in quite a while. "Thank you, Miss Hammersmith. Most of my peers think I am eccentric at best and a lunatic at worst. So it is nice to hear that coming from someone I respect."

After the two women went their separate ways, Kit thought perhaps one of the silver linings of this particular cloud was making another worthwhile friend.

Later that night, as she lost the contents of her

dinner for a third time in as many days, she was forced to reconsider the answers she'd given Cordelia. She was more than a good friend to Tom Justice.

Much more.

---

"Well, I can't tell you definitively at this point, but based on your symptoms and an examination of your cervix, I would say yes, your suspicions are correct: you're likely pregnant," Alice Landon told Kit the next day. "How far along do you think you might be?"

Kit let out a long breath. "I would say six weeks or so."

"Then it's early days. Let's wait to see if it holds." She gazed at Kit. "Do you want it to hold?"

Kit met Alice's inquiry straight on. "I'm not sure how I'm going to manage all the repercussions, especially in light of all that's going on with the father. I think I'll keep this to myself for now. But I can tell you with everything that's in me, *absolutely*. One hundred per cent I want it to hold."

Alice gave her a hug. "Then let's make sure it holds."

---

Kit's pregnancy did hold. The life she carried continued to grow, and while her stomach did not yet reveal her condition, she felt the changes in her breasts, her eating habits, and her emotions. To keep what was happening all to herself was both frustrating and empowering, and sometimes even thrilling, as if only she knew the secret to the universe.

But the reality of the situation threatened to intrude sooner than she'd hoped because Tom's trial preparations were not going well. According to Jonathan, certain elements of the case were proving difficult to rebut: the victim, Eli Porter, had been shot with his own weapon, yet suicide had been ruled out. Tom stubbornly continued to hold back details of the incident, and there was no getting around the fact that he had left the city shortly after the crime.

The letter, which only Kit and Tom knew about, would refute the notion that Tom had run away because he felt guilty of murder. Yet Kit knew Tom would not want to put her in the spotlight by making the letter public.

What would happen if she did? The press jumped on any salacious story, especially about a high-ranking family, and the Firestone name would take the brunt of the inevitably less than positive coverage. Relationships could be affected, alliances shattered, influence lost. For the sake of the family, she owed them an explanation. She needed their advice. And she would start with the true leader of the Firestone clan: her mother.

---

"It's good to see you, Miss Katherine. The missus is out in the garden with Bertrand." Geoffrey, the family's long-time butler, took her coat.

The Firestone garden had long been a source for many

of the fresh flowers, herbs, vegetables, and fruits that graced the family dining table. In the past few months, however, the area devoted to vegetables had greatly increased. A trellis had been added to accommodate a growing bush—green beans, perhaps? And row upon row of small plants were sprouting from the rich-looking soil.

Kneeling and weeding in one of the rows was a small figure wearing a wide-brimmed hat and ... wait, were those trousers?

"Mother?"

The figure turned and of course it was Josephine, her hands encased in gloves small enough to fit a child. "Hello, darling! Welcome to our little Garden of Eden."

Kit surveyed their domain. "Quite a production line you've got going."

"Goodness, yes," her mother said, standing now and dusting off her pants. At Kit's pointed look, she chuckled. "I borrowed a pair from Geoffrey's grandson. They really are the most marvelous invention. I wore them once years ago; I don't know why I stopped. You should try them. I believe you'd be much more comfortable at work."

*As if the hospital would ever allow that*, Kit thought. "Hello, Bertrand."

Bertrand paused in his raking. He looked noticeably thinner. *"Bonjour*, mademoiselle. Have you come for lunch?"

"No, no. I just wanted to talk to your slave driver about something." She turned to her mother. "Are you free for a few moments?"

"Certainly. Let's have some tea in the sunroom. No, don't trouble yourself, Bertrand. I'll get it. Just keep tilling."

"As you wish, madame."

---

The glass-enclosed room off the far side of the kitchen was warm, bright, and intimate, with a comfortable couch and chairs, a small woodstove, and a few tables scattered about. Growing up, Kit had often read there on gloomy days.

Now Josephine poked the fire to heat up water in the stovetop kettle, taking down two cups and saucers. "No more Earl Grey, I'm afraid. Strictly chamomile and peppermint."

Moments later they sat with cups in hand. "You are looking well," her mother said.

"I should be saying that about you. Honestly, you look wonderful, Mother. Do you feel as marvelous as you appear?"

"Better." Josephine sent Kit her signature smile. "I never would have believed it, but I am actually growing to love our new culinary routine. You've tasted some of Bertrand's latest creations. He really is a genius." She leaned forward conspiratorially. "But I do confess, that once, every other week or so, he prepares a farewell version of some decadent dish we have both loved over the years. We are professional mourners. We give it a proper send-off." She leaned back in her chair. "Moderation in all things, even the application of Professor Ehret's diet."

"I'm glad to hear things are going so well." Kit paused, smoothing her skirt, a gesture her mother noticed immediately.

"You are anxious about something. Tell me. Is it about our poor Dr. Justice?"

Perhaps it was the hormones now flowing through her body, but Kit took a deep breath, and to her horror, began to cry.

"Darling," Josephine said, and left her chair to hug her daughter. "It can't be as bad as all that."

"It is," Kit admitted. She described her on again-off again relationship with Tom and how she'd become a nurse because she'd felt useless compared to him. She recounted their growing affection for each other, and how, for her, at least, it had blossomed into love. She talked about the horror and uncertainty of that day in the Pavilion and how the experience had somehow changed Tom for the worse. "He was feeling so terrible those days we helped out here," she said, "and it only got worse." She explained why he'd left the city, not to run away from something he'd done, but because he was looking for answers ... and because he no longer felt worthy of Kit.

"And I know this because he sent me a letter, wanting to come back and start again if I was willing. Only I never got the letter because I had already left to warn him that the authorities were looking for him."

"But they arrested him before he could return," her mother said.

Kit nodded. "And it's been difficult for Jonathan to counter the belief that Tom ran away because he was guilty. He needs evidence to show that Tom had every intention of returning."

"Which means the letter."

"Yes. Only, Tom would be furious if I released it. He doesn't want me, or you, or anyone in our family to be connected to his nightmare. He knows what such a connection would do to my—to all of our reputations."

Josephine looked into Kit's eyes. "Do you want to be connected to his nightmare?"

*I am connected, in the most intimate way possible.* Kit wanted to share the news of her pregnancy, and yet she wanted her mother's approval, which she feared she would never have, so she kept silent. But this much she could say: "I have no choice. I love him, and I must do whatever I can to help him. I just ... I just wanted to let you know where I stand."

Josephine took her hand. "I'm sure I can speak for your father when I say that where you stand, we stand. We are with you, darling, no matter what happens. You're no doubt right that releasing the memo will lead to a flogging in the press. If you can withstand it, we can. And your young man had better get used to it."

"Oh, Mother," was all Kit could say before being swamped by tears yet again. Josephine patted her back. "Now, now. Mustn't go on about it. Someone would think you're pregnant, with all those waterworks."

Kit froze but quickly recovered, chuckling as she leaned back to wipe her eyes with her napkin. "Wouldn't that just be the cherry on top?" she quipped.

"Oh, don't tempt me with such metaphors," her mother said with a chuckle of her own. "Bertrand and I are doing our best, but we do have our weak moments, and ice cream sundaes are ever lurking, ready to pounce upon our best intentions."

Kit righted herself and stood up to leave. "One more favor?"

"Anything."

"I'd like to talk to Jonathan about all this away from his office at some point. May I invite him here for lunch?"

"Certainly. When the weather warms a bit you might enjoy a picnic in the Ruby. Let me know when you're coming and I'll have Bertrand prepare something you will both enjoy."

All the way home, Kit worried about her mother's offhand remark about being pregnant. Had she given herself away? It was one thing to have a love letter bandied about in the press, but an out-of-wedlock child, whose father was, God forbid, a convicted murderer?

No. That was no way to think. Doing all she could to get Tom acquitted was the way to think.

The only way.

---

Kit held off as long as possible, hoping that Tom's defense team could make its case without her letter, but Tom's abrupt departure from San Francisco remained a weak link in their presentation. So, on a brisk afternoon in March, she waited for Jonathan on the front terrace of her parents' home, picnic basket in hand. He looked dapper, as always, but a bit unsettled as he exited the car.

"You are always inviting me to lunch," he said.

"You are a most agreeable lunch companion," she replied. "And I guarantee you'll love what Bertrand has prepared. I'm quite famished myself."

Her mother's choice of the Ruby was inspired. They enjoyed one of Bertrand's *somewhat* healthy meals: baked chicken and asparagus, followed by a lightly sweetened peach tart. Over tea she broached the reason for her invitation by commenting on his countenance.

"You're worried. Tell me why."

He explained that while he felt sure Tom would get a fair trial without political interference, he was not so optimistic about the facts of the case, at least those he had gathered so far.

"The evidence does not lean in his favor. It has perplexed me from the start: why did Tom leave? He had to have known it would seem odd for him to do so. And yet he left his position ... and presumably you ... for parts unknown. Surely you can see how bad that looks."

*I must make him understand Tom's mindset*, she thought. *I have to put Jonathan in Tom's shoes.*

"What is it that defines you, Jonathan?" she asked, and when he seemed perplexed, she walked him through her reasoning. "If I had to guess, I'd say you are a man of principle, and reason, and most of the time, you want to do what's right. You possess the skills of logic and oratory, and you have used them quite successfully to achieve your goals.

"But now let's say your ability to reason is taken away from you"—she snapped her fingers—"like that. You can no longer assemble a series of facts and come to a logical conclusion about them. One day you wake up and that faculty is gone ...and you don't know why."

"That would be horrific. Impossible to imagine."

"Welcome to the world of Tom Justice."

She explained how the very structure they were sitting in had been an impromptu clinic just days after the quake and fires. Kit and Tom had been assigned to it for a few days, and Tom, she admitted, was angry. "Tom tried his best to hide from all of us the results of his own suffering, the inability to use his hand because of its tremor."

"What? I've talked with him several times and haven't noticed a thing."

"He would hide it from you, just like he tried to hide it from me. But I finally confronted him about it. He lashed out at me. Why do you suppose he did that?"

It took a bit of reflecting, but finally Jonathan caught on. "Because he didn't want to burden you."

"Precisely."

"So he left."

"He left. But not—and this is what I want you to understand—not because he was running away. No. Tom was running toward something—a cure, or at least an explanation. He would go anywhere, try anything, to return to the person he had been, just as you would, were you in his place."

She looked beseechingly at Jonathan. "Tom is a healer. He was born to help people. The only time, the *only* time he would ever consider harming another person would be if they threatened someone else. Especially someone he loved."

"Like you."

She gazed at him. It had to be said. "Like me."

"He left, yet eventually you did go after him." He frowned as if disappointed that she'd failed a test. "You wanted to warn him."

"You make it sound as if I wanted to help him evade the law. It wasn't that at all. Whatever Tom was feeling had hit him on a personal level, but never had it crossed his mind that he had committed a criminal act."

"You don't know that." Jonathan's voice sounded harsh.

"I do know that. I know it from the inside out. I found him, but not in time. He was arrested. You know the story from there."

"Ah but that's the problem. I don't know the story, not the whole story, at any rate. Something happened when Tom went behind that curtain at the Pavilion, and I need to know what it was so that I can best represent his side to the jury."

Kit reached for Jonathan's hand. It was much larger than hers, and warm to the touch. A strong hand. "Then you must convince him that the only person he harms by keeping the story to himself is him. Tell him ..." *Do not cry. Finish it.* "Tell him that no matter what he did, I believe it was the right thing to do, because I know him. I trust him. And I love him."

She knew the words hurt, but they had to be said. Even so, they weren't enough. Jonathan needed proof, and it was time to give it to him.

They finished their drinks and returned to the front of the mansion. As Jonathan got back in his car, Kit asked him to wait while she retrieved the letter. Handing it to him through the window, she said, "Tom will not be happy I gave you this, and perhaps neither will you. But you can tell him I wouldn't have done it unless I felt it was vital to the case. The letter was waiting for me when I returned from meeting Tom in Texas. You can tell by the postmark. It proves he wasn't running. So please, use it to prove that he's innocent."

He nodded before closing his door and she watched as he drove slowly down the long drive.

*What more can I do?* she thought. *What more?*

## CHAPTER FORTY-FOUR

The trial, held at the temporary courthouse within Beth Israel Synagogue, had finally begun. Day after day, Kit sat in the back of the room, listening as one witness after another spewed forth their perception of Tom Justice. He was curious. He was sneaky. He was a hard worker. He cared only about himself. He was caring. He was jealous. He was compassionate. He was angry.

She could only imagine what must be going through Tom's head, having so many personal details laid bare. Could anyone survive such scrutiny and come out unscathed?

Jonathan had called to warn her that the letter would soon be fodder for the press. Days earlier he had mentioned the missive in his opening remarks, explaining that it would prove that Tom's intent when he left the city was not to evade the law. But today he'd had to introduce the letter into evidence, which meant showing it to the prosecution, which made it likely the newspapers would get their hands on it. She discreetly touched her stomach. *If they think that letter is scandalous, wait until they see what else is coming!*

Throughout the trial she'd watched and wondered about the twelve men on the jury, none of whom she recognized. They all seemed like thoughtful individuals, but how could one really tell such things? Would they think less of Tom because he worked with Chinese immigrants? Would they buy the prosecution's story of his hatred for his cousin despite the women Tom had been with since? Kit tried not to dwell on that aspect; it was hardly fair to expect him to be a monk when she'd rejected him so many times.

The prosecution began its summation and she stared, dumbstruck, as they painted a picture of a horrible human being who should be strung up on the nearest gibbet. The jurors seemed enthralled by the portrayal of a selfish, mean-spirited man seeking cold-blooded revenge on a helpless relative.

It was Jonathan's turn next, and he countered with what she considered a reasoned, logical interpretation of all the facts. The so-called "murder" wasn't any such thing, only a tragic misunderstanding that happened in the blink of an eye as Tom tried to do what was right for his cousin while caught in the well intentioned but controversial "Pavilion Protocol." It had already been reported publicly, but Jonathan reminded the jurors of the Army's heart-breaking decision to euthanize terminally ill patients who couldn't be transported so that they wouldn't burn alive in the fast-approaching fire. Tom's letter to Katherine Firestone (although Jonathan didn't mention her by name) showed that Tom did not feel he'd broken the law and had every intention of returning to the Golden City. He was innocent of the crime.

It would have been enough to end it there and send the case to the jury, but Jonathan surprised everyone by having Tom take the stand. And Tom had the audacity to speak his heart and his mind openly, to tell the jury and all those present, that at some level he would have wanted to help his cousin end his life, as Eli had begged him to do. Even though Eli had not been at death's door, he'd lost his entire family as well as the use of his legs. His heart, mind, and body were truly broken and he felt he had nothing to live for. Tom explained that he hoped he could remain a compassionate man who did the right thing, even if it wasn't considered the right thing by everyone.

As she listened to his testimony, Kit struggled to contain her tears. Hadn't her dear friend Cecily struggled with the same decision, and in her own way, Bea as well? To be faced with such a choice and not feel anguish over it would be the true definition of evil.

She had never been so proud of Tom as she was in that moment, nor had she ever been so scared about the outcome of the trial.

When Tom finished, the judge instructed the jury to head toward the deliberation room on another floor of the synagogue. Kit slipped out the back and made her way to the Flood Building, where her parents had rented a large room for all of Tom's supporters to use while awaiting the verdict.

Now the proud father of a newborn, Will stood with Mandy, holding his little one and talking to Sofie Herzog, the eccentric lady railroad surgeon whom Tom had worked with down in Brazoria. Dr. Sofie was petite but full of spitfire; living in the wilds of Texas, her specialty was removing bullets without surgery. Kit imagined that if the verdict didn't go well, the lady would pull her own six-shooter and engineer Tom's escape. She had to smile: Dr. Sofie and Josephine were so much alike that her mother might very well ride shotgun.

Kit had met Tom's parents, Nan and Paul, at the start of the trial; she joined them as they stood talking with Kit's father along with some of Tom's friends and co-workers.

"How are you feeling?" she asked Nan. She and Tom's mother were of similar height and Kit wondered if her child would be as tall.

Nan Justice was a stoic woman, hardly prone to chatter, but a light shone in her eyes. "It seems a bit peculiar to say I'm proud of my son at a time like this, but I am fairly bursting with it."

Kit's eyes grew wide and she smiled. "I feel exactly the same way!"

"I can tell you do," Nan said, putting her arm on Kit's. "My boy took his time, but he made the right choice of woman to love."

Kit was too choked up to reply, choosing instead to

give the woman a brief hug. Tom had come from solid stock, and whatever happened, Kit would be proud to help pass it on.

She noticed Jonathan and his two assistants talking to each other on the other side of the room. Were they second-guessing their defense of Tom? Jonathan had done a masterful job of pleading the case and looked confident, but appearances could be deceiving. She noticed he wasn't partaking in Bertrand's lovely buffet. Then again, few people were, no doubt because of nerves. Kit wasn't hungry either, but for the baby's sake she looked for something to nibble on.

She had been there only a few minutes when her mother came up and embraced her, standing on her toes to deliver it. Then she held Kit at arm's length. "How are you holding up, darling?"

Kit shrugged, afraid that if she put her anxiety into words she would start bawling in front of the entire room.

"Well, here's something that might make you feel better." Josephine slipped a piece of paper into Kit's hand.

"What's this?"

Her mother smiled. "Read it."

Inside was a note, signed by the presiding judge, giving a "Miss Katherine Firestone" permission to visit the defendant while the jury deliberated. Kit couldn't contain her elation. "Oh Mother! How?—"

"I know the judge's wife," Josephine said, leaning in. "Now you'd best get over there; your young man probably needs his own hug right about now."

Kit barely heard her mother's words— she was already out the door.

---

Just inside the synagogue Kit was accosted by a reporter who shoved the latest edition of the *Evening Post* in her face. "What d'ya think of this, Miss Firestone?" The headline blared:

## LOVE LETTER TO SOCIALITE PROVES MURDEROUS DOC PLANNED RETURN TO CRIME SCENE

Below the headline was a rather blurry picture of Kit as she'd entered the building earlier that day.

"At least you photographed my good side," she said, otherwise ignoring the man and walking purposefully ahead.

A guard stepped to her aid, cutting off the reporter as he tried to follow. "Go on, get outta here, or I'll throw you out head first," he bellowed.

Kit sent the guard a silent thank-you and hurried up the stairs to the floor where Tom was sequestered. A police officer was stationed outside the door. After showing him her pass, she knocked, only to reveal another guard standing sentry. This one, whose name tag said "Kirby," was quite large and boasted a drooping red mustache. "Speak of the devil," he muttered.

She handed him her slip of paper. "I've been given

permission by the judge to spend a few minutes with the prisoner. I hope you don't mind, Mr. Kirby."

"Not all, miss." He gestured for her to enter and stepped out into the hall, closing the door.

And she and Tom were alone.

There were no entreaties. No recriminations. Without a word, he took Kit in his arms and she held on tightly, feeling his strength and his warmth seep into her marrow. After a moment he pulled back so that he could look into her eyes.

"I am so sorry for everything. I didn't want you to get dragged into this. But here you are, and you and your family have been so kind, to me, to my parents. I can't tell you how much—"

She stopped him with a finger to his lips. There was only one thing she needed to know. "Do you love me?"

He cupped her cheek. "You know I do."

"Well, I can't think of anything more important right now than that."

But he wouldn't let her enjoy the moment. "Katherine, if … if the verdict should come back—"

*There would be loss. So much loss. I couldn't bear it.* "No. I will accept nothing less than your acquittal. I have plans for you, you see. You're going to make an honest woman out of me, and…. and…" She ran out of bravado. "Marry me now," she whispered.

But she knew the answer before he even shook his head. He would go on protecting her until the end.

She stepped back, smiling. Reaching into her reticule, she pulled out a small lace handkerchief. "I figured as much, you stubborn man. We will just have to prevail, that's all."

He took her face in his hands and kissed her then, telling her again what her heart needed to hear, feelings she might have to live on for quite some time.

"You will always prevail, Miss Katherine Madeline Mariah Firestone. You are magnificent."

She left him standing there, wanting him more than she had ever thought possible, knowing they had never been this close, and might never be again. Knowing that she loved him more than she loved herself.

Pasting on a placid expression, she thanked Mr. Kirby and headed down the hall. Halfway down there was a ladies' retiring room that, thankfully, was empty. A small gas lamp bathed the room in a soft butter-yellow light. Some gardenias floated in a bowl, reminding her of her mother. She sat down on the small settee, dabbing the tears from her cheeks and concentrated on pulling herself together. She had to be ready for whatever conclusion the jury came to, be it good or bad. Ready to move someplace else and give her child a fresh start without the stigma of being a social pariah. Ready to live a life without the man she was meant to be with.

She tried to imagine such a life but she couldn't, because it was all wrong. It was the wrong way to think.

Instead, three words came to mind: *Fight this thing*. Whatever happens, don't put up with less than what you want. *Fight*.

Immediately she felt better. She was a Firestone, after all, and that is what Firestones did.

---

## Josephine

Everyone had been recalled to the courtroom. Josephine sat next to Edward, her hand clutching his tightly. He patted it and gave her a tender smile. "Kit will be fine, no matter what," he said quietly. "She's a survivor."

"There is only one outcome that's acceptable here," Josephine muttered. "And they'd better pick the right one."

Judge Rendell called for order and addressed the jury foreman. "Has the jury reached a verdict?"

"We have, Your Honor." The man handed a piece of paper to someone, who in turn handed it to the judge.

*Oh for heaven's sake, just read the damn thing!* Josephine barely stopped herself from grabbing it out of the man's hand.

"In the matter of the state of California versus Thomas Aaron Justice, the jury finds the defendant ... not guilty."

Josephine immediately looked at Kit, whose face radiated such joy it nearly brought Josephine to her knees. There was no raucous cry of celebration, however. The case was too heartbreaking for that. After a moment of silence, someone started clapping and the rest of the courtroom spectators joined in. At least a good man, trying to do the right thing, had been spared.

Jonathan Perris hugged his assistants. Josephine watched as his gaze turned to Katherine and Tom, who made a beeline for each other and kissed rather shockingly in front of everybody. *You will find someone, sir,* she thought. *You are a good man, too.*

"I think our girl has met her match," Edward said, and leaned down to kiss Josephine. "Just like me."

Josephine beamed at him. "I agree, you're a lucky man."

Well-wishers clustered around Tom, and Katherine stepped aside. Josephine caught her daughter's eye and grinned, receiving a beatific smile in return.

She turned to Edward. "We'd best get back to the Flood Building ahead of the others so Bertrand and I can freshen up the buffet. No doubt we'll have some hearty appetites this go around."

They made their way out the door and skirted the gaggle of reporters waiting to accost Tom. As Josephine looked back she could see that Jonathan was shepherding both Tom and Katherine down the steps. Reporters were shouting out questions.

"How does it feel to be free?"

"What are your plans now that you've been found not guilty?"

A man brushed by Josephine and ran up the steps. He didn't appear to be a member of the press; by the look of his clothes, he was a working man.

"Murderer!" he yelled. "You're all murderers! You took my son and daughter and let them burn!"

Josephine saw the flash of metal when he pulled out the gun and pointed it at Tom. "No!" she screamed in a voice that hadn't yelled so loud since her coxswain days. She rushed the man but it was too late.

The bullet meant for Tom would have hit its mark if her darling girl hadn't stepped in front to protect him.

But she did, and the bullet hit Katherine instead.

"Oh my God!" Josephine cried, and rushed forward.

# CHAPTER FORTY-FIVE

## Josephine

"She's going to be fine, my love, you'll see. We just have to let the doctors do their jobs." Josephine spoke quietly to console her husband while inside she was nearly jumping out of her skin. She *detested* not being able to help, but for once it was she and not Edward who had to maintain calm. Her dear spouse was almost catatonic with grief.

They'd stabilized Kit and taken her to the home of Redmond Payne, whom Josephine and Edward knew well. He was one of the founders of St. Francis Hospital and had generously outfitted his mansion to be used as a temporary clinic while the real facility was being rebuilt after the earthquake. Thank God it was near the synagogue. Thank God.

Tom must have held Sofie Herzog in high esteem because after the shooting, he insisted she examine Kit. Now the two of them were engaged in a heated argument. He was insisting she perform her unconventional bullet extraction technique, but Sofie countered that the damage was too severe and required a surgeon like him to go in and remove the projectile.

Josephine watched as Sofie asked Tom to hold up his hand, which he did. It held steady. There was no sign of the tremor that Kit and later Edward had told her about, the trembling that had taken him away from Kit for so many months.

"There are other surgeons," Tom began, practically begging the doctor to let him off the hook.

She wouldn't budge, however, and Josephine stepped up to support her cause.

"If Katherine were awake, she'd say you are the best there is." She took his arm and gave him a reassuring squeeze. "We could have anyone operate on her, but we want the best."

Tom was on the verge of deciding when Redmond Payne came up and murmured something to both him and Sofie.

"No!" Tom cried.

Josephine looked from one to the other. "What is it?" she demanded.

Sofie spoke up. "Your daughter has begun bleeding again. There's a question as to whether we'll have enough to—"

*At last—something I can do.* "Take mine," Josephine said.

Sofie looked puzzled. "What?"

"Take my blood. Take as much as you need."

Redmond stepped in. "Now Josephine, it's not as easy as all that. We can't just—"

"Don't patronize me, Redmond. It *is* that easy. I've had my blood identified and so has Katherine. I am almost positive they are compatible, and if they aren't, we can find someone whose blood is. Call Dr. Alice Landon if you don't believe me."

"Josephine—"

"Call her!"

Shaken by her outburst, Redmond hurried out of the room. Tom had made up his mind and he and Dr. Herzog were already headed to a room where they could scrub up.

"She's right," Redmond called to them moments later. "She's type O. They're calling it the 'universal donor.' In case we need more units, Dr. Landon is contacting other women on a list she has who are also compatible. She'll send them here directly."

Josephine had already begun to unbutton her sleeve. "I don't know why you ever doubt me," she said. "Hook me up."

---

Tom went in, found the bullet near Kit's lung and repaired all the damage along the bullet's path. She'd lost a lot of blood, but Josephine replaced some of it along with a few other donors. Josephine promised them all a grand garden party at the Firestone estate once Kit was back on her feet.

After her surgery, they were all forced to play the

waiting game. Infection was a threat under the best conditions, and after two days, Kit broke out in a fever.

This time Josephine really could do nothing, and it tore her up inside. As if Kit weren't in enough danger, Tom had told her about her daughter's pregnancy. Josephine had suspected as much, but why hadn't Kit told her when she had the chance? After all this time, was she still worried about Josephine's censure? *I cannot lose her*, she thought. *We have too much to say to one another. Too much to learn.*

But Kit's fate was out of her hands, so she focused on keeping Edward from drowning in gloom and fussed over preparing their home for her daughter's convalescence.

She also took to prayer, which had never been her strong suit. She wasn't particularly good at it, but she kept trying.

There was nothing left for her to do.

# CHAPTER FORTY-SIX

### Katherine

Kit was dreaming. She was in a lovely forest and in her hands she carried a bucket of water from a crystal-clear stream, but by the time she got to where she needed to go, almost all of it had splashed out. This happened over and over again, until a lovely lady with long white-blond hair, wearing a dress of deep red, joined her on the path and helped her carry the load. She was about to thank the lady when she heard a voice whisper "Kit darling," which caused her to open her eyes.

Tom was sprawled next to her on a chair. Although he was holding her hand, he was fast asleep. He couldn't have called her. She tugged lightly on his hand to wake him. When he looked into her eyes she asked the only question that truly mattered to her: "Am I still going to be a mother?"

"Yes," he said.

*Wait.* "This time around, I mean?"

He laced his fingers with hers. "You haven't miscarried. But sweetheart, you lost a lot of blood. There may be ... complications down the road."

"Whatever happens, she will be fine."

He chuckled. "She?"

Why were her eyelids so heavy? She could barely keep them up. "Of course," she murmured. "You're going to have two females to deal with now."

He lifted her hand and kissed it. "Does this mean you're going to make an honest man out of me?"

A moment passed. Kit was nearly back in dreamland, but she sent him a half-smile on her way out. "You'll just have to wait and see."

---

The next time she awoke it was sunset. The window was slightly ajar; she could see streaks of orange in the sky, feel the coolness in the air. Her mother was in the room, fussing with a vase of lilacs on the chest of drawers, but then she paused, put both hands on the chest, and bowed her head.

"No gardenias?" Kit asked.

Her mother straightened, smoothed her skirt. She let out a sigh. "You like the scent of lilacs better," she said. "You always did."

She came and sat by Kit. Her voice wobbled a bit, although she was trying hard not to let it. "You must never do that again. Your father is just not cut out for it."

"And you are, I suppose."

Josephine took Kit's hand and squeezed it. Her mother's hand shook slightly. "Of course I am. We are two peas in a pod, you know. Fighters."

They sat there for a few minutes and Kit knew she had to make amends for not being entirely truthful. Her pregnancy would have done much more to besmirch the Firestone name than a mere letter.

"I'm sorry for not telling you about the baby. Tom says I still have her, but I lost a lot of blood."

"But you had enough to get through it. And my granddaughter's going to be just fine."

Kit smiled with relief. "That's what *I* told him. I guess we are alike."

Kit thought about all they'd been through, all those times when she and Josephine hadn't understood each other, hadn't trusted each other. Maybe it would have been different if they'd known each other better as people, not just mother and daughter. From what little she'd read in the journal, her mother had led a life far more colorful than Kit ever imagined. She wanted to learn more about that life, and maybe she could. Starting right now.

"Mama?"

"Yes, darling?"

"Will you tell me about you?"

"What do you mean?"

"You say we're two peas in a pod, and I'd like to know why. I'd like to know *you*. So tell me. About how you grew up. About what you did … in college. About how you met Father. Everything. From the beginning."

"From the beginning."

"Yes." Wincing, Kit turned slightly to her side and plumped her pillow. "From the beginning, or wherever you'd like to start."

Josephine took a deep breath and settled in. "If you're sure," she said.

Kit smiled her encouragement.

She took a moment and began. "Well, my mother—your grandmother—was a beautiful woman and my father was a colonel in the Union army. He was quite dashing but he died when I was nine years old..."

# THANK YOU

Thank you so much for reading *Josephine's Daughter*. Readers like you are powerful, and you would be doing me a great favor by posting an objective review on Amazon, Goodreads, or other platforms based on the e-reader you use. In today's publishing world, those reviews are "golden" to authors like me.

Sharing your thoughts with others (including me!) on social media would be wonderful as well. You'll find me on **Twitter, Facebook,** and **Pinterest.** And don't forget to stop by my website (**abmichaels.com**) to learn more about my work. There you can join my Readers Group and receive a welcome gift along with monthly updates and special content.

# OTHER TITLES
## BY A.B. MICHAELS

*Josephine's Daughter* is Book Five of "The Golden City," a series of historical novels set in nineteenth and early twentieth century San Francisco during the "Gilded Age." It was a time of great upheaval and boundless enthusiasm, when scientific discoveries began to erode centuries of tradition; when wealthy individuals walked the same streets as reviled immigrants, and natural disasters leveled the playing field. From gold miners and artists to shipping barons and railway surgeons, you'll meet unforgettable characters, both fictional and historical, who must negotiate the raucous world in which they live. Other novels in the series include **The Art of Love, The Depth of Beauty, The Promise,** and **The Price of Compassion**. Summaries of those novels are listed below.

The contemporary series "Sinner's Grove Suspense" follows a number of descendants from "The Golden City" as they work to re-open the famous artists' retreat north of San Francisco known as "The Grove."

Brief excerpts from the first two novels in that series, **Sinner's Grove** and **The Lair**, can be found below. A brief description of the latest novel in the series, **The Jade Hunters**, is also included.

Each of the novels is a stand-alone read.

Thanks for reading my work—hope to see you again soon.

### *THE ART OF LOVE*
### *(Book One of "The Golden City" series)*

At the end of the Gilded Age, the "Golden City" of San Francisco offers everything a man could want — except the answers August Wolff desperately needs to find.

After digging a fortune in gold from the frozen fields of the Klondike, Gus head south, hoping to start over and put the baffling disappearance of his wife and daughter behind him. The turn of the century brings him even more success, but the distractions of a city some call the new Sodom and Gomorrah can't fill the gaping hole in his life.

Amelia Starling is a wildly talented artist caught in the straightjacket of Old New York society. Making a heart-breaking decision, she moves to San Francisco to further her career, all while living with the pain of a sacrifice no woman should ever have to make.

Brought together by the city's flourishing art scene, Gus and Lia forge a rare connection. But the past, shrouded in mystery, prevents the two of them from moving forward as one. Unwilling to face society's scorn, Lia leaves the city and vows to begin again in Europe.

Gus can't bear to let her go, but unless he can set his ghosts to rest, he and Lia have no chance for happiness at all.

### *THE DEPTH OF BEAUTY*
### *(Book Two of "The Golden City" series)*

In San Francisco's Chinatown circa 1903, slavery, polygamy and rampant prostitution are thriving – just blocks away from the Golden City's elite.

Wealthy and well-connected, Will Firestone enters the mysterious enclave with an eye toward expanding his shipping business. What he finds there will astonish him. With the help of an exotic young widow and a gifted teenage orphan, he embarks on a journey of self-discovery, where lust, love and tragedy will change his life forever.

*The Depth of Beauty* was nominated for a RITA award in 2017 in the category of general fiction.

### *THE PROMISE*
### *(Book Three of "The Golden City" series)*

April 18, 1906. A massive earthquake has decimated much of San Francisco, leaving thousands without food, water or shelter. Patrolling the streets to help those in need, Army corporal Ben Tilson meets a young woman named Charlotte who touches his heart, making him think of a future with her in it. In the heat of the moment he makes a promise to her family that even he realizes will be almost impossible to keep.

Because on the heels of the earthquake, a much worse disaster looms: a fire that threatens to consume everything and everyone in its path.

It will take everything Ben's got to make it back to the woman he's fallen for—and even that may not be enough.

## *THE PRICE OF COMPASSION*
### *(Book Four of "The Golden City" series)*

April 18, 1906. San Francisco has just been shattered by a massive earthquake and is in the throes of an even more deadly fire. During the chaos, gifted surgeon Tom Justice makes a life-changing decision that wreaks havoc on his body, mind and spirit. Leaving the woman he loves, he embarks on a quest to regain his sanity and self-worth. Yet just when he finds some answers, he's arrested for murder—a crime he may very well be guilty of. The facts of the case are troubling; they'll have you asking the question: "Is he guilty?" Or even worse …"What would I have done?"

## *SINNER'S GROVE*
### *(Book One of the "Sinner's Grove Suspense" series)*

A startling discovery when she was fourteen left San Francisco artist Jenna Bergstrom estranged from her family; unforeseen tragedy only sharpened her loneliness. But now her ailing grandfather needs her expertise to re-open the family's once-famous artists' retreat on the California coast. The problem? She'll have to face architect Brit Maguire, the ex-love of her life.

Seven years ago, Maguire spent a magical time with the woman of his dreams, only to have her disappear from his life completely. Now she's back, helping with the biggest historic renovation of Brit's career. No matter how deep his feelings still run, Brit can't afford the distraction of Jenna Bergstrom, because something is going terribly wrong with the project at Sinner's Grove.

**An excerpt from *Sinner's Grove*:**

"What the hell?!" Brit turned around when a second explosion followed on the heels of the first. He immediately wrapped his arms protectively around Jenna.

"My God, was that a bomb?" she cried. She couldn't believe what was happening. She quickly dropped her leg and straightened her dress, fear turning her passion into panic.

"I don't know," Brit said grimly. "Let's find out."

They ran out of the building, passing several workers and a few investors rushing in different directions with terror-stricken faces. The street lights had not gone out, and Jenna saw her brother across the lawn.

"Jason! Do you know what happened?"

"It looks like the equipment barn blew up!" he called as he ran in that direction. "I just called 911."

"Anybody hurt?" Brit yelled.

"Don't know yet!"

Brit took Jenna by the shoulders. "Go back to the Great House. I'll check it out."

"Not in your life," she shot back. "I'm staying with you."

Brit set his jaw and started running toward the maintenance area. Thankful she'd worn flats to the presentation, Jenna easily kept up with him. As they crested the hill, Brit stopped short and stuck out his arm to keep Jenna from running past him.

"Too dangerous!" he yelled.

She grabbed onto his arm to stop her momentum. *Oh my God— this is hell on earth.* The front two-thirds of the huge barn was a fireball shooting flames a hundred feet into the sky. And the heat was so intense, she felt as if even her blood was boiling. Smoke was everywhere, sucking the oxygen from the air. Men were shouting and running back and forth, trying to be heard over the roar of the inferno. *Please keep Jason and Da away from this*, Jenna prayed, her breathing harsh and labored.

"How's it looking, Jack?" Brit called out to the man he'd pegged to help manage the crew.

"Not good." Jack, looking disgusted, tossed a hose on the ground where it joined several others coiled haphazardly in the gloom like somnolent snakes. "Whoever did this cut the hoses. We can't get any pressure, so we're down to a bucket brigade until the fire trucks get here."

"Everybody accounted for?"

"I think so, but it's pretty crazy right now. Maybe we oughta do a head count."

Brit looked around in frustration. In the distance sirens could be heard. "Good idea," he said. "Maybe—"

"Mr. Maguire! Mr. Maguire!" Parker Bishop and Kyle Summers ran up to the group.

"What's wrong?" Jenna cried.

"I think…I think—" Parker seemed to be particularly anxious.

"Spit it out, man," Brit barked.

Jenna glared at Brit. "Give him a chance to calm down!"

"We think…we think maybe that guy Lester's still in the building!" Kyle said.

"How do you know?" Brit asked sharply.

"We were on litter patrol down around the lower bungalows. Parker said he saw him go inside."

"How could you see in the dark?" Jenna asked.

"I think it was him, but I don't know for sure," Parker hedged.

"The light wasn't that good, but we saw *somebody* go inside and close the slider. You can tell when that big sucker closes," Kyle explained. "I didn't think much of it and kept working."

"Me too," Parker said.

"No, you were on the phone, dude, remember?"

Parker nodded. "Yeah, that's right. My dad called. And then, *Kablam*! So we started running back here."

Brit didn't waste a second. "Anybody seen Lester?" he yelled to the members of the makeshift fire crew.

A chorus of "no's" came back.

"Jack, you got a master key on you?" he called out.

The man shook his head.

"Get one!" Brit yelled. He then headed toward the back of the barn.

"Where do you think you're going?" Jenna cried, grabbing his arm.

"If he's in there, there's a chance he's in the back and can't get out," Brit said. "He may not be able to get to the side door. We've got to get it open and help him out."

"But you're not going in after him, right?"

Brit paused and looked at Jenna, running his fingertip down the side of her cheek. "Don't worry." With that he took off, glancing back once before he turned the corner of the building.

Speechless, Jenna watched his retreating figure as if in slow motion. She noticed vaguely that Kyle and Parker had walked up on either side of her. Kyle put his arm around her shoulders.

"It's all right," he said soothingly. "We're here."

Jenna turned and looked up at the large, muscular young man. He had the same glittery look he'd had the last day of school. Then she looked at Parker. He was staring at Kyle and his eyes burned fiercely, just as they had that same day. Fear, slippery and cold, slid over her.

"We need to help Brit," she said neutrally, hoping her voice wouldn't betray the anxiety threatening to overtake her.

By the time she worked her way safely around to the side of the burning barn, several burly workmen were in the process of battering the side door with what looked like a large fence post. The door was already starting to buckle from the heat. When it finally gave way, smoke billowed out and Jenna watched in horror as Brit tore off his jacket, tie and shirt, soaking the latter in a nearby bucket and wrapping it around his nose and mouth.

"Don't go in there—please!" Jenna cried.

Brit looked at her briefly, his eyes communicating what words could not. Then he disappeared inside the carnage. Moments later another deafening explosion ripped apart the air.

"Nooooo!" Jenna screamed. Tears streaming down her face, arms wrapped around herself to keep from falling apart, Jenna stared in shock at the burning, crumbling building, her only words a mantra-like "please God, please God, please God."

She felt someone—Parker, perhaps—urge her back from the heat of the fire, but she couldn't seem to move. Her entire focus was on the jagged hole into which Brit had run. She couldn't believe he was gone. Wouldn't believe it. He was going to walk out again. Any second now. Any second. Any second.

### THE LAIR
### *(Book Two of the "Sinner's Grove Suspense" series)*

After her father dies in a boating incident, innkeeper Daniela Dunn must travel from Northern California's Sinner's Grove back to Verona, Italy and her childhood home, an estate called the Panther's Lair.

It's a mansion full of frightful memories and deeply buried secrets, where appearances are deceiving and the price of honesty is death. As Dani is drawn further into her family's intrigues, she has an unlikely ally in handsome Marin County investigator Gabriele de la Torre. He says he's come along merely to support her, but his actions show he has an agenda all his own.

Gabe de la Torre needs to settle old family debts before starting fresh with the woman he feels could be The One. But once Dani finds out whom he's beholden to, all bets might be off. When a mystery woman reveals that Dani's father may have been murdered, the stakes rise dramatically and Gabe realizes they're now players in a dangerous game. Protecting Dani becomes his top priority, even as she strives to figure out whom she can trust: her relatives, Gabe, or even herself.

**An excerpt from *The Lair*:**

"Nothing like a wide awake drunk," Gabe muttered an hour later. They'd gotten back to La Tana and as usual Fausta had grudgingly let them in. "Hey, you can always give us a key," he'd joked, but his aunt had simply turned around and gone back to her room.

Once in their suite, Dani had been asleep on her feet, which were a little unsteady at best, so he'd pointed her in the direction of her bedroom and reluctantly bid her good night.

*God she was beautiful.* So elegant, so feminine, even though she didn't put on airs *at all*. He'd spent the entire evening fighting the impulse to touch her everywhere, even in places that demanded privacy at the very least. He'd known instinctively that she'd get along great with Marco and Gina, and she hadn't disappointed him. Man, she was driving him crazy. He heaved a sigh. Both tired and wired, he couldn't tell which was more to blame, the alcohol or the stress of keeping his desire in check.

He reflexively reached into the small refrigerator for a beer before he realized he was already half pickled, so he opted for water instead. Unscrewing the cap, he drank half the bottle while pulling his shirt out of his slacks. To keep his libido in check he decided to focus on something decidedly unsexy. Reaching for the jacket he'd tossed on the back of the sofa, he pulled out the report that Marco had given him earlier that evening.

"I think we're on to something," Marco had told him quietly. "We found a match."

He was just beginning to scan the document when the bedroom door opened and Dani appeared. Her hair was tousled and she walked a bit uncertainly, as if she were slogging through mud in high heels, even though she was barefoot. She wore an ivory-colored cover-up of some kind and she looked nervous. "I'm ready," she said.

He looked at her quizzically. "Ready for what, bella?"

"For us...you know." He didn't have a chance to reply before she tottered up to him and threw her slender arms around his neck, locking her lips with his.

After his initial shock, Gabe took a moment to enjoy the feel of Dani's curves against him. Jesus, after all that booze his body still reacted immediately, hardening in response to her softness. She felt so damn good—like falling into the most luxurious bed when you've been sleeping on the floor all your life. He smiled inwardly at her inexperienced but earnest attempt at seduction and cursed his inner cop—the prig who wouldn't let him take advantage of her while she was intoxicated. Reluctantly he took her by the upper arms and peeled her away from his body. "Uh, sweetheart, I don't think this is a good thing to be doing..."

"What?" she asked softly but defensively. "Don't I measure up to your other women friends? Don't I? Just a little?" She stepped back and before he could stop her she dropped the cover-up, revealing a perfect—and perfectly naked—female form encased in a 5 foot two inch frame. She was biting her full lower lip, practically screaming for his approval.

An image flashed before him of Dani pregnant. She was ripe and luscious—the epitome of Woman. Instead of cooling him off, the thought of her big with child —*his* child—only made him hotter and made what he had to do all the more difficult. He looked at her a long time, so long that he could see uncertainty, followed by embarrassment, overtake her. He reached down and picked up the wrap, putting it around her shoulders.

"I...I'm sorry," she mumbled. "I thought ..." She turned to go, but Gabe took her shoulders and turned her back toward him.

"If you think for one second that I don't want to bury myself in you right now, you are sadly mistaken," he said roughly. "When you and I make love, I am going to be all over you. You are going to feel me everywhere and know when I've taken you higher than you've ever been before." He tore himself away and covered her back up. "And the next morning, you're going to remember everything I did to you and want me to do it all over again. Count on it. Now go to bed."

"But—"

"Please," he said firmly, turning her around and practically pushing her back into the bedroom. It took several minutes after her door shut for Gabe's upper brain to start functioning again. "Keep your eye on the prize," he repeated like a mantra. "Keep your eye on the prize." The prize, in this case, was a Dani who felt no regrets about whatever physical gymnastics they might partake in together. He'd waited this long for the timing to be right; he could wait a little longer, even though it was damn near going to kill him.

## *THE JADE HUNTERS*
### *(Book Three of the "Sinner's Grove Suspense" series)*

Award-winning jewelry designer Regina Firestone is proud to exhibit her famous grandmother's multi-million dollar "bauble" collection at the grand re-opening of The Grove Center for American Art. The fact that she's considering modeling the jewels in the nude like her grandmother did infuriates photographer Walker Banks, an owner of The Grove who's in charge of the exhibit. Their spat takes a back seat, however, when Reggie discovers that one of the most compelling pieces in the collection is not at all what it seems. Tracking down the truth will take the couple into the dark heart of a quest that's lasted more than a century – one in which destroying human lives—including Reggie's and Walker's—means nothing in the pursuit of a twisted sense of justice.

# ACKNOWLEDGMENTS

A big thank you to Donna Cook, author/editor extraordinaire, who told me emphatically after my first draft that I needed not one but two books to tell the story of Tom and Katherine ...

... and to Andrea Robinson, for not only her spot-on edits but her calm and supportive nature, which comes in handy when one sees a surfeit of red ink on the page ...

... and to Tara Mayberry, whose design creativity is surpassed only by her patience. I am truly blessed ...

... and to Mike, who has stepped up to the plate for me in too many ways to count; I simply would not be here without you.

# ABOUT THE AUTHOR

A native of California, A.B. Michaels holds masters' degrees in history (UCLA) and broadcasting (San Francisco State University). After working for many years as a promotional writer and editor, she decided it was time to focus on writing the kind of fiction she likes to read.

A.B. and her husband currently live in Boise, Idaho. On any given day you might see them on the golf course, the bocce court, or walking their four-legged "sons" along the Boise River. More than likely, however, you'll find her hard at work on her next book.

abmichaels.com

CPSIA information can be obtained
at www.ICGtesting.com
Printed in the USA
LVHW091125281119
638726LV00008BA/1420/P